THE BABYLON PLOT

David Leadbeater has published more than fifty novels and is a million-copy ebook bestseller. His books include the chart-topping Matt Drake series and the Relic Hunters series, which won the inaugural Amazon Kindle Storyteller award in 2017.

www.davidleadbeater.com

Also by David Leadbeater:

The Joe Mason Series

The Vatican Secret
The Demon Code
The Midnight Conspiracy

The Matt Drake Series

The Bones of Odin
The Blood King Conspiracy
The Gates of Hell
The Tomb of the Gods
Brothers in Arms
The Swords of Babylon
Blood Vengeance
Last Man Standing
The Plagues of Pandora
The Lost Kingdom
The Ghost Ships of Arizona
The Last Bazaar
The Edge of Armageddon
The Treasures of Saint Germain
Inca Kings
The Four Corners of the Earth
The Seven Seals of Egypt
Weapons of the Gods
The Blood King Legacy
Devil's Island
The Fabergé Heist
Four Sacred Treasures
The Sea Rats
The Blood King Takedown
Devil's Junction
Voodoo Soldiers
The Carnival of Curiosities
The Winged Dagger
A Cold Day in Hell

The Disavowed Series

The Razor's Edge
In Harm's Way
Threat Level: Red

The Alicia Myles Series

Aztec Gold
Crusader's Gold
Caribbean Gold
Chasing Gold
Galleon's Gold

The Relic Hunters Series

The Relic Hunters (Relic Hunters 1)
The Atlantis Cipher (Relic Hunters 2)
The Amber Secret (Relic Hunters 3)
The Hostage Diamond (Relic Hunters 4)
The Rocks of Albion (Relic Hunters 5)
The Illuminati Sanctum (Relic Hunters 6)

Stand Your Ground

To find out more visit **www.davidleadbeater.com**

THE BABYLON PLOT

DAVID LEADBEATER

avon.

HarperCollins*Publishers* Ltd
1 London Bridge Street,
London SE1 9GF

www.harpercollins.co.uk

HarperCollins*Publishers*
Macken House,
39/40 Mayor Street Upper,
Dublin 1
D01 C9W8

First published by HarperCollins*Publishers* 2023
1

A catalogue record for this book is available from the British Library

ISBN: 978-0-00-854513-0

This novel is entirely a work of fiction.
The names, characters and incidents portrayed in it are
the work of the author's imagination. Any resemblance to
actual persons, living or dead, events or localities is
entirely coincidental.

Typeset in Sabon LT Std by Palimpsest Book Production Limited,
Falkirk, Stirlingshire

Printed and bound in the UK using
100% Renewable Electricity by CPI Group (UK) Ltd

This book is produced from independently certified FSC™ paper to ensure
responsible forest management.

For more information visit: www.harpercollins.co.uk/green

For my parents

Chapter 1

With their knives sharpened, their guns loaded and, for now, keeping a lid on their rampant desires, they visited the man named Leo Barone in the dead of night, after first making sure his wife and three children were home. They moved in utter silence, embracing the dark like the pure predators they were.

'Daga,' the woman said. 'I'll need a few seconds for the alarm.'

The man nodded, resting his powerful bulk on his haunches, waiting, the very thought of bloodletting already flooding his senses far beyond their normal levels. His full name was Cassadaga, and he was a mythical killer made flesh.

'I live for this,' he whispered.

'Me too,' the woman said as she connected a home-made keypad to the door's modern digital lock.

Ivana was his partner in everything, a safecracker, a thief, and a hot-blooded murderer. Together, they had scoured Europe for the last two months, preying on the innocent where they could, moving on when growing attention forced them to.

'You think we're doing the right thing here?' Ivana asked as she worked. 'This is Italy. We should be savouring the wine, the pasta, and hot, sticky pools of blood.'

Daga knew she wasn't questioning the killing that was soon to come. She lived for it as much as he did. What she meant was should they be working for . . . *him*.

'He has the money we need,' Daga said. 'He went through the right channels. He said all the right things. As usual, my love, we take each day as it comes.'

Two months of slaking their bloody lust across nine countries had eaten into their reserves of cash. Daga was bankrolling them both and since – until recently – he'd had a ten-year sojourn, he wasn't exactly flush with cash. Still, the death spree had been worth it.

People had whispered about Daga for years, called him the world's most vicious thief. He was unkillable, a myth, a demon. Nightmare stories were told about him, repeated quietly around campfires in the dead of night.

Behave, child, or Cassadaga will come for you.

His eyes fixed on Ivana as she worked. Tall, broad and exquisite, she was an Eastern European beauty who'd crashed into his life just a few months ago and had changed everything – the whole way he worked and played. Now they were inseparable.

'Done,' Ivana said.

Daga's excitement rose a notch. They were lying inside this house, all four of them, with no idea that a horrific death was coming for them. Stretching out a hand, he pushed open their front door to be confronted by a dark hallway.

He entered. The house was utterly silent and cast in

shadow. Daga moved down the hallway a step at a time, with Ivana at his back.

'This job is for *him*,' she said. 'We don't have to finish it.'

Daga looked back at her. 'Are you saying you don't want the kill?'

'I'm saying we could easily procure our own.'

Daga frowned. Of course, she was right, and that was probably the best thing to do.

'The man's crazy,' Ivana went on.

Daga blinked, surprised at her words under the circumstances. He was under no illusions that the homicidal acts they perpetrated together were entirely rational. He enjoyed being . . . extreme.

'He has a plan,' Daga whispered. 'A good plan, as it happens. Marduk may be in prison, but he still runs what's left of the Amori, and he still has access to cash. If we help him with this, we'll be in an excellent position financially.'

'By helping him escape?'

Daga felt the attraction of the kill pulling at him, but gritted his teeth and lingered a little longer. 'Yes, he has plans,' he said. 'Plans to locate the ziggurat, find the Amori riches, take down the Vatican once and for all directly, and then kill Joe Mason and his fucking team. Now, some of that jives directly with my own cravings and, I assume, yours.'

Ivana squeezed her attractive face into a frown. 'I definitely wanna kill Mason. And the riches sound good.' Her last sentence came with a light air, as if she had sensed his irritation at their lack of forward progress. 'For now, though, let's concentrate on the blood.'

Daga grinned, a demon in the darkness. Her words stimulated him. They knew already that the parents slept in the front bedroom, the children in the back two. He flexed his muscles, breathed deeply in anticipation, and made his way across a dark front room towards an open flight of stairs in the corner. It was three a.m. Daga paused with his right foot on the first step.

'Keep it under control,' he breathed, without turning around. 'This is a big operation.'

Ivana placed a hand on his shoulder in acknowledgement. Together, they climbed the stairs cautiously, keeping to the sides so as not to make them creak. Fourteen risers later, Daga found himself on a narrow L-shaped landing. To his left, the parents' bedroom. To his right, the kids'. He turned to Ivana and nodded. She would take the kids.

Daga crept towards an open door, paused at the threshold. The room beyond was in darkness, illuminated only by the faint green glow of a digital clock. Daga stepped towards the bed and stood over his two victims, breathing quietly, letting the knife cut patterns slowly through the air above their bodies. It was a moment of power for him, carved-out seconds of supremacy when he had held the power of life or death or intense torture in his hands, the knowledge that those below him would soon live in sheer terror a source of stimulation and inspiration.

Daga reached down, put his hand across Leo Barone's mouth and rapped him smartly on the forehead with the hilt of the knife. Leo's eyes flew open, filled with shock and then with fear. Daga put a finger to his lips.

'Make no sound,' he whispered. 'Or I will slit you from ear to ear.'

Daga made Leo prod his wife awake and then made her the same promise. He made sure they could see the knife, but not the gun in its holster at the small of his back. He wouldn't want them reaching for it in some misguided attempt at survival.

'We have your children,' Daga whispered in English, with an evil taint to his voice, and then he grinned.

Leo's eyes flew even wider. His wife – a woman named Millie – couldn't help but whimper. Daga immediately ordered them to sit on the edge of the bottom of the bed so that he could reach them easier. Leo was bare-chested and wore striped pyjama bottoms. Millie wore a long black negligee that was rumpled around her legs. Daga put his knife to Millie's throat.

'Make another sound,' he growled.

Right then, Ivana herded the two kids into their parents' bedroom. Daga guessed the girl was about fifteen, the boy around twelve. They were both dressed in pyjamas, and both dashed from Ivana's side into the arms of their parents.

Daga allowed it. It was hard working with kids. They tended to act on impulse and do things an adult would never dare. Ivana came over to his side, brandishing her own knife.

'Sit still, don't speak,' Daga said. 'If we were here to kill you immediately, your blood would already soak the bedsheets.'

'And believe me, he knows,' Ivana said with a false little laugh. 'He's killed more people than Ebola.'

'Is that a friend of yours?' Daga looked at her with a wide grin.

'An old flame.' Ivana snickered.

They were already lost in their private world, where slaughter reigned supreme.

The kids sat beside their parents; that was four people lined up along the bottom of the bed. The room was silent and mostly dark. Daga liked it that way. He leaned forward so that his eyes glittered at Leo's own terrified ones.

'Which one?' he asked.

Leo swallowed hard, unsure if he was allowed to talk. 'I'm not sure what you mean,' he said finally.

'Your children,' Daga grated. 'Which one should I cut first?'

Leo's face went white. His wife sobbed. The kids were rigid. Ivana chuckled softly at his side.

Power filled Daga, the power of absolute control. He was ruthless and deadly and, with one swift decision, he could change the entire course of these people's lives.

Of course, he already had.

'It's time to decide,' he said. 'Which child. Which limb. How far in should I stick the blade?'

Daga's tone was conversational, light. Leo shook his head, unable to speak. Daga wanted to take Ivana right then in front of these people, lay her across the bed and satisfy his lust.

At least, one part of his lust.

Tension stretched inside the room like elastic. The only sound was breathing, hard and laboured. The kids had their eyes shut. Daga tapped Leo on the shoulder with his blade.

'You are Leo Barone?'

'Y . . . yes.'

'And you are the warden of Vittore prison?'

Now Leo chewed his bottom lip. 'I am.'

'You are the big dog? The boss of bosses? The head man, yes?'

Leo nodded. 'Yes, I . . . I run the place.'

Daga held his blade back as a sudden urge took him to ram it through Leo's throat until the blade pierced right through the other side. It would be a great start to proceedings. But he had other objectives tonight.

'You can make prisoners move, yes?'

'Make them . . . well, yes, I guess.'

Daga saw an opportunity to shed a little blood. He trailed the blade from the top of Leo's left shoulder to the right and watched crimson bloom in its wake. It was a shallow cut, but the blood soothed him.

'Can you, or can't you?' he asked. 'Be very specific.'

'Yes, yes, the decision rests with me. S . . . sorry.'

Hearing the man apologise as Daga cut him from left to right made the thief smile. 'Ivana,' he said. 'Get ready to cut the kids.'

Leo bit right through his bottom lip in fear. Blood welled. His eyes pleaded with Daga. 'Oh, no, I will do anything you want. *Anything*. Please don't hurt my children.'

Daga held up a hand. It was a practised move they'd done before. Normally, they would revel in the pleas, urge more and more, and then cut and start laughing. Normally, they would satiate themselves with their victims' abject fear.

Tonight was different.

Daga pretended to hold back, to appraise Leo once more. 'All right,' he said. 'You have one chance. Do you know a prisoner named Marduk?'

Leo closed his eyes and shook his head as if he'd always expected the prisoner would bring some form of bad luck. 'Of course. He's . . . notorious.'

'Ex-leader of the Amori, the group that tried to take down the Vatican,' Daga went on. 'Stole their little Book of Secrets and then some ancient body from a monastery in the alps. Captured, incarcerated, left to rot. He wants out.'

Leo gaped. 'He wants out?'

'Yeah, you know what that means, don't you? It means you're going to help me arrange his escape.' Daga waved the blade at the young girl's neck. 'Aren't you?'

Daga took a moment to assess the kids. The girl, blond hair and with a round face, was staring down at her knees, breathing slowly. Tears dripped from her eyes onto her pyjama leggings. Her mother held the girl's right hand tightly. The boy, with brown tousled hair, was staring fixedly at Ivana as if he wanted to ask her for an autograph. If he did, Ivana would gladly tattoo it on his flesh. His eyes were wide, glazed. Maybe he was in shock. He gripped his sister's left hand.

Daga didn't care. He turned his attention back to Leo. 'I know all about you,' he said. 'Marduk made it his business to know all about you. Englishman working abroad rises to the upper echelons of Italy's prison service, gets the warden's job at one of the country's most notorious prisons. *And*, you get to live close to Milan. I'd say that's a win-win. How are you finding Milan in the spring, Leo?'

The warden nodded. He couldn't take his eyes off Daga. 'What do you want me to do?'

'Me? I'd like you to die. I'd love to stick you and your fucking family a hundred times and watch you all bleed out. But we're working for Marduk, at least for today.'

'That makes you four lucky bastards,' Ivana put in.

They didn't appear lucky, sitting and crying and wiping their noses. Daga watched Leo bleed, mesmerised by the drip of the blood and the intoxicating smell. 'Do you feel lucky, Leo?' he asked.

'What do you want me to do?' Leo said. 'I can't just walk a man out of prison, can't just set him free.'

'Oh, we have a plan,' Daga replied. 'Now, sit back and relax. Let me explain.'

Chapter 2

Wherever Joe Mason picked up his gloves, that was home. Wherever he went, he always returned to the boxing gym, even if he had to build one himself.

And that's what he'd done. Since finding the Vatican's Book of Secrets and then chasing the Amori's hidden Creed halfway around the world, Sally had taken the team under her wing, employing them under the name Quest Investigations. Now they searched for and guarded relics across the globe, and they'd started to build an enviable reputation, helped somewhat by the recent discovery of the Ark of the Covenant beneath Edinburgh Castle. A month had passed since then.

Mason pulled on a pair of boxing gloves. The new set-up was makeshift, but then so was he, he reflected. A work in progress, moving slowly, day by day. There was a heavy punchbag hanging in the centre of Sally's dusty garage, a pair of focus mitts on a bench nearby for when Roxy or one of the others wanted to join, benches and weights for warming up, and a leather speed bag attached to a nearby rafter. Mason tried to use the facilities every day. He didn't need to; he was a powerful, strong but wiry man with blond hair, blue eyes and one of those young-looking faces that was often underestimated, not showing the ravages that life invariably brought.

The boxing calmed him. It was the only home he'd known for years.

That was until the new team – now known as Quest Investigations – formed unexpectedly around him. Before meeting them, Mason had been struggling desperately, trying to live with a mistake he'd made years ago – a mistake that had cost two lives, his marriage and given birth to a lifetime of guilt. Now, just over three months later, that burden was lighter, easier, though it would never disappear and nor would he want it to.

The train of thought brought his team to mind. Roxy, at thirty-three, was a free-spirited, straight-talking woman who struggled with her own demons and, more than anyone, had helped talk Mason into a better place. She was a hard-hitting rum-soaked woman who was recruited at the tender age of eighteen to work for an organisation similar to the CIA but more shadowy, an organisation that took out foreign operatives on far-off shores. Quaid, just over fifty, was an ex-British-army officer grown tired of advancing politicians' agendas. He had a craggy face with lustrous black hair and greying sideburns leaving people to wonder if he used dye up top. Sally, twenty-eight, was herself a stubborn brunette, who'd been born into money and then rebelled against it, and against her father, until his death just a few months ago. This rebellion had made her live off the grid for a while despite gaining major qualifications and working harder than anyone else at university. Now Sally worked from his old house, trying to do better than he ever did with her large inheritance. And then there was Hassell, a man who fought his memories every day, every hour. Hassell was an ex-New-York cop who'd fallen into criminal ways after his girlfriend was murdered and ended up unknowingly working for years for the man who'd murdered her. Hassell had killed the man, but there was no overcoming that kind of guilt. Hassell was stocky with short, dark hair and, at twenty-seven, was considered the 'baby' of the team.

Mason himself was ex-army and ex-MI5. He'd been working at a private security firm when he'd taken a job at the Vatican that had introduced him to Sally Rusk. That was just a few months ago. Now here he was, boxing in her garage, in the old rambling house that had been her father's, looking at a new life.

Mason started punching the bag, jab, cross and then jab, jab, cross and, after he'd warmed up, started introducing hooks and uppercuts. He moved easily across the floor, kicking up whorls of dust with his trainer-clad feet. The discipline overcame him, masking his wider thoughts under a cloud of concentration. Life was good in the bag's vicinity – it was simple and direct and all-embracing. He spent an hour working out and only stopped when he heard the approach of footsteps behind him.

'Hey,' it was Roxy Banks.

Mason breathed deeply and turned. Roxy was raven-haired, six foot two and hard around the edges, always struggling to find the softness of youth that she believed the agency had stripped from her in her teens. It was an ongoing struggle for the feisty American.

'How ya doin'?' Mason said.

'You taking the piss out of my accent again? That's gonna get you and me some sparring time, bud.'

'I wasn't,' Mason said, trying not to laugh. 'Hey, good work on the last job.'

'Flattery's gonna get you nowhere,' she started gruffly, and then relented. 'But, hey, I guess I came through pretty well in the end.'

The last job, just last week, had seen them transporting an ancient vase from one country to another, staying one step ahead of a pursuing team who were nowhere near their equal. Roxy had spotted their tail at every turn. The job before that had entailed protecting an exhibition over the course of three nights, along with two other security teams in sun-drenched Miami. Roxy had barely changed out of her bikini the whole time they were there, but she had still got the job done, still spotted the only threat that presented itself during the whole three days.

'We've certainly put ourselves on the map since Edinburgh,' he said.

'Yeah. Four jobs in four weeks,' she said, and then added: 'At least,' with a frown.

Mason started unstrapping his gloves, certain he was going to get nothing else done today. 'How's Sally coping?'

'Oh, you'll know that better than me, babyface.'

Mason narrowed his eyes at her. The nickname wasn't entirely welcome and reminded him of ribbings he'd taken as far back as high school and the army. 'Is it my fault I always look this fresh?' he said lightly.

'You must use cream,' she said. 'Anti-wrinkle lotion? What's your secret, Joe?'

'Fuck off, Roxy.'

The banter went downhill from there. Mason sighed with relief when Quaid and Hassell joined them.

'Another job?' Mason asked hopefully.

'Three,' Quaid told them. 'Sally's getting stressed that we're having to pick and choose now.'

Mason laid his gloves on a nearby table. 'Then let's go help her.'

'And how's her training going?' Hassell asked, looking down at the gloves.

Mason followed his gaze. 'Pretty good. Of course, you can train someone in a garage, in a field, in a house, as much as you like. It's real-time fieldwork that brings it all together.'

'You mean hands on,' Roxy said, yawning. 'Down and dirty.'

Mason nodded. 'You have your own specific way of expressing it,' he said. 'But yeah, like I said – real-time fieldwork.'

Hassell led them out of the garage into a bright, sunny morning. It was May in their corner of the country and spring had arrived, bringing with it the birds and the weeds and the flowers. Sally's house was a rambling old mansion, covered in ivy at the front, its impressive facade quite dominating. There were tiny windows and a recessed front door and tall plant pots on either side of a winding drive that a gardener tended to most of the week. The grounds also needed his fair hand, stretching for over two acres. Mason gazed up at the sprawling old house and wondered what secrets it might contain. Sally's dad had been a professor, a historian, and a walking register of ancient relics.

They entered the house and found Sally seated behind a pockmarked wooden desk in the study. The surface was littered with papers, a laptop was open and in use, a coffee mug was steaming at her side and her mobile phone was lighting up beside her with new messages. Sally didn't know where to look first.

'Breathe,' Mason said.

'Wish I had the time,' Sally said. 'I'm not sure working for a living is all it's cracked up to be.'

Mason pulled up a chair and sat down next to her. 'What can I do?'

Sally sat back, sighing. 'I don't know,' she said. 'We have a job coming in from England. Another from Spain and a third from somewhere in Africa. All word-of-mouth contacts. We can't take them all on.'

'You don't want to let anyone down,' Quaid said. 'I understand that.'

Mason looked at her. The tips of her dark hair were still coloured blue, but it was a far lighter tinge these days, signalling to Mason at least that her rebelliousness had softened considerably since the passing of her father.

'Let's break it down,' he said. 'Maybe we can fit more than one of them in.'

'I've tried . . .' Sally looked up at them. 'But, let's all have a go.'

'You know I need to help people out,' Quaid said. 'It's what gets me through the day.' Quaid's absolution for what he regarded to be the worst things he'd ever done whilst taking orders from the higher-ups in the army was to help as many innocents as he could. It was what he was doing when they found him in Bethlehem months ago, risking his life to bring better things to the needy.

'The England job's a two-nighter,' Mason said. 'We can crack that off and then . . . oh.'

'You see?' Sally said. 'They all want us to start tomorrow night.'

'Could we split our ranks?' Hassell suggested.

'A good shout,' Mason said. 'But the jobs require four-person teams at the minimum.'

'Is this not a good problem to have?' Roxy said then. 'Too much work is better than not enough, I think.'

'Quest Investigations needs to garner a strong reputation,' Sally said. 'Turning down jobs won't help, no matter the reason, I'm afraid.'

'I'm up for anything,' Roxy said. 'Keep moving forward, that's what I say. So long as we're doing good, I can progress too.'

Mason knew she was still concentrating on raising those barriers between this life and the last one. He said: 'Choose a job. Send the other two a nicely worded message. Don't apologise too strongly.'

Sally nodded. 'Who'd have guessed we'd end up being so popular?'

Mason knew it was about hard work and results, and they'd achieved both in bucketfuls. The dangers they faced recovering the Book of Secrets and then the Creed were still fresh in his mind. Somehow though they'd escaped death, though not without a few war wounds. They all bore the scars of their adventures, some worse than others. His broken ribs, index fingers and black eye paled in significance to the broken arm, concussion and facial lacerations sustained by Hassell. Roxy had fared worse, suffering from scorching and puncture wounds and some skin torn from her face. But they had all healed, and they were all ready to go again.

Mason was growing with them. He'd stand by them now, part of a team, a position he'd never imagined he would see again after the events in Mosul that had taken two of his best friends away. Mason found he was dealing with it now by being part of that new team, by taking the others along with him and taking responsibility for them.

Not that he needed to, he mused. They were all pretty competent in their own rights.

Sally chose a job and set about letting the other two enquiries down gently. Mason and the others read up on the new mission and decided what they needed to do, what equipment they would have to take, and started forming a plan of action. It was their way now, working together, moving together. Sally was coming into her own with the new business venture and with her training. They were all moving forward, leaning on each other and learning from each other. Mason would say he was in one of the best places of his life.

If only he'd known then how it was all about to change.

Chapter 3

Cassadaga went with Leo Barone; Ivana stayed with the wife and children. There was no greater threat. Leo's last vision of his little family was of them huddled together on a sofa with Ivana holding her knife to their collective throats. Leo hobbled to his car in a daze, moving automatically, eyes glazed, face as white as the fog that held sway over the edge of the morning. Daga knew he would need to pull Leo out of the pall of terror that currently gripped him.

'This won't take long,' he said. 'And then you'll be with them. It won't work unless you snap out of it and look human, though.'

'I'm sorry,' Leo said, starting the car. 'But it's not every day that a pair of cut-throats terrorise me and my family.'

Daga thought about that. *Cut-throats*. He liked it. The car started moving. Daga knew Leo lived twenty-three minutes from the prison. It was early. They should do it in less time because there would be less traffic. He settled back, put his seat belt on, and wished he still had hold of the knife. Not that his hands weren't deadly enough. Daga enjoyed using the knife – mostly to kill, but even threatening or slicing slightly was enough. He'd lost count of his own victims years ago.

'The plan,' he said, 'is this: you file the paperwork that enables Marduk to be removed from the prison. You organise the transport van. It shouldn't be too difficult to falsify. Marduk might be removed for many reasons: personal safety, danger to others, a medical condition. I will go with you to the cell, as Marduk will recognise me. Then, once we get him outside, I will follow the van in your car. At a predesignated point along the route, I will intercept the van and free Marduk.'

Leo swallowed hard and kept his eyes on the road. 'And then? What happens to my family?'

'I will direct Ivana to . . . set them free, of course.'

'And when you say, "intercept the van"?'

'Kill everyone except Marduk.' Daga shrugged. 'You will have to live with that one, I'm afraid.'

'Do they need to die?' Leo tried. 'Maybe you could restrain them.'

'Do your kids need to live? I think the answer is yes.'

'You enjoy killing.' It was a flat remark out of Leo's mouth.

Daga let out a deep belly laugh. 'The sum total of my world revolves around death. Nothing makes me happier than hearing that last gasp, seeing the light die in bright blue eyes, smelling the deep coppery aroma of freshly spilled blood. It is . . . my paradise.'

Daga shut up then, not wanting Leo to ponder adversely as to the fate of his kids. He wondered if Leo would address Ivana's likes and dislikes, but the man clearly couldn't bring himself to ask. They drove through quiet streets, among houses and through suburbs where Daga laid eyes on a thousand potential victims. This was his playground. He was happy killing the innocent and the frail just as much as he was pitting his wits against the highly skilled – like Joe Mason, for instance. They had fought briefly inside the Amori's shipyard headquarters. He would like to confront Mason again.

And maybe working for Marduk would facilitate that.

Daga knew he was one of the most fearsome killers on the planet. Ivana only enhanced his status, his potential. He contented himself during the drive with dwelling on past conquests, like the most recent killing Ivana and he had conducted in Nice.

Conducted being the perfect word.

The slicing of the man had been as precise as the direction of an opera. It was art in its purest form, taken right down to the raw flesh and bone. And, oh, how he had suffered. The bulging eyes, the mouth in rictus, the way he'd begged to die. Nothing had aroused Daga more in the last year, not even Ivana.

'We're here.'

Leo's words dragged Daga up from his reverie. He found they were driving through a gatehouse set in a high stone wall and then turning right into a car park. The area was relatively quiet, so Leo found a free spot near the front. Now, Daga got his first good look at San Vittore prison.

The structure had high and imposing modern walls, towering over the street outside. Daga knew it had six wings with three floors each and had been notorious during the Second World War because of the presence of SS guards who carried out inhuman treatment in one of the wings. Daga saw grey external pillars to two sides with narrow slits for windows and unscalable, smooth outer walls dozens of feet high. This was how a prison existed in the heart of Milan, by building up the extremities to make the people feel safe.

Leo cracked open a door, letting the cool morning air in. Daga saw that he had regained some composure and wasn't looking nearly as white as he had. Maybe there was hope for him and his family yet.

'I can get you through security as a guest,' Leo said. 'And take you to my office, where we can fudge the transfer request. It shouldn't be questioned in the time it takes for you to remove Marduk from the prison. I can make the transport request at the same time and have two men pull a van around to the gate. After that, you're on your own.'

Daga exited the car and waited for Leo to throw him the keys. 'Just remember what's at stake,' he said. 'Don't even think about playing the hero.'

'I won't.'

'Do you need a reminder?' Daga pulled his phone out, ready to dial Ivana.

'No, no, please. I will do as you say.'

'Of course you will.'

Daga followed Leo towards the high edifice and the main entrance doors. This was where the thief had to put on a pleasant face, play a part. He might even have to speak nicely to someone he only considered a future victim, a blood sac that existed only to potentially please him by dying a hard death. But that was the job. Marduk was paying them handsomely for this. Marduk had taken the time and jumped through the right hoops to find them, even from prison. Of course, Marduk had his own connections. Not all of them would have been severed by walls and bars.

Leo pushed through the entrance doors, waited at a cubicle, and then signed himself in. The guard behind the glass eyed Leo and then Daga as if he wanted to slice them, at least to Daga's eyes. The guy was none too friendly as he handed Daga a visitor pass he looped around his neck. Once that formality was over, Leo led Daga through security and then along a narrow passageway lined with photographs of previous wardens, maybe even some governors. Daga counted eight doors before they came to one that had a golden plaque bearing the name Leo Barone, a surname which, Daga thought nonsensically, meant 'free man'.

'Take a seat.' Leo waved him to a chair.

Daga preferred to stand and oversee Leo's work. He watched as the man seated himself behind the oak desk, pushed his laptop out of the way, and then started rooting inside a drawer. He pulled out a transfer document, squared it on the desk in front of him, and filled it in. Daga watched, counting the minutes. It wasn't a long process, but Daga felt an unaccountable dread. He didn't like to overexpose himself this way, to put himself right under the noses of the law. Daga was a wanted man in many countries, which was why he liked to remain in the shadows. Standing here, in the office of the prison warden, surrounded by prison guards, unnerved him more than he cared to admit. Both he and Ivana had decided the risk was worth the reward. Daga felt his fingers clench as if they were around the hilt of a knife, or around Leo's throat. It wasn't just bloodlust though; it was anxiety, too.

'Do you need authorisation?' Daga asked.

'Technically, yes,' Leo said. 'This isn't as easy as you might think. Full authorisation can take seven days if the governor gets involved, which he should, but if we act on this straight away, nobody should object, so long as I have the documents with me.'

Daga narrowed his eyes in suspicion and leaned against a filing cabinet. 'Are you sure?'

Leo shuddered involuntarily. 'As I can be,' he said. 'The documents should rightly have the governor's signature. I don't know what to expect. But I know . . . I know what's at stake.'

Daga swept his eyes across the room, looking for a weapon. He felt like threatening Leo again. But there was nothing on display that he could put to good use. Probably just as well in a prison. 'How long?' he asked.

'Just need my signature and the stamp,' he said. Leo looked up at him. 'When will you free my family?'

Daga shrugged. 'When Marduk is safe.'

'I . . . I want to say . . .' Leo could barely force the words out of his mouth. Daga noticed his eyes were shiny with tears.

'Keep it together, idiot,' Daga told him. 'Don't go sentimental on me now. You have work to do. Concentrate on what you're doing and maybe we can pull this off because, if we don't, it's snippy time.'

Leo squeezed his eyes closed, wiped them, and then rose to his feet. He flapped the sheet of paper at Daga. 'We can only try. Let's go.'

Daga nodded, pushed away from the filing cabinet, and spun on his heel. It occurred to him then that this was the first time he hadn't carried a weapon in years, and he felt naked without one. Still, needs must. As he'd told Ivana, Marduk was paying them well.

Leo led him out of the room, further along the corridor with the photographs on the wall and to a barred door. Daga made sure his visitor pass could be easily seen. The guards, both non-smiling, mustachioed replicas of each other, allowed Leo through without a word and stared at Daga with dead eyes. Daga welcomed the silence. The last thing he needed was to have to shoot the shit with these idiots. He tried not to show his nervousness at being under the spotlight.

Down another corridor, this one lined with bare walls, to a junction where Leo turned left. He led Daga to a new obstacle – a wall made of bars with another two guards standing on the other side. A gate stood in the middle. Leo spoke briefly to these two guards, rustled his transfer form, and then waited for the gate to be opened. It was right then that Daga saw Leo cast a sideways glance at him. Consternation and guilt manifested across the warden's face. Daga read the expression in an instant. The idiot was going to blab, to risk his family. He couldn't help it; the guy was just too weak to go through with it.

Daga couldn't accept that.

He leaned in close to Leo and whispered furiously into his ear. 'Blow this, and you're killing them. You. Not me, not Ivana. You might as well be wielding the knife yourself.'

Again, Leo's face twisted. The guilt was a palpable force, coming off him in waves. But so was the fear. It shocked Daga that the guards couldn't sense it. He whispered more devilish words directly into Leo's ear.

'Are you going to murder your family, Leo? They will die very badly.'

Leo swallowed his guilt and, with a tremendous effort, faced the guards with an emotionless expression. Daga ignored the two of them, trying not to show his face. On the other side of the bars were prison cells, some occupied, some not. The occupants looked lacklustre to Daga, as if they'd given up. He would gladly have rammed his knife through their hearts in a second. They didn't deserve to live. Daga thought you made your way in this world by taking everything you needed, ripping it from the jaws of Hell if need be, not by moping around and staring at your feet as if they might move you forward of their own accord.

One of the guards, named Alistair, the one on Daga's left who stood tall, as thin as a matchstick, was studying Leo with narrowed eyes, as if sensing that something was wrong. The eyes flicked from guilt-ridden Leo to the calm-looking Daga.

'You all right, boss?' Alistair asked Leo, still watching Daga. 'Bad night?'

Daga cursed silently, readying himself to act.

'Yes, yes, I'm sorry.' Leo forced out a laugh and tried to compose his face. 'A very bad night.'

'The kids ill?' The guard still watched Daga as he spoke to Leo. 'I know when mine fall ill we never get a wink of sleep.'

Leo shook his head. 'They're fine. Now can we hurry this along?'

That was better. That was good. Daga expected the guard to stand aside now, to open up the gate, but instead he turned his attention to Daga and rattled the transfer papers that he held in his hand.

'You'd better watch it with this guy Marduk,' Alistair said. 'He's a proper screwball. What do you want with him anyway?'

Daga's hands clenched into fists. He fought the urge

to kill. 'More questions,' he said evenly, keeping all traces of violence out of his voice. 'Marduk is a fountain of information.'

'Oh, I see.' The guard's eyes flicked from Daga to Leo as if assessing the situation. 'The last guy said they couldn't get anything out of him.'

Daga forced a shrug. 'That's true – it's why we want to try again. Now, we're on a schedule.' He turned to Leo. 'Can we continue?'

But the guard held out a hand, stopping them. 'I've never seen a prisoner transferred at such short notice before.'

Now it was all on the line. Daga prepared an attack, an escape plan. Everything was up to Leo. Either he would step up or . . . the worst would happen. The very worst.

'It . . . it's my fault,' Leo said at last as the tension stretched thin between them. 'I forgot Mr Daga was coming.' He shrugged. 'It happens.'

It was simple. It was delivered with just the right amount of humility and authority. Alistair's face changed, and he stepped aside, handing the papers back to Leo.

'Carry on, sir.'

Leo walked the length of the cell block and stopped at the far end, where a solid brick wall blocked their progress. Even from behind, Daga could tell that Leo's shoulders were suddenly taut with tension. Leo turned to his right and walked up to the bars of a prison cell before peering inside.

'This is the cell you want,' he said listlessly.

Daga stared into the dimly lit cell. A figure sat on the bed, staring back at him. From this distance, Daga couldn't make out a whole body, let alone a face. All he knew was that a shadow was rising to its feet.

Creepy fucker even in prison, Daga thought.

Marduk shuffled forward awkwardly, reminding Daga that he'd been shot through the knee by Joe Mason. Leo glanced at Daga.

'You ready?'

Daga just nodded. Marduk's face came into the light, twisted with expectation and distrust. There was a mad gleam in the man's eyes. Daga had come face to face with Marduk before and had felt nothing but contempt. This time, he shivered.

'Cassadaga,' Marduk whispered softly. 'Well met.'

Leo was staring rigidly at the Amori leader. Marduk was wearing beige trousers and a white shirt, both of which were heavily stained. His hair was unkempt. His hands were bruised and bloody, but not through fighting. Daga figured it came from grinding his knuckles into the ground because this madman was capable of anything.

'Open the cell,' he told Leo.

The prison warden had grabbed a key from the last guard. Now he unlocked Marduk's cell and let the prisoner out. Marduk stepped through like an avenging ghost, moving sideways with a floating quality despite his damaged knee, and stopped before them.

'I am free,' he said.

'I am a man of my word,' Daga said.

'You have this one's family?' Marduk's eyes glittered.

'Wife, son and daughter,' Daga said, a hint of excitement in his voice as the thought made his blood run hot. 'On my word, Ivana will chop them into pieces.'

Leo's whole body shook.

'Keep it together,' Marduk warned him. 'Do you know who I am?'

Leo nodded.

'I doubt it,' Marduk said, his voice rising. 'I am the monarch of the Amori, an ancient entity that fights the Church and the Vatican with every shred of its being. We founded Babylon, and still we—'

'Let's get you out of here.' Daga could imagine Marduk ranting on about the Amori and Babylon for the rest of the afternoon. 'We're against the clock.'

Leo turned smartly and quickly, eager to get this entire ordeal over with. He had to slow as Marduk started limping in his wake. Daga followed last, thinking how much Marduk's limp-drag forward motion reminded him of the gait of a reanimated corpse. Hopefully, the man's presence would leach some of the attention away from him. The trio returned the way Leo and Daga had come, passing by the suspicious guard, through two security gates and then along the corridor lined with photographs.

Six minutes later, Marduk tasted fresh air.

Daga tapped Leo on the shoulder, making him jump. 'Where's the van?'

'On its way.'

Daga could see the car from here. It would take less than two minutes to reach it, turn it on, and start following the van. He turned quickly to Marduk.

'Stay calm,' he said. 'We're not clear of this yet. You get in the van, and I'll free you later.'

'There is some killing to do?' Marduk's soft voice grated on Daga's nerve endings.

The mass murderer smiled. That was his kind of talk. 'Oh yeah,' he said. 'That's the best part.'

Chapter 4

Cassadaga jumped behind the wheel of Leo's car and followed the van through the prison gates and away from the grounds. The van was high and white, with black markings. It was easy to keep in sight, not that Daga was trying to keep his presence unnoticed. There didn't seem much point at this juncture. Inside the van was a driver, a passenger and then, in the back, Marduk and Leo. Marduk was in chains . . . again, cuffed to the seat. Leo was seated at his side. There had been a bit of a process to go through with the van's guards, but Leo had smoothed it out, showing that his role as prison warden came with some clout.

As he drove, Daga wondered what beautiful thoughts were running through the prison warden's head, thoughts of a dead family and butchered flesh. Thoughts of blood and pain. Sheer misery.

He revelled in it. He stayed close to the rear of the van, waiting for it to leave the city of Milan and find some quieter roads. This was the one potential flaw in their plan. He hadn't known which way the van would go, nor to which prison Leo would misleadingly assign Marduk, so they hadn't been able to scout the route. Nonetheless, he knew he would find the right time to act.

He had the utmost faith in his abilities.

He took a few moments to call Ivana. 'Are they behaving themselves?'

The woman's sultry tones filled his head. 'Oh, yes. Do you want me to hurt one of them?' She sounded eager.

'Not yet, not yet. Save it for when Leo's worth is spent. Are you having fun?'

'I'm getting bored. I've baited them as much as they can handle. Even made a few minor cuts. It's been okay . . . but eventually you have to go all in.'

Daga knew exactly what she meant. 'I'm sorry I can't be there to join you.'

'We would make love on their still-bleeding, dying bodies.'

'You make it sound exceptional.'

'But you are about to have some fun of your own without me.'

Daga glanced quickly at the van he was following. 'They will have to be swift kills,' he said regretfully. 'This Marduk . . . he's even creepier now than he was before.'

Ivana laughed. 'Somehow, those words don't sound right coming from you.'

'Are you saying I'm creepy?'

'Only in the best, bloodiest way. Not like Marduk. He's just a crazy arsehole.'

'I feel this isn't just about breaking him out of prison.' Daga turned the wheel as he passed a parked car on the inside, remaining close to the van. 'The man is a schemer.'

'Didn't the Amori disband when he went to prison?'

Daga laughed. 'You make them sound like a shitty boy band. I like it. Yes, they scattered, but don't underestimate Marduk. He's well connected and his plans tend to have a grand scale, especially in relation to the Church.'

'It hardly matters to us.'

'The money could bankroll us for years.'

Ivana was silent for a moment, thinking. 'I see what you mean.'

Daga noticed they had now left the city limits behind and were negotiating a more windy, quieter set of B roads. The van rolled through bend after bend, taking it steady. Traffic coming in the opposite direction was sparse. His attack would have to be swift and precise.

'I have to go,' he said.

'Enjoy,' Ivana whispered.

Daga placed his phone on the passenger seat, gripped the wheel hard, and peered around the side of the van. He needed a long straight stretch, but the roads were flowing left and right for as far as he could see. He wasn't a patient man, not unless he had a helpless victim chained up before him. Daga gritted his teeth, then glanced over at the tyre iron he'd grabbed from the boot and the long, sharp knife that lay beside his phone. Its blade glinted at him, making his mouth dry out with anticipation.

Ahead, the road stretched in a long straight line.

Daga put his foot down, hearing the engine roar. The little vehicle surged into the other lane, pulled up alongside the van, and then raced ahead. Daga pulled in front of the van and let his own car coast. A scan of the road ahead showed no other traffic in sight. He already knew there was none behind.

But for how long?

The issue was out of his hands. What *was* in his hands was the fate of all the men sitting in that van. He jammed on the brakes, slowing the car's pace. The van came up fast in his rear-view and then its driver too had to slam on the brakes. Its front end skewed, the tyres slipping on the tarmac. The men's faces jerked forward. Daga kept his foot on the brakes, bringing the van to a sudden halt in the road. Then he threw open his door, grabbed the tyre iron and the knife, and jumped out. A cool wind swept across the surrounding fields and battered his face. The hedgerows shook.

Daga ran around to the driver's side, beckoning for the man to open the door. The guy looked shocked, scared, but shook his head. Already the passenger was reaching for a radio. Daga was ready for that. He lifted the tyre iron and smashed it hard against the window. The glass cracked but didn't break. Daga brought it hammering down once again. This time, the glass smashed, separating into shards that dripped out of the window like ice shavings. Daga reached in with the knife and held its point pressed against the driver's neck.

'Don't move,' he said.

The passenger had frozen with the radio at his lips. He hadn't yet keyed the button. Daga smiled. 'Open the back.'

The passenger climbed down out of the van and came around to Daga's side, plucking a set of keys from his belt. Daga made the driver climb down too and then herded both men around to the back of the van.

At that moment, a white Nissan breezed past them at sixty miles an hour. Daga watched the receding car for any sign that it might have seen something awry, but nothing happened. He motioned to the van's back door.

'Quickly. Open it.'

The passenger didn't hesitate. Daga dug the point of his blade into the driver's throat, making him gasp. The passenger held up a hand as if to say, '*I'm doing it!*' Daga didn't care. Blood was close. He watched as the van's rear door opened, revealing a dark interior and two seated figures.

First, Leo rose and made his way out into the sunshine. Marduk followed at a slower pace. The passenger then closed the door back up and turned to Daga.

'Get in the car,' he said to Marduk and waited for the man to shuffle off.

Marduk left with a wry, expectant grin. He knew what was about to happen.

'My family?' Leo asked.

Daga kept his knife tucked into the flesh of the driver's throat. He could smell blood now and saw a little trickle of it run down the length of his blade. The passenger was staring at him.

'Hey . . . we did as you asked.'

Daga decided it was time to enter that part of paradise that he loved the most and moved so swiftly his victims could barely register it. He slashed deeply through the driver's throat, feeling the sharp blade's passage through skin with a deep shudder of contentment before whirling to the driver and double slashing across the man's face. The blood flew beautifully, spattering Daga and spattering the van and Leo. Strips of flesh hung from the passenger's face. His hands came up swiftly; he was screaming. Daga dropped low, slashed again, cutting the fronts of the man's thighs, then rose with the blade still travelling fast and brought its tip smashing up under the passenger's jaw so that it rammed home to the hilt. The blade passed from chin to brain in an instant, killing him. Daga left it in as the man collapsed to the ground.

Leo was sputtering, wiping blood from his face, and finding it hard to remain upright. His legs were wobbling. Daga bent over, gripped the dead passenger's skull and wrenched his blade free, watching as blood and other fluids dripped from the end. He gripped the hilt and turned to Leo.

'You were useful,' he said. 'And so were your family.'

He stepped into the man and grabbed hold of him to stop him fleeing, placed the blade over his heart, and pushed ever so slowly. Leo's eyes went wide, and he stammered.

'Please, no,' he said. 'I . . . helped you. I . . . got you this . . . far.'

'For your family,' Daga said softly, staring point-blank into the man's terrified eyes. 'You see, if you let me do this, your family survives.'

Leo was stark white with terror. Tears glistened in his eyes. He couldn't move, couldn't speak as Daga put a touch more pressure on the blade and felt the tip pierce the skin. It was a slow, beautiful compression, made even better by the victim knowing exactly what was happening.

'You will let my wife and children go?' Leo managed to say, throat cracking.

Daga continued with the pressure, feeling the skin tear millimetre by millimetre, the blood start flowing. 'Sure,' he said. 'I never made a promise to myself that I didn't keep. Now don't . . . fucking . . . move.'

Daga watched Leo closely as he sank the blade, all seven inches of it, into Leo's heart. There was a moment where the eyes went wide, where all thought focused on the pain and the impending death, and that moment stretched Daga's face in carnal lust. He forced the blade inside Leo until he could push no more.

And then Leo fell to the ground. The moment was over.

Daga took out his phone and called Ivana.

'Enjoy yourself,' he said. 'Butcher them.'

Chapter 5

The damn pain in his knee was ruining this joyful moment.

Marduk was free. Finally. Months of rotting away in that jail cell had felt like long years. Months of planning, of finding Cassadaga, of contacting the crazy, bloodthirsty thief. Of plotting beyond that . . . towards something more than diabolical.

When the Vatican soldiers and Joe Mason stormed the Amori's coastal hideout in their search for the remains of Jesus Christ, Marduk's plan to destroy the Church had come crumbling down. He'd tried, tried to release all the incriminating evidence that painted the saviour Christ himself as actually being a warrior king rather than a gift of love from the Father, but hadn't quite managed it.

First, because Joe Mason had stopped him. And second, because the Vatican soldiers had overwhelmed their hideout. Marduk had been shot as he tried to release the damning evidence, after first killing and blowing up several members of his own organisation in an attempt to kill Mason and his cronies.

Now, Marduk hurt. He hurt every second of every day. Sometimes the pain helped focus him, put him on the right path. Sometimes it drowned him, filling his mind with nothing but pure hatred and vitriol. Ever since he'd tried to steal the Book of Secrets, his attention had been on the Church. It should be destroyed along with the stain they called Christianity. The Church had more foul secrets than a sewer, and Marduk had nearly outed several of them. Of course, he'd done it all in the service of the Amori, the age-old entity that predated the Church by thousands of years and had helped found Babylon, its ancestral home.

We are the allies of humanity, not its enemies. He repeated the mantra often in his head, convincing himself. Christian scripture was a lie based on lies. But, so far, Marduk had not been able to prove that to anyone outside the Amori.

But where were the Amori now?

Scattered. Blown to the four winds by the devastating attack on their hideout, by the police forces of the world, by Vatican pressure. The Amori had put thousands of years of work into destroying the Vatican – now it seemed quite the opposite had happened.

But how could a benevolent God endure the ghastly trials of humanity? How could He stand by and watch all the pain and suffering? Surely that was proof – there was no God, and millions couldn't see it.

Marduk realised at that moment that Cassadaga was talking to him.

'I said . . . are you okay?' the thief asked.

Marduk looked down at himself, surprised at the question. 'Umm, yes. I think so. It's not my blood.'

Daga smirked. 'The blood of fools and innocents.'

The car was heading back towards Milan, presumably to pick Ivana up.

'What's next?' Daga asked bluntly.

'Next?' Marduk blinked. To him, the answer was obvious and had been for many months and years. In prison, they said his mind was not what it once had been. He'd *cracked*. Even when he was monarch of the Amori, he'd heard it whispered that some elders believed he'd lost his mind. Of course, they'd tried to oust him – to their total loss.

'We destroy the Church,' he said with vehemence.

'We?'

'Don't worry, you will get paid.'

'You mentioned you were short on funds.'

And Marduk regretted that. During the negotiations with Cassadaga, he'd made the mistake of explaining to him he had enough to cover the cost of the prison break, but would then have to make a new plan to cover further costs. Now, that lapse was coming back to bite him.

'I need you and any mercenaries we can both buy for a quick job. Remember, I am the leader of the Amori. I know where all the wealth lies. I know where to find what we need, and far more. I can set you up for life, Daga, so that you can . . . do your thing . . . for the rest of time without having to worry about funds. Imagine how your legend would grow if you're doing your thing into your sixties, maybe even seventies.'

He could tell Daga was interested. 'And how would you do that?'

'We need mercs willing to go, briefly, to Iraq. And we need ruthless bastards, like yourself and Ivana. People unafraid to kill, no matter the sex or age of the civilian. That's an imperative. There's an ancient site we need to uncover.'

Daga concentrated on the road as they hit the outskirts of Milan. 'Go on.'

'Do you know the history of the primeval Tower of Babel?'

'Vaguely.' Daga shrugged. 'Something about humans deciding to build a large city with a tower that reached into the heavens in order to get closer to God. The big man thought they were being impudent and then confounded their speech, so they couldn't understand each other and continue, inventing all the languages we have today, scattering the people across the world.'

Marduk looked over at him. 'You're more learned than I thought. Yes, that's the story behind the Tower of Babel. Any you might also know the supposed site of the tower?'

'I'm not here for a history lesson,' Daga growled.

'It's Babylon,' Marduk said quickly. 'But the whole Tower of Babel thing has been confused with the Etemenanki ziggurat. Etemenanki means *the foundation of heaven and earth*. It was a ziggurat located in Babylon and the site where the original Amori riches were buried. It's all there if we can reach it, all there for the taking.'

'On the site of this ziggurat? Even now?'

'Of course, it's very well buried in underground chambers. And we, the Amori, have controlled that region from afar all the time. We can't stop people going there, but we can influence government interference and the like. If you know the War on Terror, you will remember we even made sure the Americans built a base close by during the war to help safeguard our ancient assets.'

'I remember,' Daga said. 'Camp Alpha. Fanatics say that because America reconquered Babylon, so to speak, it now *is* Babylon.'

Marduk brushed that away with the sweep of a hand. 'It is the Amori homeland and always will be. Long before there was Iraq, we were there. Long before there was America, we were there. The Amori and Babylon were born as one.'

Daga said nothing.

Marduk went on. 'Just as importantly, we will gather the Faithful. They have a role to play in this too.'

Daga frowned. 'The Faithful?'

'Those who would die for the Amori. The true believers. We will need their help in the ultimate attack.'

'You have barely tasted fresh air for thirty minutes,' Daga said. 'And yet you are contemplating death and chaos once more.' He sounded approving.

'Contemplating?' Marduk's face twisted into an unpleasant smile. 'You are entirely wrong. My plans aren't about contemplation. They are absolute, and they will come to fruition.'

'Sure,' Daga said.

'You are thinking of my past failures?' Marduk found it hard to speak the sentence. 'Those were unfortunate, yes. But I have all my enemies in my sights now, not just the Vatican.'

'Mason?' Daga asked.

'Yes, and his team. And also, Cardinal Vallini. They have thwarted me twice. There will not be a third time.'

Marduk rubbed his knee as a spike in blood pressure increased the pain. The deep ache throbbed. He shifted his weight in the car, but it did no good. 'And I suffer for my losses,' he said. 'Every damn day.'

'Maybe you should tell me more about this plan,' Daga said.

And for the first time, Marduk smiled. 'We're gonna kill *everyone*,' he said gleefully.

Chapter 6

Joe Mason threw off his leather jacket and sank down into an armchair. It had been a long day. This morning, they'd been on the road before six, tasked with driving to Sheffield before collecting an artefact that needed delivering to Swansea in Wales and then returning to Sally's home in London. They had been the artefact's protection. It was a job similar to the recent one where they'd ended up on the trail of the Ark of the Covenant but, fortunately, this one had not turned out the same way. This one had been a safe, easy passage, a smooth job. Still, Mason was mentally tired and lay back in the armchair as the others sighed around him.

'Long-ass day,' Roxy said. 'I think I should stay at home next time.'

'Part of the job.' Sally yawned tiredly. 'And when they book Quest, they book all of us.'

Quaid poured whisky from a bar in the room's corner. 'I need a stiff one after all that driving today.'

Roxy started to say something in reply, but Mason judiciously interrupted her. 'It's good for you. Gets you used to driving in the modern world, you see. None of that manual transmission crap.'

'Still blatting on about that, are we?' Quaid sighed, taking a sip of his whisky. 'You'll never change my mind about old cars versus modern, Joe.'

'Then start using the paddle shift, you'll see,' Mason said. 'Stop driving the thing in auto. You're supposed to be a car guy, remember?'

'I am a car guy, but not your kind. Can't we coexist?' Quaid was smiling.

Mason grunted unhappily, but let it go. Some battles you just couldn't win, no matter how right you were. He checked the time, noting that it was a little after ten p.m. Opposite him, Hassell was standing behind Roxy's chair, stretching his back. Sally was already leaning over her laptop.

'Tallying expenses,' she said in response to his look.

'Do we have another job tomorrow?' Roxy asked with weary resignation. 'We've done nothing but transport artefacts and a professor or two lately.'

'Don't forget that dig we visited to ensure the provenance of that vase,' Quaid said.

'Oh, yeah, how could I forget that?'

'The good part is that we're helping people,' Quaid said. 'Every day. I need a bit of that in my life right now.'

'It's what you do,' Mason said. 'Since we met you in Bethlehem.'

'It's what I *try* to do to make up for a career of following some arsehole's orders to the letter,' Quaid said. 'Of being a victim of someone else's agenda, and thus making victims of countless men and women. I'm still trying to make up for that.'

'You couldn't try any harder,' Roxy said, reminding Mason once again that she was battling to find herself.

'How are you coping, Hassell?' Mason asked, to get the New Yorker involved in the conversation. He'd been entirely too quiet today, and Mason knew the man's thoughts went to introspective hell when he stayed silent.

'Better than working for the enemy,' Hassell said with a grunt and then a smile. 'It occupies the mind for a time.'

Mason was about to force more out of Hassell when Sally's phone rang. She looked up quickly, the blue tips of her hair flinging back against her face. Her features creased when she looked for the identity of the caller.

'It's unknown,' she said before answering.

Mason wasn't moved or impressed. It was entirely too late, and it had been too long a day to be either. He shoved himself out of his chair with a little groan and went to join Quaid at the drinks cabinet.

'Oh, hello.' Sally's voice rose a few octaves. 'I didn't realise it was you.'

Mason continued pouring his drink, but now with more than half an ear on the conversation.

'Wait, what?' Sally's voice turned urgent. 'Are you joking?'

They all turned to stare at Sally.

The historian coughed, regained her composure, and then spoke into her handset. 'Cardinal Vallini,' she said. 'I am going to put you on speakerphone.'

At the mention of the name, Mason was instantly transported back to their search for the Vatican Book of Secrets and the Amori's Creed – their version of the Bible that predated the Christian tome. Cardinal Vallini had been their primary contact throughout those events and even a friend. He had also been a close confidant of Sally's late father and a man who could gain them access to almost anything.

'Good,' Vallini said. 'Now I can speak to everyone. I have grave news, I'm afraid.'

Mason frowned. He couldn't imagine why Vallini would contact the team, couldn't imagine what it might involve. Vallini was one of the most prominent men in the Vatican.

'What is it?' Roxy asked bluntly.

'I'm sorry to tell you that Marduk has escaped prison.'

Mason's mouth fell open. He tried to close it, but it didn't work. Looking around at the others, he saw similar expressions of shock.

'You have to be kidding,' Quaid said.

'Then someone fucked up big time,' Roxy said.

'What happened?' Sally asked.

'Unclear at the moment,' Vallini all but whispered. 'But what we know is terrible. A prison warden's family targeted and later murdered. Because of that, we believe they forced the warden to falsify a prisoner transport and take Marduk out of prison. The van he was travelling in was later attacked and Marduk was freed. The transport guards were killed along with the warden, just left at the side of the road.'

'Marduk always had resources,' Mason said.

'We knew that,' Sally said. 'But he was supposed to be under special guard.'

Vallini interrupted them. 'As I said, we know very little at this stage. But the fact is – a man who threatened the existence of the Church, the Vatican and Christianity itself, as well as you people, has escaped prison. He's out there somewhere, and you can be sure he's already plotting.'

'He threatened you too,' Sally said.

'I have my faith,' Vallini said quickly. 'I have His strength and the strength of the Holy Spirit. God is with me always.'

'I have faith in myself,' Roxy said quietly. 'That's what works for me.'

Mason stepped closer to the phone. 'Do the police have any leads?'

'Nothing concrete,' Vallini told them. 'I am telling you this out of courtesy and as a thank you for all your past help. All the police know is that a woman held the family hostage, later killing them, and that a man accompanied the warden in and out of prison. They're still piecing it together.'

'Marduk could be anywhere by now.' Sally shot a glance at the curtained window, as if expecting a furtive shadow to cross it.

'He's on the run, a fugitive,' Mason said firmly. 'I doubt he'll surface for a while. But thank you for letting us know. It's appreciated.'

Vallini told them to take care and then ended the call, leaving Sally staring at the phone and then at her friends.

'He'll be hell-bent on resuming where he left off,' she said.

Mason nodded. 'I know that. We all know that. But there's nothing we can do about it. Not now.'

'He's a terrible parasite,' Quaid said. 'We should have shot him. *You* should have shot him.' He nodded at Mason.

'I did shoot him.'

'I mean properly, not in his bloody knee.'

'I'm not a soldier anymore,' Mason said. 'And neither are you.'

Quaid nodded quickly, understanding where Mason was going with this. In the army, they'd had no choice, which was partly why they fought inner demons these days. Now . . . he had every choice in the world.

'I don't think there's anything we can do,' Roxy said. 'Except take extra precautions. You'd imagine a man like Marduk will have bigger things on his mind than us.'

'Don't underestimate yourself,' Hassell said. 'When I worked for Gido on the wrong side of the tracks, he never forgot a slight, never overlooked an enemy, never let a single thing go.'

'Thanks for that,' Quaid said drily.

'You need to know,' Hassell said. 'Marduk will come for us.'

Mason tended to agree with Hassell's predicted scenario, though said nothing out loud. But making enemies happened to everyone, in all walks of life. It came with the territory.

'Starting tomorrow, we increase security,' he said. 'I'm assuming you'll be okay with that, Sally?'

Sally had inherited her father's millions and, as well as employing them, handled the upkeep of the house. She nodded without really looking up from the phone, her thoughts still elsewhere.

'And in the meantime, we have jobs to do,' Quaid said.

'Do you think Cardinal Vallini will be all right?' Sally asked, still looking down.

'In the Vatican? He's safer than we are,' Hassell said.

Sally looked up. 'Says the man who helped infiltrate that very place.'

Hassell shifted uncomfortably. 'I'm a specialist,' he said. 'It took me three months to plan and, let's be honest, the plan failed. Vallini knows what he's up against.'

Mason agreed with Hassell. Cardinal Vallini had first-hand knowledge of Marduk and all his machinations. The man would be prepared. He yawned. A long day had turned into something far worse. This was the first time in civilian life Mason was aware of an active enemy coming after him. In the army, in places like Iraq and Afghanistan, you knew the enemy was there, and that they were out to get you. It was part of everyday life. Here, at home, the scenario was entirely different. He felt unsettled and out of sorts. He felt anxious for his friends. He was fully aware that his life never seemed to run smoothly.

'Do I attract trouble?' he said out loud. 'It certainly feels that way.'

'No more than I do,' Roxy said. 'Sometimes I feel like it's the only thing attracted to me.'

Mason looked at her, feeling sadness, but then noticing the wry smile on her face. The question was – was the smile being forced? You could never tell with Roxy.

'Don't worry, everyone,' he said. 'We have weapons, and we'll have this place secured to the hilt by tomorrow night. If Marduk comes, he'll find us waiting for him.'

As he'd hoped, they all looked confident. It was the look he'd been aiming for. It showed this team had come a long way – from a ragtag bunch thrown together by circumstance into a capable unit that fused in all the right ways, and now into a cohesive component that complemented one another.

They drifted apart, each seeking their own rooms. Mason still couldn't decide if he wanted to stay here full time – there was plenty of room. But he liked his apartment in London, enjoyed the proximity to lots of local conveniences. He'd kept it on for now, unsure which way to jump. Sally's place was the ultimate closeness for work, clearly. But sometimes, it felt as if they were living on top of each other.

Still, it had only been a few months and, for most of that time, they hadn't even been here. Mason felt like he was experiencing an extended stay in a hotel, a very nice hotel for sure, but still some kind of temporary residence. The recent slew of mundane jobs was good for business, but not necessarily good for his spirit.

What are you looking for then?

He'd know when he found it.

Chapter 7

Marduk sat on a plastic folding chair in the middle of a brown desert, under a raging blue sky. It was midday. His feet were in the sand. His knee was screaming at him. Sweat and grime coated his face. His clothes stuck to his body. There was no air in this godforsaken place.

To left and right, men toiled. They knew they had to be in and out of this land – Iraq – quickly and unobtrusively. Marduk had been hard at work, quickly pulling together a small army of ruthless mercs who would obey any order, no matter how depraved, to get their cut of a decent payday. Now, they were working to put together a makeshift shelter in the lee of a mountain. Guards ranged the nearby hills with orders to hide and warn rather than challenge if anyone appeared. The air was sultry, the wind warm and full of sand particles. Marduk found that the pain in his knee meant he could barely move, not that he wanted to help anyone.

The men laboured hard. They wanted their payday as fast as possible. And there was only one way they were going to get it . . .

Marduk was playing a dangerous game. He'd almost run out of money, yet here he was, hiring fifteen ex-soldiers and retaining the services of Cassadaga and Ivana. Worse, the latter two *knew* he was short on cash. They knew this trip was an all-or-nothing kind of affair.

Marduk remained confident. The Tower of Babel – or more properly, the Etemenanki ziggurat – would provide him with all the riches he could ever desire. Which, for Marduk, was saying something. His tastes bordered on the truly lavish.

For now, though, the discomfort beat at him like a cat-o'-nine-tails. He rubbed his knee, dry-swallowed pain-killers and drank bottles of water. He asked a man to set up an umbrella over him. He sat there and brooded and thought about all the good things this momentary suffering would revive.

Marduk surveyed the landscape. It was barren, brown, and lifeless. They had two good local guides who assured them nobody would bother them out here. They were less than a twenty-minute hike away from Babylon.

For a soldier, at least. Marduk would need far longer and might even need to be carried. He'd deal with that when the time arrived. For now, he watched the mercs work, listened to their cursing, and looked for Daga and Ivana.

They hadn't been seen for a while and had offered no help to the mercs. Marduk was under no illusions about how far he could control them. He couldn't. They lived on a violent appetite, by a compass that pointed only towards the most bloodstained inclinations. But they were useful. He hoped he would soon feel confident enough in his domain to point them in the direction of his enemies.

But for now, he had to endure all *this*.

The mercs knew what they were doing and worked efficiently. Marduk felt the painkillers kick in. He saw the tent that would be his taking shape. The shade would be blissful. He passed the time by reviewing the plan in his head.

For thousands of years, the Tower of Babel had been part of Babylon's and the Amori's rich history. It was called *Babel*, according to one of Marduk's hated scriptures – the Book of Genesis – because it was there that the Lord confused the languages of the earth and scattered the people far and wide. The Creed – Marduk's own bible – attested that it had been a wonder of the world with a summit raised to heaven, a gift to their gods.

But Babel was also the Hebrew name for Babylon. And the tower of Babylon was the Etemenanki ziggurat. Nebuchadnezzar, the great king of Babylon himself, had had inscribed on an ancient monument excavated in 1917 that he had made one of the greatest constructions in the history of man, a true marvel. In 1880 another inscription had been found that stated: '*its foundations I laid out in gold, silver, gemstones from mountain and sea*.' Marduk knew this to be a reference to the great riches that were secreted under its base, riches that had never even been guessed at, never mind discovered.

But Marduk was the monarch of the Amori. He knew more secrets than most of the elders. He was a man who worshipped Babylon and the icon it had become for the world. The great Babylon. The dynastic wonder and example it presented. The Amori had turned it into the region's holy city, eclipsing Nippur. The largest city of the world, site of the Hanging Gardens, wonder of ancient times, home to Nebuchadnezzar and Alexander the Great, its name meaning the very 'gate of the gods', and home to the famous Ishtar Gate, Babylon had always been the home of the Amori and the Amori were a civilised society two thousand years before the coming of Christ.

All of that meant everything to Marduk, but the stark fact was that it also meant very little if he couldn't locate the riches in question.

Through the shimmering heat haze that hung over the desert, Marduk saw two figures approaching. Even blurred as they were, he could recognise Cassadaga and Ivana, walking together and headed straight for him. There was a strange look on Daga's face, something born of viciousness and, strangely, uncertainty.

'I see your tent is almost ready.' Ivana cast an appraising glance over Marduk's seated form and the nearby canvas structure, pointing out the fact that he clearly wasn't helping.

Marduk studied her. Ivana was a tall, broad-shouldered powerhouse, with attractive Eastern European features. She was an expert safecracker. More than that, she was a cruel killer who delighted in the murder of innocents and happily assisted Daga in his goal of killing more people by hand than anyone else alive.

'Currently,' he said, 'I work better out of this heat, and preferably loaded with painkillers and alcohol and anything else drug-related you might be able to procure for me.' He gave her a long look. 'And, believe me, for the next few days, you want me at my best.'

'You got that right,' she said quickly.

'Excuse me?'

Daga waved a hand. 'You have a problem,' he said.

Marduk was highly aware of the phrasing of Daga's statement. The word *you* told him that Daga would never be solid backup.

'What problem?'

'Ivana and I took a stroll.' Daga was talking easily and, Marduk noticed, showed no strain from the walk out into the desert and, it appeared, wasn't even sweating.

'To where?'

'To your ziggurat, your Tower of Babel. We borrowed some equipment, survival rations and a satnav, and made our way about twenty-five minutes in a northerly direction. The guides are right. This area has no life, no signs of people, no rebels, nothing.'

Inside, Marduk was seething. The first approach to the Etemenanki ziggurat should have been cautiously controlled and under cover of darkness. The success of his plan counted on risk avoidance.

'So what is the problem?' he asked shortly.

'A village has sprung up close to the site of the ziggurat, assuming your coordinates are accurate,' Daga told him. 'We counted several tents and some wooden structures, at least two dozen people. Men, women, children.'

Marduk let the news sink in for a moment. 'That is a setback,' he said finally. 'How close?'

'Well, put it this way,' Ivana said, 'if you're planning on taking all fifteen men with you, they'll be seen and heard. Just Daga and I, however . . .'

Marduk ignored her smiling face. He would need everyone for the initial dig. There would be noise. Nothing spectacular, but enough to wake two dozen sleeping villagers. 'Are they dug in?' he asked. 'I mean – do they look like they are there to stay?'

Ivana gave him a wicked smile. 'For now,' she said.

Marduk didn't really understand her meaning and didn't care. The problem was immense. If he couldn't excavate at the ziggurat, he couldn't extract the wealth.

If he couldn't extract the wealth, all these mercs were liable to kill him, with Daga and Ivana cheering them on. He watched the two killers watch him, saw them savouring every worry line that creased his face.

'Then we must take care of them,' he said. 'There's a reason I asked for mercenaries with no scruples.'

'You knew this might happen?'

'It was always a possibility. They're drawn to the old ruins like moths to flames.'

'The villagers?' Daga asked.

'Yes, the fucking villagers. They have put roots down on sacred land. They are defiling consecrated ground. That is the Etemenanki ziggurat they are corrupting with their filth – a holy, blessed relic of the Amori and of Babylon. How dare they!'

'And when you say, "take care of"?' Ivana questioned.

'I want our mercenary friends to kill them. Move on the village and kill every man, woman and child.'

'I'd bet they don't *know* they're on your ziggurat,' Ivana said.

'I don't care,' Marduk all but squealed, rising to the bait. 'Nobody crosses me and gets away with it. You hear me? *Nobody.* I will see them all butchered, murdered, torn limb from limb.' He rose to his feet, unsteady on his bad knee. 'We will send in the mercenaries. And when they are done, not a soul will remain to tarnish the eminent site. The best thing they can do is to nourish it with their blood.'

'And nourish it they will,' Daga said. 'I like the way your mind works, Marduk.'

Several mercenaries were listening to the rant, got the gist of the conversation, and wandered over. One of them looked Marduk dead in the eye.

'These are innocent people,' he said. 'Villagers, I hear. You could work with their knowledge. You could ask their consent, maybe.'

'Consent?' Marduk's voice rose several octaves and fresh sweat popped out across his forehead. '*Consent?* I do not *need* consent. I am the monarch of the Amori. This is our land, *our* land. Do not speak to me about consent.'

Marduk was breathing heavily, heart racing. He could barely control himself. His initial impulse was to smash the merc's nose and then stab him through the heart, but this wasn't an Amori HQ. It was the middle of a roasting desert hell, and Marduk needed all the help he could get.

'I didn't sign on to kill innocent civilians,' the merc continued.

Marduk resisted the impulse to lash out once again and fought to find the right words. Before he could open his mouth, Daga spoke up.

'And yet you did,' he said. 'This job was offered at a substantial rate of pay, only for those willing to follow orders to the letter. For those willing to get the job done no matter what. Those were your terms, soldier, and it's now up to you to stick by them.'

The merc narrowed his eyes, appraising Daga. The man beside him shrugged as if to say, 'no skin off my nose'. Daga didn't move a muscle, but Marduk could see that he was ready to fight, that in fact he was hoping the merc made a move.

Maybe the merc saw it too. After a few moments, he shrugged and said no more, turning away. Which left Marduk staring after him, wondering what his intentions were.

'Keep an eye on that one,' he said.

'Always do,' Daga said.

'When do we execute the next stage?' Ivana said with a grin at her own clever wording.

'Tonight,' Marduk said. 'We will kill them all tonight.'

Chapter 8

It turned out that more than one merc was unhappy with committing the atrocity.

Marduk noticed half a dozen men, all complaining, all whining about it. He couldn't understand them. It was an easy kill. What were they worried about? All they had to do was shoot and stab two dozen men and women who wouldn't put up a fight. Marduk thought it was a simple way of earning money.

And he put it that way to them.

Gathered outside his tent, he addressed them all as the afternoon waned. His simple opening comment was: '*Do you want a pay rise?*' Most of them cheered. Some of the naysayers started to smile. Marduk reckoned he had just three rebels and fifteen minus three was still a passable twelve, plus Daga and Ivana. To be fair, he knew the latter two could get the job done on their own, and he considered it. But the other mercs needed to earn their pay, and there was no better way to show them who was boss than to make them kill.

The assault on the village was decided. It was about

an hour before they were due to depart, as the sun dimmed across the western horizon, that Marduk received his visitor.

He sat on the floor inside his tent, welcoming the shade, but still hotter than a pepperoni in a pizza oven when a smaller than average merc thrust his head inside the flap. Marduk started, unused to intrusions.

'What is it?'

'Someone to see you, sir.'

'Now? Here?' His brow furrowed. 'Who could possibly want to see me here?'

'A man.' The merc shrugged. 'Says you called for him. Calls himself Keeva.'

Marduk was even more baffled. Instead of rising to his feet, which would cause him pain, he waved at the merc and attempted a smile. 'Send him in.'

The small merc nodded and then departed. Two seconds later, another figure interrupted Marduk's peace, this one the polar opposite of the merc. He was tall, at least six foot three, and wiry with long, lank hair and a bushy beard. His eyes glinted when they alighted on Marduk.

'I am Keeva,' he said, straightening to his full height.

Marduk recognised something in the glint of those eyes. 'You are one of the Faithful?'

'Prepared to serve in any way that I can, sir.'

'How the hell did you find me?'

'The Amori still check the old boards, sir. After your . . . abscondment . . . you mentioned you were returning to the Great Ziggurat. Luckily, I knew where to search.'

Marduk hadn't expected the so-called 'old boards' to be quite so active. They were, at their basic level, an internet chat site known only to the Amori. Marduk had figured that anyone still faithful to the cause would monitor the boards. He hadn't expected such fast results.

'Well done for spotting my message and acting on it. I assume you are on your own, Keeva?'

The young man nodded.

'Well, I am sure that will soon change. But for now, you are welcome. You will be the first of my special disciples, my Faithful. And you may serve me, Keeva. You will be my legs, my arms, when I cannot use them. And you will be the special one.'

'I will serve to the best of my ability, sir.'

'I know you will. And I am sure many more will soon join you.' Marduk knew others would come. There were many ways to get the word out that the Amori was back in business. For now, though, a rich odour was wafting around Marduk's nostrils.

'Maybe you could go take a wash.'

With a shuffle and a bow, Keeva turned and disappeared, exiting the tent with a *snick* of canvas. Marduk was ecstatic. The Faithful were integral to his plan and had already started arriving. After they were finished here in Babylon, he would have to come up with a more appropriate meeting point. Keeva had certainly outdone himself and deserved the glory Marduk would heap upon him soon.

Marduk wiped sweat from his brow. He wasn't looking forward to tonight's trek. He wondered briefly if Keeva could carry him, but then decided the lack of dignity wouldn't really send the right message. Marduk would get by. He was the monarch of the Amori. The coming dig at Etemenanki was the start of the downfall of the Vatican.

There were crunching footsteps at the entrance to his tent, and then another head forced its way inside.

'Ready to go,' a sullen-faced man said briefly and then

withdrew before Marduk could speak. If the man had been Amori, Marduk would have had him lashed for his insolence.

The moment he'd been dreading had arrived. He rose to his feet, felt the pain lance through his knee. Every second of pain reminded him of Joe Mason and, by association, the Vatican. Cardinal Vallini too. They would all get their comeuppance.

Outside, the day was waning. Probably early evening, Marduk guessed. They would trek for twenty minutes to this new village in the middle of nowhere and then go to the ziggurat. Work would begin tonight and it would not stop until they found something. Of course, Marduk knew his Amori history to the nth degree. He knew exactly where to look for the old treasures and, because of his standing with the secret organisation during the last few decades, knew the right people to contact to turn the treasures into hard cash.

Marduk saw that the mercenaries had formed up. There were fifteen of them, which was good, no abstentions. They knew what they were going to do. Standing apart were Cassadaga and Ivana. Marduk made his painful way over to them.

'Whatever you do,' he said. 'Don't kill Keeva. I have plans for him. Big plans.'

Daga shrugged. 'I heard one of your Faithful had turned up.'

'The first of many,' Marduk said, and then yelled: 'Now, can we get this party started?'

He received several glowers, probably from those discontents who weren't happy with killing the villagers. Marduk didn't see it as his problem. The damn civilians shouldn't be there in the first place. Let them suffer.

The small team moved out, leaving their assortment of tents behind. The sun had vanished behind dark clouds, casting long shadows over the land. The ground was hard, rocky, and brown. It gave the impression that the Hand of God had beaten it up. They walked at a decent speed, Marduk included, across the rolling landscape.

Marduk was concentrating on tonight's goal. Those thoughts were awe-inspiring and took the focus away from his agony. Keeva was walking at his side and one step back as befitted his station. Marduk wanted to keep up with the soldiers and make the journey as swiftly as possible.

They trekked through the desolate countryside. A harsh wind blew, a reminder that the temperature could plummet at any minute. It stirred up the dust, which then blew at their faces. The mercenary leader sent out scouts in all directions, making sure nobody surprised them, and the twenty minutes' journey was uneventful.

Finally, the mercs sank to the ground. Marduk gladly stopped walking and dropped with them. He was too far back to see anything properly and noticed that the ground fell away ahead. The lead mercs were lying at the top of a hill, tugging binoculars out of their packs. Grimacing, Marduk shuffled his way to the front.

On arriving, he didn't need binoculars to take in the scene below. First, the greatest thing that screamed out at him was the site of the great ziggurat. It made a magnificent imprint on the land, a vast square of darker terrain that marked the four walls, clearly visible. Marduk took a moment to experience the sheer joy that filled him. This was Etemenanki, the ancient legendary site of the Tower of Babel.

Thoughts of past glories fired his imagination. He saw in his head the vast numbers of restrained workers struggling, heaving and dying as they worked on their tower of stone. He saw their flesh and bone striving, heard the clanking of their chains, smelled their sweat and their fear. He saw the magnificent structure taking shape, the topmost temple approaching the heavens. It was Babylon in its prime, *his* Babylon, the Amori's Babylon, the jewel of all the ages. It was the greatest wonder ever built.

Even now, he saw, thousands of years later, the ziggurat still dominated the landscape in which it lay.

His attention was then dragged to the west, since that was the direction in which everyone else was looking. The ground was flat there; a narrow, winding stream split the monotony. Marduk saw a makeshift huddle of tents and small timber homes close to the banks of the stream, and though the light was dying, he made out at least a dozen shapes either sitting peacefully or walking among the abodes.

'The villagers,' someone said. 'I don't think they'd bother us.'

'A chunk of cash would silence them easily,' someone else said.

Marduk couldn't believe their disrespect. This scum of the earth was living in the great shadow of the wondrous ziggurat. Their very impudence deserved a slow death. To Marduk's mind, being shot in the head was a mercy.

'I want them all dead,' he said.

Daga and Ivana crept to his left side, knives in their hands.

'I want them all dead,' he repeated. 'Every last one of them.'

Some soldiers were already moving, scrambling down

the slope with their guns in their hands. They weren't moving carefully. They were treating the civilians as the untrained, inexperienced fodder that they were. Marduk rose to his knees and then his feet, favouring his good knee. He wanted to be among the killing. Soon, even the most reluctant soldiers were scurrying down the slope as an ever-growing darkness spread across the night sky. They were deadly shadows against the backdrop, demons from the lowest level of Hell. Marduk hobbled along behind them as the most eager men entered the village.

The first silenced gunshot rang out, and then the screams started. Figures rose and stared, wondering what all the commotion was about. Mercenaries sprang among the tents and homes. They ran down the narrow alleyways formed by the abodes. They ducked inside the shelters and grabbed men, women and children, dragging them outside by their hair or executing them where they stood. It all happened quickly in the end. Marduk couldn't keep up. He limped across the hard ground, eyes focused on the massacre, blood boiling. Daga and Ivana had raced off like man-eaters, leaving his side, not wanting to miss out on the bloodshed. More silenced gunshots filled the air.

Marduk arrived at the first tent. He smelled blood. He looked down to see the dead, upturned face of an old man. Marduk wanted to smash that old man's skull under his boots, but the pain in his knee wouldn't allow it. He contented himself with spitting on the corpse. He moved forward, threading a way through the tents. Ahead, the mercs were doing their work well. Screams rang out left and right. A long-haired woman struggled as a man held her with one hand and put a gun to her head with the other. She soon stopped struggling.

The ex-soldier grinned in her face and then pulled the trigger, letting her collapse to the ground.

A young man was rising from his knees after witnessing the murder of his mother and sister, throwing himself at two of the mercs. They let him bounce off them, laughing, and then, big men that they were, they holstered their guns and took out their knives to give him a chance. Closer to the river, Marduk smiled to see some villagers being drowned. He revelled in that kind of initiative. Closer, a male villager burst out of a tent, saw Marduk and flew at him. Marduk cringed, not ready for the attack and unable to help himself, but at the last moment something fast and shadowy flew past, grabbed the man and took him down. Marduk recognised Daga's shape even as the thief slashed his knife back and forth, opening up the villager's throat and face. With relief, Marduk sighed.

Further ahead, several soldiers were dragging the bulk of the villagers out of their tents and homes and pushing them towards the banks of the stream. It was chaos, and it was a beautiful hell. Marduk could smell fresh blood, see ripped-open bodies and the holes where bullets had smashed people apart. It was only what they deserved; he knew. The gods of the Amori demanded their sacrifice and he, Marduk, was about as close to a god as anyone was going to get.

The villagers, shoved and prodded until they lined up along the riverbank, stood with their backs to the water. Then, there was no ceremony. One merc opened fire and then all the others. Bullets smashed into hearts and skulls and faces and sent the villagers crumpling and twisting. The waters ran red. The bodies fell and twitched and bled into the ground. Marduk watched from a safe distance, licking his lips and enjoying the slaughter.

Finally, the leader of the mercs turned to him. 'All dead,' he said.

'Are you sure? I don't want even a snivelling child left alive.'

'There isn't,' Daga said from the side. 'Ivana and I took care of that.'

Marduk was glad he was in the company of such consummate killers. It made his life far easier. 'Then let's get to work,' he said.

The mercs posted four guards just in case, wary that someone may have overheard the screams. They didn't want anyone coming over to investigate. Everyone, especially Marduk, was very much aware that they couldn't remain here for long. Iraq was a powder keg, still simmering, and incredibly unpredictable. Every second they were here was a risk.

The entire team left the massacre behind and walked three minutes to the site of the ziggurat. Marduk saw they were coming upon it from the western side. Now, the mercs were all turning to him.

'Pull out your spades, boys,' he said. 'Now, the proper work begins.'

He walked to the eastern side of Etemenanki and then paced all the way to where that wall met the rear wall. There, he stopped and beckoned the others. 'Start here,' he said.

Others may have tried to find riches around the site, but only Marduk knew the exact spot in which to dig. Only he had the impeccable knowledge. He drifted away as the mercs bent their backs to the task of digging, of creating a hole in the ground. He found a rock to sit on and started rubbing his throbbing knee.

It was the first time he'd thought of it since the killing began.

What a wonderful distraction the slaughter had been. He reflected on it again now, the sound of bullets and knives sinking into flesh, the smell of fresh blood. It soothed him; it was an anaesthetic that calmed his pain.

Daga and Ivana came to stand close to him. 'Whilst we had fun,' Daga said, 'I have to ask if you need us for anything else?'

'We're bored,' Ivana said.

'Need you?' Marduk said. 'Yes, I need you. I need you for all of this. There will be good times that offset the bad, times of senseless assassination. That is coming. I want nothing more for the Vatican.'

'Perhaps it would help if you explained your plan,' Daga said.

'I can't reveal all,' Marduk said. 'I won't. It is too soon. But I will take my enemies apart. I will attack, all at once, and they won't see me coming until the moment is upon them. It will take preparation, weeks of it, dedication of the highest order, skills that will be hard to find. I will—'

'But what of us?' Daga asked. 'I know of your hatred of the Church. It doesn't concern me. You are digging our payment out of the ground. We trusted you with that. Now, I want to know what you have planned for the greatest thief that ever lived.'

'Thieves,' Ivana said.

Marduk stared at them. 'I have just the thing to keep you fully entertained,' he said. 'The perfect job.'

Daga's eyebrows rose slightly. 'Go on.'

'My plans are ongoing,' Marduk said reluctantly. 'I prefer not to disclose them right now. But have I let you down yet?'

Daga bared his teeth. 'You're still alive, aren't you?'

'Remember,' Marduk said, 'the Faithful will grow. Their number, I mean. It will grow. Today, we have Keeva; tomorrow perhaps a half a dozen more.'

'And what will you do with this so-called Faithful?'

'They are part of the same plan. You cannot underestimate their usefulness. We need them.'

'You need them.'

'The ruin of the Vatican will bring much glory for you as well as me. It will involve great bloodshed. Surely, there is no better feeling. You make do for now so that you can revel in the butchery later.'

Daga glanced at Ivana and shrugged. 'He's been as good as his word so far.'

Ivana looked at the dark landscape, her hair tousled by the wind. 'I like it here,' she said. 'The smell of fresh blood carries on the wind.'

Marduk took that as a sign of acquiescence. 'Then you're with me,' he said gladly. 'We'll see this through together.'

'Just keep the bodies coming,' Daga said with an evil leer.

'Speaking of that . . .' Marduk said. 'I'd like to tell you all about your next job.'

Chapter 9

During breakfast, Cardinal Vallini called them again.

Mason was shovelling a heaped spoonful of oats topped with fruit into his mouth when Sally's mobile phone rang. Roxy and Quaid looked up from their places by the coffee machine, a spot they hardly vacated during breakfast. Sally checked her screen.

'I wonder what he wants this time,' she said, showing them.

Hassell entered the kitchen right then, yawning, his eyes flicking instantly to the toaster. Sally answered the phone and switched it to speaker.

'We're all here, Cardinal,' she said.

'At this time? Do you people live together?'

It was meant as a joke, but Mason found his eyes flicking from face to face. They hadn't started out this way, but staying in the same house was becoming more of a common occurrence and convenience.

'We're figuring it out,' Sally said. 'What can we do for you?'

'Well, it's largely regarding our conversation of last

night,' Vallini said. 'Marduk has escaped, as you know. His whereabouts are unknown. I am sure that you know as well as I do he will waste no time in targeting the Church, the Vatican?'

Sally bobbed her head. 'I agree.'

'Don't get me wrong, we have our contingencies, our securities in place. The Vatican is harder to infiltrate than ever before. We monitor broadcasts around the clock. We are ready for anything that madman might try to do.'

'I'm glad to hear that,' Sally said, frowning as she sensed Vallini was skirting around a point. 'Are you worried about the Church?'

'The Church is the people of the kingdom of God. It is them I worry about. Like any other organisation, we need all the help we can get. It is for this reason that I am calling you.'

Sally eyed the others. 'I see. Go on.'

'I want to re-employ you, retain your services again, because I have a feeling that once Marduk figures out what he's going to do, we may need your help.'

'Why us?' Mason asked.

'Call me superstitious.' Vallini laughed. 'If you like. Call me overly cautious. But twice we have needed outside help to deal with Marduk. Twice, you have been there.'

It made sense to Mason. 'We're your good luck charm,' he said.

'Oh, I think it's more than just luck,' Quaid said.

'And I agree,' Vallini said. 'You work well together. I think our defences are better with you on board.'

Sally was thinking hard. 'Do you want us there?'

'In Rome? No, that won't be necessary. I want you on retainer until the threat has passed.'

'That'll work,' Sally said. 'We won't let our other clients down then.'

Vallini sighed. 'I can't believe that we are defending Christianity once again. This madman, this Marduk, he is the bane of all our lives.'

The words instantly transported Mason back to Mosul, where he'd lost two friends to – what he believed – was a mistake. Zach and Harry had been killed by an IED left in a house that Mason had already checked. The terrible event had haunted him ever since. It had made him leave the army, broken up his marriage and forced him into the private sector. Still, the demons came at him every night, clawing and shrieking and pulling him down under their guilt-ridden wings. After Mosul, Mason had truly believed he'd never join a team again. It was a testament to Roxy, Sally, Quaid and Hassell that he was here at all. And it had been a struggle.

For all of them, Mason knew. He wasn't the only one. Guilt and remorse and sorrow plagued them all. Maybe it was the glue that held them together. Roxy was looking for the woman she could have been. Quaid was intent on helping people. Hassell was struggling to find an answer that couldn't possibly ever arrive. And Sally . . . well, she was juggling a rebellious nature with fresh responsibilities. She'd literally been thrown into a new life, accepting her father's cash whether or not she liked it. But at least she was trying to do good things with it.

'Marduk's another in a long line of curses for us,' Mason said.

'Evil has come upon you,' Vallini said, as if quoting from the Bible. 'And it has come upon us, too. You don't know this, but we have identified the man and woman who helped Marduk escape the Italian prison.'

Mason's mind flicked instantly to the only man and woman combination he associated with Marduk. 'Don't tell me . . .'

'Cassadaga and Ivana,' Vallini said. 'It was I who identified them, since the Carabinieri did not know what they looked like until now. They are working for Marduk again.'

'That's terrible,' Roxy said.

Mason saw that as a major upscaling of the danger they were facing. Cassadaga at least was a world-class killer and had survived long enough to demand respect. He felt a shiver run through him.

'About time we started securing this place,' Sally said quietly.

They were all silent for a while, remembering how truly horrifying Cassadaga had been. He was the one person they'd all been secretly hoping they'd never have to come up against again.

'I will leave you to it,' Vallini said and then added: 'I hope to God that I do not have to contact you again over this matter. And I truly mean that.'

The team stared at each other, thoughts of Marduk and Cassadaga running through their brains, images from exploits involving the two men as fresh as newly spilt blood in their minds. There was no getting away from it.

The confrontation was coming.

It was just a matter of when.

Chapter 10

In the darkest part of the night, two killers haunted Rome.

I'd like to tell you about your next job, Marduk had said. And then he had promised them the best job on the planet.

Cassadaga had rarely been as hyped and excited about a single job. Ivana probably felt the same way. Sensuous, murderous thoughts of what they were about to do filled him, intoxicating his mind. It was acute danger mixed with bloody deeds, something that would stun the world. It was Marduk throwing down the gauntlet.

Rome breathed easily all around them. The streets were benighted and quiet, unlit where Daga and his companion walked. The Eternal City was lesser crowded around these parts, full of hidden corners, narrow streets amid the historical sights. They avoided the cameras, but Rome was not as CCTV-heavy as other cities like London. Unfortunately, the prison job had put them on the radar of several police forces, a loss of anonymity that angered them both.

But Marduk was coming through. Over in Iraq, the mercenary crew had hit upon something promising under the earth – a wide, thick stone slab that was sitting on top of something, most likely a stone staircase that led deep into the ground. Marduk was adamant that they'd found what they were looking for. The mercs were hard at work.

Daga and Ivana crossed an empty road, hugging the shadows. A fresh, chilly wind scoured the street. They could hear the infrequent rumble of nearby cars crossing other streets and junctions, more famous, prettier, historical junctions that led to unique walkways and squares, art galleries and restaurants. They heard a dog barking and a distant door closing. Pent up with adrenalin, Daga and Ivana were both still as cold as ice. There was perfect clarity in Daga's mind, and it told him exactly what he had to do.

Their biggest problem was accessibility. The Vatican was the seat of the Catholic Christian Church. The pope lived there. Most of its citizens either resided within its walls or functioned in the Holy See's diplomatic service. The bulk of the citizens were made up of the clergy and the Swiss Guard, not all of whom actually lived inside the world's smallest city. It was a choice. Luckily for Daga and Ivana, Cardinal Vallini had made the wrong choice.

He lived a short distance away.

Daga had rejoiced at the knowledge. He knew life inside the Vatican was like a royal court. A different world. The gates were locked at night and opened at six a.m. The hundred-plus members of the Swiss Guard were highly trained. But it hadn't come as a surprise to him to learn that Vallini had chosen to live apart. He was the cardinal who'd challenged most of the others over the Book of Secrets, over the Amori. He was kind of a loner and a rebel.

All of which suited Daga fine.

The two killers took their time as they crept between shadows, closing in on Vallini's home. Almost every window they passed was dark, the curtains or blinds closed. Just then, there came the noisy rumble of an approaching car. Daga and Ivana pressed themselves into the lee of a deeply recessed shopfront, pressed tightly together, staring silently into each other's eyes as the offending vehicle swept by, just a bulky shadow among more shadows. Ivana took the opportunity to kiss Daga deeply and whisper: 'We are devils, you and I, living for the kill. There is nothing I enjoy more than the sight of fresh blood.'

'And the blood of a cardinal?'

Ivana shuddered and kissed him again. The car had long gone. Daga pulled them back out into the open and continued up the street. They reached Vallini's residence, a three-storey, squat, square building that had white-painted, rough-textured walls.

Close enough to the Vatican so you could walk it. Daga took his time, aware of the heightened security so close to the Holy See. The entrance stood down a narrow alley with high walls all around, perfectly positioned for the clever thief. But Daga had an even bigger ace up his sleeve.

Ivana.

The woman was a world-class safecracker. That had been her profession, prior to meeting Daga and joining his bloody global spree. They had met high above the Italian alps in an aeroplane, Ivana by far the most competent member of his team. Something had clicked between them, something profound, and they'd been together ever since. But Ivana's skills were epically usable in their new vocation. She could gain them access to any lock, any building . . . anywhere.

Now, she shrugged the small backpack off her shoulders, extracted a small leather box that looked like a glasses case and opened it up. From inside, she plucked a set of lock picks and an electronic device that she would connect to the alarm system – if there was one – and force-reveal the numbered code. Daga never knew what to expect, but Ivana always knew what to do. She stepped forward now and peered through a narrow, door-height window.

'No building alarm,' she said. 'The apartments should be individually alarmed. For now, we just need the lock picks.'

Vallini lived on the second floor, one apartment of three. The information had come from Marduk, who had thoroughly researched Vallini – among others – during his first two attacks on the Vatican. Vallini, for his interference, was always marked for death.

Ivana straightened as the lock clicked. She opened the front door and stepped inside. To a professional, a normal, everyday lock was easy. It was one of those things most civilians ignored. Daga followed her, the two thieves hunched in case there were any CCTV cameras on the inside. A quick glance revealed the camera's position, but they knew there was no physical building security and didn't have to hurry. They crossed to the stairs and started up.

In plush carpeted luxury, Daga and Ivana made their way to the second floor. Moonlight flooded one window and cast their shadows behind them, down the stairs, twisting and elongating them so that they oozed impressions of madness. Ivana reached the landing door first and put her right hand on the handle, pausing before twisting it.

There were no sounds in the building. Nobody sane was abroad at this time of night. Ivana entered the hallway with Daga at her side, breathing easily, their eyes wide with anticipation but focused on the job. Vallini's apartment was number 5, and it lay about twenty steps ahead.

They closed in. For Daga, it was the ultimate rush. He imagined that the whole of Rome lay in fervid anticipation all around them, that the very city trembled where he walked. Ivana stopped outside Vallini's door and produced her lock picks once more. Seconds later, the lock clicked. She opened the door. There was the muted beeping of an alarm system asking for a code. Ivana quickly connected her mini processing device and waited for the numbers to flash up on the screen. It took eight seconds. Soon, the alarm was safe. Ivana stepped back and waved Daga into the apartment.

He waited in silence. It was possible that Vallini had heard the alarm's bleating and would come to investigate. They waited for a minute, but nothing happened.

Daga caught Ivana staring at him. 'We will make this the best kill yet,' he said.

'A cardinal's blood,' she whispered passionately. 'I can't wait.'

They were standing in a short hallway. Ahead lay the living room, replete with an L-shaped sofa, a small television and a large glass coffee table. The far window sported a closed pair of blinds but would have given them a view towards St Peter's Basilica. Maybe being able to see the basilica was Vallini's compromise on living outside of it. Paintings adorned the walls, most of them papal scenes or just views of Rome from afar. The only modern-day concession was a photographic arrangement looking back at Rome from the dome of the basilica. There was a small kitchenette to the left, its units gleaming. Daga imagined Vallini spent very little time here, but cherished that time with clarity, snatched moments in a different world.

To the right, a closed door greeted them. This would be Vallini's bedroom. Daga pushed the door slowly and quietly. The room beyond was dark. Soon they could make out the shape of a figure in the bed, softly snoring. Daga curled his hands into fists, warming up the fingers. Marduk had requested that the cardinal be strangled very, very slowly.

Ivana walked to one side of the bed, Daga to the other. They ripped the bedclothes away from Vallini's form and watched as the figure came awake. At first the eyes saw nothing, then they focused on Daga and still they were bleary. The terrible truth hadn't travelled all the way to the brain yet. It took another moment.

Daga saw it hit Vallini's mind. He chose that moment to grab hold of the man's right arm and drag him out of the bed. Vallini struggled but hit the floor with a bump. Daga hauled him to his feet.

'Surprise,' he said. 'Bet you weren't expecting us.'

His hand closed around Vallini's throat. He squeezed, just a little, in case the cardinal felt like he might need to scream. It was a warning, but then what else could Vallini do to escape his fate?

'Do you know who I am?' Daga whispered, face to face with the cardinal.

'*Cassadaga,*' came the shaky whisper, distorted through Daga's hand.

'I have come for you.'

'Please.' Vallini waved a hand. 'Please. Do not do this for Marduk.'

Daga loosened his grip, allowing Vallini to talk more freely. It wasn't because he wanted to listen to the man; it was because all this foreplay just heightened the anticipation of the kill.

'He has plans for your Vatican,' Ivana said from the right side of the bed.

'He wants your suffering to match the so-called *passion* of Christ,' Daga said.

'He hates me,' Vallini said. 'I understand that. But *He* is always at my side. I have the strength of the Holy Spirit inside me. You cannot hurt me.'

Daga looked surprised at the statement. He had never come across anyone that he couldn't hurt. 'Interesting,' he said. 'Does this not hurt?'

And he squeezed Vallini's trachea viciously between two fingers. Vallini shuddered and brought his hands up, trying to pull Daga away, but the killer only laughed. He squeezed until Vallini went weak.

'There,' he said. 'Where was your God, then? Did He abandon you? I failed to feel His hands on me.'

Vallini fell back onto the bed, holding his throat. Ivana crawled towards him from the right, a grin stretching across her face. She came up behind Vallini and laid a hand on his shoulder and then on the nape of his neck.

'If I touch you like this,' she said, 'can you feel it? Or does your Lord protect you from a killer's touch?'

Vallini jerked away from her. 'My faith grounds me,' he said hoarsely. 'I feel only the love of God.'

'Yes we know, we know,' Daga said. 'It all revolves around faith. But do you want to know what I have faith in?'

Vallini shied away.

'These.' Daga held up his hands and then wrapped them once again around Vallini's neck. He squeezed for a while, staring into Ivana's eyes across the top of Vallini's head. She stared back at him, sharing his contentment, stroking Vallini's neck as the life slipped out of him.

But Daga didn't end it there. Marduk had been very specific about making Vallini suffer. He removed his hands after a while and left Vallini gasping. Ivana turned on a lamp so that they could see better. Daga cracked his fingers and stepped back from the bed.

'How's your faith now?' he whispered.

Vallini sputtered and rubbed his throat. He appeared to be having difficulty swallowing. Daga leaned close to him. 'Marduk ordered this,' he whispered. 'He wanted you to know that. He also asked me to use my hands, because it's more personal. Know that once you're dead, I will slice your body up to my liking. The person who finds you will not rest easy for the remainder of their life. That is my legacy, too. Are you ready to meet your maker, Cardinal Vallini?'

He had meant it as a joke, a play on this man's love of God. But Vallini straightened his back and lowered his hands and glared directly into Daga's eyes.

'Do what you must,' he rasped.

Daga nodded. Vallini was strong, stronger than he had imagined. It didn't matter. He would still die. Ivana caught his attention behind the cardinal's back.

'Maybe I could take him halfway,' she said. 'And then you could finish the job.'

Daga smiled at her idea. He liked it. He nodded. Ivana looped her hands around Vallini's neck and started strangling him. The cardinal struggled, trying to pull away, but he stood no chance. There was a moment when the fight left Vallini's eyes, when his hands fell away. That was when Ivana removed her hands and allowed him a moment's respite, allowed the breath to trickle back into his lungs.

And then Daga took over, his enormous hands encircling Vallini's throat. He squeezed hard now, wanting to end this. He wondered briefly if a lightning bolt might hiss out of nowhere, striking him down, and then he laughed out loud. The cardinal had breathed his last. This was the end for him.

Daga squeezed until all the life left Vallini's eyes and then let the cardinal's body fall back onto the bed. He reached into his pocket and extracted a note from Marduk, a note that would shake the Vatican even as much as Vallini's murder.

Then Daga looked at Ivana. 'He's dead,' he said. 'Shall we start?'

Chapter 11

Mason ached. He'd spent the previous day hammering, twisting, bolting, securing and fastening one security device after another to Sally's property. They'd been up and down ladders, forced their way through bushes and balanced precariously along gutters the whole day. In the end, though, the toil was worth it. Hassell was the only one of them who leaned towards being electronically minded, but even he didn't fancy the idea of hooking everything up to a central hub. They had a specialist coming out today.

It was early morning, the sun just starting to announce its presence to the world. Mason started the morning off right with an hour in his makeshift boxing gym. After that, he went to breakfast and started cooking eggs whilst waiting for the coffee to percolate. The others still weren't up by the time he started eating. He didn't blame them. It had been a long day and night yesterday.

Slowly, they filtered downstairs. Sally came first, her hair sticking out in all directions. A bleary-eyed Roxy appeared next, complaining that her mouth was as dry as old churchyard bones. Ten minutes later they were a team, as Quaid and Hassell joined them, all crowded around the breakfast table.

'Another quiet day?' Roxy asked. Today, she was wearing a short-sleeved T-shirt that showed off many of the scars of her old life. Roxy's body bore several physical scars, but they didn't bother her a tenth as much as the invisible ones in her mind.

'I could do with about a week's rest,' Quaid said. 'After all that manual labour yesterday.'

'Old bones aching?' Hassell said with a smile.

'*All* of me is aching, I don't mind telling you. On the positive side though, we're as well protected as we can possibly be.'

'Short of posting a nightly guard,' Mason said. It had worked back in his army days.

'Nights are made for rum,' Roxy said. 'And bad dreams.'

'And worrying about what to do next with my father's money,' Sally said. 'Don't forget that.'

'I could probably stand guard,' Hassell said. 'I barely sleep.'

Mason finished his eggs and sat back with his coffee. The breakfast bar was full now, and noisy. His quiet morning had shattered. They had two days before their next job was due to start and, with nothing else to do, he was thinking of proposing that Sally use her skills to find Marduk. He believed the man wouldn't have strayed too far from an Amori stronghold, and Amori strongholds had been noted down throughout history. Maybe Sally could root him out.

He was about to inform them of his theory when Sally's phone rang. Again, she noted the call was coming from the Vatican.

'Cardinal Vallini?' she answered with a smile. 'What can we do for you today?'

'I am afraid this is not Cardinal Vallini,' a deep voice said. 'It is Premo Conte.'

Mason frowned. Conte was the Inspector General of the Gendarmes of Vatican City and leader of the Cavalieré, a special, highly skilled force within the Swiss Guard. He was a serious man but, as Mason had found on their last adventure searching for the Amori bible, was also a very capable one. He had helped them send a force against the Amori headquarters to take down Marduk and his cohorts.

'Conte,' he said in a formal voice. 'How are you?'

'This is not a phone call I ever wished to make. Please sit down, all of you. I have some dreadful news.'

Mason did as Conte asked, though the others just puckered their brows and asked what was wrong.

'I am so sorry to tell you that Cardinal Vallini is dead.'

Sally's mouth fell open. Tears instantly filled her eyes. 'Wh . . . what?'

'Murdered in the early hours of this morning. Murdered in his apartment. I am sorry.'

'But . . . but he knew my father,' Sally said. 'Now . . . both of them? How can it have happened?'

'Murdered?' Quaid repeated.

'It is a Carabinieri matter now. It is under full investigation.'

Mason fought the shock to find the right words to say. 'We spoke to him recently,' he said. 'He retained our services again because of the Marduk situation.'

'He spoke to me also,' Conte said. 'It is one of the reasons I am calling you. We spoke of your . . . rehiring.'

'I take it you didn't agree with him,' Mason said.

'Vallini was my boss. We may not see eye to eye on some matters, but I respect his decision. Do you have any idea who might have done this?'

Mason blinked. The answer was pretty obvious, and Conte knew it. Maybe he was chasing ghosts, trying every eventuality. 'I think we can deduce that it was Marduk, or at least someone working for him. Do you have any leads?'

'As I said, this is a Carabinieri matter.'

'But I am sure they will work with you,' Mason pressed, using the line of questioning to take his mind off the terrible news.

'We will see about that.'

Mason fought to keep his emotions in check, but found he couldn't quite manage it. He slumped back in the chair and gripped both sides of his forehead. He squeezed to ease the pressure. Vallini's death was an enormous loss, their first loss as a team, and something he really felt to his core. It was an odd, new feeling. He knew all about loss, of course, felt it every single day. But never with the new team, never in the presence of Sally and the others. Seeing how they coped was an eye-opening moment for him.

Sally wore her grief on her sleeve, openly in tears. She looked lonely standing near the table, and Mason wanted to go over to her. Roxy looked angry, the lights flashing in her eyes. She was staring around the room as if searching for an enemy to kill or a weapon to use. Quaid just looked sad, the years showing through his expression and the slump of his shoulders. Hassell looked like he couldn't believe the news, as if bad things weren't supposed to happen to this new crew. Mason felt like he'd had the stuffing knocked out of him.

'Are you there?' Conte asked into the silence.

'We're here,' Mason said for everyone. 'We're still processing.'

'Surely,' Quaid said. 'Surely you know what happened?'

Conte hesitated; they could hear it in his voice. After a few seconds, he said: 'Someone, an eyewitness, said they saw two people exiting his apartment building around the right time. No actual descriptions, but it was a man and a woman.'

Mason ground his teeth together. 'Cassadaga and Ivana,' he said.

'There's no real proof of that.'

'But Marduk did this,' Sally suddenly hissed. 'Marduk killed poor Vallini out of revenge.'

'Those two would be perfect for the job,' Hassell admitted.

'There's more,' Conte said.

Mason looked up sharply. 'What are you talking about?'

'They left a note.'

'The killers?'

'Yeah, a note from Marduk. It's personal, to Vallini.'

Mason wondered how Conte knew it was from Marduk, but let that go for now. He braced himself, because he knew what they were about to hear would be callous and cruel. 'What does it say?'

Conte cleared his throat softly and then began to read: '*A thousand years and then a thousand more, we waited. Your Bible says: "the secrets will out". But not today, and not tomorrow. You cling to your precious secrets like young children cling to their mothers. If the secrets are "out", they will surely destroy you, a fact of which you are very aware. But if I, Marduk, can't get you one way, I will get you another. My wrath will yet destroy your*

Church, your Vatican. Plans are afoot. I will kill you all soon. And I will start with you.'

Conte went silent. Mason tried to take it in. On top of the shock of Vallini's death, it was no simple thing.

'It tells us nothing,' Hassell said.

'It tells us that Marduk has a plan already, that he's implementing it,' Quaid said. 'He didn't just send Cassadaga for revenge. This is all part of some big scheme.'

'Something he's been working on in prison?' Roxy said, still looking like she wanted to murder someone.

'I'd say that's a given,' Mason said. 'The man's a fanatic.'

'Any ideas what that could be?' Conte asked. 'Did Vallini discuss anything with you before he . . . died?'

'Nothing specific,' Mason said. 'He had a feeling Marduk would be back. That's why he re-enlisted our help.'

'What can we do now?' Sally asked. It wasn't a proper question – more of a rhetorical statement.

'You can help. I will back you,' Conte said simply. 'I assume this matter takes precedence over your other jobs now?'

Mason could think of nothing more important than finding Vallini's killers and stopping Marduk. Vallini hadn't deserved to die, and bringing his killers to justice was foremost on Mason's list of priorities right now. Nothing else mattered. Stopping Marduk, and Cassadaga and Ivana, was a tangible stake they should latch on to. 'We're available night and day. Any job.' As he spoke, he glanced around at the team and saw the fierce determination in their eyes, vying with grief.

'A new man will take Vallini's place for now,' Conte told them. 'A liaison. Someone who will take up Vallini's affairs until the clergy replaces him properly. Now, I have to say, this new man is young and commands far less respect, as you can imagine. But he is all that we have for now. Do you understand?'

Conte was telling them, between the lines, that all the slack they had enjoyed with Vallini was effectively gone. They would find working with the Vatican much harder now. Of course, there was still Conte himself.

'What's his name?' Sally asked.

'Mario Gambetti,' Conte said. 'Born April 1967. He's one of the youngest cardinals in Vatican City.'

'What's he like?' Sally pushed.

'He toes the line,' Conte said. 'You won't find him taking any chances, making any snap decisions.'

'So how can we help you?' Mason said.

'Officially, you can't,' Conte said.

Mason heard the vacillation in that voice, the sense that Conte wanted all hands on deck but didn't feel comfortable asking out loud.

'So what's next?' Quaid asked.

'Officially, I can't tell you,' Conte said. 'But, as you say, Vallini re-enlisted your help. You're working for us now.'

The conversation dried up a little after that. It was only five minutes later when Sally ended the call and slumped heavily into a chair. 'I can't believe it,' she said. 'Poor Vallini. He had to go through that.'

'The question is – how do we avenge him?' Roxy asked dangerously.

Chapter 12

Mason swallowed the emotions that churned inside. 'I don't think he would have wanted us to avenge him,' he said. 'But I feel the same way that you do. How do we help if the Vatican don't officially want us to?'

'But officially they do,' Quaid pointed out. 'We have the paperwork Vallini sent to us a few days ago. It bears the Vatican seal. It enables us to carry out work on their behalf. Our company, at least.'

'What are you suggesting?' Sally said.

'That we find Marduk and teach the bastard a lesson,' Roxy said darkly.

Quaid sat forward. 'Do you remember when we attacked the Amori HQ? Cassadaga and Ivana were there. We fought . . .'

'Yeah, we fought,' Mason said. 'I remember it well.'

'That was our chance to capture them,' Quaid said. 'We let them go.'

Mason knew what he was thinking. 'Don't put yourself through that, mate. It's not worth it. And we didn't exactly let them go.'

Quaid nodded, knowing Mason was right, but his lips remained tight as if he was still blaming himself. Mason understood that they'd had their chance to take the two killers down, but there had been many other factors involved. Marduk throwing a grenade, for example, which had taken most of the team out and garnered more than a few scars.

'We have to stop them,' he said. 'For the sake of everyone else they might maim or kill. And we have to stop Marduk. This takes precedence now.'

The others nodded. Roxy rose and went to the sink, washing her hands vigorously as if trying to remove a stain. She said: 'In a terrible, warped way, Marduk is what brought us together. It would never end with him being put in prison.'

'You're saying I should have shot him through the head instead of the knee,' Mason said miserably.

Roxy suddenly looked like she'd said the wrong thing. 'I understand you could never do that, Joe. I just meant that Marduk will be our nemesis, and the Church's, until the day he dies.'

Mason nodded. 'I agree. Essentially, he is our only job now. We can't let him get away with whatever he's trying to do.'

They agreed, nodding together. Determination fired them. They were all standing, looking around the room as if they wanted to rush out and get started immediately.

'This *is* what Vallini would have wanted,' Sally said. 'Us working together to apprehend Marduk.'

Mason balanced on a raft of emotions, feeling flood-waters tearing him every which way. 'But where do we start?'

'We have no leads,' Quaid sighed. 'Just as Conte said.'

'Conte said that he would back us,' Mason reminded them.

'Which means we can investigate,' Sally said. 'But then, this isn't exactly a relic we're chasing down.'

'Even so, Conte gives us the credibility we need,' Mason said. 'So we either start with Cassadaga or we start with Marduk.'

'Marduk will lead us to Cassadaga,' Roxy said. 'I'm not so sure about the other way around.'

Mason nodded. 'Agreed. We should concentrate on Marduk.'

'Any ideas?' Sally said.

The room fell into silence. After a while, Roxy rose to make a fresh coffee, pouring herself a cup of the hot brew. It was Hassell who finally spoke up.

'We don't know where he is,' the New Yorker said. 'But we know where he's been.'

Mason frowned. 'Meaning?'

'The prison,' Hassell said. 'He just spent two months or so in prison, in a cell, with a cellmate. And we know how much Marduk likes to talk about himself.'

'About his plans?' Sally said.

'About the Amori,' Quaid said.

'He's definitely a talker,' Mason mused. 'He's proven that before. Are you thinking that he might have let something slip?'

Hassell nodded. 'The man's an arrogant narcissist who just loves to blow his own trumpet. He believes he works as a mouthpiece for the Amori, but it's just all about him.'

'Marduk *is* the mouthpiece,' Roxy said.

'Yes, he is. My idea is to go to the Italian prison where he was incarcerated and talk to his cellmate.'

Mason liked it. There was every chance that Marduk

would have revealed something inadvertently – or even on purpose – to the man. Marduk loved to stroke his own ego. And they had the authority. Premo Conte had already said that he would back them.

'And current jobs?' he asked.

'They pale in significance to this,' Sally said. 'I'll clear our schedule.'

Roxy finished her coffee and started out of the room. 'Don't need to ask me twice,' she said.

Mason paused and laid a hand on Sally's arm. 'I'm sorry about Vallini,' he said. 'I know he had a close connection to your father.'

Sally nodded, keeping her emotions in check. She rose without a word and left the room, presumably to pack.

Mason was just a step behind her.

Chapter 13

San Vittore prison sat in the heart of Milan, the high-walled, depressing chunk of concrete housing some of Italy's most notorious prisoners. Milan itself, enveloped in rich history, known for its fashion and fine cuisine as well as its art galleries, museums, its rich culture, and the archetypal Duomo di Milano, the world's largest and most spectacular Gothic cathedral, as well as sprawling world-class shopping and picture-perfect cafés, did its best to ignore the eyesore that sat just a few short miles from its classical core.

Mason and the others landed at Malpensa airport and made the journey to the prison in just over an hour. By the time they parked up in the tight visitor car park and walked to the entrance, Premo Conte had worked his magic. The officer in reception told them they'd been given special dispensation to interview an inmate named Oliver Madstone, who had been Marduk's cellmate for almost two months.

They kicked their heels in reception for twenty minutes before being led deeper into the prison, the resounding clash of every cage door closing behind them further dampening their spirits as they advanced through the cheerless void. Eventually they were shown into an interview room, where there were only two chairs – one for the prisoner and one for the interviewer – so only Sally got a seat.

Roxy shivered as they waited in silence. 'Any ideas how we're gonna approach this, guys?'

'Carefully,' Quaid said.

'We have nothing to offer him,' Sally said. 'Are we counting on the goodness of his heart?'

'He doesn't know that,' Mason said. 'And maybe he'll *want* to talk about Marduk. You know how that clown can rub people up the wrong way.'

'A prisoner is going to want something from this,' Hassell said.

At that moment, the far door clicked and then swung open. A guard led a man clad in jeans and a T-shirt into the room. The man's hands were cuffed at his back. Oliver Madstone was a big guy, thick around the waist and the neck, with chubby jowls that wobbled as he walked. His eyes were inset in the flesh of his face and gave the impression that someone else was peering out from beneath the skin, an impostor. Madstone waited until the guard removed his handcuffs and then secured them around a bar that ran down the centre of the table. The guard withdrew. Madstone stared at them.

'The fuck is this?' he asked. 'More visitors in this room than I've had in five years.'

'You're English?' The south London accent surprised Sally.

'Last time I checked. Why, you wanna get closer; have a better look?' Madstone grinned lewdly.

Sally ignored the vulgarity, but leaned away. Mason

put his hands on the back of her chair. 'We came here to ask you a few questions,' he said.

'Ask away. Take your time. Anything is better than what I have to look forward to.'

'Did you share a cell with a man named Marduk?'

Madstone pulled an unhappy face. 'That loony? Yeah, for my sins.'

'I bet he never shut up,' Roxy said, trying to build a little rapport with the prisoner. 'Kept banging on about the Amori, the Church. All kinds of crap.'

'Day and night,' Madstone told them. 'If I was a violent man, I'd have throttled him. Luckily for him, I'm in here for fraud.'

'Can you give us an idea of what he talked about?' Sally asked.

'Said he was some kind of monarch,' Madstone snorted. 'Then . . . hey wait, what do I get out of all this?'

'A bit of revenge,' Mason said. 'On a man who made your life a misery.'

Madstone glared. 'Is that it? No minimum security? No reduced time? No commissary boost?'

'I can help with one of those,' Sally said. 'A little boost into your prison account.'

'Is that it? I don't need to talk to you guys at all.'

Roxy leaned forward. 'Hey man,' she said. 'You're not a bad guy. Not a killer like half the other guys in here. Don't block yourself off mentally as well as physically. You could help many people by talking to us.'

Madstone shifted his weight, jowls wobbling. 'You sound like you've been in the same situation.'

'Not exactly, I admit,' Roxy said. 'But I know sharing helps when the Devil's calling. You need help. Remember this – you can't slay demons on your own.'

Madstone stared appraisingly at her. 'Perhaps you're right,' he mused. 'There are days when I believe my inner voice wants to kill me. In here . . .' he shivered '. . . there are all kinds of monsters. And, believe me, we're all very much alone.'

'Then take it when you can get it,' Roxy said. 'Another motto of mine. We're here right now. We can at least make your life a little more comfortable.'

Madstone sat back and sighed. 'Thing is,' he said. 'This guy, Marduk, he never stopped talking, greasing his own wheels, you know. At first, I feigned interest because the guy seemed harmless enough, and his chatter at least helped pass the time. But then he wanted me to join his damn cult.' Madstone shook his head.

'Cult?' Sally asked.

'You mentioned it. The Amori. Called himself "the monarch of the Amori". If you ask me, the guy was a crackpot.'

'For sure,' Roxy said. 'He is. What else did he say?'

'Kept rambling on about the old days, like he was part of it thousands of years ago. How he intended to destroy the Church, to ruin the Vatican, that kind of thing.'

Mason interrupted. '*Ruin* the Vatican. Those were his exact words?'

'Yeah, yeah, that's what he said.'

Mason wondered at the choice of words. Did it mean something? Of course, with Marduk, it was difficult to tell.

'This Marduk, he told me about how Jesus Christ was this noble warrior. How the Amori had manipulated and controlled the way he died. He spoke of the Church's brilliant cover-up, its Bible full of lies, the finding of Christ's body years ago. Is it all true?'

'I wouldn't know anything about that,' Mason said quickly.

'Well, he spoke with all the zeal of a fanatic. *He* believes it, you can be sure. Apparently, he came close to revealing the great secret to the world, but had the opportunity snatched from his hands.'

Mason kept quiet, his face placid, thankful that the others did the same.

'Anyway, the only other names he mentioned apart from the Amori, the Church and the Vatican were this pair of thieves he knew – Cassa, something and Ivana.'

'Cassadaga?' Quaid said.

'That's the boy, yes. Cassadaga. Apparently, these two were the worst of the worst, which to Marduk means they're the best in the world.' Madstone shook his head again.

Mason felt a trickle of eagerness. This was what they had come here to learn. The connection between Cassadaga, Ivana and Marduk was vital. 'Anything you can tell us about them would help.'

Madstone glanced at Sally, as if wondering how much more he could get on his commissary, but then eyed Roxy as if weighing her earlier words. In the end, he continued, 'Like I said, Marduk loved them. Kept regaling me with tales of the great murderer and his sidekick. Made me want to throw up. Anyway, Marduk was desperate to contact Cassadaga.'

'That would be next to impossible even for a man of Marduk's reach,' Quaid said. 'Daga is a ghost.'

'Not exactly,' Madstone said. 'Marduk has ways of contacting everyone. He kept in touch with many of his followers whilst he was inside. Called them his *Faithful*. Told me they worshipped him and would do anything for him. *Anything*. "*My Faithful would commit the ultimate sacrifice if I ordered it*," he once told me. There are some crazy people in this world.'

Mason looked at the walls of the room they were inside and thought of some of the people just beyond it. 'Too many,' he said.

'So this crazy Daga and his partner, Ivana, are contactable in just one way. Apparently, Marduk has done so before?'

Mason remembered now that it was Marduk who had introduced Daga the first time, sending him to kill those monks in the monastery and steal the body of Jesus Christ.

'He would know,' Mason said carefully.

'Marduk rambled on a lot about it,' Madstone told them. 'I don't think the guy exactly trusted me. It was more that he got used to me being there, like I was a part of the furniture, or something.'

'What did he say?' Quaid asked.

'There's a man in Paris, a real evil old goat, who facilitates just about every monstrous act you can think of. Guy's called Bellaire and apparently known only in certain circles. He's survived this long and shouldn't be underestimated, you know?'

Mason saw Madstone give them a quick glance and thought that the guy might actually be worried for them. *Compassion from a San Vittore prisoner*, he thought. *You see everything in this job.*

'Any clue how we would find this Bellaire?' Hassell asked.

'To the average person, he's as hard to track down as Cassadaga,' Madstone said. 'Or Marduk, for that matter. But when you've been living in a cage with a madman for weeks, just the two of you, you tend to hear everything at least a dozen times.'

'Tell us,' Sally said.

'It's standard protocol,' Madstone said, shrugging and fixing his tiny eyes on them. 'It's all about code words, you see. You go visit a jewellery shop in Clichy and try to buy a special watch. The jeweller is called Vintage Honoré, the watch is a 1946 Arnstadt, which doesn't actually exist. Bellaire, the jeweller, will then speak to you.'

Mason thought about all that. 'And Bellaire can contact Daga?'

'Yes, he sets up the meet, or at least a conversation, once he's vetted you and only then if he likes you for it.'

'You're talking about tracking down one of the deadliest men in the world,' Quaid said.

'Tracking down Daga would lead us to Marduk,' Roxy said.

'Tracking down Daga is an insane vision,' Sally said with genuine fear in her voice. 'I don't have to tell you how dangerous he is.'

'How the hell did Marduk accomplish all this in here?' Mason asked, nodding at the walls.

Madstone shrugged. 'Isn't it obvious? Money. The guy kept on babbling about dwindling funds, about not having enough to accomplish everything, but he sure knew how to grease palms in here.'

'So he's running out of money?' Mason said. 'That's good.'

'Not necessarily,' Madstone said. 'Marduk had another scheme. Sounded whackier even than all the other crap that leaked out of his mouth. Said he was looking for some ziggurat in Babylon – can't remember the name.'

'Why would he want to look for a ziggurat in Babylon?' Sally asked.

'A fortune.' Madstone shrugged. 'Believe me, by this time I'd stopped listening to the non-stop drivel. You see, I'm the kind of guy who retains everything. I don't forget. Listening to someone like Marduk can seriously affect my mental health.'

'Marduk's been on the run long enough to do all that,' Hassell said. 'We can't affect where he goes, just where he'll end up.'

'The ziggurat had something to do with the Tower of Babel if that helps,' Madstone told them. 'I remember because I used to think he wouldn't stop babbling. It used to make me smile.' The prisoner turned away briefly.

'Connected with ancient Babylon,' Sally said. 'The Tower of Babel is an old legend and a pretty impressive piece of engineering for the time. Many believe it is the Etemenanki ziggurat.'

Madstone started nodding. 'I think that's the name he used. Do you think he went there?'

'It's something to check,' Mason said. 'Along with this Bellaire character. I still think finding Daga will lead us to Marduk.'

'Not only that,' Roxy said. 'But Daga needs removing from the face of the earth. I'd class that as another good deed well done.'

Mason agreed, but said nothing. Madstone looked talked out, like he'd told them everything he knew. There was an expression of foreboding on his face, as if he feared having to return to general population.

Sally leaned forward briefly. 'Thanks for your help,' she said. 'I'll make sure you get that commissary top-up.'

Madstone nodded at them and attempted a smile.

'Who's up for visiting an evil old man?' Roxy said as they rose to their feet.

'Anything that brings us closer to Marduk,' Mason said.

'Strangely, it's not Marduk that worries me in that scenario,' Quaid said. 'It's Cassadaga.'

Chapter 14

The last time they'd been in Paris, they'd had the displeasure of having to explore the catacombs and come face to face with the Wall of Bones. Last time, there had been a known goal and a race against time, whereas today Mason felt the threat was more nebulous, and it put him on tenterhooks.

Marduk was planning something, he was sure. Something beyond pure revenge, which was the category that the murder of Cardinal Vallini fell into. Marduk wouldn't let it rest there, especially if he was trying to bring back the Amori.

Or these *Faithful*, whoever they were.

Mason couldn't pretend to follow the madman's inner schemings. The real truth was – he just had no clue what would happen next. Which made tracking him down vitally important not only for the sake of avenging Vallini's death, but for the ongoing survival of the Church.

They landed in Paris in the early evening, ninety minutes after leaving Milan, and cleared the airport arrivals quickly. They caught a taxi to the Clichy district, which took longer than expected, first cutting their way through the snarled-up traffic on the outer ring road, the Boulevard Périphérique, and then in the traffic jam that Paris called an inner road network, they finally decided it would be a prudent idea to get themselves a hotel for the night. The jewellery shop would have closed by the time they arrived at its door. It was a setback, reminding them that their lives didn't run as smoothly as they'd like, but it was only for an evening.

Sally found them a nearby hotel using Google Maps and paid for their rooms, though she'd be expensing everything via Premo Conte. This was a job. They were working for the Vatican. Soon, Mason sat alone in his room, planning to head down to the bar. He took a quick shower, changed, and then left his room. He immediately spied a figure already seated at one table, which didn't surprise him at all.

'Showered?' he asked, taking a seat opposite her.

Roxy held up her glass. 'In this,' she said. 'Every damn day.'

'You didn't order me one?'

'Rum's too strong for you. You're weak when it comes to the evil spirit, Joe.'

He took that one on the chin, deciding he probably agreed with her. Roxy held up her hands, caught the attention of a server, and ordered him a beer. Mason nodded his appreciation.

'How are you doing?' he asked.

'Still battling. Something I said earlier resonated with me. *You can't slay demons on your own,* I said. Well, our team proves it. I'm better at working with you guys, working together towards my goal. I feel better today than I have in years.'

'Are you where you want to be?'

'The woman I could have been? No, not yet. But she's there. I can feel her inside, struggling to show herself. It's all the baggage, you see. It keeps her pinned down.'

Mason nodded. 'What turned the tide for the better?'

'Nothing specific. Nothing I can tie down. Working with you, I know we're doing the right thing. Working towards a moral goal. I didn't have that before. I feel honest and decent these days, instead of dirty.'

Mason took a long swallow of his beer after the server plonked it down on their table and then sat back. 'Which brings us back to the shower question.'

Roxy grinned, finished her rum and signalled for another. 'And what about you?'

'Me? I'm working with a great team. But Zach and Harry still died in Mosul. I can shoulder some responsibility for their deaths, but not all. I've taken on this new responsibility now, this team. We're in danger all the time, it seems.'

Roxy smiled and looked away. 'Do you enjoy the action?'

'I know you do,' he answered.

'Sure. It keeps me on the edge of my game, where I need to be. If you're not on the edge, you're taking up too much space, right?'

Mason laughed. It was a typical Roxy comment. He drank some more of the pint and settled further into his seat. 'In the end,' he said, 'I accepted *some* of the blame for Zach and Harry. That's what helps me move forward.'

'And what next?' Roxy asked.

'You mean the team? Well, we keep on getting ourselves into trouble, don't we? I don't think any of us will rest easy until Marduk, Daga and Ivana are . . .' He paused, realising what he was about to say.

'In the ground?' Roxy finished for him.

'Something like that. Marduk's proven that a prison can't hold him.'

'There are better prisons,' Roxy said. 'And black sites.'

'Sounds like you know a few.'

'More than I'm comfortable with. You know what I was. I worked for an unknown three-letter agency for twelve years. They stripped me of my youth. I'll never forgive that. And all the other shit I went through . . . well that's in the past.' She sounded like she was trying hard to convince herself.

Mason didn't want to push her on it. 'Hey.' He turned around. 'Here come the others.'

Coincidentally, Sally, Quaid and Hassell all appeared, two from the lift and one from the stairs. Mason called them over.

The team seated themselves around the table. The bar area was fairly quiet. Just two men and one woman occupied the bar stools. There were two women talking a few tables away and a young couple seated by the window. The hum of conversation was low, and the tinny music was at a volume where most people couldn't hear it, which suited Mason just fine. The sound of a cocktail shaker was the loudest sound coming from the bar.

When they'd ordered drinks, Sally spoke up. 'An early morning visit to Bellaire sound good?'

'It does,' Mason said. 'But I think we should be extra careful. Even Madstone, from prison, warned us about this old guy. I'm thinking just two of us should go to see him.'

'Not me then,' Sally said a little moodily.

'Hey, your training is progressing just right,' Mason assured her. 'I'd trust you to watch my back already.

But I think this guy Bellaire is something different, something you need a good deal of life experience with bad guys to handle. Does that make sense?'

Sally nodded. 'I guess so.'

'Me and you?' Roxy looked at him, a shot glass poised at her lips.

Mason looked at Quaid and Hassell. 'Unless you two want to try it?'

Both men looked pleased at the offer. Mason was happy to do it. They were a team, each person equal to the other, and they should be prepared to trust and rely on everyone evenly.

'I think we should all go,' Quaid said. 'Why not? It's a democracy. This Bellaire guy won't be any the wiser if two or five of us turn up.'

Mason inclined his head, not tending to agree with the statement but taking in the team's mood. It was an important moment, he thought. Learning what the majority wanted and rolling with it.

'If that's what you all want,' though he didn't agree in principle, he couldn't see it causing them any problems.

They whiled the night away, sitting there and talking, going over the subject of Marduk and the Amori numerous times. What was he up to? Who were the Faithful? What would Daga and Ivana do next? Of course, they couldn't predict what a warped mind would do. Marduk would carry out whatever nefarious plan was in his head. There was no telling what that might be. Around them, the bar buzzed with activity; the tables becoming quite crowded; the conversations getting louder. A group of suit-wearing businessmen propped up the bar at one end, becoming noisier as the night went on, their sudden bursts of raucous laughter intruding on everyone else. Several couples leaned forward across tables in intimate conversation. Mason saw an old man and woman just sitting back in a corner, people-watching, enjoying it by the looks on their faces, and making the occasional passing comment. The bartenders flew from one highly polished side to the other, taking orders and serving drinks. When Mason checked his watch, it was a little after eleven-thirty.

'My bed is calling,' he said.

'Mine too.' Roxy was looking down at the table. Mason followed her gaze and saw five shots that she'd lined up before the bar officially closed.

'You gonna take them with you?'

'It's medicine to help me sleep.'

'I thought you said you were doing better.'

'The days are better. The nights not so much.'

Mason had never turned to alcohol to help him through the bad times. He'd turned introspective, practically unapproachable and uncommunicative. It had ruined his marriage.

Maybe drinking would have been better, he mused, and then wondered what Hannah, his ex-wife, was doing now. They had split on good terms and still kept in touch. One of the best – and worst and funniest – memories of his army days was getting ribbed by the boys because he and his wife looked very much alike, at least to an outsider. Blond hair, blue eyes, young-looking faces. Similar builds if you didn't look too closely. With Mason, all the muscle was hidden beneath the surface, making him often underestimated.

As he would be tomorrow, by Bellaire, no doubt.

The downside, of course, was that he usually had to prove himself. But Mason had become used to it through the years.

He left the table at the same time as Quaid and Hassell, leaving Roxy and Sally to chat a while longer. He made his way to his room, locked the door, and stripped down to his boxers. The room, minus air conditioning, was mafting.

Ten minutes later, he was asleep.

The next morning found them enjoying a full English at the hotel before the jewellery shop opened. Mason polished off bacon, eggs, beans, mushrooms, fried bread and hash browns, along with a pot of coffee. Admittedly, when he'd finished, he found it hard to move, but assured himself the energy would soon kick in. The team was ready to leave the breakfast room by nine o'clock.

Mason led the way out into the day. It was cool for mid-May in France; it might as well have been mid-winter. A frigid wind blew in from the east, scouring the street as if trying to scrape the top layer off. They jumped into their car. Sally pulled out her phone, just to be safe, and followed Google Maps all the way to their destination.

'Vintage Honoré,' she said.

There was an 'open' sign in the window.

Chapter 15

Inside, the jewellery shop was wide but dingy. It wasn't lit well, and the ceilings were low. Rows of watches, rings, necklaces and other items sat displayed in old glass cabinets in need of a clean. Dust choked a couple of the displays that bore old, unappealing objects that didn't sparkle. The five of them listened to the bell over the door tinkle as they entered, walked towards a display, and waited.

Soon, an old man came out from the back. 'Can I help you?' he asked in French.

'English?' Sally asked.

'Of course, like a second language.' His words might have been mistaken for a jest, but the old man wasn't smiling.

Mason studied him. He looked to be in his late sixties, wire-thin and composed of stringy muscle that hung from his bare arms. Mason could see the distended veins as if the guy had been using weights in the back. His face was a carving in severity, all deep channels and harsh lines, hair cut short and black. He moved like a man half his age and put his hands on a counter, leaning forward to study them.

'What do you want?'

Mason guessed he didn't get many customers in the shop. He didn't mince words. 'We're here to buy a 1946 Arnstadt,' he said briefly, repeating the code word that Madstone had given them.

Bellaire blinked, but otherwise didn't move a muscle. 'You must be mistaken,' he said. 'We do not keep that make here.'

Mason should have known it wouldn't be as easy as that. He shrugged and stepped forward. 'We're looking for someone,' he said. 'Some help. We were told to come here and ask to buy an Arnstadt.'

'It's a watch,' Roxy added helpfully.

Bellaire turned his flinty eyes on her as if they could shoot bullets. His mouth drew tight as he said, 'Not here.'

Mason looked around. The shop was empty apart from them. The guy appeared very assured, considering he was alone. Should he drop Cassadaga's name? That probably wasn't such a good idea. Protocol would demand that the thief's identity stay secret. What then were they missing?

'Hey, bud, you're being a bit of an ass,' Roxy said in her nicest voice. 'We've come a long way to see you. Are we missing something? Some part of the code? We've given you all we've got.'

It looked like Madstone hadn't offered the entire information, or maybe he'd forgotten part of it, or wasn't given it. Whatever it was, they weren't getting anywhere with Bellaire. Another failure. Mason wondered if they'd have to restart at square one.

Which was . . . where?

Quaid stepped forward then. 'Hey,' he said in a calm voice. 'You're Bellaire, right? They gave us your name and the name of this shop. We have at least part of the correct code. Now, I'm an obliging man. I go out of my way to help people. If you could see your way to helping us out, my friend, it'd be really appreciated.'

'Get the fuck out of my shop,' Bellaire snarled.

'Hey, Grandpa,' Roxy said in a heated voice. 'If my face looked like a nutsack, I'd be an angry bastard too, but that's no excuse to be an asshole. We gave you the damn code word. Give us what we need.'

She walked to within a foot of the old man. 'Now.'

Bellaire glared at them all, flitting his eyes from one to another. Finally, his shoulders relaxed, and he stepped back. 'Follow me,' he said.

Mason wondered if it had all been a test as the man turned and headed towards a vinyl strip-curtain that led into the back. Roxy was quick to follow.

Mason put a hand on her arm. 'I don't trust him,' he whispered.

'Me neither,' she whispered back.

Quaid and Hassell followed Mason closely as he went around the counter and headed for the strip-curtains. Nobody spoke. Sally brought up the rear. The old man pushed through first, the vinyl strips swinging back and striking Roxy's arm as she followed. Mason went next.

And found himself in a wide room probably the same size as the shop. This room held stacks of cardboard boxes, two filing cabinets, and a small desk. There was a rectangular table in the centre surrounded by four chairs. Mason could see that Bellaire had been playing Solitaire when they came in.

'You want Cassadaga,' Bellaire said from the other

side of the table. 'Many want Cassadaga. He is a popular guy lately.'

Mason was glad all the code word bullshit was over. 'Can you arrange a meeting?'

Bellaire nodded. 'I can do that. I am the only one who can do that.'

'Perfect,' Quaid said. 'We'll wait.'

'But I don't think I will do that,' Bellaire said.

Mason frowned. Roxy cleared her throat to speak. But at that moment, the fire exit door opened, and three big guys stepped through. Bellaire turned to them immediately.

'Kill,' he said.

It wasn't the sudden movement of the men that shocked Mason; it was Bellaire's quick dive. He took them all by surprise. He leapt onto the table, rolled, and came at Roxy with a knife in his hand. The American leaned back, saw the knife flash past her face and flung an arm out as Bellaire slashed again. This time, she blocked the attack with her upraised arm.

Mason moved to meet the onslaught of the henchmen. The first man tried to rush him with arms spread wide. Mason stood his ground and delivered a front kick to the man's sternum, folding him in half. As he did so, Hassell came around him, taking the attention of the second henchman. Quaid was a step behind Hassell.

Mason lashed out, striking down at his opponent's throat. The guy lowered his head just in time but caught a blow to the left eye, which made him grunt. Mason struck down at him with solid blows, hitting around the head and neck, shaking him from left to right. They were hard, boxer's blows, designed to debilitate. The man appeared to know that and fell purposely to the floor to escape them, rolled, and tried to stand.

Mason was ready for him. He waded in before the guy could settle, delivering punch after punch.

Roxy had backed away from the knife-wielding Bellaire. He was good with a blade and moved like a viper, striking quickly. She tried to put it out of her head that this man was in his sixties; he was as deadly as anyone in this room with that slashing knife.

He swung at her face, missed, and then at her chest. Then, he arrested the momentum of his attack in mid-thrust and plunged the blade towards her solar plexus.

It was a hard attack to dodge. Impossible in the space she had. Roxy saw the man's skill; she knew it was coming. She threw a hand up, smashed his wrist hard, and knocked the knife from his grip.

It flew across the room, catching the light as it spun, and clattered to the floor.

Bellaire wasted no time commiserating the loss. He flung his bony arms at Roxy, forcing her to cover up. Behind the American, Sally stood ready to join in. Roxy was very much aware of the woman and what she wanted – to be a part of the action. But it was hard to let a newly trained fighter take the lead.

Roxy launched her own attack on Bellaire.

Quaid and Hassell had engaged the other two henchmen. Both enemies were big guys in black suits, their necks as thick as a python's body. They made no sound and betrayed no emotions as they joined the fight.

Quaid went low, Hassell went high. They both struck out as hard as they could, though they were not in the same league as Mason and Roxy when it came to fighting. But they could hold their own, as these goons were about to find out.

Or not. The goons took the blows without flinching

and then waded in themselves, punishing Quaid and Hassell with body blows. The two men were driven back. It was now that Sally saw where they needed her the most.

She skipped past Roxy, then reached Hassell and used her newly learned skills not to attack the men but to debilitate them. She was fast, still learning, but she had listened well and knew exactly what she had to do. Until now, she was untested.

Hassell staggered. Sally came around him and lashed out at the henchman with stiffened fingers and fists, going for his vulnerable areas. She connected with an eye, his trachea, and his ears. The man paused in his advance, breathing heavily, to shake his head and clear it.

In that moment, Hassell was on him, punching hard. To Hassell's left, Quaid was having similar problems with his adversary. Quaid managed to trip his opponent then, sending him crashing to the ground.

Mason was aware as ever that Hassell and Quaid were the weaker fighters. As he fought, he tried to monitor them with the idea that, if they started looking encumbered, he'd find a way to step in. For now, though, they were doing okay. He wasn't comfortable with the addition of Sally in the mix, but there was nothing he could do about it. His own opponent was up and attacking quickly. Mason knew he needed to end this fast. They had to take these goons down and find out what they knew, what Bellaire knew.

He met his opponent's rush with an elbow to the face. Blood flew from the impact. The man grunted, staggered. Mason brought a knee up, doubled him over. He smashed another elbow into the guy's exposed neck. As he fell, Mason kicked him in the face.

The man fell on his spine, flapping his arms and

bleeding. Mason decided to help Quaid and Hassell but, as he turned away, the man hooked his legs around Mason's ankles and sent him crashing to the floor. Mason landed hard, banging his forehead, and saw stars. He felt his opponent climbing on top of him.

Bellaire jabbed at Roxy, showing no signs of tiring. The American let him attack and then countered, targeting his ribs and stomach. Bellaire backed away so that the width of the table was between them.

'Is the car ready?' he shouted.

'Ready, boss,' one henchman shouted back.

'Then do it.'

Immediately, Bellaire lashed out, catching Roxy with a blow around the head. The three henchmen attacked swiftly and severely, punching and throwing their weight into the battle, forcing their opponents back.

Then they turned and ran.

All of Mason's attackers ran for the fire exit. He was on the floor, twisted in pain. Hassell and Quaid were on their knees. Sally had taken a blow and was holding her head in one hand. Roxy's mouth was bleeding as she darted around the table.

'What the fuck are you waiting for?' she growled at them. 'You want them to escape?'

The team dragged themselves to their feet and took off in pursuit.

Chapter 16

The frigid Parisian air hit them like a scythe. Mason saw the three henchmen running towards a parked car, but there was no initial sign of Bellaire. The alley they'd emerged in was narrow. Where could he have gone? Then Mason saw beyond the parked car. Bellaire was jumping astride a moped.

If the old guy could have done anything more incongruous whilst being chased, Mason didn't know what it was.

The henchmen yanked open their car doors and leapt in. The moped was already starting up, a noisy hairdryer sound bouncing off the walls of the alley. Mason knew their own car waited at the front of the shop, parked the same way their enemy was headed, and gauged the amount of time they'd take to sprint to it.

They'd have to be quick.

Mason gave up the direct chase, knowing he'd never reach the escaping car and the moped in time, and ran all out for their own car. The others followed. Their enemy set off. Mason rounded a corner and saw their car parked at the side of the road ahead. He dragged the keys from his pocket and remotely clicked open the locks. He was aware of Roxy to his left, Hassell to his right, and the others a step behind. The moped emerged from the alley with Bellaire sat astride it, the old man giving them an evil glower.

'Quickly!' Roxy cried.

Mason jumped into the driver's seat. Roxy took the passenger's. Quaid, Hassell and Sally climbed into the back. By the time they sat down, he'd started the car and was jamming his foot down on the accelerator pedal. The vehicle sped off with a lurch. Ahead, the henchmen's car followed Bellaire's moped down the street.

It was a narrow thoroughfare with cars parked to one side and a few glitzy Parisian jewellery shops on either side of the street. Mason accelerated as he tried to catch up. The car's engine roared. His team leaned forward, clinging to their seats and their belts as best they could. The gap between them and their quarry shrank. Mason could see faces through the back window, faces turned towards him, the mouths open and shouting a warning. Beyond them, he could see the sprawl of Paris, the vast network of buildings and high-rises, the straight streets that joined them.

The other car sped up, reckless now. The moped was still ahead. The Parisian streets here were narrow and crowded with parked vehicles. A thin line of pedestrians wandered the walkways at the early hour. Mason thought only to stay on the tail of the escapees; he hadn't decided yet how he might stop them.

The three vehicles flew along the road. Shouts went up from passers-by at the reckless speed. Mason crept closer to the car in front. The moped was way ahead, negotiating the turns and the slower Parisian traffic far better, its only hindrance speed and the hairdryer sound of its engine that bounced off the surrounding walls to pinpoint its position. Landmarks came and went as they twisted left and right, standing out amid the sprawl of the city they glimpsed through side streets and from atop hills: the Arc de Triomphe nestled at the top of the long wide straight of the Champs-Élysées, the Eiffel Tower beyond it. Paris's extensive city network spread out in all directions.

Mason swerved onto a new road. Ahead, the splendour of Paris stretched out before him again. Then, the rising sunlight blinded his eyes for a moment before being swept aside. This was a wider thoroughfare, enabling him to creep up alongside the other car. Sally threw him a warning glance.

'Watch out for pedestrians,' she said. 'It's not like we're working for the cops here.'

Mason knew it. He just wanted the other guys to make a mistake, to slow down, to swerve. Bellaire on the moped was still in sight. Mason felt he could catch up.

As Mason pulled up alongside the other car, its windows swept smoothly down. For a moment, Mason winced, expecting guns to be pointed at him, but these henchmen didn't appear to be carrying any. They leaned out of the gap and made threats, swore into Mason's face at thirty-five miles an hour as they sped down the street.

More accurately, it was Roxy in the passenger's seat, who took the brunt of the cursing. She actually had a bemused look on her face, as if unsure what to do. Should she trade insults, ignore them?

Mason had a quick decision to make. If he sideswiped the other car, it might make it crash, render it useless, but the action might also harm a civilian. He couldn't risk that. As he drove, the decision was whisked out of his hands as the other car swerved violently into him, striking mostly at the front. Mason jammed on the brakes as the rending sound of screeching metal tore at the air. The impact shook the whole car and sent its occupants crashing into the bulkheads. Mason gripped the wheel as he felt himself thrown against his seat belt.

He fell back. The front of the car looked like an unfriendly giant had crumpled it. One headlamp was hanging by a thread. Mason goosed the gas and found that the performance of the car hadn't been affected. He pulled in behind the offending vehicle.

'What next?' Roxy asked a little archly.

They flew into a new road, passing by a finely terraced café, taking the corner too fast and screeching the tyres. Mason clipped another car in the process and the lead vehicle narrowly missed a cyclist, who shook a fist at him. Mason raced past the guy at speed.

'We stick with them,' Mason said, extremely aware that this was the only clue they had to follow.

'Won't do us any good if we get arrested,' Sally said.

'We won't,' Mason said with more confidence than he felt.

'Maybe fall back a little,' Quaid suggested. 'It's not like they're getting away. Even the moped is still up front.'

It wasn't Mason's style. The only reason he'd consider backing off was to help safeguard passing civilians. Even as the thought struck him, he eased off on the accelerator. He pulled in behind the other car and let it create a small gap. Quaid's suggestion might be worth taking on board.

The chase continued at a more sedate pace. Fine restaurants flashed by on either side. Mason took a moment to glance over at Roxy.

'That old guy almost had you back there.'

Sensing the banter, the American flipped him her middle finger. 'He was handier than he looked,' she allowed.

'And a septuagenarian,' Quaid said.

'Piss off,' Roxy said. 'He was sixty at most.'

Mason laughed as he guided the car in fast but maintained pursuit. The henchmen weren't getting away. Ahead, Bellaire was guiding his moped and looking back over his shoulder. Mason gauged the chase.

'They're gonna do something,' he said.

'They have to,' Hassell said.

Buildings emblazoned with Parisian banners flashed by to both sides, their frontages mere blurs. Parked cars were always a hazard, some protruding further than others with their wing mirrors left out. Mason tried hard not to snap any off. The driver of the vehicle ahead had no such qualms, swerving from left to right whenever he wanted to and taking car parts with him, scraping down the sides of some vehicles as if desperate to attract police attention.

'Can't go on for ever,' Hassell said.

Mason knew it. Despite the lesser speed, they were still attracting too much attention. Or rather, the car ahead was.

'What are you going to do?' Sally asked.

'Just waiting for my moment,' Mason said. 'Get ready.'

'Bellaire is the target,' Quaid reminded them. 'What he knows . . . we need to know.'

Ahead, the narrow street ended, and a wide industrial area opened up. Mason saw space to left and right, buildings set back from the road with car parks out front.

Without a word, he floored the accelerator.

Chapter 17

Their vehicle darted forward, quickly coming alongside the henchmen's car. At the same time, the narrow street widened, pavement cafés to both sides. Space appeared ahead. Mason swerved his car so that it struck the other one hard in the flank, sending it shuddering towards the empty pavement. It hit the kerb and bounced. As it did, Mason threw a glance ahead to where Bellaire was riding his moped.

The guy had his head turned, watching what was going on. He slowed. Mason turned back to the henchmen's car. It had mounted the pavement and was riding across a patch of well-manicured lawn towards a half-empty parking lot, its tyres leaving ruts in the grass. It swerved one way and then the other, churning up the soil. Mason pursued it.

The cars flew across the grass and came to a sudden halt on the concrete. Both cars shuddered. Roxy was the first to fling her door open before their car came to a complete halt. The others followed suit quickly. Mason was a second slower, climbing out from behind the wheel.

He saw the doors on the other car opening, saw the goons climbing out with fury on their faces, and took a moment to check on their main quarry.

Bellaire had come to a halt several hundred yards further down the road. Of course, he wasn't wearing a helmet, so Mason could clearly see the rage and indecision twisted across his face. He wanted to be in on this. Maybe he was furious because his cover had been blown, the passwords compromised, his business potentially lost. Maybe he was crazy because he'd have to start all over again. Or maybe . . . he was just a raving lunatic.

Mason watched him, torn. He wanted to help his team but knew the primary aim should be Bellaire. What would the old man do?

Roxy waded into the first man she saw, even as he fought to leap clear of his car. Her front kick sent him flying back inside, his whole body disappearing back through the opening. His grunt of pain lingered in the air as he vanished. Roxy followed, reaching inside the car to grab his legs and haul him towards her. He fought, kicking out, face twisted in pain. Roxy guarded herself and pulled even harder. The man slithered out of the back seat and onto the concrete, landing on his spine and the back of his head. He cried out in pain, but kept kicking. Roxy stepped towards his head, bent down, and started pummelling him. The man hit out, but his blows barely touched her.

Around the other side of the car, Quaid and Hassell confronted the other two goons who worked for Bellaire. They either leapt out faster or Quaid and Hassell weren't as quick as Roxy because they cleared the car and attacked first. Sally kept her distance, waiting for an opening. There was a bruise on her right temple from where she'd been hit before, but the pain didn't deter her. She was ready to act if needed.

Mason drifted towards the fight. The moment he started moving, Bellaire turned his moped around, hunched over the handlebars, and gunned the engine. There was the dreary sound of a lawnmower as the bike came forward, heading straight for Mason. It might be loud and practically powerless, but it could still do a lot of damage. He kept the front of his car between himself and the oncoming bike.

Instead, Bellaire aimed straight for Roxy.

Mason shouted a warning. The American spun and stepped away. Bellaire sped around the front of Mason's car, pulled to a halt in front of his own man and stepped off the bike, letting it fall to the ground with a crash.

From his back pocket, he produced the blade.

The man on the ground was out for the count. Bellaire snarled and leapt once more at Roxy, brandishing the knife and driving her around the rear of the car.

Mason surveyed the scene. Two goons were squaring up to Quaid and Hassell even as Roxy fought Bellaire. It was, potentially, an even trade-off, but Mason knew where his help was needed the most.

He flitted around the car, came up behind Quaid and hesitated. The older man was defending a few punches, tucking up with his arms and elbows covering his sides. The goon was spitting with rage as he fought, his eyes devoid of everything except the desire to commit violence. At that point, Mason knew for sure that they were dealing with local, hired muscle rather than professionals. These men had probably grown up picking on scrawnier individuals to prove their prowess and their worth. They were weak, undisciplined, and slack. Mason watched as the man threw punch after punch at Quaid, trying to plant him into the concrete, before stepping up and catching his attention.

'Hey,' he said.

The man's fury-packed gaze fell upon him. Mason struck, jabbing the guy in the cheek, rocking his head back. The guy responded by lowering his head, roaring, and charging at Mason with his hands held wide.

Just what Mason wanted. He stepped aside, tripped the guy and then landed on his back as he struck the ground. He wasted no time grabbing an arm, forcing it up at the back and breaking it at the elbow. The downed guy's pain-filled breath whistled between his lips. He slammed the concrete with his one good arm. Mason targeted his kidneys until he stopped breathing and started gasping.

Quaid had moved off to help Hassell. The two men engaged the last henchman standing. Sally was still out of the action, looking a little disappointed, but relieved at the same time. Mason turned to Roxy.

Bellaire struck at her, the knife grazing her right shoulder. There was the slightest trickle of blood. Roxy's nostrils flared as Bellaire's eyes narrowed. The old man struck again, his rangy arms straining with muscle. He moved fast and had some skills. Roxy skipped and darted out of the way, using the space all around the back of the car. Bellaire tracked her carefully and swiftly, following her every move. He struck again, targeting her ribs, but Roxy pulled out of the way at the last instant and tried to grab his wrist on the way past. Bellaire was too wily to fall for that, and twisted to the right, pulling his wrist out of the way and slashing at her flailing hands.

Roxy narrowly missed losing a finger and backed

away again, ready for the next charge. Mason wondered if she'd get angry if he moved in to help. Despite his age, the guy facing her was clearly an experienced operative. Mason paced slowly until he stood in the man's blind spot.

A last look at Quaid and Hassell. They were subduing their opponent bit by bit, sending him down to his knees and then to the ground. In front, a row of windows looked out over the parking area, but Mason couldn't see anyone taking any notice. Not yet, at least. They'd been here for just a few minutes.

He waited, watched Bellaire stalk Roxy with the knife held low and underhand. He waited for the man to attack, then darted in, kicking him in the spine. Bellaire lurched forward, somehow hanging on to the knife. He caught himself and whirled, face contorted with pain.

'If you wanna live past this morning,' Roxy said, 'you need to answer our questions.'

'This is my answer.' Bellaire sliced the knife through the air, waving it now between Mason and Roxy. 'Who wants to get cut first?'

'You're a nasty old bastard, aren't you?' Roxy hissed.

Bellaire responded by lunging forward, narrowly missing her face. Mason stepped in, but the knife swept towards his lower belly, forcing him to step aside. Bellaire was quick, but Mason had had enough. This chase and this fight had gone on for far too long. Roxy seemed to sense his impatience. She feinted to the right, grabbing Bellaire's attention. Mason saw her step into the danger zone. Bellaire committed, striking out. At the same time, Mason jumped in and drove a fist into the man's solar plexus so hard he thought his knuckles might have touched the man's spine. Bellaire gasped, choked and then folded, hitting the ground with a crunch. The knife spun away. Mason grabbed his arms and pinned them above his head, sitting astride the writhing body.

'Pass me the knife,' Mason said to Roxy.

Bellaire drew a breath. His eyes focused. When they fell on Mason, he let out a sharp snarl.

'Get the hell off of me.'

'I will, just as soon as we get some answers. We were sent to you. We used the right passwords. All we want is Cassadaga.'

Bellaire's top lip curled. 'No, you didn't. You missed out the most important part. Whoever passed on the password wasn't given the complete process.'

As Mason had thought. But none of that mattered now. What mattered was forcing the information out of Bellaire.

'You failed to mention a price,' Bellaire panted, crushed under Mason's weight. 'That's the most important part of the code.'

'I don't care,' Mason said. 'You are Cassadaga's source. You arrange his meetings and his jobs. The guy's a fucking psycho, a stone-cold killer. You already have that on your conscience—'

Bellaire spat as if he didn't care, squirmed under Mason. 'Get the hell off of me.'

'Where will we find Cassadaga? There has to be a meet point, an arrangement between you two.'

'As if I'd tell you.'

Roxy crouched down beside Bellaire. 'Listen, friend, I have a few demons of my own. But they're nothing compared to Cassadaga. You surely can't defend him. Don't you know what he's done?'

Bellaire bucked under Mason, trying to free his arms and send them flying at Mason. 'I care only about getting paid. You bastards have ruined my business.'

Mason knelt harder on Bellaire's wrists, making him flinch. 'Where do we find Cassadaga?' he breathed.

'Fuck. Off.'

Mason held a hand out. Roxy filled it with the knife. Mason let Bellaire see it glinting before his eyes.

'Last chance, arsehole.'

'No, it's *your* last chance. I have contacts. I'll see that you're all put in the ground for this. All of you.'

Mason checked his surroundings. They were drawing attention from passers-by and he could see faces at the office windows. Someone would surely call the police. Their time was now measured in minutes.

Not even a second to waste.

'I'm not gonna pretend to hurt you, to threaten you,' he said in a low voice. 'I'm just gonna do it. You still have a chance, man. A chance to do the right thing . . .' He paused briefly as Quaid, Hassell, and Sally arrived. 'You have no men left. No guards. It's just you. And if I use this knife, it's going to hurt.'

Carefully, he placed the point of the knife between Bellaire's ribs and pressed until the old man gasped.

'I'm an old man . . .' he started to say.

Roxy laughed. 'I'd say a capable old bastard,' she said.

His eyes snapped towards her. 'Anytime, bitch.'

'Cassadaga,' Mason said. 'How do we find him?'

'You must be joking.' Bellaire leaned away from the point of the blade. 'Do you know what Daga would do to me if he found out I told you?' The old man laughed grimly.

Mason was aware of the approaching sirens, of the people watching – still relatively few at the moment, of the sound of Bellaire's sharply drawn breaths and even the fact that the rising sun was giving off a little more heat. He was aware of every vital second that ticked away. They needed this lead.

'Look,' he said. 'Daga killed a good friend of ours. He's helping a madman. This all goes far deeper than any of us know. Daga will never know you gave him up.'

Bellaire's face twisted into an evil rictus. 'That bastard is a demon sent from Hell. You can't hide anything from him.'

Mason hid a surge of frustration by inserting the tip of the knife about two inches. 'Last chance.'

'Go to hell.'

Mason jerked the knife against Bellaire's flesh, drawing a sharp gasp from the man. Roxy noticed one of the downed goons stirring, walked over to him and kicked him in the head. The guy collapsed once more into oblivion.

Mason was finished messing about. He pushed the knife in as far as it would go without causing major damage.

'Answer me,' he said.

'Ah, that hurts, that *hurts*.' Bellaire found he couldn't twist away any further, couldn't escape the intrusive blade. He glared up at Mason, searching his eyes for the gravity of his intent. Clearly, he was trying to judge Mason's resolve.

'Sw . . . Switzerland,' he said.

'It's a big place,' Quaid said.

'Funny bastard, aren't you? No, there's an office. If Daga wants to meet you, he'll meet you there.'

'In Switzerland? Where in Switzerland?'

'Listen . . . can we talk about this? Daga is a seriously unpleasant guy. And shockingly precognisant. It wouldn't surprise me if he'd signed his soul over to the Devil.'

'He'd have to get in line,' Roxy grumbled quietly. 'But some of us are trying to atone.'

'Not Daga. No. He contradicts all that. I can't betray someone like him and not fear the shadows for the next twenty years.'

Mason tore more flesh with the blade. 'But we're here now, not Daga. You're dealing with us.'

Bellaire grunted in agony. 'Damn you. Like I said, go to Switzerland.' He reeled off an address. 'It's an office building, a front. You go inside and wait, then come back twenty-four hours later. Daga will find a way to contact you.'

'In the flesh?'

Bellaire shuddered. 'Why would you want to . . . maybe. In any case, that's your meet. He'll listen to what you have to say.'

Mason acted in a blur. It was all about speed now. He pushed Bellaire away, spun and started running for their car. The others followed at a pace. Roxy had to move one of the unconscious henchmen out of the way. In seconds, they were inside, and Mason was behind the wheel.

Moments later, they were gone.

Chapter 18

The evil old man had said to go to Switzerland, so the team went to Switzerland. They landed at Zürich airport, with its sweeping, modern architecture and shiny escalators, and took advantage of its parade of services and conveniences. Shortly after landing, they were climbing into a silver rental Ford and making their way towards the city of Zürich. The multicultural city by the water was an intricate mix of urban life and nature, humming with commotion by day and by night, and less than an hour from the ancient and spectacular Swiss mountain ranges.

This time, Quaid drove, still trying to wrestle with the newfangled automatic gearbox and in-car technology. Mason was beginning to think he just loved to complain about it as a way of clinging to the past. Quaid would never grow accustomed to the onward march of technology, not because he wasn't able but simply because he preferred the old ways.

Sally, in the back seat, spoke up as they drove through the outskirts of the big city. 'Just out of interest,' she said, 'and since I'm still in training, what would you have done to Bellaire if he'd simply refused to give us an answer?'

Mason leaned back and closed his eyes. This was part of the problem when you trained civilians. He'd been trained in war, for war. He'd been taught to kill or be killed by ruthless men. To be as ruthless as they were and stay alive any way he could. Bringing those attributes into a civilian situation was risky. He was no teacher.

'We're teaching you to stay alive in a combat situation,' he said. 'Let's leave the mind games alone for another year.'

'Mind games?'

'You have to make them believe you're willing to kill, to hurt, to maim,' Roxy said quietly. 'It's all in the head.'

'Well, Bellaire believed you.'

Mason thought about that. The old man had folded, but he'd done so at the last possible moment, as the cops drew near. The hard truth was, if he'd waited just a few minutes more, Mason would have been forced to back down and run. Maybe Bellaire hadn't heard the sirens. Maybe he'd got to the end of his endurance. Maybe he assumed Mason was working with the cops.

Whatever it was, Mason knew they couldn't trust a word Bellaire had told them. Even now, heading towards the address Bellaire had spilled, Mason was racking his brains for a plan B.

'Those baby blues look worried,' Roxy said to him. 'You think Bellaire was lying?'

'I think we have to follow up anyway,' Mason said. 'I don't like it, but I think that's what we have to do.'

Quaid followed the satnav on what felt like a roundabout route as they skirted the main city. They were all hungry and stopped for half an hour to make use of a fast-food restaurant on the way. Once they'd eaten, they continued their journey, which, Mason saw, was almost at an end.

'It's leading us to this warehouse district,' he said, looking left and right as they started threading their way through an old industrial estate.

'Remote and yet very accessible,' Hassell said. 'Plenty of ingress and egress routes. I'd choose this place if I was in Cassadaga's shoes.'

Mason nodded. Hassell was the expert. He watched as Quaid negotiated several more streets, taking them to the heart of the district. Finally, the car slowed and pulled up at the side of a kerb.

'It's back there,' he said. 'I drove past it.'

Mason nodded. He had noticed the building that corresponded to the address Bellaire had given them. It bore a small black number 39 on its brick frontage and a narrow, incongruous golden sign that read: *Elstead Holdings*. He studied it over his shoulder as the car ticked quietly.

'Thoughts?' he asked the team.

'We do as Bellaire said,' Hassell spoke up first. 'We go inside.'

'And then return twenty-four hours later,' Quaid said. 'Easy.'

Mason knew the building would be locked tight, but he was also aware it wouldn't be a problem for Hassell. The guy could pick his way into anything. To left and right, similar buildings stood blanketed by a similar silence. The only movement he could see was in an office ahead of them where a guy was cleaning the windows as a secretary talked to him. The little parking area in front of that building was full of cars.

Not so the one they were interested in.

'Wait for the window cleaner to finish,' Hassell said. 'Then we move.'

Mason nodded. The other side of the road was the backs of warehouses, all without windows, so it wasn't as if they were overlooked. And Hassell could find a way into the building in seconds, Mason was sure. He sat and watched the window cleaner for a while.

'He's taking his time.'

'That might have something to do with the secretary.' Roxy smiled.

Eventually, as early afternoon passed, the window cleaner made his exit, and the secretary vanished. Mason took a last look around before exiting their car, followed by the others. It was cool outside, with a cold snap in the air. Mason felt it on his exposed arms and face. He started walking briskly towards the building.

'We're meant to be here,' he said. 'Act like it for anyone watching.'

Hassell led the way, reached the door first and already had his lock picks in his hand. A few quick twists and turns of the carbon fibre sticks, and the metal door handle clicked. Hassell eased it open. Mason followed him inside, ready for anything.

The office was a dark shell, populated only by an empty desk and a plastic chair. There were no filing cabinets, no shelving, no sign that the place was in use. Mason had to assume there was some surveillance equipment inside through which they would now be observed before they left and returned in twenty-four hours. It was an obscure and roundabout way of doing business, but it had helped keep Cassadaga free for decades.

'You think that's enough?' Roxy was walking around the place, turning on the spot.

'I think they've got your good side.' Quaid smiled.

'I hope it's not a dead end,' Mason said.

'It sure feels like it,' Roxy said, staring around at the empty place.

Mason looked out the front windows. It was still quiet out there; their silver car looking incongruous parked at the side of the road. The only person he could see was a postal worker about a dozen doors down.

A car turned into the street. Mason wasn't sure why he kept on watching it – maybe it was because he had nothing else to do, maybe it was that eternal suspicion that his army days had instilled in him – but he stared at the vehicle as it cruised slowly by. It was silver, like theirs, but bigger like an SUV. The windows comprised smoked glass, but the driver was staring right at the building they were in.

Mason felt a tremor of anticipation. Was he imagining it, seeing something that wasn't really there?

Or was the driver staring right at him?

A second car turned down the street. Suddenly, it seemed rather busy outside. This one was big and brown and cruising along just as steadily as the first. It too had a driver who took a long look at the building that they were in.

Both cars disappeared around the bend at the bottom of the street. Mason kept watching. He called Roxy over. Sure enough, thirty seconds later, both cars reappeared and started back along the street.

'I think we have trouble,' Mason said.

Chapter 19

Mason watched as the vehicles came closer. The silver and brown cars passed their own, slowing as they came alongside the building. Now Mason could see the shapes of several figures seated inside. By now, they were all crowded around the window.

'Could it be Cassadaga?' Roxy asked.

'Not even he could be that quick,' Mason said doubtfully.

'Maybe this is what's meant to happen,' Sally said.

'Yes, but not in a good way,' Hassell said. 'I'll check for another way out of here.'

Hassell moved away. Quaid went with him. Mason kept his eyes out front. The vehicles appeared to be just sitting there. He could see both drivers and passengers, the lead driver of which appeared to be on his phone.

Getting orders? Who from . . . Cassadaga?

Maybe. It was impossible to say. The only thing Mason was sure of was that ten figures were now stationed between them and their car outside the building. A minute passed, and then another. Yes, this could still go either way. It still might be the right way to get to Cassadaga. But the sheer number of people out there . . .

It wasn't right. Just then, the car doors started opening. Figures stepped out into the road and onto the pavement. Mason counted ten, including the drivers. They came around the back of the car and lined up as they walked towards the parking lot.

'Shit,' Roxy said.

Mason saw it too. Almost simultaneously, what looked like seven men and three women reached under their jackets for an array of weapons. There were handguns, automatic machine guns, pump-action shotguns. These were mercenaries then, come to shoot whoever was inside the building.

'That bastard, Bellaire,' Mason said. 'He sent us deliberately to a kill box.'

Roxy nodded and dived for the floor. Mason was half a second behind, dragging Sally with him. They hit the wooden decking as the mercs outside opened fire, the sound of their weapons shattering the stillness. Bullets thudded into brick and block and shattered glass. The nightmare hail destroyed the window and the door, sending deadly fragments flying across the room. Mason couldn't hear anything except the roar and the thunder of weapons discharging, the sound of debris surging through the room.

His back was showered by the wreckage, some bits sharp enough to cut through his clothing and jab his flesh. He climbed on top of Sally, holding her down. Roxy was at his side, hands over her head. The barrage continued for what seemed like ten minutes but was probably no more than ten or twenty seconds.

When it ended, Mason moved fast.

They had their own weapons, courtesy of their new status as international relic protectors. They all carried Glocks and several rounds of spare ammo. Mason reached for his gun now, plucking it from its holster at his waistband. As he moved, he felt the debris slide off his back and watched Roxy sit halfway up.

'You okay?'

'For now.'

'They sent us here to die,' Mason said. 'Let's shatter that fantasy for them.'

Roxy was already moving. She lifted her gun over the windowsill and fired blindly. Mason moved to the left and fired through the shattered front door. He couldn't see the enemy from his vantage point. Sally was lying on the floor between Roxy and him, head in hands. Mason frowned as he looked at her.

'Get ready to move,' he said.

'Who the hell are these guys?'

'Just killers.'

'Bellaire arranged this?'

'Maybe, maybe not. It could just be an address where they send people to die. Bellaire is protecting himself from Cassadaga by sending us here.'

There was no more time for talk. The men outside were opening fire randomly now as they advanced. Bullets slammed through the openings, through the office and into plaster walls. Mason was keeping half an eye to the back, through the door where Quaid and Hassell had vanished. Where were they?

He rolled, peered around the doorframe, and sighted the approaching figures. He fired two shots, striking two targets, the shots so fast they were almost simultaneous. A bullet struck a man in the thigh, another tagged a woman in her bulletproof vest, driving her to her knees.

'They're wearing tactical,' he said, rolling back to safety.

Roxy nodded. She didn't want to pop her head up over the windowsill and open fire for fear of getting it blown off. She did lift her hand and shoot blindly again though, in an effort to drive their enemies away.

Mason grabbed Sally and scrambled for the back of the room. They couldn't stay here. He hit the back wall, turned to check on Roxy.

'I'm here.'

Together, they scooted towards the only exit in the room. At that moment, a shape appeared. Mason raised his gun.

'It's me,' Quaid yelled. 'Come on. There's a back way out of here.'

Mason shoved Sally towards him. Roxy went next. Mason turned and emptied his mag at the door and the window as shapes appeared in his eyeline. The enemy was getting closer by the second. He saw them scatter and duck, and then he headed through the back door.

Found himself in a smaller office, this one even more sparsely decorated than the last. There wasn't even a desk in this one. Hassell was waiting for them at the far side, his hand poised on the handle of a back door.

'Move it!' Roxy yelled.

Just then, Mason sensed a presence to his left. It wasn't anything to do with his five senses, more a feeling, something learned in the heat of battle. Somehow, he just knew he wasn't alone by the door. He turned, saw a black-clad pair of hands sticking through the door. The hands were clasping a gun. Mason grabbed the hands and jerked them upward just as their owner squeezed the trigger. The bullet went high, smashing into the ceiling and bringing a flurry of plaster showering down. Mason held on, jerking the hands to the floor and wrenching them hard. The owner stumbled into sight. Mason twisted the gun away, mashing the man's finger in the process. He slammed his fist into the bridge of his opponent's nose. He then head-butted the man at close range.

The figure slumped, groaning in agony. Mason would have liked to finish him, but there wasn't time. He kicked the guy in the head as he fell to the ground. Ahead, Hassell had opened the back door and was squeezing through.

Mason ran for it, half turned so that he could see behind. When he saw the next shadow filling the doorway, he opened fire again, making the shadow slink back. He kept the barrage up until he managed to slip through the back door.

Into daylight. The rear of the building was a yard surrounded by high block walls. There was a metal gate at the far end, which already stood open, with Quaid next to it. Beyond the gate, Mason could make out a small field filled with crates and packing boxes, discarded building supplies and heaps of timber.

They ran, trying to put some distance between them and their attackers. Mason flew across the yard in seconds, then waited outside the far gate, gun raised. It was all a matter of making the bastards pay for every inch of ground they gained, of making them wary at every turn. He waited for the first and then the second figure to exit the building before firing, then took them both out with headshots. The rest slunk back inside as their brethren slumped to the ground, bleeding all over the concrete.

Mason immediately turned and ran. Their enemies were thinning by the minute. The one he'd mashed in the room, the first he'd shot in the thigh, the woman he'd hit in the vest and now the two dead. They surely had to be wondering what kind of enemy they'd come up against.

They'd escaped the kill box, but they weren't yet free. They were in the field behind the building. Mason saw plenty of places where he could take cover, but would that be enough against well-armed, determined pursuers? He was already halfway through his second mag and only had two left. The others might be faring better, he supposed. Quaid was leading them, ducking behind a wobbly array of building materials that included blocks, timber, bricks, and metal pylons that stuck out at angles like sticks of chocolate in an ice cream cone. It was suitable cover and Mason scrambled behind it.

'How we doing?' Roxy asked.

'Two down, at least two injured. Five or six still able-bodied. They're well armed.'

'Who the hell are they? Bellaire's men?' Quaid asked.

Mason didn't have time to go through it all again. 'We'll deal with that later,' he said. He was peering around their barricade, waiting for the first of their attackers to appear.

He didn't have to wait long. They were coming all at once, at least six that Mason could see. They were crowding through the back gate with their guns held low. He couldn't miss. He opened fire, draining the next mag. Bullets pinged among his enemies, scattering them. At least two jerked as if they'd been hit. The rest started running for cover.

Then Roxy was firing, too, trying to pick the runners off. Hassell was also shooting. They tagged another man in the leg. Their pursuers, separated, raced for several different areas of cover. Mason lurched back as they returned fire.

Bullets pinged off the building material pile, some of them striking blocks or getting buried among the bricks. At least two rang off the jutting metal spars, triggering resonant chimes that echoed through the air. Mason waited. He looked around. Sally was kneeling with a wild look on her face. Hassell was already looking to where they could run next. Quaid was holding his gun and patiently peering around the other side of the pile, keeping an eye on the mercs sneaking around that way. As Mason watched, Quaid let off a shot.

Roxy was beside him.

'Ya think if we wound enough of them, they'll back off?'

Mason nodded. 'Yeah, I do, but they're just getting closer and closer.'

There was a lot of cover in the field, and the mercs were using it well. As he watched, a cloud covered the sun, sending a wedge of shadow over the entire area. Mason squinted harder.

'We have to move,' he said.

Quaid was already on it. There was very little ground now between them and their enemies. Quaid caught their attention and then started running towards a stack of crates, maybe eight high, that loomed precariously over the field. As he started running, a gunshot rang out.

Quaid went down.

Chapter 20

Mason's heart lurched into his throat. Quaid fell face forward into the grass, but there was no telltale red bloom spreading across his back. Mason returned fire with Roxy even as he scrambled towards Quaid.

As they approached, the Englishman sat up. There was a look of shock on his face.

'Shit,' he said. 'That was close.'

'Close?' Roxy echoed. 'We thought you'd been hit.'

'No. The bullet whizzed past my head. I guess I ducked too late, but it was a gut reaction.'

Mason reached down and pulled Quaid to his feet, still firing. 'Get moving or the next one will hit you.'

As a team, they raced behind the crates, laying down cover fire. Mason was down to his last magazine. Seventeen rounds between him and empty. The enemy were relentless as they pushed forward, now creeping behind the building pile they'd been using just a few moments earlier. Mason watched Roxy fire off a few shots.

'Make them count,' he breathed.

She nodded. She knew what he meant. Their enemies

appeared far better equipped than they were. Bullets constantly sheared the air between hideouts, slamming into the crates and tearing chunks off the wood. Minutes passed. Mason sent a look at Hassell.

'You got a way out of this?'

Hassell was scanning the terrain, looking for another escape. The field extended quite a way, becoming less cluttered as it terminated at a far road. The road itself looked busy with traffic and lay behind a high fence. Between here and there, Mason spied several more clusters of material, but hardly anything substantial.

They would have to make a stand right here.

Their enemies seemed to know it too, unleashing wave after wave of lead into their hiding place. They were pinning them down.

And seconds later, Mason understood why.

Around the corners of their barricade, mercenaries appeared. They were running hard and, mostly, blind. They came around the edges with their guns held out as if they'd been ordered to jump right into the thick of the action.

Mason reacted instantly, shooting at the bulk of the men and women. He rose quickly, grabbed a wooden spar and smashed it into his attackers. Roxy did the same at his side. They waded into the figures at close quarters. Mason dropped the timber as a man went down with blood all over his face. Roxy grabbed another by the arm and twisted until it broke, slipping around to his rear and elbowing another in the face. Mason shot a woman in the chest, the same one he'd shot earlier it seemed, and watched her stagger back and then fall to the ground, her face stretched in a rictus of pain.

On the other side of the barricade, Hassell and Quaid

were meeting another attack. Bullets flew haphazardly, most of them hitting the ground or skimming high into the air. Everyone was grappling for something, the figures too close to bring their weapons to bear. Sally was at the centre of the barricade, her back to it, staring from side to side with wild eyes.

Mason tripped one man and then threw another into the one beside him. He took several punches and escaped the thrust of a knife quite by accident as one man pushed him out of the way of an attacker.

He fell back. A man kicked out, striking Mason's shins. The pain stabbed through his brain. Mason ignored it. There were four men and a woman in front of him. Roxy was there, too. It was a melee of arms and legs and bodies. Nobody could shoot for fear of hitting a colleague. Roxy kneed one man, grabbed hold of his neck, and twisted. He fell, groaning. She punched another in the face.

Mason couldn't hold them back. There were too many. He knew that as soon as the enemy got behind him; it was game over. There was too much space. They could just step back, draw their weapons and fire. The only way was to keep them in the choke points around the side of the barricade.

But they were losing the battle. One man slipped past Mason and ran into the open, already reaching for his gun.

Sally stepped forward. She fought like she'd been taught, capturing the man's attention with hard jabs and searching for vulnerable areas. The guy wore Kevlar and a bulky jacket, so it wasn't easy getting through. He was trained too, and able to guess Sally's every strike. He didn't fall back.

But she slowed him down.

Mason had already fallen back a little. Now he stepped back some more. Three of his opponents were on their knees. On the other side, Quaid and Hassell were holding their own. From somewhere, there came the sound of a gunshot, a merc taking a potshot, trying to take someone out. Mason grabbed one man and hurled him into the rest, watched them all stagger. To the left, he saw two mercs push their way past Quaid and Hassell, moving out into the open. Sally was still diverting the attention of the other one. Mason saw their tentative safety net falling apart.

Leaving the closer battle with Roxy, he moved away and lifted his weapon. He was a fast shot. He fired off two rounds. The bullets crisscrossed those fired by his enemies in the air. Mason felt the tug of hot lead pass through his jacket. The sensation sent fire through his brain, fear that wouldn't chase away. That was how close he'd come to getting shot. Mere inches.

His own bullets struck true, one smashing into the arm of a merc, the other striking another's Kevlar tactical jacket. Both men fell to their knees and Mason ran towards them.

On the way, he passed Sally.

He wanted to help, leaned towards her. The merc struck out and Sally blocked. Mason was a few feet away. He slammed a fist out at the merc, making him stumble. He ran on, reached the two he'd shot, and waded in.

Using his knees, he sent them both crashing to the ground. To his right, Quaid and Hassell were taking on just two mercs and matching them, grappling for weapons and throwing punches when they could. Mason fell on his opponents, giving them no chance for respite. He smashed the first in the face with the butt of his gun, saw the blood fountain, and then turned to the other.

The guy was already on his knees, reaching for a weapon.

Mason flung himself at the man, grabbed the gun hand and broke it. The gun slipped away. Mason knocked his opponent unconscious with a few well-aimed punches and then swivelled, trying to take in every aspect of the battle in one go.

The man fighting Sally appeared to be doing the same. He could see what Mason saw. That only three other mercs remained in the fight, all being held at bay by Roxy. Including him, there were just four mercs remaining.

The man appeared to make a split-second decision. He waded into Sally, grabbed her roughly by the neck and started hauling her towards Roxy. Mason jumped to his feet. Right then, Roxy fell to her knees, staggered by a punch to the gut, and the three mercs pushed past her to join the fourth who had hold of Sally.

To her credit, Sally fought back hard, making him regret his decision. It was only when one of the other mercs stepped in that they were able to subdue her.

Mason raised his gun. 'Let her go. Let us go. You're done here.'

'You won't shoot as long as we have her,' the merc she'd been fighting said. He had a thick accent, possibly Croatian. Mason wondered what the hell he was doing.

'We're taking her,' the man said.

By now, Quaid and Hassell had paused. The two mercs they were fighting backed off and came around to join their brethren. They were all injured, most of them limping. Sally struggled in her captor's grip.

'Don't follow us,' the merc said. 'We will shoot her in the arms and then the legs.'

'You're making a mistake,' Mason said, hiding the fear he felt for Sally. 'They sent you here to kill us. Do anything less than that, they'll kill you.'

'You don't even know who they are.'

'Maybe not, but I have a good idea. And I know anyone connected with Cassadaga won't brook any slip-ups.'

The merc blanched but then recovered. 'Cassa who?' he said.

As one, the mercenaries started moving away. Mason kept his gun trained on them. Roxy was back on her feet, her face dark with storm clouds. Hassell and Quaid walked to his side, all holding their guns low.

'What do we do?' Quaid asked.

'We won't be letting them take her,' Mason said.

The sun came out from behind the cloud that had passed over it, lighting the scene for a few moments. All four mercs started walking away with Sally – two of them covering her with their guns and two covering Mason and the others. The man holding Sally had a firm and severe look on his face, as if he wasn't exactly sure he was doing the right thing.

Mason wasn't about to let this happen.

Chapter 21

Mason waited until the mercs were out of sight and then started running, taking a different route through the stacks of crates. He bypassed the mound of building materials at the same time as the running mercs, but stayed out of sight using the crates. Roxy, Quaid, and Hassell ran with him, staying low.

It was a desperate sprint. They reached the building first, slipped inside before the mercs appeared. Mason started the quick dash through to the other side, traversing first the back office and then the front room. Through the shattered windows, he could see the mercs' vehicles parked at the side of the road outside.

A dozen plans ran through his head.

They were only seconds behind the mercs, who were dragging Sally along with them. They flew through the front room and were then outside again. Mason knew he was out of options.

'What's the fucking plan?' Roxy hissed tautly.

In moments of high stress, they deferred to him. Mason

had once said he never wanted to lead a team again, but circumstances just kept putting him in charge.

'Have you got some bullets left?'

They all nodded.

'Then shoot these bastards when they come out the bloody door.'

Mason flattened himself against the wall a few feet from the broken door. Roxy went to the other side. Quaid and Hassell separated and copied their movements. Mason listened hard. Already there were sounds of the mercs coming through the front room.

Mason readied himself. The first merc came through the door, backing out, dragging Sally along with him. Mason didn't hesitate. The whole situation was incredibly fluid. He placed the barrel of his gun close to the guy's head and fired. Even as his body spasmed and jerked, Sally struggled with the other mercs pushing her outside. From the right, Roxy shot another merc through the face, aiming high. Mason jammed his gun into the armpit of the next merc, careful to avoid the vest, and opened fire.

All that was left was the main merc who had grabbed Sally.

He still had hold of her, but shock and fear now clouded his features. Mason shoved his gun point-blank into the man's face.

'Let her go.'

'Back off or she dies.' The merc's eyes were wild. He lost his grip on Sally but held his gun pointed straight at her, his finger poised on the trigger. Mason could see the white flesh, showing that he already had some pull on it.

Sally stood like a deer caught in the headlights, unable to move, her arms spread out at her sides.

Roxy made it clear she had her gun aimed at the back of the mercenary's head.

Mason put some pressure on his own trigger. 'Stand down,' he said carefully. 'You don't have to die here today.'

The merc rolled his eyes from Mason to Sally, clearly in turmoil. Around him, the bodies of his colleagues lay in pools of blood.

Mason didn't want to kill this man. He didn't want to risk Sally's life. The seconds passed between them as if they were being dragged through thick, oozing mud.

'I won't tell you again,' the merc hissed through tightly drawn lips.

'If she dies, you die,' Mason said. 'If she lives, you live. The choice isn't a hard one to make.'

The merc's face twisted in indecision. Mason could see a huge, chaotic battle going on in his eyes. Surrendering certainly wasn't his style. On the other hand, he wanted to live. Mason wondered whether to push him even harder.

But the man's aim never wavered. The barrel of his gun stayed pointed constantly at Sally's face.

'You can't win this, man,' Hassell said, taking a few steps away from the wall. 'Look at the firepower.'

It was a ploy, something to take his attention away from Sally, something that might give Mason or Roxy the chance to act. The merc didn't fall for it, but he'd been holding the same position for some minutes now. He was sweating, and Mason saw his arm shaking. He wouldn't last much longer.

'Hey,' he said, still trying to defuse the confrontation. 'Hey, stand down.'

'I'm walking away with her.'

'No. No, you're not.'

'Then I'll shoot her where she stands.'

The merc strained, his whole body pressing forward, the gun wavering in his hands. Mason was a hair's breadth from pulling his own trigger. In the chaos of his mind, he was also very much aware that this man, this sweating mercenary, represented their last genuine lead. Bellaire had sent them into a corner to die. They had nothing. Mason's mouth was dry, his tongue practically stuck to the roof of his mouth. He could almost taste the man's indecision.

Until now, she'd been unaccountably quiet, but it was Roxy who stepped forward then, putting her gun away and catching the merc's eye.

'Nobody wants to kill you,' she said. 'Not here and now. We want answers from you, yes, but that doesn't mean you can't go free when we're done.'

The merc blinked at her. 'Answers?'

'Put the gun down and let's talk.'

'I don't trust you.'

'And I don't blame you. But what else is there to do?'

Mason knew they were at a dead end. The clues that had led them to Bellaire had fizzled out the moment he betrayed them. Of course, they shouldn't be surprised that the evil old man had scuppered everything. He was an associate of Cassadaga.

And then there was the terrible thief himself. Their only way of getting to Marduk. Even now, Marduk would be plotting against the Church. It was as certain as the fact that night followed day.

Mason decided to take a chance.

'What's your name?' he asked.

It was an incongruous, dangerous question. The merc still had a good pull on the trigger. His eyes were wide and bloodshot. There was also the passage of time to consider, because Mason was sure the police would be on their way. What they really needed to do was get the hell out of here and interview this man elsewhere.

'My name's Gabriel.'

'Well, Gabriel,' Mason said. 'How about we stow our guns, get in our car, and run? The cops will be here any minute. Does running work for you?'

Gabriel's face smoothed a little as he took on board what Mason was saying. His eyes didn't look so wild anymore. There were sirens in the wind, getting closer by the second. For the first time, he looked away from Sally.

'I'm taking a lot on trust here,' he said.

'So are we,' Roxy said. 'Now give me the damn gun.'

She reached out a hand. Gabriel folded and plonked it into her hand. Sally let out an enormous sigh of relief and started to shake. Mason walked up to her and grabbed her before she fell down.

'Sorry,' he said. 'But we must hurry.'

It was a strange sprint to their car with Gabriel at their centre. They made the silver rental Ford in a matter of seconds and bundled their way inside. It was a tight squeeze, but it wasn't as though they'd have to travel too far.

Mason jumped behind the wheel this time, staying silent. Nobody said a word. Their focus was on getting out of the area. A quick look around assured him that nobody was watching them – at least not discernibly. He knew that furtive eyes, somewhere, would be upon them, perhaps even noting down the licence plate. That couldn't be helped for now. He started the car and drove off, first losing them in the network of roads that crisscrossed the industrial estate and then following signs for Zürich's city centre. At no point did they see a police car, but they heard the sirens close by.

It was a little after five p.m. now and the roads were busy with rush hour. Mason wasn't sure exactly where to go and nobody was talking in the car, so he pulled into the first fast-food restaurant he could find and made his way around to the back of the car park. Finding a space beneath overhanging trees, he pulled the car in and switched off the engine. It wasn't dark outside yet, but the trees did a good job of blocking out the light, making the car's interior dim.

The first thing Gabriel said was: 'I could eat.'

Mason actually agreed with him. Sally and Hassell volunteered to collect some fast food and, fifteen minutes later, they were all sat in the car, eating and drinking their way through cola and burgers and nuggets as if they were all old friends.

Mason finished his burger before speaking. 'Gabriel,' he finally said. 'I realise this is about as strange as it gets, but now we need to talk. Why were you at the office today?'

Gabriel blinked as if he didn't quite know what to say. 'Well, to kill you, of course.'

Mason nodded. 'I figured that. Okay, wrong question, I guess. Who sent you?'

'Wait . . .' Sally said. 'You were there simply to kill us? Not to capture us, not to interrogate us?'

'Orders were clear. Terminate anyone found inside that building. It's a pretty smooth operation. All the orders come down the phone lines.'

Mason delved deeper. 'What do you know of Cassadaga?

Of Marduk? Somebody must pay your wages. Is there something new happening, something big?'

Gabriel finished his box of French fries before answering. 'I've heard of this Cassadaga,' he said. 'But I thought he was a myth, a figure dreamt up to scare weak minds. The things they say about him . . .' He tailed off. 'Are you telling me he's real?'

Mason nodded. 'We've met him. He's as real as you or I. And all those stories? They're real too.'

Gabriel couldn't stop a shadow of fear crossing his face. 'Please don't tell me I work for him.'

'In a way . . . you do. The building is a kill box, probably designed by Cassadaga and others. Their *associates* probably have orders to direct people to places like that, people who don't pass the test. And then they call you guys in.'

'It makes sense. We work for an organisation called Wineth, always on retainer and primed to move at a moment's notice. We work shifts with other men and women, always on call, and are primarily based here in Zürich, but there are other units placed around the world.'

'What can you tell us about Marduk?' Mason asked again.

'Seriously, I do not know who that is.'

Mason wasn't surprised, but he felt a stab of despair. Where could they go next?

'Anything about a prison break?' Hassell asked.

Gabriel looked blank. 'Who escaped?'

Mason didn't answer him. Instead, he continued to push. 'You work for a big mercenary network, right? One connected to Marduk, I assume, since it's connected to Cassadaga. Has the network picked up any new jobs recently?'

Gabriel frowned as he considered the question. 'Yeah,' he said. 'Yeah, there was one big one.'

'Where?' Quaid asked.

'Babylon,' Gabriel said.

Chapter 22

Now it was Mason's turn to frown. 'Babylon, Iraq?'

'Yeah, do you know it?'

Mason did. They'd been there not so long ago, and Roxy had come close to death. Not only that, but Babylon and Marduk were inextricably entwined. He didn't mention that now. 'You were there?' he asked.

Gabriel shook his head. 'I only know because the job wiped out most of our resources for a few days. They sent a lot of mercs down there for a short period. I was on call pretty much twenty-four hours a day. It was a big op, dozens of mercs all at once. When we questioned it, we were told some big dude had paid for an op in Babylon.'

'Some big dude?' Mason repeated.

'Yeah. When the boys got back, they were subdued. Something happened, something they wouldn't talk about. They said it was all sanctioned by some crazy lunatic who ran the job. He was there, on site, telling them what to do.'

'Did he have a name?' Mason asked.

'And what exactly did they do?' Roxy put in.

'I didn't press them much,' Gabriel admitted. 'They're mercs. The boys and girls didn't really want to talk about it; I could tell. Something bad happened, like I said. Nobody ever mentioned the dude's name.'

Mason's brows knit together as he thought. The coincidence of Babylon with Marduk was hard to ignore. Marduk was – or had been – the monarch of the Amori, whose home had been old Babylon for thousands of years. Why would Marduk return there now?

'You think he's gone back to the motherland?' Quaid was clearly thinking along the same lines.

'We can't be sure,' Mason said. 'But it sounds that way.'

'This Marduk has a history with Babylon?' Gabriel asked.

Mason nodded. 'A big one. And he's as batshit crazy as they come. Look, mate, we really need your help here. Marduk has no conscience, no scruples. He'd torch a christening if he thought he could get something out of it.'

Gabriel nodded. 'I've worked with plenty of men with loose morals before,' he said. 'You just keep your head down, do the job, and get the hell out of there. Live to fight another day. You worry about the cost to your own soul later.'

Mason had also worked for people with agendas, and he knew Quaid had fought against the same issues. Quaid more than him. Mason knew where the ex-British-army officer's head would be.

'I get it,' he said. 'We've come up against the same thing.'

'You think something similar happened in Babylon?' Quaid asked quietly.

Gabriel nodded. 'It had to. Nothing else would dampen spirits like that, especially since they were on a big payday for a short duration of work. They came back, fully loaded with cash, and not a smile between them.'

Mason thought through what they knew. He wanted to believe that the 'crazy lunatic' in Babylon was indeed Marduk. It made perfect sense. The obvious problem was that the op was over.

'Any ideas at all what they were doing over there?' he asked.

'Lots of digging,' Gabriel said. 'I heard them talking. They were involved in digging around some old pyramid or something. Took them days. Now, things are coming back to me. There was talk of another crazy dude and a female sidekick, real killers even hardened mercs were afraid of. Maybe that's your Cassadaga?'

Mason didn't like that term. *Your Cassadaga* was entirely accurate. But he said nothing.

'So they dug around for a few days,' Gabriel went on with a shrug. 'Made a discovery. Apparently the crazy dude – the *original* crazy dude – got real excited about it. Took a load of them down some secret passageway. Came back with something wrapped in sheets. Probably a load of old junk.'

'Why do you say that?' Quaid asked.

'You know what these history types are like, always searching for some crusty, dusty old piece of crap.'

Sally remained quiet, but Mason could tell it was with an effort. He wasn't sure if she wanted to defend herself or her father.

'Any idea what was under the sheets?' Roxy asked.

Gabriel shook his head and continued eating his burger,

munching away like a condemned man eating a last meal. Maybe he thought he was.

'Don't worry.' Quaid reached out a compassionate hand and placed it on the man's arm. 'We won't hurt you.'

Mason wondered at the gesture. Quaid's principal aim in life these days was to help people. He'd been doing it when they met and he was still doing it, even their enemies, it seemed. Mason considered everything Gabriel had had to say.

'So you don't know if it was Marduk? You don't know if it was Cassadaga? You don't know what they were looking for?' He sighed. 'Is there anything you *do* know?'

'Anything that can help us?' Quaid said.

'Only the obvious,' Gabriel said.

'Which is?'

'The mercs,' Gabriel said. 'Obviously, I know them all. I can give you the name of the leader. The man who led the op.'

Mason thought about that as Roxy said, 'That's not a bad lead.'

It wasn't exactly a direct line to Marduk, but it was a step closer to the Babylon operation itself.

'What's his name?' Mason asked.

'Brett Curry,' Gabriel said.

'And where would we find this Brett Curry?' Roxy asked.

'You're gonna let me go, right? No funny business?'

'Despite the fact that you tried to kill us, that you were part of a team sent to destroy us?' Roxy said. 'You mean despite all that?'

Gabriel stopped eating suddenly and nodded. 'Yeah.'

'Would you?' Roxy asked, looking dangerous. 'Would you have shown mercy?'

Gabriel frowned and then nodded. 'Sure,' he said.

Mason knew he was lying. This man was an order-follower and a money-grabber. Same as most mercs these days – they did what they were told and kept their mouths shut.

'You're not gonna kill me,' Gabriel said abruptly. 'I can read you all. You all got issues far worse than mine. No way will you add to your burdens by killing an unarmed man.'

Mason nodded. 'All we need from you, mate, is a way of contacting this Brett Curry.'

Gabriel nodded. 'I know Brett, of course. He's a team leader, and I worked with him a couple of times. Good soldier. I can probably arrange a meet, but you'll have to pay him.'

Mason wasn't surprised. Once a soldier became a merc, he was all about the money. 'You have his phone number?'

'Sure do.'

Mason leaned forward. 'Let's have it.'

Chapter 23

Once they'd left Gabriel behind alive in the car park, they drove to another parking area and sat back to review what they knew.

Mason watched as the dimming light of early evening spread across the skies. It was a cloudy day anyway, the clouds leaden with rain, and the sun had long since given up trying to control the heavens. Shadows lay across the land. They passed through an industrial area and then circumvented a large skate park, finally ending up close to an area of woodland where there were a few quiet car parks. Not entirely empty – there were still people turning up to walk their dogs and head out for a jog – but it was about as discreet as it was going to get.

Quaid kept the car running, letting the heat warm them. 'What a day,' he said shortly, attempting a bit of levity.

Mason appreciated it, but they had a lot to discuss. 'Bellaire sent us to our deaths,' he said. 'If we had more time, I'd love to go back and pay that old man a visit.'

Roxy nodded eagerly. 'I'm with you whenever.'

'But what would you do?' Quaid asked them. 'Kill him? I don't think that's what you want to do, Joe.'

Mason knew Quaid was right. He'd never kill in cold blood. 'Maybe just slap him around a bit,' Roxy said.

'Either way,' Mason said. 'We came out of it with something—'

'Brett Curry,' Roxy said helpfully.

'Yeah, Brett Curry. And a whole lot of info about a guy who may or may not be Marduk.'

'He needed something from Babylon,' Quaid said. 'Something clearly hidden and probably old. He needed it badly because, despite being on the run, he transported an entire mercenary team there and dug it up.'

'Wait,' Sally said quietly. 'This is . . . horrible. There's a news report centred around Babylon. Of course, it doesn't get a lot of international publicity these days, but you only have to search for Iraq and Babylon, and you'll get the latest news. Someone recently wiped out a small village, its inhabitants shot or knifed to death. The working theory is that "a force of mercenaries rampaged through there, out of control". Of course, they'll have bullets and shell casings, evidence to work with, but they will never know who controlled those mercenaries.'

'I wouldn't put it past Marduk,' Mason said. 'Is there any explanation as to why they were killed?'

Sally shook her head. 'Wrong place, wrong time, is the general consensus,' she said. 'But that's just newspaper theory. There's no hard evidence.'

Mason put it aside for now. 'What do we know? That Cassadaga and Ivana broke Marduk out of prison. That Marduk has apocalyptic plans for the Church; that one of the first things he engineered was the death of Cardinal Vallini. The first step in his master plan, I guess. He needed something from Babylon to start the entire process. What that might be, we can only imagine.'

'And following the breadcrumbs to Cassadaga hasn't worked,' Hassell said from the back seat.

'We should have expected that.' Mason blamed himself a little. 'Daga hasn't stayed off the radar for over ten years for nothing.'

'Though if he knew how careless Marduk was with his secrecy,' Hassell said, 'maybe Daga would think twice about working with him.'

Mason nodded. 'It would be nice to tell him, but I don't think anyone gets a sit-down conversation with Daga. And the proper focus should still be Marduk and what he might have planned.'

'What do we tell Premo Conte?' Sally asked.

Mason remembered they were still working for the Vatican. Conte could ring at any time for an update. 'Tell him we're working on it,' he said blandly.

'Which brings us back to this merc who led the Babylon operation,' Roxy said. 'This Brett Curry.'

Mason looked at the scrap of paper he held in his hand. It held the number of the team leader. It had been verified by Gabriel, who had made a quick call in front of them. All they had to do was ring the guy and set up a meet.

'You really think a merc captain is gonna help us find Marduk?' Quaid asked.

'He's the last chance we have,' Mason said.

'Let's hope he's forthcoming, then.'

'We have what he wants,' Sally said. 'Money. He'll talk for the right price.'

Mason listened to their conversation. There was some discussion around Marduk and how well protected he was; some comments about the number of mercenaries he had around him and how close they could get working alone, but mostly it was about the hatred he held for the Vatican, and what he might do next.

The Amori, his people, had scattered after the raid on their African HQ. They had proven to be no trouble since. What resources could Marduk seriously call upon if he had no followers, no loyal people working for him? It would, no doubt, be a question running through the monarch's own head.

Mason took the time to clean his gun, breaking it down without thinking and then reassembling it quickly. The action was ingrained in his mind, as deep-rooted as breathing. He noticed that Roxy soon followed suit.

'Let's get on with it,' he said, smoothing out the piece of paper with Brett Curry's phone number on it and pulling out his mobile phone.

Chapter 24

Mason had expected Brett Curry to be based close to Zürich, since he was the team leader of the locally based mercs. It turned out he resided in Dübendorf, a suburb of Zürich, and agreed to meet them in a busy area for a price. Curry turned out to be American, but the suburb comprised thirty per cent foreign nationals, so the young man would fit right in. They agreed to meet the next day at a coffee shop situated close to the train station.

Brett Curry looked to be in his late twenties, a fit-looking man wearing a tight T-shirt despite the chilly day, black cargo shorts and comfortable-looking trainers. He might have just exited the gym. His hair was cropped short, almost to the point of non-existence, and there was the slight shadow of a beard on his chin. Mason had known many young men in the army who grew beards on patrol to make them look older or to save on the inconvenience of shaving. Almost always though, when they got home, the clippers came out.

Curry sat with his back to the shop window, surveying the street. He was expecting five people to meet him, so when they appeared out of the nearest parking area, his eyes locked on them straight away. They didn't veer away for two whole minutes as Mason and the others approached.

When they reached his table, a waitress appeared. She was efficient, carrying a small pad of paper and noting all their drinks down. Hassell ordered a croissant, too. Soon, they were seated comfortably around the table, facing Curry.

'You Mason?' he asked.

'How can you tell?'

'You have the look. These guys don't, except her.' He raised his chin at Roxy. 'But she just looks crazy.'

'Fair assumption.' Roxy folded her arms.

Mason looked left and right. The other tables weren't so close that the occupants would overhear their conversation and, in any case, there were only two other people seated close by – a woman and her daughter who were quietly chatting.

'I'm Mason,' he said.

'Good. You said you wanted information regarding the Babylon op and would pay for it.'

Mason nodded. 'Are you okay with that?'

Curry frowned at him. 'You mean ethically?' The man shrugged. 'I don't give a rat's ass, to be honest. The client was crazier than *she* looks.' He nodded again at Roxy. 'Crazier than a box of frogs.'

Mason described Marduk to him. 'Is that your client?'

'Sounds like him, yeah. The guy never shut up, not for a minute.'

'Was there anyone with him?' Hassell asked.

'Oh, yeah. Two very dangerous-looking people that we all steered clear of.'

They all stopped talking and leaned back as the waitress brought their drinks. Mason took a gulp of strong black coffee. A car passed slowly along the street behind them, its engine burbling. The smell of Hassell's warm croissant made Mason wish he'd ordered his own. None of them had eaten a proper breakfast yet, and he'd been too intent on studying Curry to think to order something.

Curry took a sip of his own drink, also a black coffee. 'Dude called Cassadaga and a woman called Ivana. They were seriously warped. I always thought Cassadaga was a myth until I met him on this op.'

'What did they do?' Sally asked.

Curry looked unsure for the first time. 'Is that really what you came here to ask me? And I haven't seen a millimetre of cash yet.'

Sally took out a wad of cash from her purse and flashed it surreptitiously at him before replacing it. 'You'll get it at the end,' she said.

'Right. Well, what do you really want to know?'

'What the hell were you doing in Babylon?' Mason asked.

'I have no problem answering that. Like I said, the dude, this Marduk, was a real whacko. He doesn't deserve protection. Some of the things he did . . .' Curry trailed off and took a long gulp of his coffee before going on. 'The guy wanted to survey this ziggurat, a particular one. Said he had something important buried there. No . . .' Curry frowned. 'He actually said something ancient and vital had been buried there thousands of years ago and he was going to get it. Of course, we hear clients babble all the time. We just wait for orders and carry them out.'

'And what were his orders?' Sally asked.

'To dig. He pointed out the right place, and we dug. For days. Sure enough, eventually, we uncovered a door that led deep underground. This Marduk fella – he jumped inside without fear and led the way. He must have found what he was looking for because he was a happy camper for the rest of the trip.'

'Any ideas what that might have been?' Mason asked.

'Oh yeah, the crazy fucker never shut up about it.' Curry finished his coffee and signalled the waitress to bring him another. 'You see, it all hinged around this ziggurat called Etemenanki, I think. It's ancient, or it was. It's just a ruin now. Marduk called it the Tower of Babel sometimes, though I'm sure that was all a myth. Anyway, first he wanted to dig and then he wanted to explore. To be fair, crazy or not, he sure knew what he was talking about.'

'Went straight to it?' Quaid asked.

'Yeah, as if he'd buried it there himself thousands of years ago.'

'So he confided in you?' Sally asked.

'I think "confided" is the wrong word. I'm pretty sure he thought we were all dumb grunts. This Marduk was a talker, loved to blow his own trumpet.' Curry went quiet as the waitress brought him another coffee and then started drinking it the moment it landed on the table.

'Can you tell us what he discovered?' Mason said again.

'Sure. It was mostly jewels. Lots of them. I was behind him when he made the discovery. It was kind of surreal. We were following a passage carved out of the bedrock, a narrow passage with damp walls and moss and lichens. It smelled musty. You could sense the age, sense that we were the first visitors in thousands of years. You had to stoop to prevent your head from hitting the top of the tunnel. It wound for a while, and everyone was quiet for several minutes. ' Curry took another drink. 'There were about eight of us down there, though Marduk didn't need any bodyguards. He walked unerringly, albeit with a limp, maybe from the memory of something he'd been told. I don't know.

'We passed a couple of offshoots, dark tunnels that led in different directions, but Marduk just ignored them. Like I said, the going was tricky, but it wasn't too tough. We crossed two fissures maybe four feet wide. Marduk had trouble with those. They could have gone straight down to the bowels of Hell for all we knew. One guy slipped, but the others caught him. We suffered no casualties on that trip.' Curry went abruptly silent for a moment, as if reminded of something. His face took on a haunted look, but then he seemed to remember where he was and shook himself. 'Where was I?'

'Crossing a fissure,' Roxy said.

'Yeah, we continued down and down, winding under the old ruins of the ziggurat. They built it in the sixth century, maybe even as a way to hide the riches, but—'

'How the hell do you know so much about this pyramid?' Roxy asked.

'Not a pyramid,' Curry said quickly. 'And I know so much because, later, I read up on it. Just googled the Etemenanki ziggurat. Marduk piqued my interest. I got to wondering if it really was the Tower of Babel, the one from the Bible. But the dates don't really add up.'

'You sure?' Quaid asked. 'History can be pretty loose with its dates.'

'Nobody knows how long it was there to be fair, not really. Nebuchadnezzar, the famous Babylonian king, was supposed to have rebuilt it. Academics reckon the tower wasn't built in a month or a year; but instead came from a long history of ongoing constructions, destructions and reconstructions. Its origins date to 2000 bc, a date that Marduk appeared to know very well.'

'Go on with your account,' Mason said.

'Sure, well, to cut a long story short, we came eventually to a wide chamber. It was cold by now, freezing cold. The air wasn't great. Some guys were complaining, but I didn't pay them much mind. I was too focused on Marduk, wondering where the madman had led us. He stood there for a while in the entrance to the chamber, head lifted, as if listening to the sounds of voices, maybe thousand-year-old ghosts. Who knows? He wasn't in any hurry. He started pacing forward slowly, moving his head from side to side. Maybe he was praying or chanting or whatever the hell he does. I stayed clear. By now, I was wondering what the hell was really going on. This was clearly a dead end. Had he brought us the wrong way? Had he cracked up? Did he even remember we were there? Anyway, after a while, he shone his torch in a particular direction . . .'

'As if he knew where to look?' Quaid said.

'Exactly. He must have been told by someone, maybe his boss.'

'Marduk is the boss,' Hassell said softly. 'But the Amori had elders, maybe. They must also have had a monarch before Marduk.'

'Knowledge passed down through centuries,' Curry said. 'It makes sense.'

'What did Marduk find?' Roxy asked the mercenary.

'The far side of the chamber was a rock fall composed of ledges. Hundreds of them. Perhaps they were once full of treasures, I don't know. But Marduk's flashlight picked out the one ledge that held something. At least, the only one I saw. He walked over and knelt and raised his arms. I stayed back, wanting nothing to do with it. The men stayed behind me. Marduk picked up a chest the size of a small suitcase. It was black with a bronze lock that Marduk didn't bother with. He just wrenched the chest apart, dug his hands inside, and came up with this vast assortment of jewels. They glittered in our torch-light, lots of different colours. It took our breath away. Marduk didn't seem to care that he'd just shown a fortune to a bunch of mercenaries who were fully capable of taking them away from him. Maybe that's a sign of his madness.'

'Plus, he had Cassadaga,' Roxy said.

'That too. Though the thief and his sidekick had some business up top and disappeared. They wanted nothing to do with creeping around underground anyway. So, Marduk lifted handful after handful of jewels, muttering to himself. Something about money and fortune and revenge. I didn't catch it all. Eventually he seemed to tire, put the necklaces and bracelets and all the rest of the stuff back in the chest and wrapped it all up in a blanket. Then he shoved it under his arm. I was still waiting by the entrance. Marduk walked up, pushed past me, and started heading back the way we came. Like he wasn't interested in the old chamber anymore.'

'He's a man with a one-track mind,' Mason said.

'No reverence, no sense of duty,' Curry said. 'No wonder this Amori crumbled around him.'

'He was a poor leader,' Mason agreed. 'But, in part, that was because of his madness. His terrible desire to exact revenge on the Church.'

'So that's really what he wants? Revenge?'

'It consumes him all day, every day.'

'How can you be so sure?'

'We've run into him on more than one occasion,' Sally said. 'He's the kind of man who would sacrifice his own daughter if it meant defeating the Church. In fact—'

'I see,' Curry went on quickly. 'Well, he led us back out of that cave network and once again into the open. He found Cassadaga, asked him to stand guard, and then went to his tent. Never saw him again. The next morning, we were told the op was over.'

Mason thought about what Curry had told them. It was enough to earn the money, but he couldn't help but wonder if there was something else.

'Did Marduk mention his intentions?' he asked. 'We know he wants to destroy the Church and the Vatican. Was there anything else he might have said that stands out to you?'

'He kept on talking about the Faithful.' Curry shrugged. 'But in no particular context. The Faithful are coming, are here, are all we need, that kind of thing. A man turned up, tall with a beard. I think he was called Keeva. Marduk took to the Keeva like he was his own son. I don't know their actual relationship.'

'And Keeva was one of the Faithful?' Mason asked.

'Yeah, he called him that. He said there were others. Keeva was the first of many. He also mentioned infiltrators.'

Mason frowned, thinking hard. 'Any clues as to their purpose?'

Curry shook his head. 'It was just a comment or two. Nothing major. Perhaps it meant nothing, the ravings of a madman.'

Mason nodded. 'Maybe. But we've learned to take everything he says and does seriously. If Marduk mentions infiltrators, then there will be a reason.'

'Well, I saved the best for last.' Curry finished his latest coffee and signalled for a new one.

Mason was still sipping his first. 'What do you mean?' he asked.

'Marduk couldn't help himself, you see. We've already established he's a talker. Well, as we climbed out of that hole in the ground, as we met Cassadaga, he was already chattering about his next move. He pulled out his phone. Spoke to a guy who clearly knew him and had been waiting for the call. They talked crap for a while, but then Marduk got down to business. We were close to the tent by now and he waved at Cassadaga, I think, telling him he wanted to be alone. That Cassadaga didn't look like he gave a shit. But Marduk just kept talking, and I heard everything he said through the walls of the tent.'

'Which was?' Mason asked immediately.

'Basically . . . that he had the goods and wanted to sell them through some lavish auction in Monte Carlo.'

Mason blinked. 'He *what*?'

'The guy he was talking to must have been his broker or something. Marduk told him to inform the auction house that he was ready, to invite only the richest and most influential clients, and that even Monte Carlo had seen nothing like what he was about to bring.'

'Did he mention a date?' Quaid asked.

'No. Nothing like that. It was a conversation overheard for about thirty seconds. What I said is what I heard.'

'It sounds like Marduk recovered the jewels to turn them into cash,' Mason said. 'Which means the bastard's broke. He needs more money to bankroll the next move, whatever that might be. He intends to get it through this auction.'

'Which may already have happened,' Quaid said.

Mason didn't think so. In any case, it would be easy enough to check. He stood up so fast the table shook.

'We need to move,' he said.

Chapter 25

Outside the smoked-glass floor-to-ceiling window, the golden lights of the luxurious city shimmered.

Marduk stood with one hand touching the window, his body leaning forward. The lights calmed him; they let him think. It was a little after ten p.m. in Monaco, the small principality that sat on the French Riviera. Interestingly, to Marduk, the sovereign state was the second smallest in the world, after Vatican City. It was also one of the costliest and richest places in the world. Perhaps even more famous is Monte Carlo, a neighbourhood soaked in sunshine, wealth and thousand-dollar bottles of bubbly.

Marduk felt at home here. This was his most longed-for lifestyle. Though he was first the monarch of the Amori, he knew that his position granted him certain luxuries. After all, he was a supreme leader. He was currently reflecting on his life, and how it had changed since he tried to destroy the Vatican by stealing the Book of Secrets.

Marduk was alone in the hotel room, which was large and opulent. He had paid for it on one of the few remaining credit cards that worked for the Amori. The bills were racking up; the cards were filling up, but Marduk wasn't about to turn into a peasant now. He knew he deserved the very best.

The lights were out. The room sat in silence. Marduk stared out across the city to its harbour and beyond, past the opulent yachts in the bay, beyond the dark, rolling Mediterranean to the distant horizon where the sea met the sky. There, his thoughts roiled in turmoil.

Jail had given him time to plot and plan, to reflect on the best courses of action. Of course, he was currently on the run, an escaped prisoner, and it wouldn't do to show his face properly here or anywhere, but Marduk still had many moves to make.

The auction, for instance. He was behind the sale, but his broker, a man named Harold Toussaint, would be the face. Toussaint knew nothing of the real Marduk; he only knew that a very rich and influential new player had come to town and would line his pockets handsomely if he carried out a few simple tasks.

Marduk was drinking expensive red wine. It came with the room. He reflected on the past, from the time he'd ruled the Amori with an iron fist to the time he'd been deposed and then when the raid on their African HQ tore the organisation apart. Marduk blamed the Church. Already, he'd exacted his revenge on Cardinal Vallini, his only regret that he couldn't be there to witness the horrors wrought upon the man. Marduk would have loved to have seen that.

This new, insular life didn't really agree with him. But it was worth it to take down the Vatican once and for all. All manner of discomforts were worth that. Marduk's thoughts turned to Keeva, the Faithful one who'd turned up in Babylon. Seeing Keeva there was a sign that Marduk was doing the right thing. His own bible was the Creed, the Amori book of religious texts, and it had been around long before the despicable Bible. Marduk revered the Creed and followed its guidance and its word throughout his everyday life.

Marduk turned away from the window and walked a few metres back into the room, stopping before a low coffee table. On the coffee table was the chest he'd taken from the chamber beneath the ziggurat. The chest was open, its contents glittering darkly in the dimly lit room. Marduk dug into the wealth as if he was excavating sand, grabbed a handful of the jewels and let them slither through his fingers. There was an awful lot of it, a mountain of treasure. It felt good. Marduk delved in again and again, feeling the wealth that was rightly his. A smile stretched across his face.

What was next?

His agenda was long and complex. Already, the Faithful were coming forth. He'd been contacted by four more besides Keeva and had told them to stand by, stand close, and be ready. They were invaluable to his plan. The additional money that would soon come in would pay for the infiltrators who, also, were imperative to the plan. It was a strategy that the Vatican could not withstand.

One of the big questions he couldn't yet answer was – *should I rebuild the Amori?* Should he even try? They'd been overthrown, ousted. They'd scattered to the winds so easily. Marduk wondered if they were even worthy. The answer was – *if they are worthy, they will find their way back to the fold. Back to me.* He wouldn't turn anyone away.

He would instead make use of them.

Marduk still retained the services of Cassadaga and Ivana. He had ensconced them in a lesser suite, where they'd be getting up to unimaginable evils, no doubt. Marduk knew how tenuous his thread on life currently was, how unstable was the ground on which he stood. It would only take one member of the public, one cop to recognise him and his universe would come crashing down. He intended to disguise himself, and Monaco was one of the best places in the world to do that. Was anyone really themselves here, out on the town, or were they grinning caricatures of themselves, dripping in the prosperity that they clearly wanted everyone else to see, the whole lot of them putting on a show for the world?

Well, Marduk could play that game too. The ziggurat, Babel and Babylon were now behind him. The future was on its way after the night of the auction. Marduk agonised only that it wasn't coming fast enough.

He called Harold Toussaint.

'Are we ready?'

'Oh, hello, sir. Good to hear from you. If you mean the auction, then yes, I believe we are ready.'

'The rich and the powerful?'

'Have been invited, cajoled, and promised great things.'

'The authorities?'

'Coaxed the right way. Informed that we are hosting a very high-level event. All the high-society names have been dropped. Entrance to the event will be smooth and simple. Any local authorities will be intensely discreet.'

Which didn't exactly help Marduk. He'd prefer to see clearly the men he was trying to avoid. 'Do they really have to be there?'

'Of course, sir. We hardly want criminals infiltrating our event, do we?'

Marduk coughed. 'Good point. No, we don't. That would never do. And when will the event take place?'

'Two nights from now. I hope that's acceptable, sir?'

It certainly wasn't, but Marduk could do little about it. He would have to sit in anticipation a while longer. He tried to console himself, knowing that attracting the right clientele to the auction would take time, and in the long run, only benefit him.

'Two nights then,' he said. 'Keep in touch.'

'Of course, sir.'

Marduk ended the call, his mind turning. He thought about everything he'd lost, everything the Vatican had taken from him. The Amori had had a global reach, their fingers in countless pies. He wondered who had filled the void that they left, if anyone. He wondered if he should look at starting a new organisation. Something fresh based firmly around his own beliefs with him as the head of state.

Time would tell. For now, Marduk again satisfied himself by rifling through the contents of the chest.

If they knew what was coming, the Vatican and all its cardinals and guards would shiver in their boots.

And, though frustrated, Marduk smiled in the darkness.

Chapter 26

The call came in shortly before they left Zürich.

'It's Premo Conte,' Sally said tersely.

Mason understood her abruptness. The Inspector General of the Gendarmes of Vatican City, leader of the Cavalieré, was essentially their boss, a boss they hadn't been keeping apprised of their progress. Conte was highly capable and had earned their respect a dozen times over during their last encounter with Marduk, but he wasn't exactly a patient man.

'Answer the phone.' Mason shrugged. 'He deserves to know.'

Cardinal Vallini had been Conte's friend, too.

'What have you got?' Conte's words blasted out of the speakerphone.

Mason was currently driving them to the airport. He thought about treating Conte with kid gloves, maybe trying to brush him off, but then caught Roxy staring at him in the rear-view mirror. The last time they'd tried to fob their boss off – Patricia Wilde – it hadn't ended too well. They'd both been sacked from their jobs.

'We tracked Bellaire to his shop in Paris, made him talk. He supposedly gave us Cassadaga. We were to meet through an office in Zürich.' Mason took a deep breath and then told Conte the rest of it, finishing with their promising lead in Monte Carlo.

'You're no nearer to catching up with Marduk than you were a few days ago,' Conte said.

Mason sighed. 'Conte,' he said. 'We're in the middle of a fluid investigation. You know how it goes, setback after setback, until you find what you're looking for. We're making progress here.'

'Did Bellaire or this Curry guy give you any sign of what the Vatican is up against?'

Mason thought about the so-called Faithful and the infiltrators. 'None,' he said.

Conte took a deep breath. Mason imagined the tall man in his tailored suit leaning forward. 'You wouldn't be hiding anything from me now, would you?'

'Have you heard anything from your side?' Mason asked, changing the subject.

'I'm calling you back to Vatican City,' Conte said. 'I think a face-to-face is long overdue and we can talk more openly here.'

Mason let out a long sigh. 'Conte,' he said. 'That won't accomplish anything.' He knew Conte liked to throw his weight around, liked to impress on everyone who was in charge. The guy could be insufferable, but he was also extremely useful. Mason felt exasperated by the man.

'We're on our way to Monaco,' Roxy said from the back seat. 'You can't make us turn around now.'

'It's time-sensitive,' Quaid put in.

'Everything is time-sensitive,' Conte said. 'Even my

lunch is time-sensitive. To be honest, I'd rather see you back here. Get a better feel for what you know.'

Mason pulled into the airport parking area and found a space. He sat there with the car engine running. 'All right,' he said. 'You win. Listen, we're headed for Monaco right now. We're sitting at the airport, and we can't let Marduk jump any more steps ahead of us. We're close – we know where he is. That's *our* investigative skills at work. But as for what we know—' He bit his bottom lip and thought about what he wanted to say, and then he told Conte all about the Faithful and the infiltrators.

'They could already be among you,' Roxy said bluntly.

Conte was silent for a while, digesting Mason's words. 'This changes things,' he said. 'We should look at any new starters in the last few weeks.'

'I'd go back months,' Quaid said. 'Marduk has been planning this from prison since he got arrested.'

'And Cassadaga?' Conte asked. 'That demon haunts my dreams. We all live in a world where atrocities are visible. It's what makes us live in constant fear and anxiety. But he is a law unto himself. *Let no evil befall us*,' he chanted softly. '*Be our safeguard against the wickedness and snares of the Devil.*'

Mason was slightly taken aback. So far, through all their dealings with Conte, he'd never come across the religious side of the man, but he guessed the more you got to know someone, the more transparent they became.

'Daga is with Marduk,' he breathed. 'We're closing in on him too.'

Conte said another prayer, more a warding spell than anything born out of fear. He finished with the words,

'*Burn all these evils in Hell,*' and again went quiet. Mason waited for him to ask his next question.

'Do you recall the name of Cardinal Vallini's successor?' Conte said.

Mason thought back. 'Mario Gambetti?' he said.

'Yes, as I mentioned, one of the youngest cardinals here. He's with me, learning how we work. It's unfortunate that he comes into his role at this time of crisis. Unfortunate in many ways,' Conte added quickly. 'I'd like his input on this.'

There was a moment's silence, and then a voice, slightly surprised, spoke up. 'I think your team is doing a standout job.' The accented words came through clearly. 'I think it would be best if you carried on to Monaco and attended the auction.'

Roxy shifted in the back seat. 'I like him,' she said.

Mason couldn't agree more. 'Then that's what we'll do,' he said.

Conte was quick to break in. 'Why?' he asked. Maybe he was making this a teaching moment.

'Look.' Mason switched the car off and prepared to depart. 'We don't have time for this. Marduk is already ahead of us, planning this auction. He's deeply involved in his master plan, which, as you know, concerns the Church and the Vatican. We're boarding this plane right now, Conte.'

They started walking across a car park that was wide open to the elements. A chill wind scoured it from east to west, sweeping among the cars and making wind tunnels of the spaces between them. Mason zipped his jacket up.

'Are you *planning* on attending this auction?' Conte asked, the question a concession on his part.

Mason wondered if it would even be possible. 'If we can find a way in, yes,' he said. 'I imagine it will include an awful lot of high society.'

'Riff-raff not included,' Roxy said. 'That puts you lot out.'

Mason glanced at her. 'Roxy will blag us a front-row seat,' he said. 'I have no doubt.'

Conte grunted, sounding unconvinced. 'I may be able to pull some strings,' he said. 'As you are no doubt aware, the Vatican is held in high regard across Europe. If I can locate the whereabouts of the auction, I should be able to get seats.'

'It would be better not to mention the Vatican too loudly,' Quaid said. 'This is Marduk we're dealing with.'

'Marduk just wants filled seats,' Conte said. 'He won't be checking too closely. But I'll be discreet, of course.'

'It shouldn't be too hard to locate the auction,' Sally said. 'Check for anything Babylon-related that's sprung up recently.'

'I have the right contacts,' Conte assured them. 'I will make the enquiries.'

'But let me source the tickets,' Sally entreated him. 'It's for a good reason and something worthwhile I can put my father's money towards.'

'That is unnecessary,' Conte started saying. 'The Vatican can—'

'Oh, it is necessary,' Sally told him. 'For me. I struggle with the best ways to use his money. This is one of those.'

Mason was walking with the phone cradled in his hand and held out in front of him. Quaid was walking a step behind. 'And maybe we can help these people stay clear of Marduk's influence,' he said. 'I would call that a win, too.'

It reminded Mason of Quaid's constant battle to help others. Quaid's battle defined his current state of mind.

'We can try,' he said. 'But, essentially, we move on.'

His words came from the heart, from the place he lived where chaos reigned. Mason's stimulus came from stopping all the bad guys, to atone for the deaths he thought he'd helped cause in Mosul. Zach and Harry, and the way they'd died, were always on his mind. He'd checked for that IED a thousand times, again and again in his mind and, each time, he'd found it. They were still breathing the same air as him, still walking the earth. But it was all a lie, a joke, a dream. They weren't here anymore and, even though he'd learned to move on, to grow and make fresh memories, the guilt and the agony he felt over their deaths would never diminish. Mason fought to keep their memories alive every day, at the same time as trying to overcome his own culpability.

Roxy was at his side, as she always was. 'Keep smiling,' she said lightly, having developed that uncanny knack of knowing when he was hurting.

'Some days are harder than others,' he said, then sighed. 'Shit, I mean, some *minutes* are harder than others.'

'I know,' she said. 'But we gotta fight through it.'

'Well, we are fighters.'

'One foot in front of the other.'

'Every damn day.'

'And what do we do?'

'Don't listen when the Devil's calling.'

Roxy nodded with satisfaction. 'I've taught you well.'

Mason laughed. 'You're barely functional,' he said.

'I have my moments,' she retorted.

'Good and bad,' Mason said.

'Same as anyone,' she said. 'At least we're normal enough human beings in some areas. It's where we're headed that worries me.'

'Monaco,' he said.

'Funny,' she replied. 'You know what I mean.'

They were nearing the terminal now, the wind still rolling at them eagerly. Mason thought about what Roxy was getting at.

'I do,' he said. 'I feel that we're doing all we can. All of us. Each one of us carries burdens. It's the way we deal with them that counts.'

'Don't sweep them under the mat, but don't deal with them head on,' Roxy said. 'That's where I'm at.'

'And you're winning,' Mason said. 'You've raised those barriers between today and the past. You win every day, Roxy.'

'I wouldn't go that far. Sometimes I take a huge step back. But it's better than it used to be.'

Sally could overhear their conversation and joined in at that moment. 'I must confess, I'm in turmoil,' she said. 'Using my father's money to bankroll our business makes me feel like a bit of a hypocrite. It's why I want to pay for Monaco. I left home to rebel against what he was, what he did with his wealth and all the hangers-on who surrounded him, but here I am now . . .' She spread her hands. 'Sorry to intrude,' she added.

'It's no problem,' Mason said. 'We need a good team therapy session. You should remember that you're doing a good thing with your father's money, putting it to better use. It's not being squandered.'

They were at the terminal entrance by now and pushed their way inside, where it was a lot warmer. Mason searched for the right check-in desk.

'Monaco,' he said. 'Do you think this ragtag crew will fit in?'

'Funny we should be speaking of money,' Sally said. 'Because it's gonna take an awful lot of it to make that happen.'

Chapter 27

The night of the auction started by making Mason feel uncomfortable.

It all began when they entered their hotel rooms the day before to find a lavish environment waiting for them. Mason wasn't relaxed in such opulence and didn't want to be. It wasn't him. He contented himself by making a very nice coffee and checking out the view that stretched beyond the floor-to-ceiling windows. Monaco was a picturesque, grand old city, surrounded by high hills and composed of a bountiful stretch of beach, a glittering marina and countless restaurants, hotels and houses that the world admired. As Mason looked over the town, he saw the hustle and the bustle, the everyday businesses and the civilians walking the streets. It was the same as any other town, just draped in wealth.

He drank his coffee and made another. If nothing else, he could get used to wonderful coffee. He waited for Sally to call, knowing that she was trying to source them some suitable clothing. Apparently, here, the clothes came to you. You didn't have to walk for hours trailing your way through expensive stores. Sally knew the game, and she knew the world. She probably didn't like it, but needs must.

Mason had been measured for a suit and shoes and everything else. In the afternoon, he'd received a phone call from Premo Conte, telling him that five seats had been reserved at the hottest, newest auction in town, which Sally had then needed to procure using her father's money.

'Are we sure it's Marduk?' Mason had asked.

'I'm sure. The description of the auction offered to the public at large includes the words: "*recently discovered treasures from one of Babylon's most ancient sites*". It also includes "*riches from the great and mysterious Tower of Babel*".'

'I am so annoyed with all this,' Sally said. 'These so-called riches, this treasure, should be on display in museums and available to all scholars, not being clandestinely sold to private collectors. It's so wrong.'

'But his greed has enabled us to catch up to him,' Mason said. 'We're right on the bastard's tail.'

'Don't waste all our efforts now. This kind of private auction also makes my blood boil,' Conte said.

Mason shook his head. 'Not one for pep talks, are you, Conte?'

'I don't believe in them. Do you really need more motivation?'

Mason remembered Vallini's murder. He didn't need any further motivation and said so. His motivation continued to rage like a furious bonfire inside him, his desire for revenge as powerful now as it was when he'd first heard the terrible news. Conte signed off with a rather forced 'good luck', and left Mason alone to his thoughts. It had taken a great deal of effort and many setbacks to get this far. Later that night, the team met in the restaurant downstairs and tried to make sense of the fancily worded meals. Mason ended up with veal and veg whilst the others just ordered steak and chips. The food was perfect, so good it took Mason's mind away from the job at hand for a while. He finished it all off with several bourbons.

'To this time tomorrow night,' he said.

The toast echoed around the table. They were ready. Mason didn't think Marduk would actually attend the auction – the man would have to be suicidal to show his face openly in public. But he thought he'd have agents stationed inside and, if they could be spotted, they might lead back to Marduk. The auction house would also have details of the seller, and Hassell was a master at breaking and entering. They would have to be ready for anything on the night of the auction.

And still, there was Cassadaga lingering in the shadows. Mason imagined *he* would be mad and arrogant enough to turn up at the auction with Ivana in tow. He'd probably be there on the lookout for fresh victims. But that couldn't be helped, and it might not happen. Mason could only deal with what was in front of him.

The auction.

The rest of the night before passed quickly and uneventfully. Most of them retired to their rooms early. Mason kept Roxy company in the bar for an hour or so before taking his leave. The American still doused her waking life in rum, still fought the past with the present, but had a brighter outlook these days. Mason had seen no recurrence of the malaise that had beset her in that graveyard in London.

The next morning, the day of the auction, dawned beautifully over Monaco. Mason's bedroom window faced east across the sea and treated him to a magnificent sweep of crimsons and golds that sparkled off the rolling blue waves like precious diamonds. He sat on the edge of his bed, watching it for a while. After that, he headed down for breakfast and then reconvened with the others in Sally's room.

'The auction house is on Boulevard Princesse Charlotte,' she told them. 'It normally focuses on rare and collectible timepieces, but also has a private room hired, we assume, by Marduk. They have an HQ and showroom that hosts a discerningly curated variety of world-class collectibles. It's the best of the best.'

'Oh, I'm sure we'll fit right in,' Roxy said.

Mason wondered how she'd handle wearing a dress. 'How'd the fitting go?' he asked.

Roxy eyed him like she'd eye something she was about to crush. 'Fine.'

'Just "fine"? Is that it?'

'I guess we get used to wearing our everyday clothes,' Quaid said. 'I'm going for the James Bond look tonight.'

'Well, you're in the right place,' Hassell said. 'We're not that far from the Casino de Monte-Carlo.'

'Oh, I know, and I fully intend to grab my special James Bond cocktail before the night is over.'

'Play a little poker?'

'I might be persuaded.'

Sally sought to regain their attention. 'Be serious,' she said. 'The clothes are ready. The taxi is booked. We need to arrive at seven p.m. on the dot. I have our invitations to hand.'

'Conte came through,' Mason said.

'Yes, he did, though I daresay if I'd had to, I could have leaned on some of my father's old connections to get us in.'

Mason nodded, aware that was something Sally would never want to do.

'Do we even have a plan?' Hassell asked. 'I can study the auction house and its surroundings for the best means of exfil and infil but knowing the parameters would be better.'

Everyone looked at Mason, again making him feel slightly uncomfortable. 'Well . . .' he said. 'Do we think Marduk will be there?'

'In the shadows, yes,' Roxy said. 'But not overtly.'

'I don't think so,' Sally said. 'Not at all. Much too risky.'

'We have to work with Sally's theory and hope that Roxy's is right,' Mason said. 'Rent a vehicle and park it close in case we have to follow the seller's agents at the end. Identify those agents and watch them every step of the way. Try to get close, find out who they're talking to. Hope to hell Cassadaga and Ivana don't turn up.'

'And if they do?' Hassell asked.

'Stay the hell away from them. Maybe he won't recognise us.' Mason shrugged at their cynical faces. 'He's a busy murderer at the end of the day. But we can't control that. We can only control Marduk's grasp over the auction through his agents.'

'And . . .' Hassell knew there was more to come.

'Yeah, I'm afraid there has to be a contingency plan in case none of those agents lead us to Marduk. I'm gonna need you to break into the auction house's office.'

'During the auction?'

'That's your call. I'm guessing it'd be easier after it's

closed. If we wait, we run the risk that Marduk will simply vanish afterwards. The auction house's office is bound to have details of the seller, copies of bank accounts and addresses, even a return address in case something doesn't sell. Or a collection guarantee. Either way, they should have something that leads directly to Marduk.'

Sally's western-facing room looked over twisting, narrow streets and roads, overlooked by the high hills that bordered Monaco. Mason stared down now, watching life go by. He felt isolated not only by the distance and the hotel room, but also by lifestyle. Tonight, he would put his life on the line.

They drifted apart. They spent the rest of the day chilling, walking, getting lunch, acting like tourists. Mason gravitated to the usual haunts rather than trying something new. Food from Starbucks, a snack, and a bottled water from a bakery. The time soon passed. It intrigued Mason that they'd all chosen to spend the afternoon separately; it revealed that everyone still needed their alone time.

As another evening embraced the extravagant principality, Mason and the others dressed for the auction in their rooms and agreed to meet down in the lobby at 18.30. Mason wore a dark blue bespoke designer suit along with a pencil-thin tie and slip-on Guccis. The entire ensemble felt off to him. Maybe the outfit was just too tight. He was used to wearing baggier clothing.

Outfit?

He smiled at himself as he checked the mirror. It felt like an outfit, something out of character he wore to conceal the real man underneath. The word *costume* would work better. He combed his hair and patted it down, pulled his shirt from under his cuffs. He was ready.

Tonight, they would finally defeat Marduk.

Chapter 28

They gathered in the lobby, all dressed in the finest clothes that everyone except Sally had ever seen – all looking distinctly uncomfortable.

Quaid had embraced the new *Casino Royale* Bond look, everything from the tux and the shirt to the Omega watch. He'd even restyled his hair. Hassell had gone for passably neat and practical, knowing he would have to go to work tonight. Sally wore a knee-length white dress festooned with sparkling sequins and a diamond necklace that might blind a man with its radiance. She wore jewellery on her wrist and her right ankle too and carried a clutch purse that bore a large golden V for Valentino.

It was Roxy who took his breath away.

Ever since they'd met, Mason had felt that there was something more between Roxy and him, something that might flourish given time and if nurtured the right way. He hadn't pushed it – that wouldn't be the right thing to do – but he was sure something was there, something unspoken. And now, he wasn't sure if he was just surprised by seeing Roxy in entirely different clothing, a new persona shining out of her, or if she'd got even further under his skin.

Roxy was frowning at him. 'What the hell are you staring at?'

'I was thinking it's a damn sight better than when we first met.'

She gave him the finger. 'Piss off, Mason.'

He coughed, trying to hide his shock. Roxy wore a tight black dress that fell to her knees, shiny heels and carried a glossy purse. Her makeup was light, just enough to highlight her features. Her eyes and black, silky hair went well with her accessories, shining like polished jet. When she moved, for Mason at least, she seemed to draw all the light towards her.

He dragged his gaze away, feeling odd. They were all overcooked in some way, made up for the evening's activities. Mason glanced self-consciously at the others, but they were all looking away.

The taxi arrived. They jumped in and directed it to the auction house. Darkness had fallen across Monaco and its neighbourhood of Monte Carlo. Multicoloured lights were illuminating along the streets, lights from homes and restaurants, bars and shops. They passed the marina, which was a chaos of unlimited wealth. Grandly illuminated multimillion-dollar yachts nudged into narrow berths. Waiting staff dressed in suits carried silver platters between decks. They curved around the Casino de Monte-Carlo with the Café de Paris to the left and passed between black bollards along a route that took them further west and onto a wider street. Soon, the taxi was pulling up outside the auction house, the driver turning in his seat.

'Collect later?' he asked in passable English.

Mason shook his head. They weren't sure where they'd be after this auction finished, but it was doubtful they'd be jumping into a pre-booked taxi.

They climbed out into the evening. Mason pulled his jacket around him as the wind cut through the streets. The glittering lights ahead marked the entrance to the auction house. All along the sloping street, limousines and taxis and expensive-looking cars were pulling up, disgorging men and women clad in all their finery. They sparkled under the streetlights like a procession of jewels as they started filing towards the open door.

'See that?' Quaid nudged Mason. 'Parked two cars to your left? That's a Ferrari 275 GTB/4 from 1967, I'd say. Now that's a proper car.'

'I'd be surprised if it makes it to the end of the road,' Mason came back.

Quaid glared at him, horror-struck. 'How can you say that?'

'Anyway . . .' Mason made a point of looking around. 'Where've you left the Aston?'

Quaid looked like he was attempting to hold his tongue. They were caught in the flow of people now, filtering towards the entrance where two large men in suits were checking everyone's invitations. Walking towards the auction house was like walking towards the sunlight. Sally removed their invitations from her purse and showed them at the door. Mason followed her inside. Soon, they were all in, milling around the lobby. Threading their way through the guests came waiters and waitresses carrying silver trays loaded with sparkling champagne and canapés. Mason refused both, thinking he'd need to keep a clear head tonight and might need to move fast. Roxy accepted a glass and a small pastry, which she despatched in about two seconds and then pulled a face.

'Not what you were expecting?' Mason asked.

'Not even close. But I can wash it down with this swill.' She swirled the champagne in its glass.

'Heathen,' Mason said with a grin.

More guests were arriving by the minute, which seriously raised the noise level in the lobby. Soon, it wasn't worth talking. About five minutes after that, an inner door opened and a man in white gloves and a dark suit ushered everyone through into another room. Mason wasn't bothered where he sat, but he was keeping an eye out for Marduk and Cassadaga.

There were simply too many heads and faces bobbing among the crowd to make a proper ID. Mason funnelled into the auction room with the crowd and found a seat, making sure he was near the end of an aisle. Sally sat next to him as the others found nearby spots.

They'd been handed a programme at the door. Mason scanned it for information as the noise of conversation swelled all around him and his nose was beset with the thick, varied scents of countless perfumes and colognes. The glossy pages were full of jewels, each page dedicated to two or three, but Mason wasn't looking for information on the gems. He flicked through the book and carefully read the inner and outer leaves.

Not a single reference to the seller.

Of course, remaining anonymous in this kind of environment was probably a given. Mason imagined it happened all the time. He placed the programme on his lap and took a few moments to scan the room.

His focus was on identifying three faces. Marduk – Cassadaga – Ivana. Mason took his time flicking over the crowd. He counted ten rows of seats arranged either side of a wide middle aisle. There were also people standing at the back and down the sides of the room. For now, the chatter continued.

'See anything?' Sally muttered under her breath.

'Not a bloody thing,' Mason replied.

'Still hoping Marduk might be here?'

'Sure,' he said. 'But not really believing it.'

'He could be in disguise.'

'I doubt his ego would allow that,' Mason said honestly. 'I really do.'

To his left, across the aisle, Roxy and Quaid were also perusing the crowd, doing their best to look nonchalant. All around them, people in long dresses and suits and glimmering gems chatted and flicked through the programme and looked impatiently towards the front of the room. Mason guessed the time to start was approaching.

He noticed that Hassell's seat was empty.

Didn't even see him go.

Mason knew Hassell was a master at exfil and infiltration, of staying unobtrusive under the radar. He would blend his way expertly into the back rooms and beyond. And the best time to get there was before the auction started whilst the guests still mingled and stood round and wandered from place to place. By the time the auction began, Mason knew he'd be back in place.

At least, that was the hope.

Hassell loved his job. It was the only thing that stilled the clamour inside his head. He was firmly in the zone now, standing in the auction room with hundreds of people roving left and right around him. He walked among them, using them as cover, making his way to the far end of the room where a lectern stood on a raised platform. Clearly, the auctioneer would stand here soon. Hassell saw doors to either side of the stage, both standing open. He had moves to make here. Plenty. If he got caught, there were many excuses he could think of, including the old faithfuls – 'just nosing around' or 'looking for a restroom'. In here, with this clientele, where nobody wanted to upset the patrons, it would work. He chose the door to the left, made sure nobody was watching, and then slipped out of the auction room and into a new one.

Hassell found himself in a long, white-walled corridor. There was nobody about. He made his way down, spotting two doors to the right and two to the left. Ahead, the corridor ended at a closed, eight-panelled dark-oak door. Hassell quickly checked the rooms to left and right.

Small offices, unmanned, populated by desks so tidy they looked like they never got used, leather chairs and a single filing cabinet, which he rummaged through. All four offices looked the same.

Hassell approached the oak-panelled door. He pressed gently on it, relieved to feel it move. He pressed harder. The door opened to reveal another corridor and even more rooms, two with their own doors standing open. Hassell was about to dash quickly to check them when he heard voices from ahead.

One of the closed doors opened.

Hassell quickly ducked back, leapt into one of the sparse offices and hid under the desk. He stayed still and quiet, crouching low. Soon, he heard voices and footsteps in the corridor. They passed without stopping.

Hassell gave it twenty seconds. He then rose and exited the office and made his way back into the second corridor.

Without pause, he checked the new rooms, finding two cluttered offices, both marked 'Manager', and two filing rooms. He saw he had his work cut out. The filing cabinets in here were wide and heavy-looking.

So far, he'd seen six filing cabinets.

Of course, a file lying on a desk with the heading – Marduk – would be perfect. It would make Hassell's day. But what he faced here was an overwhelming wealth of information. There had been a chance – a chance that the auction house was small and kept just a few records. Seeing all these cabinets – and now rifling through them – made Hassell bite his bottom lip. There was no chance they'd get lucky, he knew. The task was insurmountable, a waste of time. He flicked through file after file, hoping he'd get lucky, hoping he'd see something suspicious and all the while wondering if he was about to get caught. The manila folders flicked past his eyes, name after name, client after client. If only they had a name to go with, one of Marduk's aliases. It was a fruitless task. Hassell soon realised that he was going nowhere fast.

Thinking he'd be better off staying out of prison, Hassell exited the offices after several more minutes of flicking through files and started making his way back to the auction room. It didn't take long, and he only had to duck into a nearby room once. The woman he saw walking past through the crack of the door was too busy looking at her mobile phone to notice anything out of the ordinary. Hassell paused at the main door and then walked back into the auction room as if he owned the place. A few gazes flicked his way, but nobody seemed to think anything of the suited man who exited the back rooms.

Hassell caught Mason's eye and shook his head, then drew his thumb slowly across his throat.

Plan A was a washout.

Mason tried to blend with the beautiful crowd, a task that wasn't as easy as he imagined it should be. He might have dressed like them, but that didn't make him a part of the jet set. There was etiquette, a way of sitting, Jesus, even a way of holding your damn programme. So Mason just sat there and didn't even try to fit in; he made sure he watched every corner of the room. And he knew, from experience, that men like him, men who fought in wars and used violence, and had a certain mindset that always focused on protecting innocent people from the harm evil men and women could do, had their own certain look, an aura that could unsettle a civilian. The quality of the soldier surrounded him like a force field, and there was little he could – or wanted to – do to filter it out.

Across the way, he could see the same air around Roxy. She looked tense. The woman who sat next to her, dripping in jewels, kept giving her looks that ranged from suspicion to fear, and then respect, when Roxy briefly talked to her. It changed again as soon as Roxy's head turned away.

Mason waited. The room filled up to the brim, the hum of conversation now quite deafening. Finally, there was a movement near the front. Three men appeared and started making their way over to the lectern.

Mason made a last sweep of the room.

Chapter 29

The auctioneer, as Mason had expected, was good at his job. Both clear of speech and sharp of eye, he would be trained in a discreet form of crowd control and would also be a bid watcher. He would have to know the local laws inside out and, for this place, have a reputation second to none and perhaps even be an expert in jewels and jewellery. Mason saw the art of the auctioneer at its finest.

Everyone took their seats. A hush fell over the room. Mason sat with his eyes forward, but flitting from side to side. He saw nothing suspicious and was still certain Marduk would have agents here. If they couldn't identify them in the next hour or so . . . then Marduk would probably walk away from all this a rich man.

But there was always the money trail to follow.

Mason turned to his programme, saw the first lot, a small collection of ancient gems presented in an archaic chest.

Sally spoke up immediately. 'I know this one from my research. Known as the Pharaoh's Ransom, it's a trove that belonged to a famous Akkadian king and queen. Very old, for as we know, the Akkadian empire was the first ancient empire of Mesopotamia.'

It was the first of ten such lots. The auctioneer started his spiel, and the audience sat silently, taking notice. Mason was at the stage where he didn't know quite what to do. Was this as close to Marduk as they were going to get?

Had Marduk somehow seen him in the crowd?

Anything was possible. Mason tried not to listen to the numbers being shouted out by the auctioneer, hear Sally's explanations of the various treasures she knew, tried not to see the hands being raised up and down the room, for everything he saw and heard was another cornucopia to line Marduk's war chest.

Ten minutes passed. The auction continued.

Marduk watched the auction through a large screen mounted on a smoked-glass coffee table in the middle of his hotel room. The video feed was mounted at the back of the auction room. The audio was clear, the images sharp. He sat on a plush leather chair, the footrest up, laid back, with Cassadaga and Ivana standing behind him.

'Listen to that,' he crowed. 'All our prayers are answered.'

'One million two hundred thousand,' the auctioneer said, pointing at a woman in the audience who was holding up a paddle.

It was still the first lot.

'My own prayers don't generally include the acquisition of wealth,' Daga said. 'They are more . . . visceral.'

Marduk cringed a little at that, getting the meaning and not liking Ivana's brief chuckle. He knew money didn't move Daga; it was the main reason he felt reasonably comfortable having the cut-throat standing beside him. 'It's quite the full room,' he said.

Daga and Ivana said nothing, but they continued to watch the feed. The auctioneer finished lot one at around one-million-five, and then started immediately on lot two, a cluster of emeralds that dated from the Akkadian empire, purportedly to have belonged to a famous king. Marduk had been loose with his descriptions after having the chests all dated to the correct timeline.

And he had foregone speculations offered by the auctioneers of the grander wealth he might accumulate if he waited a while and got everything properly catalogued and dated. He wasn't bothered about vast wealth – he just wanted enough money to carry out his plan.

'Look at them.' Marduk waved at the screen. 'Preening. Flaunting their assets. Products of a world where the Church holds sway.' Marduk seemed to have forgotten the lavish hotel and sumptuous room that surrounded him. 'With nothing better to do than spend their millions.'

'Is this not what you wanted?' Daga sounded confused.

Marduk fought to speak through an additional pressure in his brain. Sometimes he found it hard to concentrate. His hatred and his anger thickened like fog, taking over and making it impossible for him to think clearly. All he saw was the old animosities laid bare, the torment the Church had been laying on the Amori for countless years.

'Of course,' he said after a while, staring at the crowd.

Something had caught his eye.

Suddenly, he saw clearly.

'No way,' he whispered. 'I do not believe what I am seeing.'

His tone of voice must have sounded sufficiently shocked or dumbfounded for Daga to take note. The thief said, 'What is it?' immediately.

Marduk stared hard, his eyes fixed on the head of a man seated in the fifth row from the front. The picture quality was good. When the man had turned around just now, searching the room, Marduk had got a clean look at his face.

'Joe Mason,' he whispered. 'That is Joe fucking Mason.' His right index finger jabbed at the screen.

Both Daga and Ivana leaned forward.

'It certainly looks like him,' Ivana said.

'It *is* him. The man who gave me this limp. The man who thwarted our plans in Africa and started the downfall of the Amori. Why is he here?'

Marduk went abruptly quiet, biting his lip until the blood flowed. Inside, he seethed. Thanks to this man, the Amori's global efforts were ravaged. In truth, he couldn't fault the man's efforts. His attack on the HQ and his previous quest to find the Creed had been valiant and ruthless. But Marduk admired nobody. Someone like Mason ought to be crushed, like the cockroach he was. After Africa, the Amori had folded quickly, some fleeing into hiding, others bending and breaking under police interrogation, many betraying their fellows with little persuasion. The ensuing investigations had taken down most of the Amori.

All thanks to Joe Mason and his damned crew.

All right, he thought. *So maybe it's not as black and white as that.* But Mason was a major reason Marduk had lost everything, including his well-planned vengeance on the Church. What the hell was he doing here now? At Marduk's resurrection. At the most important point of his life so far.

'I don't know how,' he said. 'But he's found us. Look there, the rest of his team.' Marduk jabbed at the screen. 'I recognise them all now. Roxy Banks. Sally Rusk. Paul Quaid. Luke Hassell.' All names engraved on his psyche as if they'd been pressed there in molten fire and left to harden. 'I don't see how they could have tracked us down.'

'Someone blabbed about the auction,' Daga said. 'That's what happens when you use mercenaries.'

'No sign of the cops, though,' Ivana pointed out. 'If Mason was sure about this, about you, he'd have the authorities all over that place. You remember Africa.'

Marduk couldn't get Africa out of his mind. Mason had brought dozens of crack Vatican troops to storm his hideout. He'd also used the local cops. Ivana was right. Mason was here without backup.

'Interesting,' he said.

The auctioneer called out the start of lot five. They were halfway through. Marduk had lost track of the total. His entire being focused wholly on one man.

'He may think he's tracking us,' Daga said. 'But he's right where we want him.'

'He's very close,' Marduk said.

'Exactly,' Ivana said.

'He may know where we are, who we're using inside the auction. I don't like the fact that he's just sitting there . . .' Marduk started jabbing furiously at the screen. 'Inside my fucking auction . . .' *jab, jab, jab* at the plastic. 'Thinking he's still alive.'

'Calm down,' Daga said. 'If he knew where you were, the cops would be here already. If he knew anything except the location of the auction, he wouldn't be just sitting there with his team. This is good for us. We can use this.'

Marduk fought to relax the tide of hatred that was flooding his brain. He resorted to concentrating on the money, on the plan, on the actions of the Faithful that were to come. He focused on the downfall of the Church.

'How can we use it?' he finally managed to say.

'We do what we do,' Ivana said in a silky-smooth voice.

Marduk turned to look at her. 'You can't kill them at the auction.'

'Why not?'

'Just *look* at it. Half of Monaco's elite are sitting right there. You can't just waltz in and start . . . slashing.'

'Do you want Mason dead?'

'I want them all dead.'

'He won't live past midnight.'

Marduk checked his watch. It was a little after eight. 'You have a plan?'

'Usually, it's killing everyone we can get away with,' Daga said. 'And then disappearing. But we can't do that and look after you. I guess we'll just have to focus on Mason.'

'The world's greatest killer focusing on Joe Mason.' The pressure in Marduk's brain eased. 'I like the sound of that.'

Ivana pressed her body against Daga's and smiled. 'As do I.'

Marduk thought about everything he was trying to accomplish. It was a tall order, and maybe a man newly broken out of prison should look at a set of different priorities right now, but the downfall of the Church was his reason for living. This was everything he needed to accomplish, and he'd happily die succeeding.

'Will you kill him at the auction?' Marduk noted the screens were full of people.

'And disrupt your plans?' Daga said. 'I don't think that's a good idea.'

Can they help themselves? Marduk wondered but didn't say it out loud.

'We've never properly hunted Mason before,' Ivana said, still smiling. 'This should be quite satisfying.'

Marduk was still staring at the screens, at the back of Joe Mason's head. To think this man had tracked him all this way, had somehow got his hooks into him again. Maybe killing Cardinal Vallini so early in the project had been a mistake. The act had probably raised more attention than Marduk needed at this point.

'But the plan is still intact,' he said aloud.

Daga looked at him. Marduk had seen that look before on others. The man thought he was crazy but . . . more importantly, was still happy to work for him. 'Hey,' he said, aloud. 'It's a well-known fact – people who talk to themselves are geniuses.'

Daga nodded, but didn't look bothered. Ivana was still holding Daga, but now staring at the screen. By now, they were up to lot six. Marduk was already a very rich man, thanks to the Monte Carlo elite. He wondered how they'd take it if they actually knew what they were financing. Would they care?

Marduk would have liked to have kept all their details, the buyers, but unfortunately the auction house kept all that stuff secret. And, with the Amori disbanded, he didn't have the wherewithal to unravel their security.

Terrorism on a shoestring, he thought. A project that would develop from a minuscule thread and become the thick rope that would finally hang their false God from the neck.

It was coming.

Chapter 30

Mason watched everything like a hawk, regularly turning in his seat to see if he recognised anyone. Already, they were on lot seven. The evening was drawing to a close. Mason had seen movement in almost every chair tonight. Many people bidding six- and seven-figure sums for the Babylonian jewels. He had also seen several people leave the room, including a guy who'd been sitting next to him. Clearly, not everyone was interested in Marduk's haul.

Mason was becoming increasingly frustrated. Sally, seated to his right, concentrated on every lot and watched the buyers. She'd already explained to them that one of the lots had once belonged to Nebuchadnezzar and had been cherished by his wife. Now, as another lot was presented, she sat on the edge of her seat.

'Another one,' she said. 'These are the Spheres of Akkad. Akkad was the capital of the Akkadian empire. The spheres came to Babylon two thousand years before the birth of Christ and never left. Before now, we did not know where they ended up.'

Sally flicked her eyes from the buyers to the auctioneers to anyone in the room who watched closely. She saw no obvious sign of anyone who might be Marduk's agents. Whoever they were, they were keeping an extremely low profile.

Mason watched the buyers, wondering if Marduk might later target them. It didn't seem likely, but then any information, no matter how small, could be helpful. He cast a glance over to where Roxy, Quaid and Hassell sat across the aisle. Quaid gave him a slight shake of the head.

But they couldn't come this far and then lose it all. They couldn't come this close to Marduk and leave empty-handed. Marduk's stench was all over this auction; he was close; he was watching. They were probably within minutes of their enemy, of a man obsessed with destroying the Church, and yet they could do nothing to prove or prevent it.

Why not contact the auction house itself?

But Premo Conte had already done that. The house assured him they had carried out all necessary checks and, because they had cleared the seller – and the auction was underway – they slid behind their many veils of security and secrecy and reputation. All they really wanted was a smooth, profitable auction.

Mason listened to the auctioneer and watched the audience. They were on lot nine of ten, something Sally had referred to as the Pearls of Enheduanna, a powerful priestess who had held sway in Akkad. Their opportunity was slipping through his fingers as quickly and easily as the smooth pearls. He sensed movement to his left and in the row behind, and two new people were shuffling into place to watch the auction. Two latecomers.

Mason cast a glance to his left.

Not latecomers.

Shock lanced through his body like a spear, penetrating him from head to toe.

Cassadaga had squeezed into the seat next to him, a smug smile plastered across his face. Mason remembered that face from a few months ago, remembered it stretched in a rictus of anger and covered in blood.

A brief glance back affirmed that Ivana was now seated behind him.

What would they do?

He didn't have long to find out. The auctioneer finished lot nine and called for lot ten. As he did so, Daga leaned over.

'You knew we were with Marduk,' he whispered. 'You knew the danger.'

Mason shuffled around so that his hands and arms were as free as they could be whilst he faced Daga. There was something strange about facing one of the world's deadliest killers, something that filled him with a potent mix of anxiety and adrenalin.

'We're here for you too,' he said evenly.

'For Ivana and I?' Daga looked genuinely surprised. 'Do you know how many men and women have tried to emulate you?'

'No, but I'm sure you're gonna tell me they're all dead.'

'Not all of them. Some we left alive so that they might suffer more.'

Mason could hear the auctioneer announcing lot ten as if from the bottom of some distant tunnel. All his focus was on Daga and the man's lethal hands.

'Why don't we talk about Marduk?' he tried. 'What's he up to?'

The black pitiless eyes fixed on him. 'Schemes. Conspiracies. Ploys and ruses. He is consumed.'

Watching Daga, Mason could see Roxy, Quaid and Hassell in the row across the aisle. They were all on the edge of their seats, ready to act. Roxy had Ivana in her sights. Around them all the fast pace of the auction continued, the rustling of the audience, the murmur of those using phones to bid, the bark of the auctioneer. It felt to Mason that the bidding was becoming more frantic the closer they got to the end of the auction.

'Another maniacal plan?' Mason said. 'That guy's gonna get you killed.'

'He's living his best life.'

Mason saw no sign of a smile hovering around Daga's lips. The guy had probably never smiled in his life.

'What's he planning this time?'

'He won't like what's happening here. Too soon, he'll say. But I only take notice when it's time to kill.'

'Like now?'

'Like now.'

'In the middle of all these people?'

'You should be scared, Joe Mason.'

'Why? Because the great evil spirit Cassadaga has come for me?'

'You shouldn't mock your murderer.'

'I see someone with all the faults and weaknesses of a man. There's nothing special about you.'

'Shall we see?'

Daga moved so fast all Mason saw was a blur. But he'd focused on the man's hands. He saw the thrust and just assumed Daga had produced a knife. Mason caught the wrist close to his own stomach.

Daga's strength was phenomenal. Mason could barely

hold him back. Focusing now, he saw the blade nestling close to his flesh, low down. Their silent struggle began as the auction went ahead all around them.

'Three hundred thousand,' the auctioneer shouted. 'Can I hear three fifty?'

Daga leaned in, pushing the blade. Mason's muscles screamed as he barely held it at bay. Ivana was chuckling in the seat behind. Sally was on the edge of her seat, not sure what to do. Mason clutched his hands around Daga's wrists and tried to force the blade down.

'Four hundred,' the auctioneer said. 'And now I have five. Can I hear—'

Mason tuned him out. It was life or death. Daga's facial expression never changed. The blade wavered inches from Mason's stomach.

'Six hundred thousand,' the auctioneer said.

Mason saw Daga was giving him no choice. Their powerful, unseen struggle couldn't go on like this. Insanely, Ivana was leaning forward, whispering something in Daga's ear. The thief's face betrayed nothing. He remained as impassive as granite. Mason jammed the knife down towards his seat, then stood up, twisted and pulled away from Daga.

Immediately, people turned to stare at him, some with their mouths open in objection. Mason stumbled into the chair in front of him, his hip striking the back of a man's head. In the next instant, Daga rose from his seat.

Knife in hand.

And now his face was distorted with hatred. He flew at Mason, bringing the knife down fast, striking at Mason's neck. Mason stepped forward, deflected the blow and threw a hard right into Daga's ribs. The thief didn't even flinch, but punched out with his free hand and bore down on Mason.

At the same time, Ivana exploded into action. She leapt out of her seat, backing up Daga, and would have attacked Mason too if it wasn't for Roxy's fast thinking. The American jumped out, hurdled Quaid, and then sprang across the aisle, hitting Ivana around the midriff. The two women went sprawling, rolling across two people's laps.

The auction room went into an uproar. People started shouting. Some saw Daga's knife; others just saw the violence that was erupting. Chairs scraped back everywhere, some falling over. Men and women rose quickly to their feet. Some tried to see what was happening; others tried to calm the offenders down. The auctioneer was already shouting for security.

Mason twisted free of Daga, picked up a chair and flung it at the man. The legs hit Daga's face, stunning him. The knife disappeared for a moment, slipped back into Daga's waistband.

Roxy had one knee on a chair, balancing as she threw punch after punch at Ivana's head. The other woman had covered up, hands raised, but now kicked out at Roxy's free leg. The blow connected. Roxy winced, reset herself. Ivana fought back. To their left and right, people backed away, filling the aisle. Quaid and Hassell were cut off from them. Quaid started helping those who looked scared, ushering them in the right direction as he stepped closer and closer to the aisle.

Screams filled the air. A group of security guys rushed in. Mason faced Daga, the two men circling each other carefully. Daga removed his blade again just as a security guard came running up.

'Stop!' the man yelled.

Daga flicked his knife. The blade passed through the man's neck like butter. The man never even saw it coming, but was suddenly falling, holding the flesh of his neck and seeing thick spurts of blood soaking the ground before him. It appalled Mason. He'd barely seen Daga move. He put another chair between them, knowing he couldn't help the fallen guy. More security was coming, and Mason waved frantically at them to back away.

They didn't take any notice of him.

Three burly guys in suits came at Daga. They hadn't seen what happened to their colleague but knew something wasn't right and felt safety in numbers. Daga saw them coming from the corner of his eye and didn't hesitate. He flew at them, slashing left and right. His knife plunged into the first man's chest, came out and thrust in a second time in the blink of an eye. Before that man even fell, Daga was on to the second. He swept the blade at the man's neck. Blood sprayed. The third man's eyes went wide as he saw what was happening. He wasn't prepared. He flung both hands up to ward off Daga's attack, saw the knife slash across his arms and wrists.

Mason moved too, trying to intercept Daga, trying to save the guard's life. He reached the man an instant too late and then had to defend himself against Daga's sudden onslaught. The guard staggered back. Mason swerved away from the attack, picked up another chair and threw that one straight at the thief.

The chair knocked the knife out of Daga's hand. The man grunted. He didn't stop his attack. He came at Mason with fists and feet striking out, pushing Mason back.

Roxy stepped into Ivana, grabbed the woman by the neck and squeezed. Ivana struck at her, smashing her arms and wrists, but Roxy just grimaced. She didn't let her grip loosen. Ivana had stopped smiling by now and was fighting for her life. She staggered left and right, crashing into chairs. A large man to her right moved towards the fight, as if seeing Ivana as the victim. Roxy's face must have changed his mind, for he veered off as he came within touching distance.

The auction house shuddered to the sounds of terror, the aisle filled with running people, the walkways around the edges crammed full of jostling men and women. They swarmed out of the exit; they surged through the back rooms; they fell out of the fire exits.

And inside, the bloodshed continued.

Chapter 31

Mason saw the madness take hold of Cassadaga. It lit the man's eyes from within, firing those hellish pits. One moment he was fighting cleverly, sensibly, the next the bloodlust had taken him, and anything that moved was fair game. It wasn't a gradual process either; it was a sudden spark of madness that leapt through the thief like black flame.

Mason thought the change might give him a chance. But then Daga was targeting random men and women, going after them with flashing hands and feet, and Mason saw that he would have to be the deterrent, the protector. He would have to get in between Daga and his prey.

Daga struck out, kicked a man in the thigh and brought him down. He chopped another across the neck, smashing his larynx. He was about to grab a woman's hair, haul her back and put out her eyes when Joe Mason got close enough to attack. Mason filled Daga's vision. The people flowed all around the two combatants.

Mason ducked his head and punched, throwing out hard boxer's strikes. Daga covered up, not wanting a broken rib or damaged kidney. They fell across the aisle, through the crowd and into the other row of seating. There were chairs everywhere, obstacles trying to trip them up. Mason doubled down on his attack, keeping Daga occupied.

A fleeing woman struck Roxy. The impact loosened her grip on Ivana's neck. Her hand slipped away. Ivana coughed and backed off, almost doubled over. Roxy didn't let her recover. She kicked a chair at the woman's shins. The chair hit hard, making her cry out. Roxy was a metre behind the chair, leaping at Ivana, who backed away again, just trying to create a little space. Roxy struck at the woman's face, targeting her eyes and throat. Ivana stumbled, fell to one knee. Roxy didn't fall for it. She knew all the tricks. Shit, she'd invented a lot of them herself. She let Ivana linger on one knee, picked up a nearby chair and threw it at the woman's head.

Ivana rolled out of the way, came up with both fists raised. It was a good job, as Roxy was immediately upon her, striking out right and left, using her knees and elbows in close quarters.

Behind them, Quaid was dragging people up the aisle and helping them through the crush. He couldn't help it; he was wired to act this way. He could see Mason and Roxy holding their own, staying on top of their respective fights, and his overwhelming urge was to give aid to the fleeing people. At his side, Hassell was struggling to push through the crush and get to Roxy.

From the other side of the auction room, Sally watched both battles. She wasn't crazy enough to get involved, to think she could stand up to either Daga or Ivana. This wasn't her battle to get caught up in. She watched the exits, watched the auctioneer and his assistants, watched for the arrival of the police. It wouldn't be long.

And, as much as she longed for it, longed for someone to stop Daga, she agonised lives would be lost. Daga seemed unstoppable, a killing machine. Only Mason could stand up to him, and even Mason was making little headway.

Daga snarled, eyes flashing. His hands flicked out, catching Mason in the temple and driving him back. Daga didn't press the advantage. He couldn't stop himself from lashing out at another civilian, taking him down to the ground and kicking him harshly in the ribs. Mason came back in a hurry and drove him further up the aisle.

Towards the door.

The fighters moved with the crowd, much to the crowd's terror, caught up in the flow. Quaid grabbed and helped up the civilian Daga had felled, the man gingerly holding his ribs. Quaid urged him to ignore the pain and move quickly. He turned to the next person and pulled them faster into the stream of people.

Hassell finally broke free of the crowd and clambered across rows of seats towards Roxy. Ivana saw him coming. She attacked with a flurry of blows, raining her fists down onto Roxy's skull and shoulders, creating some space, and then stepped past the American to face Hassell.

Hassell was momentarily shocked.

Ivana kicked out, catching him between the legs and felling him. Then she whirled to meet Roxy's next attack. Both women stumbled on a mass of chairs, falling among the upturned legs and backs. Still, they lashed out, catching each other across the face. Ivana was up first, pushing her way towards the exit.

Daga was watching Ivana's battle, too. Mason kept seeing the thief's eyes flicking in that direction. It was an interesting telltale, proving that Daga had feelings for Ivana.

He didn't want to see her hurt or captured. Mason might be able to work with that.

He noticed Daga was also steering them gradually towards the main exit.

The doors that led to the lobby were currently wide open, held that way by the flow of people. Shouts and screams filled the air and people pushed and shoved their way to the front. Rich or mega-rich, it didn't matter, everyone was equal in the crush.

'Give it up, Daga,' he tried.

The thief didn't even reply. He was too intent on hurting people. He struck out carefully at Mason, driving him back, and then hit out at passing civilians, enjoying himself.

Minutes later, the battle had left the auction room and was crossing the lobby. There was more space in here, and it felt more airy because the ceilings were higher. There was the glass frontage too that looked out onto the street. The floors were made of shiny white marble, the walls painted white to look as spotless as possible. Daga looked like he was trying to get blood on them.

He grabbed a man by the side of the head and rammed him into the wall. The man's eyes fluttered closed, but Daga held him there, pulled the head back and would have rammed him again if Mason hadn't waded in, forcing Daga to drop the man and defend himself. Mason found his blows blocked and defended and then had to back away as Daga sought to blind him with several sharp jabs to the eyes.

At the glass doors, Roxy and Ivana were engaged in a wrestling match. Each had hold of the other around the neck and was trying to force their opponent's head to the floor. Hassell ranged around the back and kicked Ivana in the leg, trying to topple her. The woman's leg buckled, and she fell. Roxy landed on top of her, stuck in the doorway, bearing her to the ground.

It wasn't pretty. People stumbled over them left and right. Women wearing jewels and men sporting expensive blazers trampled them without care. Roxy found that the only way was to roll out of the lobby and into the street, going with the shoes, and then standing her ground as she forced herself upright.

Ivana was rolling too, this time straight into Roxy's feet. As Roxy got her balance, Ivana took it, sending her back down to the ground. Roxy hit hard, landing on her spine, the impact taking her breath away. Ivana chose the opportunity to clamber on top of her.

'Now I will kill you,' she said.

Roxy fought off a wave of pain. Her eyes had blurred, but she tried to focus on Ivana's face, which was just inches away. She brought a knee up, rolled, and tried to throw Ivana off, but it was Hassell punching in from the right that rattled Ivana's ribs and forced her to climb off.

Roxy jumped to her feet.

Mason followed her outside, still engaged in combat with Daga. It was cool, the streets slick out here. Drizzle filled the air. Mason's face was coated with water the second he stepped outside. The night air resounded with the sound of approaching sirens.

'They're gonna put you in jail, Daga,' Mason said. 'For ever.'

'I will die first,' Daga snarled.

Mason had heard that before. He'd heard it all across Iraq, night and day, from the throats of his worst enemies. There was little worse than fighting in a foreign country against its inhabitants and trying to kill them. But what made it better, made it more acceptable, was fighting alongside men and women you thought of as your friends. You were all highly trained, as well equipped as you could be, but the biggest comfort was your comrades in arms, your colleagues. When you were fighting against an enemy that was prepared to die for their cause, you needed strength in numbers and a certain peace of mind.

And tonight, Mason had his team. They were with him. Roxy and Hassell were targeting Ivana. Quaid was ushering people to safety, following his heart and his gut. Sally was helping people get free and keeping an eye out for the police. She was talking to security people, probably warning them off, trying to save their lives.

Mason separated from Daga on the glossy street. The thief wasn't even panting. Mason's heart was beating wildly, his hair soaked. The drifting drizzle floated between them, droplets illuminated with blazing light and flashing like fire.

The thief's eyes were still wild, focusing on every civilian, on every runner at the same time as engaging with Mason. It was impossible to tell which way he was going to jump – at Mason or at innocent people. Mason had experienced nothing like it.

Ahead and to the right, Ivana and Roxy were locked in a similar kind of combat, Ivana striking out at any passing civilian who strayed too close. Quaid was herding them away. Hassell was coming at Ivana from her blind side.

Roxy found her focus and her objectives changing. The fight with Ivana had not only moved, but it had also changed parameters several times. Now, as the woman targeted running people, Roxy concentrated on saving them.

Ivana punched out at a passing woman, aiming for the ribs. Roxy grabbed the woman by the coat and twisted her away. Ivana went to trip a tall man who ran past holding his partner's hand, but Roxy struck right at that moment, diverting Ivana's attack into a defence. She was protecting people, saving them, working hard to defend those who hadn't come here to fight. And it felt good. Every person she saved was a shadow on Ivana's soul. It put the other woman off her game, frustrated her no end. Roxy wasn't quick enough to stop Ivana from grabbing a blond woman around the neck, but she was strong enough to force Ivana away from her, enabling the woman to break free and run.

This was how she used her skills to save ordinary people. This was how she raised new barriers to guard against the old memories. This was how she eclipsed the sins of her past, the sins they made her commit.

Ivana came at her, sweeping low. Roxy evaded her, kicked out, and caught the woman in the thigh. Ivana grimaced. She rose to her feet, saw another passer-by running down the road to her right and, crazily, turned her attention from Roxy to leap at him. She tackled him and bore him to the ground, raining down blows at his face and neck. Roxy was a split second behind her, lashing out at Ivana and causing her enough pain to turn away from the man. Roxy saw redemption in the focus of her attacks.

Mason was dealing with a similar situation with Daga. Thank God there were no guns involved. This could easily have become a bloodbath. The good news was that the sirens and the flashing red lights were a lot closer. Daga had taken out another security guard, leaving him prone on the floor but, thanks to Mason, still breathing. People ran past them, pounding down the slick road, dampened by the rain, some screaming as they saw the men and women fighting.

Daga's face was becoming increasingly less ecstatic. He knew the chaos was soon going to end. His eyes fixed on Mason's for the first time in a while, instead of roving among the fleeing civilians. Mason tried to ignore the aches and pains that Daga had inflicted on him.

'You failed,' Mason said, trying to distract him further.

'I have had my fun.' The corners of Daga's lips turned up.

'Marduk will be angry with you.' It was a sentence designed to raise Daga's hackles, maybe make him make a mistake.

It worked. Daga's eyes flashed. His guard went down. He spread his arms, opened his mouth to say something.

And Mason attacked.

He hit hard from the front, driving in with a knee and an elbow. The knee struck Daga's sternum, the elbow a cheekbone. Daga grunted from the pain but didn't flinch. He stumbled back about three steps. Mason was close up, twisting his body to deliver punch after punch as quickly as possible. This was his best chance to take Daga out. The thief doubled up and then fell to one knee. Mason was standing over him.

Daga lashed out, sending a low punch at Mason's groin. A sickening wave of pain lanced through him. He fought against it, but couldn't help falling to his knees.

Face to face with Daga.

The thief head-butted him. Mason felt his nose crack.

Again, the pain debilitated him. Rain splashed down his face. He swayed backwards.

Daga's eyes were dangerously close, the thief sweating heavily and panting, slicked with blood, not all his own. He rose and Mason sought to rise with him, but couldn't quite make it to his feet at the same time. He reached out, but there was no one around to help him up.

'Next time,' Daga said, 'I will kill you slowly and painfully.'

Mason wanted to deride him, to tell him to stop being a cliché, to highlight his failures, but couldn't quite summon up the strength to speak. Finally, he got to his feet, swaying.

'Next time,' Daga said again, and was gone.

He didn't vanish like they do in the movies, but he yelled at Ivana, got her attention, and then turned to run with the tail end of the crowd, heading towards the rain-slicked back streets. After a minute, even Mason lost sight of him.

His first thought was for his friends. Roxy was staggering across to him, her knuckles bruised and bloody. He saw Hassell wavering back and forth as he, too, attempted to make his way over. Quaid was standing amid the milling crowd, having saved dozens from the hands of the killers and urged even more to safety. Sally was walking across, her own hands slicked red where she had tried to staunch blood.

Despite it all, one word flashed continually in Mason's mind.

Failure.

'We should get out of here.' Hassell's first words spoke of the ex-criminal's state of mind.

'The cops are almost upon us,' Roxy said.

'We have nothing to hide,' Sally said. 'We're working for the Vatican.'

'They mean it's more of a time issue,' Mason said between gasps. 'We'd lose hours just cutting through the red tape.'

With that, they started hobbling towards the same back streets that Daga and Ivana had used, which Mason saw as highly ironic. The crowd and some still-running people shielded their movements.

'CCTV will reveal our faces and identities,' Quaid said. 'But by then we can have Conte make a call.'

Mason nodded and wished he hadn't. 'Does my nose look bent?' he said.

Roxy narrowed her eyes. 'Looks odd,' she said. 'Want me to snap it back?'

Mason shuddered. 'God, no.'

'Someone's gonna have to do it and the sooner the better, while your adrenalin's still firing. I'd rather it be me.' She looked serious before adding, 'And I'd take no pleasure in it.'

Mason slowed as they entered another side street. He thought he'd seen movement ahead. It was dark all around them, the vault of the night sky above offering no light. Darkened shopfronts and restaurants stood to each side, their frontages plastered with rain.

'Wait,' he said.

'What is it?' Roxy frowned at his tone of voice.

'I thought I saw something ahead.'

Sally moved into their midst. She'd been hanging back, thinking. 'What kind of something?' she asked.

'Figures. Two of them.'

'You don't think . . .' Roxy let the sentence hang.

'Crap,' Quaid said.

Mason wiped the rain from his eyes. 'I can't be sure,' he said. 'It was a fleeting glimpse. But I swear I just saw Daga and Ivana.'

'But that means . . .' Quaid began.

'Yeah, we're being hunted,' Mason finished.

Chapter 32

Mason stood in the glistening night, knowing their next decision would mean life or death.

'These are his streets,' Roxy said. 'His environment. He thrives in situations like this.'

Mason didn't move, his eyes fixed on the place where he'd seen the movement. He couldn't be sure that it was Daga, but then . . .

. . . what if it was?

'Form up,' he said.

His team made a circle around him, watching every direction. Mason, trusting them, took his eyes off the street and put cupped hands to either side of his nose. This was going to hurt.

'Happy to help with that, Joe,' Roxy said again. 'You should really have someone do it for you.'

Mason grunted. Roxy was being far too insistent, almost as if she looked forward to it. Mason took a deep breath, fixed his palms on either side of the dislodged cartilage, and pushed as hard as he could. Instant pain lanced through him, and he couldn't stop the bellow escaping.

The noise of it seemed to flow up at the skies along with the spear of pain. He heard a crunch. Tears blinded his eyes. For a second, there was so much pain he couldn't breathe.

Then it was over. He looked up to find Roxy staring at him.

'Shit,' she said. 'You've bent it the wrong way. Now it's twice as bad.'

Mason knew enough to give her the finger and wipe the tears from his eyes. He winced at the remembered pain and the cracking sound as his nose went back into place. He looked back the way they'd come, saw lurid, flashing lights painting the walls back there.

'Can't go back,' he said. 'Can't go forward.'

'Can't stay on these side streets,' Sally said.

'We should go somewhere public,' Hassell said, always thinking. 'Somewhere very public.'

'In Monaco?' Mason said. 'I know just the right place.'

They retraced their steps to a side road that was well lit and started down it when they saw several groups of people wandering ahead, clearly revellers. It was relatively close to the main street where the cops were now situated, but not dangerously close. Of course, they knew Daga would track them, stay in the shadows, and follow, hoping for an opportunity to strike . . .

. . . if it even *was* Daga out there.

Mason believed it was. Daga would do this: double back to strike and kill and maim the same night. They hurried along the back street in close formation, ready for anything, until they caught up a few loud groups and then slowed down.

Quaid spoke as they walked. 'I had to go with my calling back there,' he told them. 'Daga and Ivana were targeting members of the public. I couldn't let them all just run into the violence.'

Mason squeezed his nose to gauge how tender it was. 'You helped a tonne of people, mate.'

'Thanks. I couldn't turn my back on them.'

Roxy joined the conversation, her voice low. 'I did well, too. We all did. We all helped save people. I think . . . I think I had a breakthrough.'

Mason didn't stop his surveillance, but glanced at her. 'Seriously? Fighting Ivana gave you closure?'

'I wouldn't go that far,' Roxy said, eyes roaming. 'I felt something shift inside, a barrier probably, replaced by something; I just don't know what yet. And it wasn't fighting Ivana that helped, it was helping her would-be victims.'

Mason nodded. He'd also saved many from the hands of Daga. 'Those two,' he said, 'are about as far removed from reality as it's possible to get.'

'All that,' Hassell said. 'Everything we did. And we failed.'

Mason had been trying not to think about it. They'd lost any chance of finding Marduk. Was there any way forward from here?

'For now, let's survive,' Sally said.

Conscious that Daga and Ivana might well be tracking them, they stuck to the main, well-lit streets, Mason leading the way. Twice he saw shadows move to their left, something dark coalescing with something darker, and was forced to direct them back to the main road. They emerged several hundred yards away from the cops, but still with partygoers milling around. It was a busy night in Monaco.

'Where are we going?' Roxy asked once. 'Assuming we're not leading the murderers back to our hotel rooms.'

'To somewhere Daga won't go because it's too public even for him,' Mason said. 'To the most famous place in Monaco.'

They threaded their way through the streets and walked alongside the harbour for a while. They walked up a long hill, a constant stream of cars passing to their left. When they reached the top, Mason indicated to an old building to the right.

'Casino de Monte-Carlo,' he said. 'Spruce up.'

They might be wearing splendid-looking clothes, but they were a bedraggled bunch. They smoothed their jackets and dresses and wiped their faces free of rain and any smears of blood that might remain. They slicked down their hair. To gain entry, they had to look respectable. Mason led them around the side to the front.

Built in 1893, the casino offers a wide, warmly lit edifice accessible by a series of rounded-off stairs that lead through impressive front doors to a marble-paved atrium surrounded by over two dozen Ionic onyx columns. The gaming rooms are decorated with stunning architecture, stained glass windows and striking paintings. Mason had never visited before, but if there was anywhere he didn't mind losing some money, it was here.

They took a moment to scan the streets all around. The entire area was packed with people. Café de Paris was now to their right and the brasserie to their left. Mason walked up the steps, nodding at the doormen.

Inside, it was cool, air-conditioned, the high golden ceilings swallowing most of the noise. People were standing everywhere, and sets of doors to the left led to the gaming rooms. Mason headed towards the tables he could see.

'You drowning your sorrows?' Roxy asked him.

'We lost this round badly,' he said. 'I don't honestly know where we go from here.'

Inside the gaming room, it was noisy and crowded. Mason saw a bar to the left and headed straight for it. Ten minutes later, they all had drinks and were seated in plush chairs around the front of the bar. A low table sat before them.

'Is this public enough for you?' Mason asked rhetorically.

'I feel like we're hiding,' Roxy said. 'I don't like it.'

'Hiding in plain sight,' Hassell said. 'I do like it.'

'The dark is Daga's domain, the night his playground,' Quaid said. 'Let him have it. We'll take it all back tomorrow.'

Mason leaned forward. 'He had all the advantages out there,' he said. 'This way, we take it away from him. It's not about running. It's about being wiser.'

Still, they kept their eyes peeled. They eyed and inspected and measured every figure that entered the gaming room. They vetted every newcomer and the people he or she arrived with.

'We lost Marduk,' Quaid said finally. 'So where do we go from here?'

'It's a big setback,' Mason admitted.

'We get Premo Conte to lean on the cops to lean on the auction house,' Sally said. 'They have to give up Marduk's details.'

'Already been tried,' Mason said. 'Didn't work. And besides, by the time they got anywhere, Marduk and his money will be long gone.'

'Follow the money,' Hassell reiterated.

'Marduk could be gone already,' Sally said.

'The auction house probably works quickly,' Mason said. 'But not that quick. Daga interrupted the auction anyway. They're probably still waiting for some monies to be transferred.'

'Which gives us a few hours,' Hassell said.

'Maybe a day.'

They drank their cocktails in silence for a while, watching the flow of people and those who lost at the gaming tables. The atmosphere inside the casino was highly charged, the beautifully dressed people enjoying themselves. There was some faint, unobtrusive music playing in the background. Mason watched the room and racked his brains.

It can't end here.

Daga had shown his hand too early. In a way, the thief had failed too. But though he worked for Marduk, Mason knew that even the Amori leader was not arrogant or dumb enough to reprimand the thief. With Daga, you got what you saw.

'I have a thought,' Hassell said. 'We've hit another obstacle, but there still might be a way around it.'

Mason studied every face that passed or turned their way. Yes, they were keeping a low profile, but that didn't mean Daga wasn't hunting them.

'Spit it out,' Roxy said.

'Premo Conte,' Hassell said. 'He arranged for us to attend that auction at very short notice. That means he leaned on someone.' Hassell looked from face to face. 'Do you see? He leaned on someone inside the auction house.'

Sally nodded. 'Makes sense. I think I know what you're saying.'

'If Conte can get us an introduction to this person, then we can use whatever means we can to lean on him again.'

'Lean on him?' Sally asked.

'Whatever it takes,' Hassell said. 'Marduk's still gunning for the Vatican.'

'And for all we know, the only thing he's been waiting for is the money,' Quaid said with an ominous tone to his voice. 'As soon as he gets it . . .' Quaid trailed off.

The table fell into silence. The loud noise of the casino washed over them as they sipped their colourful drinks. Quaid had gone for the Bond martini, shaken, not stirred, and made with Royal Standard as opposed to Beefeater. Roxy was on the rum, after flirting with a special concoction the casino called a Vesper. The others had ordered standard drinks. Mason noticed that his was going down rather quickly.

Torn between wanting to order another and keeping his wits sharp, he scanned the room. This place had a style and charm all its own. It was intoxicating. He thought about what Hassell had said.

'We lean on the guy at the auction house,' he said. 'I like it. How about we call Conte now and tell him that?'

'It's a little late right now.' Sally checked her watch.

'Just shows we're doing our job,' Mason said. 'He'll want an update, anyway.'

Sally pulled out her phone.

Chapter 33

They stumbled out of the casino into the light of early morning, Mason quickly checking his watch. It was a little after six a.m., and they'd spent the entire night inside. The morning air was crisp and clear and fresh. He filled his lungs with it. Casino Square was quiet as the grave, just a few early risers – or late revellers – wandering around and a single car winding its way up from the town below. It was quiet, surreally so, after the all-night hubbub of the casino. Mason shielded his eyes for a moment as they adjusted to the light.

'Back to the hotel?' Hassell suggested.

'Yeah, and surveillance all the way,' Mason said.

They used every scrap of skill they'd accumulated through the years to meander their way from the casino to their hotel, making sure they weren't being followed. Hassell's expertise came in useful, as did Mason's and Roxy's. They doubled back several times, and took wrong turns, waited for minutes behind corners, but eventually ended up standing outside their hotel, satisfied that sometime in the night Cassadaga had relinquished the hunt.

They entered the lobby, knowing they weren't going to get any sleep, but content to freshen up. Before they could cross the wide, airy space, Sally's phone was ringing. She stopped next to a row of potted plants to answer it.

'Yes?'

'Is that Sally Rusk?'

Immediately, she put the call on speakerphone and ushered them all to a quiet area of the lobby. 'Yes, who is this?'

'You don't know me. I am Daniel. I work for a certain, um, auction house.'

'Premo Conte asked you to call?' Sally said.

Daniel coughed. 'In a manner of speaking,' Daniel said with a rich English accent. 'I organised your tickets last night.'

'Good.' Sally held the phone tighter. 'Can you speak freely?'

'Yes, I can.'

'We need information. I'm guessing it will be . . . classified. Can you help us?'

'That depends on what you need.'

'A man,' Sally said, thinking hard. 'He's the owner of all that Babylonian jewellery, the seller from last night. We need his name and his address here in Monaco.'

Daniel drew in a deep breath. 'That's highly confidential information.'

'I realise that.'

'Until now, all I did was get you some tickets, but now you're asking me to break the law. I could lose my job, maybe go to jail. I could—'

'Calm down, kid.' Roxy leaned towards the phone in Sally's hand. 'Take a breath. Why did you get us those tickets?'

'Why?'

'Yeah. Something must have made you do it, and I'm guessing it wasn't for the love of Premo Conte.'

Daniel managed a small laugh. 'No, it was purely for the love of money.'

Mason liked that. It made the man easier to read. 'Conte bribed you?'

'I guess you could say that.'

Sally spoke quickly. 'All right, well, that's still on the table,' she said carefully.

'The tickets were easy. What you're asking is going to be super hard.'

'Can you do it?' Mason asked.

'I need to think about it.'

'Would it help if you knew that this man is a criminal?' Sally said. 'Wanted by the police?'

'You could really help,' Roxy put in.

'This would be to help track him down?' Daniel asked.

'That's exactly what it would be,' Mason said.

'Who are you people?'

Mason thought about that. After a few moments, he said, 'We work for Conte on sensitive matters. Things we don't want the public at large, or even the authorities, to know too much about. All we need from you is a name and an address.'

Daniel was quiet for a long time. Mason was torn between wanting to prompt him and pushing too hard. The fact was – they'd already tried breaking into the place using Hassell. The New Yorker had told them he'd need hours to go through all the files, to track Marduk down that way. What they really needed was an inside man.

'Daniel?' he said finally.

'How much?' he asked.

'How much did Conte pay you?' Sally asked.

'Five hundred.'

'Then how does five thousand sound?'

There was a sharp intake of breath. 'Pretty good,' Daniel admitted.

'We need that information as soon as possible,' Mason said. 'The man in question may leave Monaco at any moment.'

'I'm a keyholder. I can go in early,' Daniel said. 'There's always plenty to do. I've done it before. It just might be possible. It all depends how quickly I can find the right file.'

Hassell made a face. 'Tell me about it.'

Mason kept his voice low, since there were now others in the lobby and sound travelled inside. 'Will you do it?'

'I'll try.'

'Good man. As soon as you're done, call us. We'll be waiting for you.'

Daniel coughed. 'If I haven't called you by ten a.m. the deal's off.'

The line went dead, leaving Sally staring at a phone with an empty line. She looked up at the others. 'Our best chance,' she said with a wry shake of her head. 'It's a small hope.'

Mason knew he needed to decompress, to take a few moments alone. They exited the elevators and then parted, heading for their rooms. Mason closed the door behind him and then leaned against it, sighing. It had been a hell of a long night. Worse, they had failed.

Again.

It's never going to be a case of just jumping from clue to clue, he thought. During their last few missions, they'd learned that. He tried to focus on the positives from last night – Roxy claiming she'd made a breakthrough, all the lives they'd saved, that they'd faced Cassadaga and lived.

Mason showered, changed and lay down on the bed. It was seven-thirty a.m. He was hungry. He spent an hour dozing and then swung his legs off the mattress, put his shoes on and headed down to the breakfast room, half expecting to see Roxy propping up the bar as he went past but, for once, the American wasn't there. Mason helped himself to a large, cooked breakfast, a mug of coffee, and then took a table. Soon, the others turned up. They talked, they ate, but nothing could make the time go faster. It crawled by. All they thought about was Daniel and of what he might be doing, of Marduk and where he might be. After breakfast, they took a walk to the harbour with takeaway coffees clasped in their hands and leaned against the railings, staring at the expensive yachts.

'You think Marduk's still here?' Mason asked.

Sally nodded as the wind tousled her hair. 'I do,' she said. 'Last night's fiasco set him back.'

It was nine forty-five.

'Everything will change if we get an address,' Mason said, the words as much to stimulate himself as the others. The slow passage of time was edging towards their deadline, and now they wanted it to go slower, fearing that ten a.m. might come around and they wouldn't hear from Daniel.

It was nine fifty-five.

The sea glittered, the waves rolling and lapping against concrete moorings and stirring the enormous yachts. Seagulls dipped and soared, squawking and making wayward patterns against the blue vault of the skies.

Service staff were cleaning the decks and the windows, one man bringing a sleek car around for its owner to drive. Another man, dressed in a suit, was sitting alone on deck, breakfast laid out before him, staring out to sea as if searching for something even his wealth and influence couldn't conjure.

'It's gone ten,' Sally said then. 'That's the deadline.'

'Give him a few minutes,' Mason replied. 'He might have got held up.'

Time passed. There was no phone call. Mason sipped his coffee and scanned the marina, chilled now by the rising wind. He checked his watch. Daniel was ten minutes late. It didn't look good. For all they knew, Daniel could be in police custody.

'He said he was going in early,' Sally fretted. 'We need to come up with a plan B.'

'Plan B?' Roxy stared at her. 'We barely have a plan A.'

Mason tried to clear his head. It wasn't working. Everything they'd done in their search for Marduk had led them to this harbour at this moment. It couldn't all be in vain.

'Give him a few more minutes,' he said.

'There comes a time,' Quaid said, 'when you have to get past it and move on. I think we're there now.'

Mason wondered if they could just turn up at the auction house and talk to Daniel face to face. They could, but it was hardly fair to the kid. Mason wouldn't push someone into doing something they didn't want to do.

Out of nowhere, and loud across the tranquil marina, the ringtone of Sally's phone chimed. Mason jumped, even though he'd been hoping for it. Sally answered the call and put it on speakerphone.

'Daniel?' she said.

'Yes, I have the information you want.'

'We thought you weren't ringing back,' Roxy said with relief in her voice.

'I got caught up in something, but I got the name and the address. Are you ready? I don't have long.'

'Sure,' Sally said, finding her notes app on her smartphone as Quaid pulled a pen and paper from his pocket. 'Go ahead.'

'The man's name is Jon Utu, and he's staying in one of Monaco's best hotels.'

Sally's eyes narrowed at the mention of the name. She typed it into her phone as Quaid scribbled it down on his pad. Daniel spent a few seconds reeling off the name of the hotel and the room number and then hung up, asking them to wire his money across as soon as possible. Sally looked down at the name she'd written on her phone.

'Utu,' she said. 'It makes sense.'

'Why does it?' Quaid asked, also studying the name.

'Utu is a Babylonian god,' she said. 'He appears in the Epic of Gilgamesh and helps him defeat an ogre. He's portrayed as riding a heavenly chariot that looks a lot like the sun. Most importantly, he was responsible for dispensing heavenly divine justice.'

Mason nodded. 'That links perfectly to Marduk,' he said. 'It's what he thinks he's trying to do.'

'Utu is a major god,' Sally told them. 'Outliving the Babylonian empire by thousands of years and only diminishing when Christianity suppressed the Mesopotamian religion.'

'One more reason for Marduk to hate Christianity,' Quaid said.

'So this Jon Utu is Marduk,' Roxy said, with steel in her voice. 'Let's go pay him a visit.'

Mason pushed away from the railing and threw his empty coffee cup in a nearby bin. 'Today,' he said. 'We can end this.'

Chapter 34

They moved fast. They returned to their rooms, pulled out their weapons and took an inventory of what spare magazines they had left. Mason had two, as did Quaid, but the others were all down to their last mag. They pocketed their guns and the magazines, made sure their gear was packed in case they needed a fast getaway, and then met down in the lobby. Sally made a quick call to Premo Conte. The Inspector General of the Vatican Gendarmerie asked them to hold off until he'd assembled a team.

'We can't wait that long,' Mason told him. 'Marduk could vanish at any moment. Just get ready to smooth things over with the local cops.'

They didn't wait for an answer. In less than two minutes, they were out the door and into the cool day. They ordered a large Uber and told the driver the name of the hotel they wished to visit. Then they sat on the edge of their seats.

The driver told them it would be a drive of fourteen minutes.

Mason hoped with all his heart that Marduk would still be there, waiting in his hotel room for the money to come through. There was no reason to think he might have left, no immediate threat to him. Marduk had to think he'd won. The only fly in the ointment was Cassadaga and what the thief might have told him about last night.

Could it be another trap?

Mason didn't think so. Marduk was entirely too full of his own importance to think of luring them with an alias. The taxi sped along the relatively quiet roads. Mason's heart beat fast. Soon, the car was pulling up outside Marduk's hotel, a grand mix of modern, fresh, elegant and old-world. The team jumped out of the taxi and then started up a set of the stairs, finally pushing their way into the lobby. It was open and roomy inside, the check-in desk situated across a wide marble floor. Mason ignored it, trying to look like he belonged. He strode across the lobby to the elevators.

'Room 119,' Sally said. 'First floor.'

Mason nodded. He already knew. The team made ready as the door closed and the lift travelled the short distance. Out in the plush-carpeted corridor, they followed the wall plaques to their target room, saying nothing. On the way, Mason saw a used tray and a metal food dish sitting over a used plate. He grabbed it all up in his left hand. When they arrived, Mason and Roxy removed their guns and took point.

Roxy did a three-countdown on the fingers of her free left hand.

'Breakfast, sir,' Mason shouted, knocking at the door and holding the tray up to the peephole so that it blocked out everything else.

He heard nothing at all for long seconds, but then a voice shouted from the other side. 'I didn't order any breakfast.'

Marduk. Undoubtedly, Marduk.

Mason reared back, then leapt at the door, his right foot lifted. He kicked out as he reached it, putting all his strength into the onslaught. The door splintered under force, rocking back into the room. Mason staggered to the left, dropped the tray and fell, striking the doorframe with a crash. Roxy didn't stand on ceremony; she just clambered over him and rushed into the room.

Quaid and Hassell rushed in behind her. Mason dragged himself up off the floor and, seconds later, his shoulder pounding in pain where he'd collided with the doorframe, followed them into Marduk's room.

It was chaos. Marduk was there, stumbling back down the corridor towards the bedroom. The man had a shocked and angry look on his face and was limping badly. He wore a shirt and black trousers, the shirt unbuttoned to the waist. Roxy's gun targeted his chest.

'Stop, asshole,' she said.

They'd captured him. Mason felt elation, although he wasn't surprised to find Marduk waiting for his money to be transferred. The madman had to wait somewhere – where better than in all this luxury.

Mason strode down the hallway as Marduk backed up. The room was well lit, sunlight flooding through the far windows.

'Be careful–' Mason began.

As they entered the bedroom area, shadows flew across the room. It wasn't that his team weren't prepared for it, it was that the shadows hit so fast and expertly.

Something struck Roxy from the left and she staggered

against the wall, maintaining her grip on the gun. Behind her, Quaid was also struck and went sprawling to the floor. Further back, Mason could make out what happened.

Two figures who knew exactly what they were doing had attacked his friends from their blind sides. Marduk was far from alone in this hotel room.

Daga and Ivana were with him.

Mason aimed his gun at Daga. 'Stand down.'

Behind him, Sally was coming through the doorway, her own gun drawn. Hassell had his back to the wall, covering Ivana. There wasn't a moment to take a breath. Daga reached down, stamped on Quaid's arm and wrenched the gun from his hand.

'After you,' he said in a voice dripping with malice.

Ivana threw her weight on Roxy's spine, making the American cry out loud. Still, she held on to the gun, rolling under Ivana's weight and striking out at her. Mason sighted on Daga.

Tension crackled between them.

'Drop the gun,' Mason said.

'I'd rather fire it,' Daga said. 'But I don't do guns.'

Impossibly quick, Daga threw it at Mason. Then he reached down, grabbed Quaid and put a knife to the man's throat. 'Now,' he said. 'You put your gun down.'

Quaid struggled, but Daga had him in a vice-like grip. The older man could barely move and, when he did, the edge of the knife pressed into his flesh.

'Don't do it,' Quaid gasped.

Marduk had reached the far side of the bedroom, expression wild, and was scrabbling around a coffee table back there as if searching for something. Mason hoped it wasn't another gun.

'If I shoot . . .' he warned Daga.

'He dies,' the thief said.

'No. *You* die.'

Ivana was gripping Roxy's wrist that held the gun. She was squeezing hard. The two women tussled on the floor. Mason concentrated on Daga. He knew there was no morality there, no sense of right and wrong, only the cold-blooded conscience of a malignant killer. In fact, it was worse than that. Mason believed Daga *did* know right from wrong, but delighted in the evils he performed.

It was Marduk who broke the deadlock. The man brought up a gun of his own, held it out, and started limping forward. The gun shook badly in his hand, travelling unconsciously from Daga to Mason. Mason's first instinct was to shoot the madman.

But Marduk opened fire first. The bullet ploughed through the air between Daga and Mason, smashed into the door and blew splinters out into the corridor. The gunshot was loud in the hotel room, punishing Mason's ears like tank fire. He fell to the floor. At the same time, Daga rose, getting in between Marduk and Mason, and dragging Quaid with him. The older man struggled, but was no match for Daga's brute strength.

Marduk yelled out a warning. 'Move out of the fucking way!'

Daga smirked. 'Now,' he said. 'Watch.'

And he started drawing his blade across Quaid's neck. Mason's heart jumped into his throat. He saw the blood start to flow. He tried to aim the gun, but Daga was hidden behind Quaid. There was only one option available.

Mason would have to shoot Quaid.

He squeezed the trigger. In that instant, Marduk, in his madness, reached Daga and sought to elbow the thief aside just so that he could get a bead on Mason.

Daga wasn't expecting it. The knife slipped away. Quaid wrenched himself from Daga's grip, falling to one knee. Mason saw the disorder erupting between Marduk and Daga. He could have opened fire, but the confusion was too intense. Nobody knew what was going to happen next, and a lone bullet could hit anyone. Quaid was struggling. Hassell was darting in from the right. Daga was staggering as Marduk pushed past him, gun still wavering.

Mason ran at the gun.

An instant before Marduk opened fire for the second time, Mason grabbed his wrist and wrenched it towards the floor. He wanted to break it but didn't have the angle. The gun ripped from Marduk's grip, though. Mason unbalanced the limping man with ease, and then threw him aside, discarded rag, straight at Hassell, who caught hold of his shirt and spun him right into the wall. Mason now faced Daga.

The thief slashed, but Mason was already past him. He wanted to free Roxy, even the odds a bit. He kicked Ivana in the spine, sending the woman lurching forward and over the top of Roxy's head. The impact knocked the gun from Roxy's hand, but she could sit up. Mason got a quick snapshot of the melee as he turned.

Sally was standing by the door, which was still half open. She had a gun in her hand but didn't know where to aim it. She couldn't open fire. There was too much chance of collateral damage. Quaid was undeterred by what had happened to him and was starting back towards Daga. The thief was turning with the knife in his hand, eyes locked firmly on Mason. Hassell had changed tack and was now angling for Ivana, stepping around Roxy. The American herself was kneeling upright, taking in the chaos.

Marduk was shouting at everyone, the gun still swinging in his hand.

Mason flung himself to the floor. The action seemed to galvanise Daga into doing something besides attacking. With a grimace he whirled, caught hold of Marduk's gun hand and twisted it, relieving him of the weapon.

'Idiot,' he said. 'You will kill us all.'

Mason used the precious few seconds to act. This was no longer a point and shoot situation. He'd freed Roxy; the American was already confronting Ivana. Now, Daga was coming at him. Before Daga could get there, Hassell turned and attacked. Daga lashed out, striking Hassell, but the American was ready and blocked the attack, ducked and came at Daga from a low angle. He rose with his head, smashing his skull into the side of Daga's face. Daga staggered into the left wall. Hassell was on him in less than a second.

But Daga was ready. He loved and embraced the pain. It didn't bother him. He slipped down under Hassell's attack and jabbed the man in the ribs and then the kidneys. He rolled, giving himself space, then leapt to his feet just as Mason reached him.

Mason was ready. He balled his right hand into a fist and used every ounce of training and experience he had to throw a punch at Daga's jaw. It struck hard and true, sent the thief backwards and straight down to the floor.

Daga lay supine, out cold, not moving.

Mason's fist hurt, his knuckles throbbed, but he didn't acknowledge the pain. With one proper punch, he'd laid the scourge of the world out. Daga had seen it coming too, but could not dodge out of the way. Mason took a few seconds to make sure the thief wasn't bluffing and then turned. Marduk was staring at him as if he was an antichrist or, in Marduk's mind, maybe Jesus Christ. Ivana was engaged with Roxy, neither having seen Daga go down. Mason moved on to the next job.

Marduk.

The leader of the Amori held up a hand as if in warning.

'Stay away from me.'

'Why? Your little bodyguard's out for the count.'

'I am the monarch of the—'

'Yeah, yeah, blah, blah, the monarch of who-gives-a-fuck. I know. Y'see, mate . . .' Mason moved towards him. 'I just don't care.'

Marduk covered up, cowering. He wasn't the monarch Mason had first come up against. He didn't have the defiance, but then he also didn't have a powerful organisation at his back. 'You're going back to jail,' Mason said. 'But first . . . what do you have planned?'

A smirk crossed Marduk's face. 'We meet again, you and I,' he said, completely ignoring the question.

'Yeah, the last time didn't go so well for you.'

'You shot me like a coward. You brought cowards with you, sinners all. Those who believe in dead things. Jesus, the saviour, the redeemer. The Holy Spirit,' Marduk spat. 'It is all so many lies. Only the Amori and the Creed show the right and true way. *Ours* is the only gospel that matters and this, you will see.'

Mason shook his head. 'I don't care.'

By now, Roxy and Ivana were struggling hard. Hassell came in behind Ivana and took her out at the knees, sending her to the floor. Quaid was there to help, too. Mason saw the fight coming to an end.

And then, incredibly, Daga rose to his feet.

Chapter 35

The thief swayed in place, spitting blood and teeth from his mouth.

Mason stared disbelievingly. He'd doled out some hard punches in his time and had thoroughly expected Daga to be out for a good while longer. But the thief was up, shaking his head and grimacing.

They couldn't leave him be. There was still a gun on the floor. Mason reacted quickly, but Daga was faster, suddenly aware and active. He didn't reach for a gun, but leapt at Hassell, tore the man away from Ivana and threw him into the wall.

'*Move,*' Daga shouted.

Perhaps it was pre-planned. Mason wasn't sure. But Ivana suddenly redoubled her efforts, forcing Roxy away. Daga smashed Quaid across the back of the neck, sending him to his knees. By the time Mason was there, Marduk reached the room's only window, a floor-to-ceiling single pane of glass that stood partly open.

'Do it,' Daga said.

Mason threw another punch at him. Daga blocked it,

spat in his face, and then kicked out. Mason stumbled away. Daga and Ivana ran past, now backing away from the major fight.

Marduk picked up a chair and threw it at the window. The glass shattered outward, the flow of shards surging to the ground below. Mason remembered they were on the hotel's first floor.

Marduk used the chair to clear any remaining daggers of glass from the frame, then limped to the window. He stepped onto the frame with Daga and Ivana at his back. Mason saw him hesitate.

'*Do it,*' Daga snarled again.

Marduk leapt out into space. Before Mason could reach them, Daga and Ivana had followed, not evaluating the jump, not gauging their landing, just running and leaping out into thin air. Mason pulled up short when he reached the window just a short way behind Daga.

Looked out.

Marduk had landed on the soft lawn below, his bad leg crumpling beneath him and forcing him to roll and roll into the nearby hedges. He was holding his leg and grimacing, but otherwise looked unhurt. The distance wasn't that far. Ivana had landed and rolled too and was now picking herself up. Mason saw Daga hit the grass and fall to one knee, then catch himself and start running towards Marduk.

The street outside was quiet, although some traffic was running along it. Mason considered the jump. If those three could make it, he was sure as shit that he could too. He climbed onto the sill, saw Daga glance back. Met the thief's eyes.

Daga moved quickly to where he thought Mason would land. The threat was obvious. At the moment he landed, helpless to defend himself, Daga would take him out. Ivana was already flagging a car down by stepping into the middle of the road.

Mason hesitated.

Marduk had limped to the pavement. A car rolled up in front of Ivana, who sped around the side and yanked open the door. She pulled the driver out, kicked him in the head, and threw him into the gutter.

Only then did Daga leave his post.

Mason gauged it quickly. There was no way he could stop them. Jumping out of the window must have been a desperate escape plan, but it had worked. He felt the others at his back.

'We have to get the hell away from this room,' Roxy said.

Mason knew it, too. They would be caught up in bureaucracy, unable to operate properly. Mason cursed and turned away from the window.

'Go,' he said.

Marduk was furious. He wanted to kill something. That idiot Ivana had thrown the driver to the gutter, otherwise Marduk could have smashed his head in. *Mason. Joe fucking Mason.* At every turn, that demon turned up, threatening to destroy all of Marduk's plans. The problem was – he was a hard man to kill.

Many had tried, including Marduk and even Daga. Marduk seethed in silence for a while as Ivana drove the car.

Daga clutched and rubbed his jaw where Mason had struck it. For a moment there, when Daga fell, Marduk had thought he was done for.

'I want Mason dead,' Marduk said.

'Join the damn club,' Daga growled.

'No, I mean, I want you to go back right now and murder him. And his crew. I want them all to stop breathing.'

Ivana, driving, looked over at Daga. 'Are you okay? He got you pretty good in there.'

Daga didn't look especially pleased to be reminded that Mason had knocked him out. 'I'll take more than teeth from him when we meet again.' He swallowed blood.

'Didn't you hear me?' Marduk ranted. 'I want them all dead. *Now*.'

Daga turned to him with a snarl. 'Don't talk stupid. We barely escaped. You fired a shot. The authorities can't be far away. Going back is the last thing we could do.'

Marduk fumed. 'So Mason escapes again.'

'Yes, for now. But he's living on borrowed time.'

Marduk struck the seat beside him. Sweat poured from his brow and his knee hurt where it had buckled underneath him when he'd hit the grass. The pain had been like a lance flashing through his body. He rubbed it now, groaning, sweating.

'He should be dead,' he couldn't help but grumble.

Daga wasn't in the mood. Marduk saw the man's empty hands close into fists and knew he'd pushed the mad thief too far. He leaned back and held up his hands.

'All right, all right, I'll leave the death dealing to you.' He tried to sound nonchalant but quaked inside.

Daga turned away, staring fixedly out the front window. Ivana drove aimlessly, just getting them lost in the streets of Monaco. Marduk knew they'd have to ditch the stolen car soon. Had he left anything of importance back in the hotel room?

No. Everything important was on his phone.

And, as if to reinforce that thought, his phone gave

out a soft chime. Marduk glanced at the screen. There was a message from the auction house.

Lot one proceeds transferred.

Marduk's heart leapt. Here it was. Everything he'd been waiting for. With resources like this came the collapse of the hateful Church.

Another chime.

Lot two proceeds transferred.

A grin stretched across his face. He couldn't help it. Ivana was staring at him in the rear-view and shook her head.

'You are one crazy fuck,' she said. 'What are you smiling at?'

He grinned at the broad-shouldered woman. 'My plan is coming together.'

'The money?'

Marduk nodded.

'Then you can pay us everything that you owe us?'

Marduk nodded again, but felt his smile falter. 'I still need you for the duration of my plan.'

Daga sighed. 'I'm getting bored. I need someone to kill.'

That tempted Marduk to say, '*Kill Mason*', but he managed to hold it in. Although the next stage of his plan could proceed without Daga and Ivana, their presence would make things far easier. As they drove, the profits from lots three, four and five were paid into Marduk's account.

He was fluid. He had wealth. Everything he needed was in his possession. Why waste any more time?

Excitement rushed through him like a tidal wave. Suddenly, all his aches went away, and he was on the edge of his seat. He felt as if Daga and Ivana were his best friends. He was at one with the world.

'All that digging around the Etemenanki ziggurat proved fruitful,' he said. 'If I wasn't monarch of the Amori, I'd never have known about the riches that lay beneath the sands, beneath the great Tower of Babel. I have succeeded.'

Some part of him knew he was being boorish, but that didn't bother Marduk. He was above such things, and better than most people. 'The great destruction of the Church can begin,' he said.

More chimes. All the lots came in, even lot ten, which had been partially interrupted by Daga's impatience. Marduk was now done with the auction house and could move on. He could control his money through his phone, but still preferred a physical station to work from.

A place from where I can start the attack . . .

From which they will never recover.

It was time. Excitement overcame him. He twisted in the seat and leaned forward. 'Can we get to a hotel?' he said. 'I need a base to work from.'

Daga shook his head. 'We dump the car first,' he said. 'And then we should leave Monaco.'

Marduk ground his teeth in frustration. 'Is that necessary? I like it here.'

'We've outstayed our welcome,' Ivana said. 'But Nice is close by.'

Marduk's only proper concern was starting his attack on the Church. But it was complex and bristled with many moving parts. Maybe now wasn't quite the right time to begin. With an effort, he reined his urges in.

'Nice?' he said. 'How far is that?'

'Not far. You'll be scheming again in no time.'

Ivana pulled over to the kerb. They left the car parked in a quiet street in between two trucks. With luck, no one would notice it for hours. Ivana then ordered them an Uber, which would transport them to Nice.

Marduk ran through his plans. To date, four more Faithful had come forward to join the original man – Keeva. That was the perfect number to start with. Marduk was ready, and they were ready. They would play their part soon. Not every asset was in place, but it wouldn't take much effort to make it so.

The Uber driver took them out of Monaco and on the road to Nice. True to Ivana's words, the drive didn't take long. Marduk was soon climbing out of the stuffy car into a crisp day and directing them all to a luxurious hotel. After walking there impatiently, he paid for two rooms, split up from Daga and Ivana, and then rode the elevators to the top floor. He deserved the best. With every step, his anticipation grew. Marduk entered the room, enjoying the copious feeling of extravagance that it offered. He crossed to the window and stared out.

A good, commanding view of the city.

He made his first call to a man named Kroll.

'Update me,' he said, offering no introduction.

Kroll answered immediately and deferentially. 'We are awaiting funds for the last of the preparations, sir.'

'I can have funds with you momentarily. How far away are you from action?'

'Two days, sir.' Kroll was the man Marduk was using to bring everything together. Kroll was the plan's supervisor, someone trusted to handle all the fluid aspects and make them slot together at the same time.

'Two days? That seems quite a long time.'

'Our assets have been waiting longer, sir.'

It was true. It had taken a while for Marduk to search

the ziggurat and then arrange the auction house sale. 'Two days then,' he said. 'Are the Faithful ready?'

'Most of them,' came the irked reply.

'Is there a problem with the Faithful?'

'The job they have vowed to do is not an easy one,' Kroll said. 'They need some cajoling.'

'Then get on with it.'

Marduk didn't let Kroll go straight away. He went over a few more aspects of the plan. He told Kroll to notify his tech guru that Marduk would send him a video soon, a video that would then need forwarding to those who mattered in Vatican City. Finally, he asked to speak to Keeva.

The young man, the first of the Faithful who had travelled all the way to Babylon to meet him, spoke in a halting, submissive voice.

'I am here.'

'Keeva,' Marduk said warmly. 'You are the first, my most treasured servant. Your time is almost here.'

'I am ready.'

'In two days, you will become glorious,' Marduk said. 'A light shining in the centre of the darkness. As will the rest of the Faithful.'

'I am happy.'

'Then, my servant, you shall be fulfilled. The Creed speaks of the Faithful, of those committed to helping the Amori. You were with us in Africa, yes?'

'I was one of the kitchen's chief chefs. I recall vividly the moment of the brutal attack.'

Marduk shuddered. 'As do I. All my plans lost in those terrible moments. The Church will pay for what they did to us. My God Project will undo them.'

'Your God Project?'

'You are already a part of it.'

'It is all that I want.'

'And you shall have it. And I shall rejoice.'

Marduk ended the conversation soon after, content that Keeva was still the best man for the hardest job. He then ended the call to Kroll and set up the phone so that it showed very little detail of the hotel room he occupied. Eager with anticipation, he pressed the record button.

'I am Marduk,' he began, addressing the camera. 'And I am the monarch of the Amori, the true bane of the Church. I will be your downfall, your destroyer, the Satan that you fear. You cannot defeat me, for I have over four thousand years of knowledge and know-how behind me. I am ready,' he said. 'Ready to show you I cannot fail, that there is no one true God, that your Jesus Christ was in fact *not* the saviour of humanity.'

Marduk leaned forward so that his face filled the screen. 'That will be me,' he said. 'The end of your days is nigh.'

Chapter 36

Mason and the team made themselves scarce. The battle in Marduk's hotel room had been loud and had caused a lot of damage that they didn't want to be associated with. They escaped on foot and then took a taxi to a place where they could regroup over a late breakfast.

Mason ordered a Full English before speaking. They sat in the far corner of a snug little café along the Avenue de Monte-Carlo, leaning in close so they could not be overheard by the place's other patrons. The café smelled of cooked bacon and strong coffee and, through the front windows, they could see almost all of Port Hercules.

'We're screwed,' Roxy said vehemently. 'We lost that rat bastard and now he has everything he needs to carry out his plan.'

Mason couldn't see a way forward, either. 'There has to be something,' he said, trying to stay optimistic for the team. 'A way forward.'

'I must admit,' Quaid said, 'that it feels as though we've tried everything. We are only five people. Maybe we need help, after all?'

Mason blinked at him. 'Help? Who'd you have in mind? James Bond?'

'I could live with that,' Roxy said with a grin. 'Or a younger Pierce Brosnan. Whatever works.'

'I was thinking more along the lines of Premo Conte,' Quaid said. 'The Cavalieré.'

'The special officers of the Vatican Gendarmerie,' Mason said. 'They aren't gonna help us catch up to Marduk.'

'But Conte needs to know that we lost him,' Sally said.

Just then, Sally's phone rang. She answered it in low tones, conscious of the people sitting close by, but the general hubbub of conversation inside the café drowned out her voice.

'Hello?' she said again, forced to speak louder.

'This is Mario Gambetti.' It was the new young cardinal who'd taken Vallini's place.

'Oh, hi.' Sally sounded taken aback. 'What can we do for you?'

'We need you here,' he said. 'Something has happened.'

Mason felt his heartbeat double. 'What?'

'I am sending you a video clip now.'

Mason waited as Sally took out a pair of earphones, plugged them in, and listened to the video clip. 'It's Marduk,' she told them. To Gambetti, she said, 'This was emailed to you?'

'To the Vatican, yes. It tells us Marduk is ready to act.'

Sally passed her phone around so that they could all listen. Mason felt angry because they had let it come to this. Marduk had slipped through their hands more than once. 'You want us to come there?' he asked.

'We want your perspective. Inspector General Conte says you can help. You have done so before.'

Something was coming, something bad. Mason guessed the best place they could be was at Vatican City, fighting it. Of course, Marduk may well be en route along with Cassadaga and Ivana.

'Is everyone on board with this at your end?' he asked, remembering that during the Book of Secrets incident, Vallini had had immense trouble getting the cardinals to embrace his point of view.

'Not enough, I'm afraid,' Gambetti said. 'Another reason Conte wants you here.'

Mason had wanted to hit something for some time now, preferably a punchbag that could take the damage. Losing Marduk, Daga and Ivana had riled him up no end.

'You're not saying much, Joe.' Roxy was watching him closely.

'It's not what I do,' he said. 'I don't rant and rave, don't shout about our losses. They're down to me as much as anyone.'

'Conte's asking for help,' Sally said. 'I think we should give him ours.'

'We work for the Vatican,' Mason said. 'At least for now.' Looking back on the last few months, it was working for the Vatican that had got them to the position they were in now. 'But what can we do to help?'

Gambetti said nothing for a while, then sighed and asked them to make their way as soon as possible, before ending the call. Clearly, both he and Conte needed backup.

Their breakfast arrived, smelling delicious, and with it more black coffee. Mason ate and drank his fill, saying nothing else. When he was done, he pushed the plate away and regarded the others.

'We're on Conte's side,' he said. 'No matter what. If Conte wants us to stay there and convince those other cardinals that Marduk's off his rocker and planning something terrible, then that's what we do. Agreed?'

'I don't think we'll have to convince them of anything,' Sally said. 'Marduk will act pretty soon.'

Mason guessed she was right. Nevertheless, he respected Premo Conte and wanted to offer him every courtesy. And being invited to help the Vatican was no small thing.

'Let's hope we get there in time,' Roxy said morosely.

Her words galvanised Mason, made him want to get moving. She was right. Once Marduk received his money, he'd be solvent and able to do anything he wanted. He kept an eye on them until they'd all finished eating.

'Are we ready?' he asked. 'One big, last push. This time, we stop that madman.'

Chapter 37

Time passed. Rain and sleet bombarded Rome so hard it seemed to be trying to wash away a multitude of sins and goodness too, all at once, in one terrific deluge. Vatican City stood stoically beneath it, washed clean. The skies brooded by night and day, hanging heavy with the promise of more to come. Thunder and lightning swept the city, noise and light stalking from east to west and beyond.

Joe Mason and his team arrived before it all started and went straight to Premo Conte, who was passing through the barracks of the Swiss guards when they called him. Immediately, he gave them clearance, and they turned to their right across St Peter's Square and passed through a security cordon. Conte stood right before them.

It was three p.m. in the afternoon. In his video call, Marduk had given the Vatican two days, which meant that something would happen tomorrow. They had a little time to come up with a plan. The team had travelled under their official guise and could retain their firearms, albeit stowed away for the flight. Mason was hoping Conte would resupply their ammunition from the Swiss Guard's armoury.

But what next?

What were they expecting? What could you do to stop someone as ruthlessly determined as Marduk?

Premo Conte was tall, broad, and wore wraparound sunglasses and a tailored suit. He walked up to them outside the barracks and stopped suddenly, regarding them.

'It's going to rain,' he said. 'We should go inside.'

Mason, surprised, followed him towards the nearest door. Around them, the profound quiet of Vatican City away from the tourists reigned, the spaces relatively empty, but Mason had only to look back over his shoulder and peer through the massive Doric colonnades to see that the hustle and bustle of sightseeing Rome wasn't far away.

'Is there any more information?' Sally asked as they walked.

'Everything that can be done is being done. We don't know what's coming. It is hard convincing some cardinals and the police that anything is coming. The gendarmes, the Carabinieri, they have their own security structures and there has been no warning of anything happening. No chatter, no leaked information. No signs of any sort. I have told them that Marduk is an unknown entity working alone at the top. I have told them his circumstances, of having to wait for the money, but they simply do not believe that anything could have flown under their radar. My station, it seems, doesn't give me the credibility I'd hoped for.'

'But they're on alert, right?' Hassell asked.

Conte nodded. 'To a point.'

'The politics of Italian police forces.' Sally sighed. 'I have heard it is both complex and harsh.'

Conte walked through a door into a busy office. He hung his coat up and moved inside. Mason shrugged out of his leather jacket, hung it up next to Conte's and then moved further into the room, which appeared to be a communications hub. Men and women sat at desks, some with headgear, talking to a dozen people around Rome and the world. The walls were bare and functional, the windows tinted.

'We don't have long,' Conte said. 'Let's get to it.'

He led them to a smaller room, closed the door and asked for a debrief. Mason and Sally gave him a rundown of everything they'd done since learning of the murder of Cardinal Vallini.

'And what would you do next?' Conte asked at the end of it all.

'Find Marduk,' Mason said. 'This all ends with his capture. Without him, there is no way forward for our enemy.'

'Thousands of hotels in Rome,' Conte said. 'Not to mention other residences up for rent. Where do you suggest we begin?'

Out the window, Mason saw the start of the rain. It hit the pane with a splat, four big droplets, each one striking before sliding down. Seconds later it began in earnest, the view outside obscured by sheets of liquid.

'Ignore that,' Conte said. 'It is the least of our worries. Do you really think Marduk has plans to destroy the Vatican tomorrow?'

'It is his reason for living,' Mason said. 'He will do it.'

'*He will do it?*'

'Unless we stop him.'

Chapter 38

They thrashed it out with Conte and then found a nearby hotel with spare rooms saved for the Vatican. They slept and then met for breakfast. When he woke, Mason found he was thinking of today as the day of judgement, zero hour. It was the day that Marduk would attack the Vatican.

When would it happen?

They ate and drank coffee and then made their way across the road to St Peter's Square. It was early, and the rain had let up, though the dark hanging clouds promised much more to come. They splashed through puddles across the square towards the barracks, where Conte appeared to have set himself up. He'd told them it was far enough away from his main office to let him breathe and to keep the jackals who demanded his time at bay. Today, he couldn't spare a second for them.

It was eight a.m. Mason and the others spent a little time watching Conte work. They were ready to act, ready to seek Marduk at a moment's notice, a force on hand to track the enemy down at the slightest hint of a clue.

Mason tried to shake off the failures that had beset them so far; they'd almost captured Marduk, only to be beaten by circumstance and luck.

Hours passed. Mason got sick of the cramped space, the endless noise, and wandered out of the barracks, back through the colonnades and into St Peter's Square. It was around ten a.m. and the place was already buzzing with tourists. A light drizzle filled the air.

The sky was dark, threatening, as if sensing Mason's mood.

As was the entire atmosphere that hung over the Vatican City and Rome itself.

He went back inside. More time passed. Lunch was a pre-packed sandwich whilst they stood and listened to fresh intel. None of it led to Marduk. Their police liaison was next to useless, offering no information. Still nothing happened. The atmosphere inside the barracks was laden, heavy with anticipation. Everyone in there expected something to happen and every minute that passed increased that expectation and added to the sense of time slipping away.

In the middle of the afternoon, seeing a break in the rain, Mason again slipped outside, desperate for some fresh air and a few lighter moments to allay the feeling of unbearable tension. It had been raining until recently but, for now, a shaft of sunlight had broken through the cloud cover and was blessing the square with its radiance.

This time, Mason had taken Sally with him.

'I don't think we're doing any good here,' she fretted. 'We're standing about, waiting for something to happen.'

It felt like they were on the back foot. Mason said, 'What else can we do? We've exhausted our investigative limits. Sometimes, you just don't get what you want.'

'My father would never have understood that, but I do,' Sally said, referencing the wealthy late Professor Rusk. 'I saw it every day.' Sally's was such an odd story, Mason reflected. Born into privilege, rejecting it, running away and then reconnecting with her father only to see him murdered. But he was glad that she'd stood up for what she believed in.

'Do you regret any of it?' he asked, thinking of his own story, losing friends in Iraq, the failed marriage that resulted, the long years drenched in guilt.

'Sometimes,' Sally said honestly. 'The regret comes and goes.'

'That's a direct and truthful description of what most of us feel,' Mason said. 'Me included.'

Sally opened her mouth to say more, but, as she did so, an explosion rang out across the city. Mason was checking his watch at the time, so the exact hour was emblazoned into his brain.

15.05.

And then a second explosion filled the air.

Chapter 39

A cold and terrible silence fell over St Peter's Square.

Mason scanned every horizon he could see, looking past the irregular roofs of buildings and the semicircle of Doric columns. People were standing around, looking in all directions. Nobody wanted to accept the truth of what they had just heard.

'No,' Sally breathed. 'It can't be . . .'

The double explosions finally stopped echoing around Rome. Whatever had happened had been large. Mason squinted, now seeing a rising column of black smoke to the south-east. He saw another one rising to the north-east, just a thin column spiralling into the sky. It could be anything. It might be a gas-main explosion, but the timing of it warned Mason otherwise.

They ran back towards the barracks.

Inside, all hell had broken loose, men and women shouting into their phones and at each other, trying to be heard. Premo Conte was standing at the front of the room, overseeing all, with three of his special cavalieré at his side.

'Smoke,' Mason told him. 'Rising above the city to the east. Two columns. Do you have access to CCTV here?'

'Only local,' Conte said. 'We're reliant on the press and the police, I'm afraid.'

'Increase the security around Vatican City,' Roxy said. 'Do it now.'

'We've already gone down that route,' Conte said. 'It's at an all-time high. Swiss guards, cavalieré and gendarmes are deployed.'

There were monitors fixed to a wall. A man shouted, slapped his computer screen and sent an image flying across onto a monitor. It was the first picture of an unfolding incident across the city. The first media vans had arrived on the scene.

Mason saw an L-shaped row of buildings about three storeys high. Black bollards lined the street outside each house, essentially there to stop cars from parking on the pavements. It appeared to be an upscale, urban street. Mason could see twisted wreckage amid a lot of flame and black smoke, something that had passed between the bollards and hit the front of a house. Whatever it was had detonated massively, causing widespread damage, breaking windows and scarring the front of many residences, as well as ravaging the row of cars parked at the kerb outside.

'It's a motorbike,' one man said. 'Look, you can still see the rear wheel.'

Mason looked closer and saw that the man was right. The wreckage was about the right size. Someone had driven a motorbike through the bollards, up to the front of the house, and detonated it. He couldn't tell if there was a body close to the bike.

The camera panned away, showing the rest of the street. Seconds later, a woman sitting on the right side of the room shouted out and sent another image across to a monitor.

'Site of the second explosion,' she said.

Mason saw a similar scene. The wreckage was the same, causing two people to speak up immediately and speculate that it was another bike. This time, the burning debris lay snugly against a shopfront at the end of a residential street. Glass and block and mortar had been gouged out of the edifice, giving the impression that a bomb had hit it rather than a motorcycle.

'What the hell are we seeing?' one woman asked.

The camera zoomed in closer, its operator now pushing people out of the way. Mason saw something he recalled from his time in Iraq and had hoped never to see again.

A burning body. Someone had been on the motorbike when it hit the building.

Mason turned away as a collective gasp rang out around the room. Roxy looked at him.

'I don't like the look of that,' she said. 'And I don't mean the burning body.'

'What *do* you mean?' Conte asked. 'Speak clearly and quickly.'

'Everything that the burning body and the surrounding evidence implies,' she said. 'That guy was clearly carrying an explosive.'

Mason switched his attention back to the first scene. The cameraman there hadn't zoomed in close yet. Flames licked the front of the building. He knew exactly what Roxy was suggesting.

'Suicide bomber?'

'That's right.'

People stared at her. Conte stared at her. This was Rome. This kind of thing didn't happen in Rome. Conte tried to manage the situation.

'Information will roll in,' he said. 'Stay calm. The important part is to analyse it skilfully, to manage it. Do not let yourselves become overwhelmed.'

'We can't be sure,' someone said.

'We can't be sure of anything until we are,' Roxy said. 'This might have nothing to do with Marduk. Of course, he most likely has his filthy little hands all over it.'

Mason studied both scenes. The burning bike and body in the second scene were being picked out gruesomely by the cameraman as if he'd forgotten he was livestreaming to the nation. Smoke and flames covered most of the tableau, smoke roiling to the sky. First responders were arriving and rushing through a crowd that had formed. Mason wasn't surprised to see at least half the crowd with smartphones held in the air, recording what was happening. There were wounded people, all covered in debris and dust and blood, some trying to help others with their hands, with their words, with anything they could. Others were just holding the hands of those who didn't look like they'd make it.

'So you're saying someone is just driving motorbikes into things?' Conte looked like he was willing to play Devil's advocate. 'Why?'

Mason checked his watch. Ten minutes had passed since the first explosion. 'Check your perimeters,' he said. 'Repeatedly in Iraq, they used things like this as a distraction.'

He saw disbelief stretch across several faces.

'Check your perimeters,' he said again.

Conte ordered it. Fingers started flying across keyboards, thumbs raised in the air as people affirmed that all was okay. They made calls. Nothing seemed out of the ordinary throughout Vatican City. All was quiet and normal.

'Shit,' someone said.

Mason immediately glanced over at the man who'd spoken. He was short-haired, wearing thin-rimmed glasses and staring hard at his computer screen. 'There's been another one,' he said. 'A third.'

'An explosion?' Conte asked.

'Yeah, a big one.'

Mason waited. Tension crammed the communications room as if it was jostling for space. Minutes passed. Mason glanced out the window to see a dreary day filled with rain again. Nothing was happening out there; they might as well be isolated in the North Pole. He looked back when someone shouted, '*There!*'

A video feed was flicked rapidly across to another monitor. Now there were three ongoing feeds. The third showed another smallish, flaming wreckage lying in front of a large store. The store's double glass doors had been demolished, glass and mortar strewn for yards around. Mason saw that the entrance was bent to hell, the inside a mess of debris.

This time, the rider had been thrown free, but it was clear he'd been on the bike at the time of detonation.

'Has to be the rider,' Roxy said. 'He's wearing a crash helmet, blending in whilst he drove up. People, these are suicide attacks.'

'Marduk,' Hassell said.

'We have to look at it from that angle,' Conte said. 'But what exactly is he up to?'

Mason thought of the word *distraction* once more,

but didn't repeat himself. His own experience with war outweighed everyone else's in this room, with the possible exception of Roxy, though she was a different breed of warrior.

'Emergency services deployed to all three,' a man said. 'Cops are going apeshit. They're talking about a major terrorist event.'

They won't be far wrong, Mason thought.

Was this Marduk's plan? To use suicide bombers? And where had they come from? There had to be more to it.

'This isn't done yet,' Quaid said. 'Not by a long shot.'

'It's getting closer,' someone said.

Silence weighed heavily on the room as a fourth explosion rocked Rome. Mason saw another monitor now filled with close-ups of skyrocketing flames. The carnage, the devastation, the terrible aftermath.

'Ten blocks from here,' a man said.

Mason had had enough of watching monitors. Conte had told them not to get overwhelmed, but it was an overwhelming feeling, faced with all this death and destruction flashing from one monitor to another. He needed to be out there in the real world, helping. He spun on his heel, strode to the door and left the room, hearing Conte's irritated question – *where's he going?* – but offering no answer. He left the barracks and made his way back to St Peter's Square, where the sheer amount of space gave him solace. It was wide open, vast, giving him a sense of freedom.

Mason breathed deeply. He didn't want to look up, to spot the columns of black smoke rising over Rome, but his eyes were drawn to them. The most recent explosion, the fourth, which had happened at the famous, towering Castel Sant'Angelo, the mausoleum of Hadrian, just minutes from the Vatican itself, an old fortress now under new attack. The black smoke rose thickly nearby, roiling like a poisonous snake away to his left.

Were the attacks purposely getting closer to the Vatican?

He didn't know. He couldn't know. If this was Marduk, then it was a purely evil endgame. Mason turned as a young man came up to him.

'I am Cardinal Gambetti,' he said. 'The inspector general wants you back in the communications room.'

Mason appraised the young man who had replaced Vallini. 'When did you turn up?'

'Oh, about two minutes ago.'

'Listen,' Mason said, not ready to be pushed around just yet. 'I think—'

His words were drowned out as a massive detonation shook the ground. Mason reacted instantly, grabbing Gambetti and forcing him to the floor. He didn't look left or right, didn't look up, just tucked his head and arms in and kept hold of Gambetti. The explosion reverberated around the square.

Immediately after, alarms rang out, those of cars and businesses, those of countless office buildings, strident through the suddenly silent air. Mason looked up. He didn't want to, scared of what he would see. But there was no choice; this was moving forward, putting the past in the past.

'Oh, God,' Gambetti breathed.

The explosion hadn't happened inside the square, though it had felt that way. Mason saw a pile of burning wreckage lying up against one building that circumvented it. The pavement all around the explosion was populated with the wounded and the dead. Cars that had been passing were either standing askew or, in one case, completely blown over. Flames licked up the façade of the closest building.

The utter silence was just as loud as the preceding explosion.

Then the screaming began. The lament for the injured and the lost, the trauma of the incident hitting everybody hard.

Mason pulled Gambetti to his feet, knowing they had to get out of St Peter's Square.

'We have to get to Conte,' he said. 'This is only the beginning.'

Chapter 40

Keeva's conscience was clear. He wanted to do this. It was the right, just and virtuous thing to do. He was the first of the Faithful, not only the first to arrive, to pledge his life to Marduk, but the first of the small contingent of men and women that Marduk had elevated to that status. Keeva's job was the most important.

He blended with the crowds easily, a simple tourist; baseball cap perched stupidly over his head, a large, heavy rucksack clasped across his back. He wore a denim jacket and black jeans and comfortable boots. He was one of them, which was ironic because all his life he had never *been* one of them.

Now . . .

Keeva's had been a long, lonely, painful life. He recalled every savage moment of it, sometimes relishing the hurt that they'd caused him because it made him more determined now. It made him love the Amori – and Marduk – the only stable ground that he'd ever found, even more. Keeva had been a fifth or sixth child, he couldn't even remember, in a family brought up hard in the back streets of Marseille. When they weren't stealing, they were looking for something to steal or trying to appease the gang that owned their father. Keeva remembered a time when he'd given himself to the gang leader as a willing victim just to stop the torture that grim-faced gang members were happily doling out to the man. They never killed him, but he was never without a broken bone.

The gang hated their father because he had rejected them, refused to join. Keeva had seen his life go from bad to worse, had seen his mother unable to cope and turn to drugs and alcohol, thus becoming dependent on the very gang they refuted. He had seen her after she overdosed, stretched out on the kitchen floor, not breathing. That was when his father had given up and stopped looking after his boys.

Keeva joined the gang that had created the circumstances that ensnared his mother, eventually killing her. He joined along with his brothers to give his father a break but, one year later, his father was dead anyway, it appeared of a broken heart. Keeva did the gang's bidding again and again, slowly losing his humanity. It was worse when he saw his brothers embracing the violence, the brutality of it all. Keeva found he couldn't come to terms with that.

Nevertheless, there were some good people that he came into contact with. When Keeva worked as a debt collector, he met a flirtatious girl who liked him, someone he could talk to, but after several visits he knew he couldn't let her get dragged into his world and never saw her again. It was like that. You kept those you cared about safe by leaving them alone, by distancing yourself from them. The gang lifestyle brooked no fondness and no sentimentality. If they thought you were weak, they would eat you alive.

Keeva endured it for years, trying to hold on to even a shred of decency. What he did every day and night assaulted his brain. It was years after his father had died and after he'd lost touch with all of his brothers that he came across the Amori.

Somehow, the gang butted heads with the shadowy organisation. For the first time, Keeva saw something stronger than the gang, something the gang feared, and it energised him like the strike of a lightning bolt. Somehow, he had to get closer to the Amori.

He managed it. He befriended a woman who later turned out to be a remote security agent. What that meant, Keeva never really understood, but he did understand that the woman could get him closer to the Amori and that the Amori were always on the lookout for capable new members.

It was like being poached for a job. They discreetly contacted him after he expressed an interest in them. He sat in a dingy office and answered questions; he told them about his past, his ties to the gang, the violence that surrounded him every day. The man he spoke to assured him they could relocate him to someplace the gang would never find him and procure him a job, but he had to be devoted to the Amori. He had to prove that he could follow the Creed.

Whatever that was.

Keeva agreed to all of it. Why wouldn't he? Here was a way out, a future. He'd never look back.

And it all worked out for him. He ended up working out of some incredible hideout in the depths of Africa with an amazing shoreline. He trained to be a chef.

He left all the blood and the carnage and the destruction behind him and embraced the Amori virtues. He read the gospels night after night, devoured the Creed, and embraced it as a way of life. His outlook changed. His *brain* was altered by the new life, by the peace and freedoms and tranquilities that it offered. The Amori had been around for thousands of years, and now he was one of them. The Amori was going nowhere.

Keeva had found a home.

Working in the kitchens, serving up increasingly sumptuous dishes and earning high praise for it, Keeva forgot about his old life. Violence was not a part of the Amori way, he decided, knowing his job insulated him but caring little. All he did care about was that he was living his best life. They let him walk the shoreline, explore the surrounding forests landward, to watch streaming TV, and get limited access to the internet. It was a structured life, structured by tiers. His boss answered to another man in charge who was just three tiers below the monarch – Marduk. Of course, Marduk had been deposed, and another man came to be in charge, but Keeva always thought Marduk was the one with all the right credentials.

The change of leadership was the one thing that worried Keeva. He didn't like change anymore.

And then came that terrible, fateful night when his entire world revolved again. As far as he knew, they were doing nothing wrong. The Amori lived out a peaceful existence far removed from the chaos of life. Of course, they had to get their funding from somewhere, but Keeva just assumed it was from a bunch of wealthy patrons. He still did.

Why had *they* attacked the Amori compound?

They.

They were the authorities, the establishment, the destroyers of his new world. They came in carrying guns and using them frequently. They shot men and women indiscriminately, men and women just trying to stand up for their rights and wielding only knives and machetes and pots and pans as surely they were entitled to. Everyone was entitled to defend their own realm.

Keeva wanted none of the fighting. He'd seen enough ferocity to last him a lifetime. He wouldn't get involved, especially when he saw his fellow chefs and servers gunned down with their weapons still in their hands. Keeva's stomach turned and his life changed. This had been beautiful; it had been stable and perfect. Far removed from his past. This had been a place of healing.

But the Amori were wiped out that night. They disbanded. Their outstanding leader – Marduk – was whisked away, the whispers said to jail. *Why?* For living as they wished, for living apart? Keeva didn't understand any of it.

Ironically, it was his past life that helped him escape that night.

He had the old skills, the in-built ability to vanish into the dark, starry night, slipping between bodies like a wraith, not seen, not heard, not found. He disappeared into the jungle and made his way to the nearest town, just a man wearing a strange white outfit carrying a handful of dollars he'd been able to grab and nothing else. Lost again, alone, he was a man ripped from his home. He lay low; used his skills to later return to the Amori site, but saw only authorities swarming over it. *Why, oh why?* And where had everyone gone? Some hadn't survived the terrible attack, but others surely had. Did many others escape as he had? Keeva had no answers and no way to get them. He stayed in the town until his money ran out. He then hiked to another town and another until he came to a major population centre. He didn't know its name. Once there, he was forced to resort once more to his old skill set, to theft and enforcement and banditry.

It destroyed him inside.

With money in his pocket, Keeva started searching for the remains of the Amori. He simply couldn't believe such a deep, far-reaching organisation with so many members had just vanished overnight. Of course, living alone and with means, he now used a laptop and had access to the entire internet. He saw the news. He listened to stories about Marduk and what he had been planning. He wondered if the Vatican attacked the hideout. It seemed plausible to Keeva.

In that case, he owed the Vatican an extreme debt born of hatred.

Keeva kept his focus on Marduk. He found and joined forums where stragglers from the Amori enterprise still conversed. Some of what they said was interesting – they spoke of the Vatican, the Bible and expounded on the past four thousand years or so.

Other discussions were of no interest to Keeva.

He followed certain individuals on the net. He hung on their every word. They were devout believers like him. They talked about messages coming from inside Marduk's prison, messages that spoke of Faithful and infiltrators and the coming vengeance against the Church and the Vatican. It wasn't over yet.

They would retaliate. They would have their vengeance.

And then Marduk did exactly as he said he was going to do. He escaped that prison and started on the long road to vengeance. He called for the Faithful to attend. Of course, he needed them, needed their devotion and expertise. Keeva knew instinctively that he was one of the Faithful; he had lived and breathed the Amori without faltering for many years now. They were his world. What happened to them made his head hurt, made all the turmoil inside churn as though the tines of a mixer were spinning, crunching through his brain. Everything was scrunched up in there; he couldn't think straight, and it hurt.

The forums guessed Marduk was going for the riches he knew were buried in Babylon. These were good, knowledgeable people. Some even said they were thinking of going to join up. Keeva decided the first night, almost instantly. He wanted to help Marduk gain his vengeance with all his heart.

And so . . .

. . . it had all come to this.

Walking through Rome with pounds of explosives strapped to his chest and even more nestling in his backpack. Keeva saw faces in front of him, to left and right, but all he really saw was the face of Marduk, the features of the man he saw as his monarch, his king, his mentor and chief and – even – father. Keeva saw a child skipping along to his left. The child wore a red jacket and had braids in her hair. Keeva felt something, a tug on his heartstrings. He should warn her to get out of the way, warn her parents perhaps. But he couldn't do that. The whole point of this exercise was the surprise it would bring. Keeva was the first of the Faithful and he wouldn't let his master down.

To his right, a young boy carried a teddy bear and tried to grab hold of the pushchair that his mother was wheeling where an even younger boy sat. Keeva was among them, sometimes touching them. He forced his way through the crowd, his destination just ahead.

Behind him, the evidence that the other Faithful were doing their jobs hung over the city. Keeva had heard the explosions, had turned to see the black pillars of smoke that somehow reminded him of the state of his soul. Keeva was a wicked man trying to do good. He *was* good, but something had gone wrong. Marduk was trying to right that wrong. It was a complex equation, but Keeva knew what he had to do.

The fourth explosion rang out then, just a few hundred yards ahead of Keeva and to the right. Keeva didn't react, but stood there, staring at the devastation whilst all around him people either ducked or started screaming or pulled out their mobile phones. He was a rock amid the surge as still more pushed past him, trying to get away from the scene, fearing more devastation. Keeva didn't blame them. He stood stoically in the crowd as they flowed past and then, steadily, he started walking forward once more.

Everywhere, people were running. Some ran towards the carnage, others ran away. Sirens and alarms were going off. The sound of crackling, burning fire and the stench of acrid smoke filled the air. Keeva knew that another of the Faithful had successfully completed their mission. He was happy for them, happy that they'd found peace and a better life, happy that they'd embraced the teachings of Marduk and the Creed and had gone willingly into the next world where everything would be a thousand times better.

Keeva hoped for the same thing.

This vendetta Marduk had with the Church, this so-called God Project – it was all-consuming, all-empowering.

Keeva became aware now of the great basilica ahead of him, the wide square that fronted it. The space was enormous. There were so many people. He found that if he sped up to overtake a child or a group of youngsters, he just came across another cluster of them.

Keeva entered St Peter's Square.

Despite the space, the world was shrinking all around him. This was it, the end of the line. Keeva didn't remember many happy times, but those he did recall reared up to haunt him now – sultry nights in Marseille, slipping from bar to bar, not drunk, but happy with the moment, living life while life breathed all around him. In those times he loved well because death was so close, death had a stranglehold on him, a stranglehold the Amori broke.

Until the Church took it all away.

Keeva walked across the square. He took one look back, saw the devastation that the motorcycle had caused. It was bloody, broken mayhem. People's lives changed in an instant. The landscape marred. One minute, a busy stretch of street where people walked and talked and laughed every day; the next, irreversibly tarnished for ever. Nobody would ever forget what happened there today.

Keeva felt the weight of the backpack across his shoulders. It weighed heavy, and not just physically. He didn't know exactly what was inside, but he knew what it would do. As fortune had it, the explosion had cleared many people away from St Peter's Square. And, as Marduk said, this wasn't all about killing people; it was about distraction and terror and diversion. The Faithful were paving the way for what was to come.

Keeva was happy to give his life to Marduk. The Amori had given him the best months of his life, a time when he had actually begun to dream about a future. Of course, it was all gone now, so why was Keeva still even here?

Concealed in his pocket was the detonator. Keeva grabbed hold of it now, let his finger roll over the button. With a last look in every direction, and waiting for a break in the flow of people all around, he closed his eyes, said a prayer to the Creed, and detonated himself.

Chapter 41

Gambetti pulled Mason back. 'We should go help those people,' he said, pointing to where the bike had just exploded. 'It's only across the square.'

Mason knew the young cardinal was right, but also that he was wrong. Human decency pulled him in the devastation's direction, but he was also aware there was only one way to put an end to it all. By finding and stopping Marduk.

Right then, the others appeared behind him, running up to him. 'Are you okay?' Sally shouted in his ear.

'Yeah, yeah, we're fine. This is Gambetti.'

'Oh my God, those poor people,' Quaid said, and Mason knew exactly what the man was going to say before the words spilled from his mouth. 'We have to help them.'

Sirens and the sound of screaming were everywhere.

Roxy was already moving past them. 'I'm going over there.'

It was pandemonium. Mason couldn't see through so many running bodies. He rose, started following in

Roxy's footsteps. They started crossing the square. He could see Swiss guards, police who'd been close by, hundreds of civilians out of the corner of his eyes, but he centred his focus on the motorbike wreckage and everything around it. There were people on their knees with their hands out, holding the outstretched hands of the wounded and the dead; people applying pressure to wounds. There was one woman who looked like a doctor, racing between patients. There were body parts and flames and burning flesh and it was everything you didn't think about too deeply, everything you compartmentalised. It was the horror hidden away in the closet, the thing under the bed, the darkness that tapped on your bedroom window deep into the night. It was horror and hell and a scene from a diabolical *other* world.

Mason and his team ran towards it.

Still, he couldn't shake the feeling that Marduk was planning further atrocities. He hoped Premo Conte was attending to that.

Halfway across the square, Mason saw a young man. He was standing there, head down, a rock amid the flow. Perhaps he was so traumatised that he didn't know what to do. Mason wanted to go to him. His legs started forcing him in that direction. But there were other, far worse off people just ahead, and Mason gritted his teeth and kept running. He ran away from the youth standing in the centre of St Peter's Square.

And, seconds later, that youth exploded.

It was overwhelming, destructive, shattering. It bore them to the ground, throwing them about like rag dolls. The deadly shock wave battered them as they rolled.

And as quickly as it happened, it ended.

Mason's senses were shot. He lay staring up at the skies, thinking, *I see the sun; I see the sun; I see the sun,* because it was the most comforting thing that came to mind. His limbs were unresponsive. There was a buzzing sound in his brain. Were the arms lying on his stomach even his?

And suddenly everything clicked back into place.

Sound returned. The buzzing faded. At first, there was a blessed silence. Even the wail of sirens faded into the background. *I am Joe Mason,* he told himself. *I am here to help, to fight, to prevent more . . . more . . . attacks.*

He sat up, head spinning. He was unhurt. His legs and arms functioned; his brain was sharp. *Oh God, the others!*

It felt like déjà vu. A flashback. He remembered when the bomb went off at the HQ in Africa. Then, he had feared for their lives. Now, he scrambled to his feet and ran to them. First, Roxy, lying on her side, her hands out in front of her. She stared fixedly at them as if trying to count fingers. When Mason reached her, she looked up.

'Are you okay?' he asked gently.

'Yeah, sure, I think so.'

Second, he scrambled across to Quaid. The Englishman was sitting up and shaking his head, looking groggy. 'I'm good,' he said. 'The blast was far enough away.'

Hassell and Sally were lying on their backs, staring at the leaden skies where thin shafts of sunlight tried to make a breakthrough. They were unharmed, at least physically. Mason's next port of call was the cardinal, Gambetti.

Leaning over, he hooked arms under the cardinal and helped him sit up. 'How are you feeling?'

'I don't know. What happened?'

For the first time, Mason looked to where the explosion had come from. He didn't quite know what he expected to see. The area was clear except for scorch marks on the ground that spread in all directions like evil, pointing fingers. There were some sickening remains several yards from the scorch mark. But there were also other people lying closer to the site of the explosion, people screaming, people crawling away.

Mason lifted Gambetti up and started running, trying to reach a young man with blood on his reaching hands and on his face. Mason's legs felt unsteady. He had to slow down. The world flipped, and he found himself on his knees. He ignored it, took a deep breath, and hurried over to the crawling man.

'Are you hurt, mate?'

'I . . . I think so. My legs . . .'

Mason took a hard look at the guy's legs. They were fine. It was the trauma, affecting everyone in different ways. 'Hold there,' he said. 'Sit up. Rest a while. You'll be fine.'

Roxy ran past him one way, Quaid the other. They raced to the sides of people who were clearly hurt. Sirens blared across the square. Mason looked back, saw ambulances pulling up and paramedics climbing out. There weren't enough. Here, now, in the heart of Rome and Vatican City, there weren't enough ambulances. The sense of horror inside Mason swelled. His eyes focused on the faces of the paramedics. He saw the despair in their expressions.

All around, he saw a contrasting mix of high activity and quiet death. He saw men who were clearly undercover agents pulled from pillar to post. They were dressed as civilians but carried weapons; they were trying to help the wounded; they were shouting into handheld radios. Cops were everywhere. Mason raced off to the next injured person.

Ahead, Mason could see the entrance to the basilica itself. It was being guarded by rows of gendarmes and the Swiss Guard, all with weapons drawn, men who couldn't leave their posts to go help the wounded. He could only imagine what they were thinking, how they were coping. He saw civilians headed towards the basilica, towards the Doric columns, towards nearby buildings.

But were they civilians?

How could you tell?

He sat up, hands covered in blood. His legs were hurting, his back ached. His head was still spinning. There was chaos and carnage all around him, something akin to a battlefield. It all took him back years, back to a different time that held both terrible memories and good. He hadn't ever expected to experience something like this again.

What now?

Had it grown into something that was too big for his team to handle? Marduk had clearly been planning this for some time; he had the personnel, the resources, the loyalty of those who had already given their lives. Of course, the Amori infrastructure had already been in place. It can't have been too hard to tug on that.

Mason's phone rang. It was Premo Conte calling.

'Where are you?'

'In the square. We're all okay.'

'I need you back here. It's crazy.'

'It's pretty bad out here, too. We're helping whoever we can.'

'Don't you want Marduk?'

Mason gritted his teeth. *Of course we want Marduk!* But he could feel someone's blood drying on his hands. 'We're saving lives, Conte.'

The man signed off, clearly under pressure and, possibly, not trusting himself to speak. Mason saw a body in front of him, clothes that were charred. He saw movement beyond that, a woman trying to shrug a backpack off, the backpack shredded by shrapnel in a way that might have saved her life.

'What do you have in there? Kevlar?' Mason helped her with the backpack.

'Wood,' she said. 'Planks and shapes. I was transporting all the composite parts of a scale model of a boat.'

Mason shook his head. He was grateful, but also shocked at how fate worked. How did one person live while the next died? He could say the same about the incident in Mosul that had ruined so many lives. How had Zach and Harry become the ones who walked into the IED? It could have been a dozen others, it could have been Mason. He'd inspected the house first. Why did one person die in a storm of violence that passed another person by?

He pulled the woman away from the epicentre of the blast. She was bleeding from the ears and from the mouth. He helped steady her and made sure she didn't see what lay around her. 'Rest,' he said. 'The paramedics will be here soon.'

Already, they were making their way across the square. Some had stayed to attend to those injured in the motorcycle explosion, whilst others headed this way. More ambulances were arriving. Mason rose to his feet and looked around, seeing St Peter's Square bathed in lurid flashing lights from one side to the other, reflecting the reds and blues. It was now eerily empty of passers-by, an enormous space.

His eyes fell once more on the basilica to the west. The doors were closed, the lines of guards that stood outside looking imposing in front of the tall columns that supported the building. They were stationed at the top of the steps. He imagined there were more guards at other entrances. Mason saw the civilians were closer now, at the bottom of the steps, and appeared to be gesticulating as if asking questions. Where had the civilians come from? Possibly the side streets to the south after having walked through the columns.

The guards shouted at them, telling them to vacate the area. Mason watched. When Roxy looked up, she saw him staring and turned her head in the same direction. A cloud passed over her face.

It was incredibly violent when it happened. Even as Mason looked on, the civilians reached under their coats, pulled out guns and pointed them at the guards. They rushed forward, assaulting the front doors of St Peter's Basilica. They opened fire, their bullets strafing the air and the building in front of them. Guards twisted and fell. The sound of gunfire slammed across the square from side to side, causing a heavy silence and people, struck with terror, looked up to see what was happening now.

Guards returned the fire. Bullets flew. Men and women sprawled across the steps that led to the basilica. The attackers closed in, running hard and firing constantly. Almost instantly, more guards and undercover agents and cops started converging on the assault from the sides and the rear, pulling out concealed weapons as they ran, but the attackers were plentiful and they advanced even though they took fire and died. Mason saw at least two dozen of them running up the steps.

He rose to his feet. What the hell could they do? If they raced in to help now, they might get shot by the guards. He noticed Roxy and the others staring at him.

Make a decision.

'We can't join in,' he said. 'Nobody knows who we are.'

Unless . . .

Gunfire reverberated across the square. Those genuine civilians close to the fight were running and screaming. The attackers won their ground hard, falling quickly, twisting in death throes on the steps, but the line of guards that stood before the doors had been thinned out now. Only nine men were left standing.

Against fourteen attackers.

'We have to help,' he said. He looked around for Mario Gambetti. 'Come with us,' he said. 'You can vouch for our identities.'

'Me?'

'Yes, get moving.'

'But I could be anyone wearing the garb of a cardinal,' he said.

True. Mason thought about it. 'Won't they recognise you?'

'They should,' Gambetti conceded.

'Then come with us.'

Mason gathered himself, breathed deeply, and went to help the Swiss guards in their defence of Vatican City.

Chapter 42

Marduk had the best view of all.

It started with one motorcycle. Marduk was with the rider all the way, swerving and swaying through the thick traffic, almost colliding with a car's metal bumper – that would have been catastrophic – but staying upright. The rider wasn't particularly accomplished by any means – in fact, this was the first time he'd ever ridden a bike. Marduk was pinning a lot on the man's uncertain skills.

He sat in a plush chair, his aching leg elevated, but was along for the ride through the body cam that they'd attached to the man's vest. They'd fitted all the Faithful with body cams – including Keeva – so that Marduk might glory in their sacrifice from close range. His lips were dry in anticipation.

The first rider's body cam showed him veering off from traffic, mounting the pavement and passing between two startled ladies. Marduk laughed at the looks on their faces and the way he imagined they'd try to berate the rider.

Only this time, they wouldn't have a chance.

Because the hard wall was coming up, the end of the line. The rider flew at it without slowing down. The brick and the block, the surrounding glass, filled the camera lens. A second later, the camera went blank and Marduk heard the sound of the explosion echo across Rome.

What a vantage point, he thought. *What a show. I can see and I can hear and I'm sitting in comfort in this hotel room with my bodyguards at my back.*

Bodyguards?

A dubious statement. Cassadaga and Ivana weren't the most reliable of shields because they were so . . . unpredictable. Of course, he couldn't have anyone better beside him in a fight, but it was their other proclivities that worried Marduk. At any moment, they might decide they wanted to go out and make a kill.

Daga was bitching about the teeth he'd lost in the fight with Mason. Ivana was coaxing him into another kill to help reset his mind. Marduk reminded them they were here to protect him and should stay in the room. Neither of them looked happy about it, but Marduk reminded them of the bigger picture, of the wealth they were due that, after today, would set them up in their murderous ways for the rest of their lives. Both nodded, and Marduk went back to watching the TV.

The second of the Faithful exploded gloriously. Marduk clapped. He was so happy that his long-planned strategy was working, or at least appeared to be. Two open laptops were tuned to news channels and showed emergency services and police racing to the scene. That was a good start. Yes, he knew security across Rome would be heightened because of the attacks, but there was no doubt in his mind that – with more to come – resources would be taken from the perimeter of the Vatican.

Which wasn't exactly required for his plan to work, but it would help.

All this for a few less men to deal with. All this because he could, to prove that he – Marduk – was still the monarch of the Amori and at war with the Church.

'Your suicide riders are doing their jobs?' Ivana asked from the back of the room.

Marduk didn't look at her. 'As expected. They will all succeed.'

'You mean they will all die?'

'That *is* their job.'

'For you.'

'Yes, for me. Who else? I am worthy of their sacrifice, am I not? It is *their* Bible, their Book of Exodus, which proclaims we take "an eye for an eye". The Creed has no such equivalent, but we are dealing with Christians here. We will deal with them as they suggest, harshly.'

'I must say,' Daga said drily, 'your Creed is missing a trick there.'

Now Marduk swivelled to look at him. 'The Creed contains the highlights of old Babylonian law, which is a subset of cuneiform law. Babylonian law has received a lot of archaeological attention through the years simply because of the wealth of information available. Now, this law postulated that a hurt individual, or their relative, would take unforgiving vengeance on the person who caused the injury. Perhaps even worse vengeance to the point of death. The Creed softened that commandment. The worst crimes, of course, those punished most severely, were crimes against the monarch.'

Marduk turned back to the screens that were arrayed before him. The third of the Faithful was cutting through traffic as though he was in a race, narrowly missing cars and vans and making even Marduk wince. Through the wide window to his right, he could see one column of smoke snaking up towards the sky. It was beautiful. It was all because of him. The Church's day of judgement was here, and there would be no hereafter for them, no eternal life. They would simply be . . . dead.

Marduk rubbed his hands together, unable to stop grinning. He cheered when the third of the Faithful exploded. The anticipation was running through him in warm tingles. He ordered champagne and popcorn. He slipped his bare feet into warm slippers and tied a soft, plush robe around his waist. Then he lounged back with arms dangling across the arms of the chair.

'This is my moment,' he said. 'Every explosion, every death, every drop of blood is a win. I simply cannot lose this day.'

He sniggered at the sight of blood that slicked the floor at one scene, cheered when the news channel's cameras showed the devastated bike. He licked his lips when the fourth of the Faithful approached his final destination.

From the back of the room, Cassadaga watched him through narrow eyes.

Cassadaga was a lot of things, but he was no fool. He knew when the writing was on the wall. Marduk was spiralling out of control, worsening with every minute and fresh scene of devastation that flickered across the screens, lost in the quick and carnage-filled progression of death.

Daga put a hand to his mouth and touched the two empty spaces where Mason had knocked his teeth out. The pain didn't matter; it was the ignominy of it all that made his blood boil.

Ivana saw him and slapped his hands away. 'Stop that,' she said with an odd compassion in her voice. 'You'll make them bleed again.'

The killer regarded her softly. He viewed Ivana through rose-tinted glasses. She was his soulmate in terror, his one loyal companion. They understood each other in life and – even better – in death . . . in the death of others, that was. Ivana was the only person on this earth who could get away with slapping him in such a manner.

'They don't even hurt,' he said grumpily.

Ivana pulled out the sharp, long blade she kept holstered at her waist. 'Do you think he'd notice if we slipped away?'

Daga smiled knowingly at the blade. 'To do what?'

'That which we do best together.'

'Death and madness reigns throughout Rome today.'

'And there's nowhere I'd rather be.'

Daga nodded and grabbed her, pulling her close. He ground his hips against her, feeling his passion rise. She held the knife between them. The more he saw the terrible images on the TV, the more he wanted to rush out the hotel doors and find someone to kill.

'Do you think he'd mind if we did it right here?' Ivana breathed.

Daga glanced over at Marduk. 'I doubt he'd even notice. He's way too far gone.'

Ten minutes later, Daga was readjusting his jeans and Ivana was pulling herself up from the back of the couch. Marduk had turned around once, averted his eyes, and then shouted out a warning that Keeva was approaching the centre of St Peter's Square.

Daga had watched the explosion over Ivana's shoulder. The sight of it spurred him on. When he and Ivana were decent again, he stood back and watched Marduk enact the next part of his plan.

'My infiltrators,' Marduk said into a handheld radio. 'Attack.'

The message would need relaying by several people across the city because of the short-range radios they possessed. But it wouldn't take long for it to reach its intended target. Daga knew Marduk had thought of everything.

Currently, the man was ecstatic, rapturous after seeing the explosion in St Peter's Square. He had screamed out when it happened, a euphoric moment that filled his body with joy. He'd fallen to his knees as if in worship and now couldn't take his eyes off the TV. There was a media camera focused, by chance, on St Peter's Basilica.

Marduk saw his attackers begin their assault.

Daga and Ivana had other urges. It was time to act on them. Daga drew Ivana to the back of the room and started whispering in her ear.

'This room is a kill zone,' he said. 'And that man will not come out of all this alive.'

'His plan's working.' Ivana looked towards Marduk.

'Yes, that's not the point. He's gone mad . . . well, even madder. Can't you see? The guy's totally off his head.'

Ivana watched. It did indeed seem that the sequence of events, the success of the attacks, had stretched Marduk's sanity to beyond breaking point. He was on his knees, hands on his head, chewing his lips until they bled. He held a radio in one hand, the bringer of death to some, a glass of sparkling champagne in the other. He cackled, he cheered, he laughed as if misery and blood and slaughter were the gods he worshipped.

'It's the end of the road for him,' Daga said. 'No matter how many casualties he causes, he can't possibly win this.'

Ivana squeezed his hand. 'Did he pay us our money?'

'Most of it, yes. Enough.'

'Then we should leave him to his butchery and go spread some of our own.'

Daga grinned. 'It should be prime pickings tonight,' he said. 'With the authorities engaged elsewhere. It gives us more scope to have more fun.'

'Then what are we waiting for?'

Without a word, they turned and walked away from Marduk, abandoning the mad monarch to his crazed plans, shedding any responsibilities that might tie them to him. They made sure their weapons were at hand as they approached the hotel room door.

'It feels . . . perfect,' Ivana said. 'We are walking into a city already floundering in death.'

'We will also make a mark,' Daga said.

Ivana opened the door and led the way out of Marduk's bedroom all the way down to the lobby below and then out into the street.

'Which way?' she said.

'I don't care,' Daga said. 'Just lead me to fresh blood.'

Chapter 43

Mason and his team ran towards the basilica's entrance after putting Mario Gambetti at their fore. The cardinal's face should be recognisable to the Swiss guards and should prevent any incidents of friendly fire. Of course, the team looked like civilians and so did the attackers, so things could still get messy. Mason had already noticed that the attackers had shrugged themselves into bullet-proof vests. And most of them were wearing backpacks.

He ran fast, not drawing his weapon yet. They approached the remaining Swiss guards, standing in a line across the steps that led to the front doors. Some were on one knee, others sheltering as best they could, but still exposed up there. Two more had already fallen. The attackers were sweeping across from Mason's left and were closing in quickly.

Gambetti cried out, 'Do not shoot us. I am Cardinal Gambetti and these men and women are here to help!'

That would have to be enough. Mason was thankful for the cardinal's bravery. Not every man of the cloth would have done that. The Swiss guards glanced at them as they tried to protect the doors to their magnificent church.

Gunfire rang around the square.

And then it got worse. Mason saw another wave of attackers running in from the same direction as the first. They had gathered outside the square with their backpacks and weapons and body armour and had outfitted themselves quickly. The police who had noticed them were now being gunned down.

Mason yelled out a warning and veered to his left. He drew his gun and started shooting as a wall of people ran at him. His team stood at his side. Bullets flew between them. Mason dropped to the floor, still firing, and pushed in another mag. They were too exposed. He scrambled back to the furthest arm of the colonnade, using it for cover. Behind him, the Swiss guards fought their attackers on the steps.

Bullets tore chunks out of the concrete above their heads. Mason couldn't fire blindly around the pillars. There was no telling where his bullets would end up. He crouched and waited for the gap to diminish.

Which it soon did. Mason already knew that the attackers were no special forces team or even a bunch of mercenaries. He could tell by the way they ran and held their weapons, by the way they conducted themselves. They weren't trained; they were civilians with guns. More of Marduk's so-called Faithful, perhaps. He ducked as bullets flew around the corner of the colonnade, but then heard running feet. He tripped the first man who appeared. This guy sprawled to the ground in front of those following, effectively bringing them down too. They were all running as fast as they could, their guns held out every which way and just firing off shots.

They weren't disciplined, weren't prepared or used to action like this. They went sprawling as they ran into each other.

Mason stepped around the corner, Roxy at his side. They fell into the heap of men and women and started clubbing heads with their weapons. When a gun rose near to them, they shot the owner. A fist struck Mason across the face. He fell to the side. He leaned on the man beneath him, grabbed another's wrist, and tried to subdue both. Roxy fired her weapon twice, bringing a man and a woman down.

Behind, Quaid, Hassell and Sally also had their guns drawn. Gambetti sheltered behind them, the steps to the basilica at his back. The Swiss guards were still fighting there, scattered. Mason concentrated on his own battle. Only half of the attackers had fallen in the scramble.

Mason struggled to subdue them all.

The man with the badly scarred face walked in the rear of the second wave. He was the most important, the man who would matter. His brain was filled with dark visions and hatred. He worshipped the Amori and longed for the old days, the days when he had fitted right in. Marduk promised a return to those days. All the scarred man had to do was . . . destroy the Vatican.

He moved with a purpose, fired up. His muscles ached with tension. He wore a large backpack but hadn't bothered with a Kevlar jacket. He didn't care one way or the other. He was a big man, stout of chest and of stomach, with arms that might have been an impressive size if they were made of anything other than flab. He lumbered along in the rear, but his position was not down to his size. It was because all the others – the doctors, the politician, the stay-at-home mums, the counsellors and the accountants – had to protect him. That was their job. He ran in their wake as best he could.

He carried the biggest backpack.

And when they reached the end of the long row of colonnades, he fell to one knee, unhooked his heavy backpack and deposited it on the ground. He unzipped it quickly, catching part of the material on the weapon inside.

When he saw it, he breathed deeply, happily.

So perfect.

It shone. It was 40 millimetres in diameter, 950 millimetres long and weighed around 6 kilograms. The end was flared. The scarred man had trouble extracting the weapon from the rucksack; it only just fit. When he had it lying on the ground, ready, he reached back into the rucksack to extract the smaller grenade.

This was 70 millimetres in diameter and weighed around 3.5 kilograms. It would travel out of the launcher at 115 metres per second. It would ignite after 10 metres and sustain flight for up to 500, but that wouldn't be necessary.

The RPG would make fine holes in the façade of St Peter's Basilica.

The scarred man quickly assembled the weapon and used the optical sights. The steel was cold in his hands and against his right cheek; the weapon balanced nicely on his shoulder. He was still situated at the back of the fighting pack. Nobody had even noticed him yet.

Which was the aim.

He settled, wondering if Marduk would be pleased, wondering if this blessed shot would bring about the hallowed resurgence of the Amori. Even if he didn't survive, the scarred man was at peace, knowing that he had done his part.

He was ready. He had a second grenade at his feet.

The scarred man pulled the trigger. Not having used an RPG before, he expected some recoil, as he'd seen with guns, but surprisingly there was none. The only feeling he experienced was a sudden lightness as the grenade left the tube.

That, and elation.

*

Mason heard the woosh and hiss of the RPG. Shock flooded his system. He hadn't heard that sound in years and had never expected to hear it here, not even on this day. He looked up, attention taken away from the man beneath him, just in time to see the grenade impact one of the basilica's front doors. What followed was a massive explosion and a spray of fire and a trembling of the ground. The detonation assaulted his ears. Deadly debris flew in all directions. The grenade blew the door off its hinges, destroying it and sending wreckage back into the basilica.

Mason's eyes flitted towards the source of the RPG.

Already, a big man was fitting a second grenade into a launcher. The weapon looked like a toy in his hands. Mason lined him up in the sights of his Glock and fired. The bullet took the man through the forehead, between the eyes. The man toppled over, and the RPG fell to the ground with him.

Instantly, one of his companions scrambled to pick up the weapon.

Mason shot him, too. He pulled away from where he was, extricating himself from the battle there, and dashed over to guard the fallen weapon. Behind him, smoke wreathed the front entrance to the basilica.

The Swiss guards were faltering on the steps, almost overrun. In the midst of it, but staying detached from the fighting, was Cardinal Gambetti. Mason respected the man for staying put, although his face was grey with fear. One of the Swiss guards remained close to him.

Mason stood his ground as another man ran for the grenade launcher. The man was too close to shoot. They traded blows, but the man was no fighter; he was no boxer either. Mason delivered a couple of body blows and then a devastating uppercut that laid him out cold. To the right now, Roxy and Hassell were struggling with men and women. Hassell was on the floor with another adversary. Sally had her gun drawn, but had not used it yet. Mason could see the indecision in her.

It was then that Mason saw something that sent a river of ice slithering down his spine.

They were coming from the right, two of them. Walking fast. They wore heavy jackets, and they were sweating. Two men, with their right hands hidden in their pockets, their thumbs on the buttons of detonators. Their eyes were wide and wild, their faces like alabaster. Two men who had one purpose: to walk out into the middle of St Peter's Square and cause mayhem.

The twin explosions rocked the air, shook the ground. Fire sheared up towards the sky. Debris flew for hundreds of yards in all directions. Mason fell to his knees, and not just because of the percussive blast. Even in Iraq, he hadn't seen this scale of mayhem.

And now came a third wave of attackers, all fully armed. There were too many now, Mason saw. They would overwhelm his team and the Swiss guards within minutes. Already, they were lucky they hadn't been winged by a stray bullet. Already, they were living on borrowed time.

Mason fixed another mag into his Glock. He could see the strain in the faces of the remaining Swiss guards as they sheltered behind bodies, behind a planter, behind a lone tree. He could see Cardinal Gambetti still standing tall, praying with his hands together. The priest did not falter.

Sudden shouts struck the air. Mason spun around. A stunning sight met his eyes. From the left, from the direction of the barracks, they came. Dozens of Swiss guards and gendarmes were flooding in from that direction, their guns held at shoulder height, their eyes steely with determination. Not just that, but Mason could see the cavalieré too, the special officers of the Vatican Gendarmerie, running in a stream alongside the regular guards. Like the cavalry, they swarmed towards the battle.

Galvanised, Mason swung back to the fight. He raised his weapon. The extra attackers were already here. A bullet flew past Mason's shoulder. He didn't back away from the fallen RPG. Roxy flung herself at three running men, bringing them all to the ground. Hassell and Quaid tangled with three more.

And it was then, right then, that Mason heard the desperate voice of Premo Conte.

'*Mason! Mason! They've caught Ivana! We need you to help with her now!*'

Mason whirled. Conte was almost in his face. 'What? How? Where?'

'No time,' Conte panted, holding a gun in one hand. 'She's three blocks away. Get there now. They're gonna interrogate her on the spot and you and your team might hear something invaluable. You guys know her and Daga as well as anyone.'

Three blocks? Mason could run it in minutes. At that moment, the cavalieré came rushing by and ploughed into the attackers. There was the sound of crushing bodies and gunshots and yelling and groaning, all echoing across the wide expanse of St Peter's Square.

Mason shouted to his colleagues. He yelled their names at the top of his voice, saw them disentangle themselves from the fight and come over, all looking bloody. He told them what Conte wanted.

'Fuck, yeah,' Roxy said. 'Let's interrogate that bitch right now.'

Around them, the battle raged. Mason had never seen anything so surreal. Conte gave them an address and then rushed off into the fight. The Swiss guards on the steps took a slight breather as their reinforcements arrived in the form of gendarmes. There was a heart-stopping moment when three attackers broke through and raced for the front doors of the basilica but, in that moment, Cardinal Gambetti read their intentions. He roared, picked up a weapon, and fired before they even reached the steps.

Mason had never seen anything like it.

He turned and viewed the quieter span of St Peter's Square.

'Ivana,' he said. 'This is our last chance to stop all this.'

Chapter 44

Cassadaga and Ivana chose to take advantage of the night's distractions to cause their own brand of mayhem elsewhere. They left the lunatic, Marduk, to his own machinations and exited the hotel. It was only when they were outside that they turned to each other, their faces swept by the cool wind and spattered by a faint drizzle, to make the mutually beneficial decision on their destination.

'What do you fancy?' Daga asked. 'Anything special? Indian? Italian? Chinese?'

Ivana's nostrils flared at the thought of the kill. 'Oh, how about an eclectic mix?' she said. 'What do you get in a pub these days?'

Daga started walking. 'Warm bodies,' he said. 'Warm bodies and lots of blood.'

They were euphoric. Marduk's grisly mayhem had whetted their appetites for more, for a hugely personal 'hands-on' experience. Daga knew want and need were overcoming caution and vigilance, but he didn't care. The police had their hands full tonight.

And he and Ivana would be through the pub in a matter of minutes.

Leaving something crimson and fantastic in their wake.

They would walk the slick streets and find a pub at random. It was all about fate now, especially for the soon-to-be victims. It was about being in the wrong place at the wrong time: that different corner turned where you went one way instead of another, that whim that took you in a different direction, that last-minute phone call or argument that delayed you. Those who waited for death in the pub right now were there through destiny, luck, and providence.

Daga passed the first pub with its dour façade and bright lights, the smell of beer pouring through its open front door, and turned to Ivana. 'What do you think?'

She snapped her fingers as she chose on a whim. 'Move on to the next.'

If they'd known, everyone crammed inside would have uttered a prayer of relief.

Daga grinned, loving the fact that he held the power of life and death in his hands. He knew Ivana did, too. They were kindred spirits, soulmates in murder, and would never be separated. They would kill together for ever.

His own reputation was already fearsome enough. Stories had accumulated around him. He was invincible, could kill you in under a second. He was older than the grave and bathed in blood and came every ten years to rip the hearts out of women and children.

Great myths, he thought.

On to the next pub. Daga didn't like the look of this one. It was too small. They needed at least a decent-sized space to work their magic. Around them, what night life there was still left in Rome and not in pubs wandered the street, most of them looking shell-shocked. Why they weren't all running home as a terrorist incident unfolded, Daga did not know. He guessed the general public had become a little immune to tragedy and terror these last few years. It was all they ever saw on their smartphones and tablets and televisions. Thrust into their faces every day, every night. They were dulled to it, the impact lost through constant bombardment. That was why they still packed the pubs as the Vatican quavered in fear. They wanted to watch it together on TV.

Daga stopped. Ivana was to his right and linked his arm. A pub sat on their left, double doors open invitingly. It looked quieter than the other two, as if some patrons had left sensibly. But, through the front windows, Daga could see several dozen people that were still inside.

'Perfect,' Ivana said.

'It will be.' Daga smiled.

There was a doorman. Daga's right hand poised over the hilt of his knife. If the man threatened to search them, he would be the first to die. But the doorman, looking bored, barely glanced at them. Daga climbed three steps to reach the doors and then walked inside. Ivana was a step behind him.

The noise of conversation met his ears, the yawping of a few drunks in the corners, the quiet music in the background. A barman and woman stood serving drinks to patrons lined up at the bar. There was room to walk between tables.

Ivana looked at the line-up along the bar. 'I can work there,' she said.

Daga chose a path between tables where he could

move quickly and efficiently. 'I'll see you near the back doors,' he said.

'I'll watch your progress,' she said.

Daga slipped his knife free.

Together, they started work, Daga's head swimming with visions of blood. He stalked to the nearest table, thrust out and stabbed a man in the neck. A woman sitting next to him received a chest wound. The man across from her, eyes wide, rooted to the spot, was caught across the throat by a wide slash. The woman seated next to him managed half a scream before Daga severed her windpipe.

He leapt to the next table, people too caught up in their conversations to notice the swift demon in their midst. They were laughing, heads thrown back, staring at their partners or at their companions' partners, drinking from their half-empty glasses. They saw no threat in their vicinity and some probably didn't even know what was happening at the Vatican.

It all gave Daga the time he needed.

To his left, Ivana was treating those lined up at the bar like a buffet line. She walked down them, stabbing three times into each back, aiming for arteries and kidneys and seeing the start of the blood flow before she moved on to the next in line. Some reared, others cried out suddenly and reached for their wounds, others grunted and fell forwards, already dying. One man just collapsed to the floor. She delighted in rushing along the line.

Daga reached his third table. A quick look back showed the fruits of his labour: people dead and dying, lying slumped next to their favourite drinks. He'd spilled their blood in less than a minute, but even so, people had seen.

There was something running through the crowd in the bar now, something raw and terrified and painful that manifested like a living thing. It was the knowledge that there was a killer in their midst, and that only a few people had noticed. It was these people who raised the alarm, though, starting to shout and scream and to yell out warnings. Daga loved the transformation from happiness to terror; he loved that moment his prey realised it was in deadly peril.

The downside was that his death-dealing was almost at an end. For now.

The third table was aware of him coming at them. A man rose, pint glass in hand. Another threw a shot glass at Daga's head, soaking him. The women were screaming, though one was reaching for her handbag as if she had a weapon inside.

Maybe she did.

Daga hadn't lived this long by taking unnecessary risks. He backed off quickly and looked for Ivana. His knife dripped red at his side, spattering the floor. Ivana was halfway along the line at the bar, thrusting and stabbing, and Daga now started towards her. Another table was in his way. He slashed out as he passed, injuring a man and a woman.

Finally, a man rose to confront him. Daga smiled grimly. The guy was wide and beefy, wearing a black leather jacket. His scarred face looked like it had been in a few fights before. Daga didn't hesitate. He grasped his knife in the underhand position as he'd been originally taught and stepped in to the guy, slashing left and right. His opponent tried to block, tried to grab his wrists, but he was too slow. You should never mess with a knife. Daga opened up his chest and then his right cheek and let him sink to the floor.

He didn't have a lot of time.

But he had bathed in blood, in terror, in dominance, and that was good. He was a dozen steps from Ivana when it happened.

One second, she was stabbing happily, her blade thrusting in and out of soft flesh, the next he thought the screams and yells that were filling the pub must have alerted someone. Two men turned at the end of the bar. They saw what Ivana was doing and took action. Daga immediately recognised military trained men and felt a chill in his heart.

Between them, the pub's patrons had risen to their feet, getting in the way. Daga could not reach Ivana.

She hadn't seen the two guys either. She was happily centred on her next victim. Daga yelled out a warning, but it was lost in the din, the din he'd helped to create. He looked around. People were pointing at him, yelling. Some had mobile phones to their ears. The bar staff were on their phones. People had slumped to the floor everywhere and there was the fresh, coppery scent of blood in the air.

Daga viewed the scene as dispassionately as he could. The question was – could Ivana take out the two grunts? They came at her now, and Ivana saw them out of the corner of her eye. She stepped back, but they were already on her, one man grabbing her left arm, the other her right. They bunched their free hands into fists and slammed them point-blank into her face. Ivana's nose exploded. The next punches were at her ribs, and even from here, Daga could hear breaking bones.

Ivana slumped, but she fought hard.

She twisted and pulled the knife free. She caught an attacker across the left bicep, making him yelp, and then slashed at the other. He twisted her arm, breaking it. Ivana yelled out in pain. Daga could have kept going; he could have fought his way through the crowd and confronted the men, but already he could see that Ivana had lost. She was falling to her knees. Daga was twenty feet away from her and stuck behind at least a dozen individuals.

But the way to the pub's rear door was wide open.

He despaired. He couldn't lose his soulmate. His companion in blood. But Ivana was lost; she was lost already. The grunts had her. They had already disarmed her. Daga could hear sirens approaching. He could see lights flashing in the windows. Damn it, if the cops hadn't committed every resource to the Vatican. Damn them to hell. Daga cut quickly to his right, pocketing the knife and pushing through a small crowd. He saw the rear of the pub. He saw the fire exit door back there. A few people sat next to it and looked as if they were preparing to bolt. That suited Daga. The more people fleeing this pub, the better.

He pushed his way over to them, yelled out a warning, told them to run. One man pushed the bar down on the fire exit door and fled. A woman followed him. Daga followed them, rushing out into the night. Cold air struck his face. His hands dripped blood, as did the sleeves of his jacket, but it all just looked black in the darkness. Nobody could tell. He ran with a group of five, staying close. He ran into the darkness of an alley that stretched along the back of the pub and other establishments.

But Cassadaga didn't run far.

Instinctively, he knew what would happen.

It wouldn't take long before someone recognised Ivana, some local cop who was good with faces. It wouldn't take long before they connected her presence to Marduk. And Daga knew exactly what would happen then.

The cops needed Marduk.

Daga was way ahead of them and needed to stay that way.

Carefully, he manoeuvred his way through growing throngs of people back to the scene.

Chapter 45

Mason's veins filled with fire. He was fervent, bubbling over with purpose. The attack on the Vatican was still ongoing. He and his team, forced to leave it behind, to leave the valiant Swiss guards, gendarmes and cavalieré and Cardinal Gambetti behind, had raced across the length of St Peter's Square, holstering their weapons, with a gendarme among them. Conte had given the gendarme an order, to vouch for Premo Conte's authority in questioning Ivana. He would push for Mason and the others to be allowed to interrogate the prisoner. Of course, the question of Conte's authority in Rome was a grey and problematic prospect.

But Ivana had knowledge about the ongoing terrorist attack. Surely common sense would prevail.

The cops on site knew that. They had been told to wait the ten minutes it would take Mason and his team to get there. Already, in his head, Mason was forming the questions he would ask.

The early night air, filled with drizzle, surrounded them and kept them cool. It was welcome. Mason ran through the growing darkness. They crossed streets, crossed roads, pushed through crowds of onlookers with their phones out, each one trying to capture something out of the ordinary whilst ignoring the police advice to move away, to go home, to take care of their own lives. Mason pushed past them, following the gendarme, who had directions to where they were holding Ivana.

It was a narrow street with parked cars on both sides. They could already see the site of the mayhem because a large crowd had gathered outside. Onlookers were blocking the street and the pavement, making Mason force his way through.

They reached the police cordon.

The gendarme pushed underneath the yellow tape, turning and waving Mason and the others along with him. They urged the first police officer to meet them to go grab a supervisor. The supervisor was told to get hold of the main boss on site. The gendarme produced a note written by Premo Conte and then dispensed some knowledge – he told them all about the part Mason and his team were playing in tonight's madness, including that they worked directly for the Vatican Cavalieré.

'I am Chief Inspector Luca Esposito,' the site boss said in English. 'Come with me.'

Mason followed in Esposito's footsteps. The chief inspector was a tall, spare man whose jacket appeared to be too short for him, whose trousers looked too tight. He was one of those people who couldn't get anything to fit right off the shelves and didn't earn enough to have everything made bespoke. His fingers were long and currently resting on the handle of the gun that was thrust into his belt.

Esposito led them to another man. 'Inspector,' he said. 'Tell them what we have. In English.'

'Two local men captured this woman in the bar of this pub.' The inspector gestured over his right shoulder. 'Overpowered her. She went on a killing spree inside, murdering at least three people and injuring many others before being stopped. She won't talk. We used facial recognition and have linked her to many crimes, including the escape from prison recently of the terrorist Marduk, who's linked to tonight's attacks on Vatican City. We put the word out hoping she may have information that someone might be able to use.'

'Thanks for your cooperation.' The gendarme again introduced Mason and his team, asking for the chief inspector's indulgence for a few minutes.

'You want me to let them interrogate her?' Esposito sounded dubious.

'You are interrogating here right now, are you not? Right here, in the street, surrounded by all these people.'

'If the bitch has information that can stop the Vatican attacks,' Esposito said, 'we will use all means to uncover it.'

'We know her,' Mason said. 'We've fought against her before.'

'Did you find Cassadaga?' Quaid asked.

The chief inspector stared at him. 'We know of this mythical killer she runs with. He is also in the surveillance videos. No apprehensions yet. It is only a matter of time.'

Mason cast his eyes across the crowd, searching for a murderer. 'He won't be far away. He and Ivana are inseparable.'

'He will want her back,' Roxy said.

The chief inspector looked wary. 'If I were him, I'd be dozens of miles from here by now.'

'Then you don't know Daga, or Ivana,' Mason said. 'Please let us talk to her.' His tone constrained by the pressure that was on him, the knowledge that the Vatican guards were still fighting to protect the building and their lives, the knowledge that every second counted, the knowledge that Daga couldn't be too far away and might act at any moment. 'Please,' he repeated.

'It can't hurt,' Esposito said, face grim. 'She's a murderer. Hasn't spoken a word yet. Despite . . . our pressure.'

Mason followed the chief inspector quickly around the side of a police van so that they were out of sight of the crowd. The pub in front of them had windows through which they could see many cops and plain-clothes detectives working. He wiped the still-falling moisture from his face and turned to the van.

Esposito slid the side door open.

Ivana sat inside, her face bloody, her hands clasped together before her in handcuffs. She was leaning forward and staring at the floor, but looked up when the door opened. She seemed surprised to see them.

'Joe Mason,' she said.

Esposito shook his head, clearly bemused that the first words out of her had come after the appearance of the newcomers. Mason stepped up into the van and saw two armed officers seated to the right, both with their guns drawn.

'How hard have you interrogated her?' Roxy asked.

'We asked questions,' Esposito said. 'She has broken ribs, arm and nose. We haven't allowed her any painkillers.'

Roxy glared at him. 'Painkillers? Damn, dude, is that it? This woman is one of the worst serial killers in

Europe's history. She has information on an ongoing terrorist incident, and you've denied her *painkillers*? Wow, that's just great.'

Mason crouched in front of Ivana. 'For now,' he said, 'we don't care about you. Not in this moment. We don't care about Daga. We just want Marduk. Where is he?'

'I don't know any Marduk,' Ivana answered, her broad shoulders moving from side to side, her accent thick.

Mason leaned closer. He could see her broken nose, her hanging arm, the way she winced because of the pain in her ribs. He knew she didn't want to move, not even a millimetre. 'Tell me what we need to know,' he tried again.

'You can't hurt me,' she said, sneering.

Mason moved aside as Roxy entered the van. 'No, but I can,' she said and grabbed hold of Ivana's good arm, twisting it slightly. 'This is a friendly warning,' she said and then yanked on the arm. Ivana's face went slack, and she cried out in pain.

'That was your good arm,' Roxy said. 'Just a little tug. I can do far worse.'

Mason slid the van door closed behind them, shutting out Esposito. The last he saw of the man's face, Esposito looked glad to be out of it.

'Where is Marduk?' he asked again.

To his right, the local cops sat in silence. They knew exactly what Ivana had done and what she was capable of. Mason hated Roxy taking the lead like this – it could set her recovery back if she reverted to her old ways – but he knew she was the best person for the job.

'Daga will come for me,' Ivana said.

Mason believed it. He was waiting for it. Daga and Ivana were far too intertwined to be dealt with singly.

He tried to hide his revulsion as he thought about them murdering Cardinal Vallini, and of all the other things they'd done during the last few months.

'If Daga comes, he will die,' Roxy said.

'Daga?' She chortled. 'You can't kill Daga. The man's immortal. A myth made flesh. When he comes for me, you will wish you were already dead.'

'In that case, tell us what we want to know,' Roxy said. 'It can't hurt.'

'Speaking to you is like having my wrists dragged along cut glass,' Ivana spat. 'You disgust me.'

Mason felt shock, despite himself. Hearing words that actually defined this woman, hearing them thrust out of her own mouth against him, was both confusing and surprising. He didn't know quite how to respond, so spent a few moments in silence. Ivana was going to have to be induced.

Roxy was way ahead of him. Her fist shot out, smashing Ivana in her already broken nose. Mason understood that the punch was the least cruel of the punishments Roxy could have doled out and understood why she chose it.

Ivana bellowed and tried to bring her hands up to her face, but the cuffs attached to the seat stopped her. Her head rocked back as more blood flowed.

'Bitch,' she said, her voice unnatural with pain. 'You will pay for that.'

'You get another every time you don't answer our questions,' Roxy said, now leaning forward and grabbing Ivana's throat. She bunched her fist again.

Mason said, 'Where is Marduk?'

'Fuck you.'

Roxy punched her again. This time Ivana's head flew back. She screwed her face up and screamed, but not just in pain. There was anger there too, frustration and hatred and immense disappointment that she had let herself get caught. Her eyes brimmed with fury. 'You will get nothing from me.'

Her voice sounded nasal, deep. Roxy didn't hesitate to punch her again, although Mason could see the American's reluctance to do so. He put a hand on her arm, staying the next punch.

'We'll give you a minute,' he said. 'Consider your next answer carefully.'

Esposito was banging on the van's door. Mason slid it open to see the chief inspector's face along with his colleagues' all looking up expectantly. The chief inspector was practically gnashing his teeth.

'What do you have?' he asked.

'We've barely started,' Mason said, mostly for the benefit of Ivana. He quickly slid the door closed again and turned to the captive.

'Same question,' he said.

This time, to mix it up, Roxy didn't even wait for a reply. They had to be constantly on top of Ivana, showing her they not only meant business but that there would be no let-up. She punched Ivana as her mouth opened, tearing her own knuckles in the process. Ivana grunted and spat blood.

'You don't have long,' Mason said. 'From here on in, it's just gonna get worse.'

'There is nothing you can do,' Ivana said.

'It's not Daga we want. It's Marduk,' Roxy pointed out.

Ivana stared at her, blinking.

'Surely Marduk can't be that hard to give up. You did it before, at the African HQ, remember? You and Daga just ran away. Why can't you give him up this time?'

Ivana frowned, as if the thought had only just occurred to her. She licked the blood from her lips. 'But what do I get if I give him up?' she said.

What could they actually offer her? Ivana had committed some of the worst crimes imaginable. Mason was in no mind to offer her any leniency and, of course, he had no jurisdiction anywhere.

'What do I get?' Ivana hissed.

Mason opened his mouth to reply, but then a terrifying scream sounded from outside the van.

Ivana grinned.

Chapter 46

Cassadaga infiltrated the crowd surrounding the police vans that were stationed outside the pub he'd just helped Ivana run amok in. The blood hadn't yet dried on his hands and sleeves. It was still tacky, still the blood of someone who had, hopefully, died at his hands. He trod warily, keeping his head down and his hands in his pockets. He started on the edge of the sizeable crowd that was gathering around the scene. To begin with, he was behind them all, looking at the backs of a hundred heads, but then he pushed through them. Oh, it was such a pleasure and a pain. The killer was in their midst. How he could have so easily slipped out his knife and started slashing arteries, how he could have sunk his blade into their ribs, their kidneys, their throats. The opportunity sang to him. It called him like a siren's song. But Daga clenched his teeth and held back. The only thing more important to him at the moment than blood-letting was Ivana.

And Ivana was sitting in that middle van, he knew.

Daga counted the cops. He saw five ranged around

the perimeter, watching the crowd, an unknown quantity in the vans and at least a dozen in the pub. There were crime scene cops and normal cops and the higher-ups all represented. Daga didn't look too closely; he stayed flitting among the crowd, finding the taller people and using them as cover. He fought to keep his true desires hidden, concealed from the masses at least this time. He ran his fingers along the shape of his knife beneath his clothing. He could feel the sharp blade and knew exactly what he wanted to do with it.

And then, as he struggled with a decision on what to do, on how to free Ivana, everything changed. Before Daga's stunned eyes, one of the people he wanted to kill most in all the world turned up.

Joe Mason.

And with him, his colleagues.

Daga watched, his eyes like black lasers. He saw Mason converse with a cop who appeared to be in charge, saw the whole group traipse up to the van where Ivana was being held, and then saw nothing more. They were all hidden around the other side, but the meaning was obvious. Mason was going to try to get something out of Ivana, and Daga knew exactly what it was.

He wondered. What if . . .

. . . what if . . .

No. They wouldn't agree to it.

Ivana for Marduk.

Maybe they would.

Daga could hear gunfire echoing from St Peter's Square even now. He knew what Marduk was sending against them and, even though Marduk would eventually lose, the authorities didn't know that. Shit, even Marduk didn't know that. Or didn't want to believe that he just didn't have enough resources to take on the Vatican and Rome's police forces. But he would do a lot of damage in the process.

Daga could offer to help stop all that. Would the cops give him and Ivana an even chance?

No way.

Even considering it was ridiculous. But he didn't want to continue without Ivana. They were joined at the hip, inseparable. Over the last few months, she had got under his skin so much that she had become an extension of him. He didn't work as well without her.

What to do?

Daga had killed and killed. It was his destiny, his way of living. Death was a lifestyle. Perhaps . . . the time had come to try something else.

Daga hesitated. This was world changing for him. Was he really going to negotiate with the cops for Ivana's release?

You have to.

The simple answer was: he couldn't carry on without her. Daga took a deep breath, steeled every nerve in his body, and pushed purposefully through the crowd. He knew both he and Ivana had a wealth of information to offer and that they could stop the attacks with just a few words, with the location of Marduk's hotel. They had an awful lot to offer. It would be a shame not to get to kill Joe Mason, but maybe that could come later.

Daga reached the edge of the crowd. He stood behind a tall, wide man still not one hundred per cent committed. The van was right before him, just twenty strides away. Ivana would be inside, just on the other side of that thin metal sheeting, and she would be thinking of him, consoling herself with remembered bloody deeds. He knew it. They were soulmates.

Having decided to give up, to bargain for Ivana's release, Daga suddenly remembered why he had been born. He remembered everything he'd done ten years before he met Ivana. The thrill of a messy kill, the blood-lust, was what he remembered. He knew, in that moment, what kind of man he was.

Blood before dishonour. Death before surrender.

Daga's vision swam red; it swam with visions of slaughter. He couldn't give that up. It was overwhelming. He needed to act on it now, right now. He drew his knife and stuck it in the spine of the big man concealing him. He whirled to the left and slashed at a woman's arm before racing for the yellow tape that cordoned the crime scene off.

A woman screamed.

Daga fell on top of the first police officer.

Chapter 47

Hearing the scream, Mason shot to his feet. Roxy was already sliding the door open. Ivana was chuckling softly.

'Now you will reap hell,' she said. 'At least *I* am not afraid of the Devil.'

Mason followed Roxy out of the van. Hassell, Quaid and Sally were nowhere in sight. There were cops disappearing around the front. Mason could hear yelling and grunts of pain coming from the other side of the van. He drew his gun.

Together, he and Roxy sprinted around the front.

A terrifying sight met their eyes. Mason saw the heads and shoulders of several cops, maybe six or eight. Quaid and Hassell were standing on the fringes of the group. Something was moving in their midst, something incredibly fast. Mason saw glimpses of it, a head there, a shoulder, a body . . .

. . . a wraith.

At least I am not afraid of the Devil.

Cops were falling. Mason pocketed his gun. He couldn't use it here because of the crowd gathered all around.

Daga would know that. He pushed forward, pushed past Hassell and Quaid and two officers. He had Roxy at his side and was grateful for it. Who could want for more? The shape ahead shifted from side to side and cops fell left and right, some clutching their chests, others at their throats. Arterial blood painted the air.

And then Mason was face to face with the Devil itself.

Cassadaga was a portrait in slaughter. Blood dripped down his face, his chest, his trousers. His face was livid, his eyes as big as mini suns and just as bright. This was Daga in his element, in all his terrible glory. When he saw Mason, he paused.

'You,' he said.

Mason took the only advantage he could think of. He didn't stop to talk. He lunged at Daga, going for the wrist that held the knife. His fingers clamped hold of it and slipped off because of the blood. Daga slid to the side and lunged. The blade thrust past Mason's ribs, but only by its own width. Daga threw a punch. Mason was ready for it and welcomed it. Punches he could deal with. He blocked it and stepped in, again targeting the knife arm. He grabbed it, ducked underneath and tried to twist it behind Daga's back, but the thief was ready, spinning and moving with Mason.

Right then, Roxy made her move.

She ran and barged into Daga, knocking him right off his feet.

'I'm nothing if not a blunt instrument,' she said.

Daga hit the tarmac. Mason tried to jump on the man's chest, but he was incredibly quick. Mason had never seen anything this quick. By the time his knees struck the tarmac, Daga had rolled out of the way and was leaping to his feet, blade already thrusting. Mason yelled out in pain when the edge slashed across his left bicep, cutting deep. He couldn't help but flinch backwards.

Daga attacked. He would have killed Mason right then but for Roxy's intervention. She hit the thief again, barrelling into his left side and sending him sprawling back to the ground. Daga might be quick, but Roxy was just as fast. Before the thief could move, she was stamping on the back of his thigh and then raised another boot to bring it down onto his spine.

Daga rolled. He swept the knife in an arc. It sliced through Roxy's boot and parted her flesh. She didn't react; it was as if she didn't feel the pain. She brought the boot down anyway, but Daga deflected most of the blow with one hand, sending it to the right of his body.

Mason was gripping his bicep, blood squeezing through his fingers. He had to help Roxy now, push their advantage whilst Daga was on the back foot, and he didn't flinch. He wasn't afraid of the Devil either. All around them cops were gathering, some with guns drawn even though they couldn't use them. Daga scrambled backwards.

'I will kill you all,' he said.

But Roxy was already climbing on top of him. It wasn't pretty, but she was effective and that was how she'd been taught. Mason too. He flung himself to the ground and targeted Daga's legs, punching as hard as he could into the meat of the man's thighs. Roxy hit his midriff. Daga resisted as much as he could but was unable not to react to the punishment. He thrust his knife down at the top of Roxy's head.

She rolled.

Daga overextended. Mason grabbed his wrist and broke it easily. The knife slipped into Daga's lap. The thief ignored the broken wrist and staggered to his feet.

Roxy bowled into his chest, knocking him flying, the two of them slamming into the side of the van, Daga's head hitting first. Daga let out a yell of pain and looked suddenly woozy. Roxy made sure of it by punching him in the face.

To compound it, Mason stepped up and did the same. Roxy grabbed Daga by the throat and held him in place as his legs buckled. Mason looked around.

'Cuffs,' he said.

Right then, there was a terrible yell, something born of pain and murder and the end of something raw and incredible. Mason whirled, thinking, *what now?* But he should have known.

It was a nightmare made of flesh.

It was Ivana, still cuffed, but crazy. Ivana was a broad-shouldered, strong woman and running at speed, screaming at the top of her voice. Her hair flew in contrails behind her. She barged first one cop out of the way and then another, a killing machine in full flow. She was running too fast, or so Mason thought. She appeared to stumble, fall to her knees, but he saw she was only scooping up a fallen gun. Ivana grabbed it with both hands and then rose and continued her run. The gun waved in his face.

Ivana fired. Bullets flew to either side of Mason's head, thudding into the side of the van. They missed him and they missed Roxy and Daga, passing to left and right. By then, Ivana was just feet from Mason.

He ducked, heaved, and threw her right over the top of him. She sailed through the air, struck the van in the wake of the bullets, and slithered to the ground. But she wasn't done. She had a fire in her that was born of desperation and the endgame. She knew this was her limit. Ivana barely landed on the ground before flinging herself at Mason and trying to wrap her cuffed hands around his neck.

'She's gone berserk,' Roxy said. 'You'll need a bullet to stop her.'

Now Daga was struggling too. He was feeding off his companion, feeling the same fury, the same will to go down in blood and flames. He flung his head back, hit Roxy's nose, and turned around. He kneed her in the stomach and grabbed her throat with his good hand.

Mason knew the only way to disable Ivana was to target her most vulnerable areas. He took punishment from her, took the blows and the bruising attacks, waiting for that one opportunity. It came within seconds. Her eyes were exposed, her nose too. He jabbed stiffened fingers into her eyes, punched her throat and saw her stop fighting. It was as if he'd put her on pause. Her whole body stiffened and then she slumped, retching. Mason drove her face into the ground.

It was still far from over.

Roxy regained control of Daga. The cops were pressing in, guns drawn, wanting nothing more than to shoot Daga in the face and avenge their dead colleagues. Mason saw a chance to let them do just that.

He hauled Ivana to her feet. He threw her up against the side of the van. And then he turned to Roxy.

'Kill Daga,' he said.

Ivana's eyes flew open. To be fair, so did Roxy's. She stared at Mason. 'Do you know what you're asking me to do?'

It wasn't just the instruction, he knew; it was what it would cost her personally.

He nodded. 'Kill Daga. Just end that motherfucker's life.'

Roxy frowned and closed her eyes, as if steeling herself, as if trying to decide whether to follow Mason's order. The surrounding cops didn't move; they watched. Their bulk shielded everything from the crowd.

'Kill Daga,' Mason repeated.

Roxy grabbed Daga's own discarded knife. She held it in one hand, made sure Daga couldn't move, and then plunged the knife into his heart.

'NO!' Ivana screamed.

Roxy arrested her plunging attack at the very last instant.

'Where's Marduk?' Mason said once more.

'I'll tell you, I'll tell you,' Ivana sobbed. 'Just please don't kill him. Don't hurt him. I couldn't bear the thought . . .'

Mason heard Daga's gasp as Roxy pierced his breast with the tip of her knife.

'We're waiting,' he said.

Chapter 48

The attacks were continuing. The Vatican was under siege. The streets of Rome ran red. Mason and his team raced through the darkness towards Marduk's hotel. How much did he know? How much could he see? They couldn't tell, but they knew they were going to stop this even if they had to rip his heart out.

The car stopped outside the hotel. Mason saw the shadow of the Colosseum some way off to their right. There were no tourists out tonight, not anymore. The streets of Rome were wet and cold and empty.

Mason stepped out of the car, followed by his team. A group of five cavalieré exited a following car, carrying their guns openly. As a team, the group ran towards the hotel's lobby.

'Two men, stay here,' their captain said.

Mason pushed into the lobby. They made their way over to the front desk and showed credentials. The manager was waiting for them, having been previously alerted by Premo Conte. The computer screen before him was immediately turned towards them. It showed Marduk's photo and, next to it, a room number.

They had him.

They took the elevator. It was a strange, silent journey. Mason just wanted the damn thing to hurry. It deposited them on the third floor. They all squeezed out and into the corridor and started making their way to Marduk's room.

Mason was counting. It had only been minutes since they'd pulled up. Mason could hear TVs blaring through the doors they passed, all tuned to the media coverage of St Peter's Square. It must feel surreal to the watchers.

Halfway up the corridor they came to Marduk's room. Mason stood aside as the cavalieré prepared to breach. They counted to three and then forced their way into the room, smashing the door back against the interior wall. They flooded inside, yelling at the tops of their voices – a shock-and-awe attack. They had their weapons aimed and were happily prepared to use them. Mason and the others followed the contingent of cavalieré.

At first, Mason saw only the backs of the soldiers. But, as he moved further in, he got a feel for Marduk's lifestyle. The opulence. The richness that he loved to surround himself with. All in the name of the Amori, Mason thought drily.

There was an enormous bed, a dressing room, and a sitting room. There was a double-size bathroom, a grand shower and lots of gold-coloured furnishings. Their boots sank into the deep pile carpet.

But there was no Marduk.

Mason jabbed at his Bluetooth earpiece. 'Not here,' he said. 'Do you have anything outside?'

Inside, he was cursing, screaming with anger. How the hell had Marduk slipped away? As they moved further into the room and, in particular, the sitting room, they saw why.

'He has quite the array,' Sally said. 'Monitors. Laptops. Cameras.'

Mason could see many screens set up across two desks and even resting on a couch. Some showed the battle in St Peter's through what could only be a body cam. The image was moving in time to a person's body. Others showed points of view that could only originate from fixed cameras. Two of those views were of the lobby downstairs and the steps outside the hotel.

'Bastard saw us coming,' Quaid said heavily.

Mason held his tongue. Among the laptops were dozens of mobile phones, all cheap plastic burners. There were also three handheld radios. As the cavalieré started talking, Mason held up a hand and put a finger to his lips.

'Outside.' He beckoned them.

Once outside the room, he spoke up. 'Those phones,' he said. 'The radios. Clearly, it's how Marduk is communicating with his Faithful in the field, the attackers. In his hurry, he left them behind and they're probably still active.'

'But where did he go?' Hassell was still searching the room.

'One thing at a time,' Mason said. 'I think, if the radios and phones are still active, we can end this attack. Or . . .' he added, 'at least try.'

'How?' a man asked.

'Simple,' Mason said. He walked back into the room, scooped up a radio, and pressed the side button. He spoke into it clearly. 'End attack. It's finished.'

He didn't wait for a reply. He picked up the next radio and repeated his words. Soon, the cavalieré were picking up all the phones and doing the same thing. It took them just a few minutes to speak into all the phones, and all the while, they were staring at the screens.

It didn't happen at once. First one body cam showed a man lowering himself as if falling to his knees and then placing a gun before him. Another body cam showed a man suddenly turning from the fight and fleeing in the other direction, running at speed. Seconds later he fell, cut down, probably by a bullet. Still another body cam saw a man raising his hands and waiting as a Swiss guard approached. The cavalieré breathed sighs of relief, and one man cheered.

'It's over,' another breathed.

Not even close, Mason thought. Where was Marduk?

They returned to the main room. Seconds later, their comms crackled into life. 'We might have him,' one man stationed at the front of the hotel said. 'Taxi driver reports seeing a man with a gun running for the Colosseum just a few minutes ago.'

'Was he limping?' Mason asked.

'As a matter of fact, he probably was,' the answer came. 'The taxi driver said "staggering". The report was quite clear.'

Mason wasted no time. If Marduk was headed for the Colosseum, then they had to be hard on his tail. They raced out of the room, hit the stairs, and pounded down them. Roxy was a step behind, the others just a step behind her. They still had their guns drawn. They hit the lobby and dashed across, pushing through the entrance doors. They flew down the steps and started running across the wide road.

The Colosseum stood ahead in shadow and darkness, draped in history, the largest amphitheatre ever built. Mason could see dozens of burnished windows glowing in the dark, the upper attic hidden by the black of night. Mason rushed across the quiet road to find an entrance.

There were eight people with him, two men left back at the hotel. They found an entrance and used lock picks to open the padlock. Clearly, Marduk had found another way in. One of the cavalieré questioned why Marduk would come here.

'A lot of entrances and exits,' Hassell said. 'I've used it myself once before. Marduk's looking to flee.'

The special officers gave Hassell an odd look, but let it go. They pushed their way through a creaking iron gate. Inside, they split up, hoping to cover more ground and take some of the advantage away from the madman.

Mason crept through the dark on the other side of the wall. Some parts of the interior were illuminated; others lay in total darkness. He had Sally at his side.

'Stay low,' he said. 'Don't forget, he has a gun. Assume he wants to use it. He'll be moving fast, or at least as fast as he can.'

They swept through the darkness, clearing space after space, hugging the interior wall because it cast a gigantic shadow and helped conceal them. They stopped and listened often. Because they were looking for them, they could see the shadowy shapes of their companions clearing other areas. It was a fast, slick undertaking. They all moved through the interior of the Colosseum without slowing down.

Mason saw the shadow staggering ahead and knew it had to be Marduk. He couldn't see the man clearly, didn't know for certain, but it was the awkward gait, the lopsided limping pace that the shadow used to slip through the night. The shadow headed for the Colosseum's farthest exit.

Mason's heart leapt. He made no noise. He was that soldier again, surrounded by danger. Survival depended on stealth. He glided between shadows, closing the gap relentlessly. Marduk was intent on reaching that far exit, more focused it seemed the closer he came. Mason turned to Sally.

'Stay behind me,' he said. 'I need to get as close to him as possible without sound.'

It was all muscle memory. It was training, ingrained within him. He flitted through the night, closing in on Marduk with every step, now the vengeful wraith himself, intent on stopping his intended target. How close could he get? His gun was drawn, but he wouldn't just shoot Marduk in the back. He should . . . but he wouldn't.

Marduk reached the far wall and started heading for the nearest exit. The only time he looked back, Mason was luckily wreathed in deep shadow. Mason was just ten steps away. He took a quick glance around, saw nobody beside him. Marduk lurched faster, the gun at his side passing between light and dark.

Mason moved to within three feet.

'Stop,' he said. 'Drop the gun.'

Marduk jerked as if he'd been electrocuted. He didn't turn around, just pulled up. He raised his head. 'Is that you, Joe Mason?'

'Drop it. I have a gun and would love to shoot you.'

'So we meet again. Old antagonists reunited. You've shot me before, but I don't die that easily.'

And Marduk turned slowly until he faced Mason. The gun, held low in his right hand, pointed at the ground.

'Use it or lose it, asshole,' came Roxy's voice out of the darkness. Mason saw her closing in from the left, gun raised.

Marduk had a strange look on his face, something between acceptance and regret. He flicked a glance at Roxy, and then focused his attention on Mason.

'Did you stop the attacks?'

'Every one of them. You're finished.'

'Maybe,' he said. 'But the Vatican and the world will never forget what happened here today.'

'Your legacy,' Mason said. 'Blood and death.'

'The Amori die with me,' Marduk said. 'Over four thousand years of history, born in ancient Babylon. It all ends here tonight.'

'Good,' Mason said. 'Go for your gun.'

Death was written all over Marduk's face. He wouldn't be captured tonight. They weren't taking him alive. He was the monarch of the Amori; he had tasted prison and he didn't like it. He knew they'd never let him see the light of day again.

'I am the last of the Amori,' he said. 'Christianity is a plague that has outlived us, but it is a plague that cannot thrive for ever.'

And he raised his gun surprisingly quickly. It wasn't Mason who shot him; it was Roxy. The American was fast, faster than he could have believed. Her bullet smashed into the side of Marduk's head and sent him tumbling to the ground, the half-raised gun with him. Mason felt a moment's grief that it had been Roxy who pulled the trigger. He would gladly have taken that burden and wanted to.

It was done; it was over. Here, in the shadow of the great Colosseum, in darkness, under sodden clouds, they had rid the world of another great evil. Marduk would never have stopped until he brought the Church crashing to its knees. He was better off where he was. Mason made sure he was dead and then stepped away from the body as the rest of his colleagues and the cavalieré came running up.

'Is it over?' Quaid asked.

'I finished it,' Roxy said.

'Ah,' Quaid said.

With Marduk lying dead at their feet and his dogs of war called off, Mason felt a surge of relief. In the end, through adversity, they had succeeded. They had ended the reign of a madman and – hopefully – severed any hold that the Amori still had on this world. It was a good win.

But Marduk had left behind a terrible legacy. As he'd said, the world would never forget what happened here today, and they'd never forget the name of the man who made it all happen. Perhaps that was Marduk's only victory – infamy. Mason's biggest hope now was that the authorities could repair all the damage that had been done, but he was sure Premo Conte and his colleagues could get right on with that.

It would be no easy task, repairing the bomb damage that had been done to St Peter's Square and the front of the basilica, and other areas of Rome. It would take the best stonemasons and builders the world had to offer and even then, it would be fraught with difficulty, time-consuming and expensive. The papal enclave had been damaged on the outside only; the interior was intact, but it was the exterior that drew the world's eye, chiefly by way of the tabloids and news channels. Such massive repairs would require a delicate balance of media information management, something the Vatican was not unskilled in.

Mason turned his back on the dead body and walked away. His team fell in alongside him. There was no immediate chatter, just a great sense of relief. Eventually, though, Roxy broke the silence.

'Every time we work for the Vatican,' she said, 'we almost die. I think there's a lesson in there somewhere.'

'A message,' Quaid said.

'I can't imagine what it is,' Hassell said with a smile.

Mason looked askance at Sally. 'So what is it next? Back to relic protection?'

'More than one job has come in during the last few days.'

'Do they sound dangerous?' Roxy asked.

'Yeah,' Quaid said. 'Because if they need the Ark of the Covenant moving from Edinburgh Castle, you know we're the right team to do that. Right?'

Everyone laughed. Mason listened to their banter and knew they'd all got through this in the right state of mind. They were all broken, but they weren't shattered. They all had hard work to do, but it was a work in progress.

Together, the team was stronger, a thought he'd never have expected having just a few months ago, before he met them.

Together, they were stronger.

THE END

NOW READ ON FOR EXCLUSIVE BONUS CONTENT FROM DAVID LEADBEATER

Author Q+A

1. What inspired the Joe Mason series?

I wanted a story with a new, diverse bunch of characters who got together during an actual adventure. Joe and Roxy came together first and bounced off each other well. After that it was just a matter of creating the right circumstances for the others to join the team. I've wanted to centre a story around the Vatican for some time. It's something I've stayed away from until now, but when I got the idea for a Vatican Book of Secrets, the ideas started to flow.

2. Which character in the Joe Mason series is your favourite and why?

My favourite character is Roxy! I love her attitude, her boldness and how, during the writing, she constantly surprises me. Sometimes I have no idea what she's about to say or do and then her next action just jumps off the page! It really helps to have a character so fresh and diverse that her actions can make you laugh even as you are writing them. I think so blends well with the team and helps keep them straight.

3. Do any elements of your own personality end up in your books?

Not that I am consciously aware of, but I guess some traits must come creeping through. I tend to live vicariously through my characters. I find that sometimes I *want* to perform the same actions as my characters but unfortunately that's never really possible!

4. *The Babylon Plot* sees the return of Marduk, leader of the Amori. What made you want to bring this character back?

I knew all along that Marduk's story wasn't finished. He was too big and too evil a character to let fade away. He wouldn't just stay rotting away in a prison. He would find a way to hit back at the Vatican and the church, no matter what. That thought inspired me to write *The Babylon Plot* and engineer Marduk's new line of attack. Also, I wanted to see out his storyline to the deadly end.

5. Joe Mason's team is constituted of very different people, and yet they all have forged great relationships. What message do you want the reader to take away from this?

My own ideas around this is that it's all about the right people and the attitude they bring with them to the mix. You can't choose your family but you can choose your friends who, then, can become family. Much of my writing centres around a team forging a bond that makes them feel like family. The Joe Mason series is no different in that respect.

6. How did *The Babylon Plot* evolve as you wrote it? Did you decide on the ending before you started writing?

I always sit down and write a full chapter by chapter breakdown before I start writing page one. I find this helps me overcome any kind of writer's block. If I get stuck I simply look at the breakdown, see where I'm going next, and keep writing. So I always knew what would happen at the end. It was just a matter of getting my characters to the right point at the right time to make it happen. I do like to keep a rigid structure to my writing.

7. What was your favourite part of the story to write?

I loved the part where they all went to Monaco. It was great fun to write and research and I loved immersing my characters in that world. Of course, it didn't fit them well and it made them all uncomfortable. But that was also fun to write. I enjoyed fitting my characters into that lavish, crazy world and will seek to put them out of their comfort zones again. Monaco is so the opposite of what my characters enjoy that it was quite fun, but quite daunting, to take them there, especially in the glittering world of the auction they ended up in.

8. Do you have any advice for budding writers in this space just starting out?

My advice would be to sit down, write the outline and then the plot. Next, write the story before doing anything else. Get at least the first draft down on digital paper. The next step – and this is essential – would be to get a good editor, however you seek to do this. If you're publishing independently it's still possible. Work together with your editor to polish the best story possible. Take their advice and look at the story objectively, even if you feel you don't want to. There's a lot of compromise to be had. Then it's all about cover design and blurbs and creating a strong presence online. Social media is important these days so get yourself on there and start interacting with your potential readers. It's not like the old days when you sent your favourite author an email or a letter and never got a reply. An author should be very available today, networking with their audience. Make your story as polished as possible before releasing it out into the world and then grow a thick skin, because, no matter what anyone has told you, you will get all manner of reviews. In addition to this, I would say visit as many places in your story as possible. I realise that's not always possible, but the more intimate knowledge you have of a place the better you can describe it and ultimately immerse your reader in it.

9. When you are not writing your own books, what kind of fiction do you love to read?

My favourite set of books is the Agent Pendergast series by Douglas Preston and Lincoln Child. I've lost count of the number of times I've read them and am currently going through them once again. I love the character of Pendergast, the detail in the research, and the dark, brooding stories that often appear supernatural only to end up with a perfectly believable ending. If I'm not reading Preston/Child I tend to gravitate towards Thrillers and enjoy the work of Scott Mariani and Clive Cussler to name a few. I like anything with an archaeological slant, as evidenced by my own stories! In addition I also like the crime thriller work of Robert Crais, as he sprinkles a great amount of humour through the dark worlds he creates.

A stolen treasure.
A secret society.
Danger is waiting in the shadows . . .

Don't miss the third gripping and fast-paced action adventure in the series.
Available now!